GOTTA BE BAYOU

BADGES OF THE BAYOU

ERIN NICHOLAS

THE BADGES OF THE BAYOU SERIES

Gotta Be Bayou (Spencer & Max)
Bayou With Benefits (Michael & Ami)
Red, White & Bayou (Wyatt & Trudy)
Always Bayou (Beau & Becca)
Stuck Bayou (Theo & Savannah)

ABOUT THE BOOK

How do you get over a woman you never should have been,
ahem, **under** *in the first place?*

Just when Spencer Landry had decided to forget about Maxine–
Max–Keller and their one hot night together, there's a threat
made against her and Spencer's protective instincts get all riled
up. Again.

So now they're shacking up on the Louisiana bayou and
pretending to be in love so he can keep Max safe until the guy is
apprehended.

Considering their chemistry and that he can *not* stop thinking
about the gorgeous-and-doesn't-know-it, smart-mouthed, bold-
and-yet-vulnerable redhead, this could be a fun few days, right?

Nope. She's all wrong for him.

And she hasn't forgotten he can be kind of a jerk.

Sure, the naked-times are great, but he told her exactly what he wants— a bubbly, sweet school teacher who bakes him brownies and loves to cuddle—and Max ain't it.

Max not only doesn't bake, no one has *ever* called her sweet. And cuddling? *Shudder*.

Plus his bossiness is super annoying for someone who's been taking care of herself all her life. But now they're stuck together and dammit, besides being hot and very good with his mouth, Spencer is pretty irresistible with baby goats, little kids, and attempts at baking. And don't forget alpha-protective. All of which makes her stomach feel very swoop-y. No wonder her clothes keep falling off.

But this is a *temporary* situation and they're only faking it. So falling for the guy is a terrible idea.

She really should have kept that in mind.

PROLOGUE
BAYOU TONIGHT

"Why do I want you *so much*?"

Spencer was aware that the words he said gruffly to Maxine Keller sounded drunkenly slurred. Leo Landry's moonshine had that effect on mouths and tongues. But it also worked as a sort of truth serum.

The clear, potent, homemade concoction that could be used to unstick frozen windows, and as an antiseptic on wounds, was also delicious and could make a man spill all of his deepest, darkest desires.

That was no secret. People knew it would happen before they took even the tiniest sip. But they kept sipping.

Spencer should have known better.

"Because I'm clever, witty, bold, and beautiful?" Max asked him.

She was all of those things. For sure. But he frowned as he studied her face, including the tiny, mischievous smile tugging at her lips.

"I don't think that's it."

She lifted a brow.

But seriously, he met clever, witty, bold, and beautiful women all the time.

Okay, maybe not *daily*, but often.

Max had deep red hair, and big green eyes—that often flashed at him with irritation, as a matter of fact—and smooth, creamy pale skin, and amazing breasts.

Yeah, he was a breast guy, and this girl had *perfect* ones.

She was gorgeous, no doubt about it, and he'd had the impression from the first time he met her that she didn't even know it.

But no, it wasn't all of that. Whatever was drawing him to her was something he couldn't put his finger on. Something he *almost* understood, but couldn't quite define.

And it was making him fucking nuts.

It was why he'd pulled her away from the wedding reception going on inside the building behind her and why he now had her alone in the shadows. He needed to figure this out. Because he'd been thinking about her for months, even though he'd tried not to. And he'd almost convinced himself that whatever he'd felt a year ago had disappeared.

Then she'd shown up at this wedding, with her hair up in some sexy twist, wearing a black dress—who wore black to a summer wedding anyway?—and the air had been sucked out of his lungs and he'd thought, *well, fuck.*

"You're...different," he finally said.

Damn Leo's moonshine. *Different* wasn't the right word. But Spencer couldn't come up with the correct one.

"I am," Max agreed. "Why do you seem puzzled by that?"

"I'm not puzzled. I'm... annoyed."

"Annoyed?"

"Yes, annoyed."

He reached up to cup her face, her silky, warm hair falling over the backs of his hands. He leaned in and nuzzled her temple. "Why do I think about you all the time?"

But he didn't give her a chance to reply. He kissed her instead, moving his mouth over her forehead, where he placed a kiss in the center, then he kissed down her nose to her lips.

Heat shot through his body, settling low in his gut, and he pressed closer.

She didn't protest. She opened her mouth with a tiny sigh that made his cock jerk, she gripped his shoulders and arched her lower body against his as he leaned in, and she met his tongue with a bold stroke.

She was delicious. She tasted like the same moonshine that was muddling his brain. But her soft lips, the hot, wet inside of her mouth, the way her tongue met his without hesitation, and the way she leaned into him made him feel like the moonshine was burning through his veins.

He shouldn't be surprised by her reaction, he supposed. She'd come outside with him willingly.

They'd known each other for nearly a year, though he hadn't seen her in several months. They'd worked a case together last year in his capacity as an FBI agent. He'd been called in to help his cop cousin, Zander, with an illegal animal trading ring. Max was an investigative journalist assisting Caroline, her friend and the woman Zander would fall head over heels for, in gathering information about that ring.

Together, they'd taken the bad guys down and rescued several illegally kept exotic animals, including a number of big cats.

He lifted his head from the kiss and stared at her. They were both breathing hard. She looked a little dazed. He *felt* a little dazed.

His hands were now sunk deep in her hair at the back of her head, and her hands rested on his hips. He had her pressed against the wall of Ellie's bar and was leaning into her. She didn't seem bothered by the position. She didn't push him away. Or tell him to fuck off.

"Do you bake?" he asked.

It wasn't completely dark here. Besides the moonlight, light spilled from the tall lamps illuminating the parking lot in front of Ellie's. It was certainly enough to see the way Max's eyes widened slightly. "I do not."

He frowned. "You don't bake *at all*?"

"Nope."

Despite that answer, which was *not* the one he'd wanted, he dipped his head and took another taste of her. Her lips were soft, and she sighed again as he stroked along her bottom lip. God, he fucking loved that.

He felt her fingers curl into his sides, and he couldn't help but tip her head slightly and deepen the kiss.

He kissed her for nearly a full minute before lifting his head again. "Not even brownies from a mix, like the kind you get from the store, where all you have to do is add like one egg and water and stir it?" He was aware his words were running together, and he hadn't paused once during that entire thought.

She ran her tongue over her lips. "I don't bake anything at all, Spencer. That seems important to you, though."

He nodded. "I'm looking for a woman who can bake. Cook in general. But baking is a big deal for sure."

It had to be the moonshine that made that sound so stupid. Or maybe it was just saying it out loud. He wasn't sure he'd ever spelled that out for any other woman he'd dated. Or said it to any other person, for that matter.

"You have a Betty Crocker fetish?"

He frowned deeper. This made sense. It did. He was sure of it. Well, *pretty sure* of it.

He needed to explain this. "No, I just really like coming home to good food. So I want to be with someone who can do that. So when I come home from work, we can have dinner together."

"You eat brownies for dinner?"

"No." He shook his head slightly. He *would* eat brownies for dinner. But he wanted other things for dinner and then brownies after. "But I like having brownies there."

"You are aware that that sounds sexist as hell, right?" she asked.

He *was* aware of that. Now that he'd said it out loud. Even when he was drunk, that all sounded like misogynistic garbage. But it wasn't.

He swallowed and frowned, focusing on her nose, determined to make this make sense. It wasn't that he had some old-fashioned idea about gender roles or that he believed the kitchen was a woman's place or that he had mommy issues, or… anything like that.

He just thought having a normal routine at home was important for countering the not-normal, sometimes-terrible stuff he saw and dealt with at work. But he had crazy hours and didn't get home at a decent enough time to be in charge of meals. He'd happily be in charge of other things, though.

"I do laundry and stuff," he blurted. "I iron my own shirts and pants. And I'll do all the grocery shopping. And toilets. I can scrub toilets."

Her soft puff of laughter was warm against his lips, and it reminded him how much he liked her lips, so he lowered his head and kissed her. She gave another little sigh, and he was lost for a full sixty seconds again, tasting her, feeling her.

This time he slid his hands from the back of her head, down her neck to her upper back, and then down to her hips, where he pulled her closer, pressing her against his thick, hard cock. This woman turned him on more than he could remember being turned on in a very long time.

But she doesn't bake.

He lifted his head. "I'm just not a very good cook myself. Or baker. Never learned. And I don't have time. I work weird hours."

She pressed her lips together. But she nodded as if she understood.

Well, that was good. He needed her to understand.

"I really like casseroles too," he said.

Again, that sounded stupid out loud. *Why does she need to know that, Spencer?*

Well, if I want to marry her, we should talk about who's going to make the casseroles, right?

Could inner voices get drunk? He thought maybe his was drunk.

Or maybe being drunk was just making this all seem stupid. Maybe it was a perfectly legitimate thing to say in the middle of a make-out session and made total sense to her.

"Casseroles?" she repeated, looking at him like he was a dumbass. "So, baking again."

Okay, maybe it wasn't just the being drunk.

"Yeah, you know, like chicken and rice and broccoli. Or enchiladas. In my opinion, enchiladas are a casserole. Casseroles have multiple ingredients that are baked together all in one pan, and they make the whole house smell really good when you walk in the door. Same with lasagna. I will fight you on that."

Again, she was staring at him as if he was missing a few noodles himself. But he wasn't. He was more than slightly drunk, but he was very sure about what he wanted. When it came to casseroles, anyway.

"I don't want to fight about that."

"Okay, good," he said.

"This is all very specific," she said.

"I think it's good to be upfront and honest in relationships."

Her eyes went *very* wide at that. "I have never made enchiladas in my life. I can't even remember the last time I *ate* enchiladas," she said. "And I want to be very clear about this point... Spencer, are you listening?"

He nodded.

"I have no intention of making enchiladas at any point in the future." She enunciated that all very clearly. As if he was five. Or stupid. Or drunk.

He scowled.

That was not going to work out. He could not be this obsessed with a woman who not only didn't know how to make enchiladas but didn't *want* to.

He needed to think about this, but it was proving to be very difficult. He really should've stopped with one shot of moonshine. Not two. And certainly not five.

Since he needed a moment to muddle through his thoughts, he bent and ran his mouth along the side of her neck. God, she smelled amazing. And the skin here was so soft against his lips. And the sound she made now? Ten times better than the sound she made when he kissed her. This was not just a sigh. This was a moan. And it shot heat from his chest to his gut to his cock.

So he did it again. He dragged his scruff-lined jaw up and down her neck, placing kisses every inch or so. "I think I'm addicted to the feel of your skin," he said gruffly.

"Spencer," she said again with a little moan.

His name on her lips made his cock ache. He wanted more of that. Maybe he didn't like enchiladas as much as he thought he did.

He lifted his head. "Do you like dogs?"

She opened her eyes and blinked at him as if trying to keep up with what he was saying. "Dogs? Of course, I like dogs."

Okay, that was good. That was very good. "I really like dogs."

She nodded.

"Do you have a dog?"

She dragged in a little breath. "I don't." The slightly dazed look cleared, and her eyes widened. "Is this another thing on your list for the perfect girlfriend?"

He nodded. "Pets are good."

Dammit, this moonshine was making him sound like an idiot.

But pets *were* good.

"Pets are great. I don't have one because I have an erratic work schedule and never had a pet growing up, so I'm not that familiar with taking care of one. I didn't feel like it was fair to an animal to bring one into my life."

He frowned, studying her eyes. They were gorgeous. He loved green eyes.

That was not something he had been aware of before this moment, but it was true. Apparently.

"You never had a pet growing up?"

She shook her head. "Nope.

"Not even like a fish or hamster?"

"If I had, I would've counted that as a pet, and I wouldn't have said that I didn't have a pet growing up."

It occurred to Spencer that Max was possibly much less drunk than he was. And that she might be getting annoyed with him sounding like a dumbass.

Thinking over the fact that this woman he could not seem to get over did not bake and not only did not have a pet now but had *never* had a pet, he absently lifted a hand and traced his thumb along her right collarbone.

She gave a soft sigh at that too and seemed to arch a little closer.

"What TV shows do you like to watch?" he asked.

Before she could answer though, he lowered his head and placed a kiss where his thumb had just been. Even the skin on her collarbone smelled great and was soft. He stroked his lips back and forth along the spot and felt her arch closer, her breasts pressing against the bodice of the dress she wore.

It was black.

She was the only woman at the entire wedding in black. She could have just as easily worn this outfit to a funeral. But the color made her skin look even creamier. It was held up only by spaghetti straps, and Spencer lifted a hand and hooked his index finger under the strap that crossed the collarbone he was currently giving a lot of attention to. He pulled it off her shoulder, suddenly needing even *more* of that skin, and followed the strap with his mouth, kissing over the curve of her shoulder, then down to the bare, silky skin where the dress gaped over the upper curve of her breast.

"Spencer," she whispered hoarsely.

His hand drifted down to cup her breast, and she whimpered slightly as he ran his thumb over the hard tip of her nipple.

Absolutely perfect breasts.

"Thank you," she said with a breathless laugh.

Ah, he'd said that out loud.

Damned moonshine.

He lifted his head. "It's true."

"Maybe that's why you like me even though I don't bake or have a dog."

He continued to cup her breast. "Maybe. That makes sense. But it feels like more than that."

A tiny wrinkle formed between her brows. "Does it?"

He leaned in to kiss her again. With his mouth against hers, he said, "Doesn't it?"

"Kind of, yeah."

He kissed her deeply this time. His tongue stroked in firmly along hers, his thumb teasing her nipple, his other hand dropping to her ass—which was also pretty damned nice—and pressing her up against him.

He wanted her. It didn't make sense. But he did. Badly.

Her hands slipped under the edge of his shirt, and it was only then that he realized she'd untucked his dress shirt from his pants. She ran her hand up his back, and he shuddered at the feel of her palms against his bare skin. She moved around to his sides and then to his abs, stroking and arching against him and kissing him back with as much enthusiasm as he was kissing her.

He was too drunk to take this any further than making out. He was aware of that. But this was pretty damned good. He knew he wasn't going to be getting over her anytime soon, and this was going to be a very nice memory to keep with him until he saw her again.

Because, dammit, he was gonna have to see her again.

Maybe when he was sober he could make some sense out of

the fact that he wanted her so badly when she wasn't at all what he was looking for.

The strap of her dress slipped lower on her arm, the front of the dress falling away from her breast. Okay, so that had required a tiny bit of a tug from him, but then he was lowering his mouth, dragging it over her jaw, down her sweet neck to that delicious collarbone, where he gave her a little nip, before continuing down to first circle her nipple with his tongue, then give it a little suck.

This time when she gasped his name, it was not quiet.

He felt her hands go to his fly and the button and zipper give. Her hand tucked into the front of his pants. Her palm skimmed along the flesh that was so hard it was nearly painful before he finally came to his senses.

He grasped her wrist, halting her stroke.

He just held her still, breathing hard for a moment before lifting his head and pulling her dress back up—though not before drinking in the sight of her naked breast. Then he pulled her hand from his pants and pressed it against his chest, staring into her eyes.

"I'm too drunk for this," he said roughly.

That seemed to take her a moment to process, but she pressed her lips together and nodded when she did. "Dammit. Okay."

He let go of her hand and zipped his pants. Then he braced his hands on the wall on either side of her head, keeping her between him and the building.

Still, she did not seem intimidated by the move. She just stood staring at him, still breathing a little hard.

"What do you like to watch on TV?" he asked, repeating his question from a few minutes earlier.

He wasn't sure why that was what he chose to say. Or, rather, he had an *inkling* of why, but it wasn't entirely clear. Kind of like every other thought he'd had since he'd stupidly taken that fifth drink of moonshine.

"I don't watch much TV at all."

Another knife to the heart.

"So, no baking, no pets, no TV."

She lifted a shoulder. "Pretty much."

"And your level of interest in any of those things in the near future is...." He'd let her fill in that blank, though he had an idea of what her answer would be.

"Very low."

He studied her for a long moment. There was definitely something there. The idea of not seeing her again just didn't feel right.

"Even lasagna?"

"I live a pretty full life without making lasagna now. I'm not sure that I have a burning need to change that. I mean, I'm not necessarily anti-lasagna. But I am pretty sure I'm anti-making-lasagna-myself," she admitted. "That seems like a lot of work. And I'm guessing there are about a dozen restaurants that make and deliver great lasagna in New Orleans."

Yeah. He could take her to one of those. Or have her over to his place and have some delivered.

He didn't want to do either of those things.

Not because he didn't want to see her again. Not because he didn't want to eat lasagna with her. But because those weren't the main points here.

"Do you even like enchiladas or lasagna?"

"I'm more of a burger girl, I'll be honest."

He sighed. "Max," he said.

"Yes, Spencer?"

"You are so not my type."

———

MAX DIDN'T SEEM shocked by that revelation. "You don't like burgers?"

"Love burgers. Burgers are not great delivery food. Buns get mushy, tomatoes and lettuce wilt, fries get cold."

"Well, you need to not get the lettuce and tomato. For one thing."

He sighed. "I'm not a big delivery guy anyway. I like sitting down to meals cooked in my own kitchen. Growing up, that was the way my mom made everything better. We'd walk in the door, the whole house would smell amazing, we'd sit down to awesome food, and it was a reminder that no matter what bad shit happened outside the door, there was calm and care inside."

Wow. Okay, so that had been a pretty good explanation. Despite the moonshine.

Max seemed to think about what he'd said for a moment. Then she said, "But you don't cook."

"No, but my girlfriends do."

She clearly did not have a response for that.

Spencer wasn't sure what to say in follow-up.

He was currently single. That had been true for about a month. His mom had saved him by cooking for him several times, but he'd been going out to restaurants, and he had resorted to some takeout and delivery. But it wasn't nearly as good.

He should probably hire a housekeeper or an assistant or just someone to stop by at the end of the day and put dinner in the oven for him. He could do that, he supposed.

His gaze dropped to Max's lips.

He could definitely do that.

Though he'd *really* like to still have the cuddling-on-the-couch-with-a-dog-while-watching-TV-after-dinner part that he found so nice and comforting.

But he also loved sitting on the balcony with a beer. And reading in bed. Lots of relaxing, appreciate-the-little-things activities. It wasn't *all* about the food.

Maybe he should tell her that he always did the dishes and made incredible margaritas and gave amazing foot rubs.

"So, you should know—"

"So, I guess—"

They spoke simultaneously and were interrupted by the sound of a cell phone ringing.

Spencer frowned as Max dug in the pocket of her dress and withdrew her phone.

He hadn't even realized the dress had a pocket.

And it was midnight. Who was calling her now?

She glanced at the screen, then back at him.

"Well, I need to take this. It's been very nice dancing and making out with you and figuring out all of the reasons why we definitely should not date. I do admire a guy who knows exactly what he wants, though. So good luck finding your dream girl."

Then she ducked under his arm and strode several feet away to take the call.

Spencer stood frowning at her back.

He should let her walk away. He should definitely say, "Well, clearly this isn't going to work out, thanks for clearing that up so maybe *now* I can stop thinking about you."

Instead, when Max tucked her phone back into her pocket, he called, "You okay?"

She spun, clearly surprised that he was still there.

"Yeah, just need to head back to New Orleans."

"You are not driving. You've had too much to drink."

"I ordered an Uber."

"Hang on, and I'll take you."

She laughed. "You're way too drunk to drive me."

"I'm not gonna drive you. My brother will take us. Wyatt lives in New Orleans and will be going back there anyway. He knew he was driving home tonight, so he hasn't been drinking at all."

"No, that's okay. The car's only two minutes away."

Spencer scowled. "Dammit, Max. Let me just go get Wyatt."

"Spencer, I'm fine."

"It's midnight. You're gonna get an Uber back to New Orleans alone?"

"That was the plan all along. I got down here with an Uber. I expected to drink a little, so I knew I wouldn't be driving myself home."

"Just hold up one minute. Wyatt's just inside. He's going back to the city anyway."

She blew out an exasperated breath. "I get myself from point A to point B alone all the time. You're sweet to worry, but I'm fine."

"I'm not done with you."

Okay, that sounded a little demanding. Bossy even. And was it true? He was the one who had just laid out all the reasons she wasn't right for him. Why wasn't he done with her?

She propped a hand on her hip. "Listen, the making out was great, and I had a good time, and I'll admit I was kind of hoping to see you tonight, but not only do I not bake, but now, knowing that it's actually on a list of things you *require* in a girl-friend, the chances of me ever doing it have gone down to zero."

"Knowing what will make me compatible with someone is a good thing. It saves time and heartbreak. Knowing what you need in a partner and what you are looking for in a relationship is a mature way to approach dating."

"Mature? Okay."

He could *sense* the eye roll even across the distance in the dark.

"Aha!" He pointed at her and then had to correct when his finger wanted to point too far to the left of her. "You *do* care that I have a list of things that mean I can't date you."

She shook her head. "That's not what I'm saying."

"Admit it. It annoys you that I have some things I want that you can't give me."

Her brows arched. "Well, I'll admit annoyed *is* something I'm feeling. Maybe not for exactly the same reason that you think."

"Are you annoyed that you know I could give you an amazing orgasm, but you can't give *me* brownies?"

Okay, that didn't sound good. Fucking moonshine. That was

absolutely not the way he would've phrased that if he'd been totally sober.

"Actually, you know what?" she asked. "I think that you should *cling* to that list of criteria. I think that you should be absolutely unwavering in those requirements. I think that you should not even speak to women who cannot make brownies or enchiladas. And I think you should definitely start with me."

Just then, a car pulled up, and the window rolled down. "Max?" the driver asked.

"Yep," she answered. She turned back to Spencer. "Bye, Spencer."

She got in the car, and it pulled away before Spencer's brain could slosh through the moonshine fast enough to say, "Dammit, Max, wait!"

With a growl, he turned on his heel and marched into Ellie's bar. "Wyatt!" he bellowed.

Everybody on that side of the bar, mostly the Landry family, gathered around the big table toward the back corner, quieted and pivoted toward him.

"Where the fuck is Wyatt?" Spencer demanded.

"Right here, holy shit." His brother stood up and pushed forward. "What's going on?"

"I need to go to New Orleans."

"'Kay. I'll be ready to go in a little bit."

"We gotta leave now."

"Why? What's going on?"

"Max just left. I have to go after her."

It was about then that Wyatt seemed to realize how drunk Spencer was. A knowing smile graced his little brother's face. "I see. Why didn't you just go *with* her?"

"She didn't invite me. She said she could go alone."

"Then maybe we should let her go alone." Wyatt clapped him on the shoulder. "Come over and have a drink with us. Or maybe some coffee. Water?"

Spencer shrugged his brother's hand off. "I need to be sure

she's okay. She got a sudden phone call and needed to take off. It's midnight."

"But she didn't want you to go with her, bro. I think you need to let her go."

Spencer frowned. "I just want to make sure she's okay."

Wyatt's eyes narrowed as he studied Spencer's face. The brothers were close. It was just the two of them, and they were only a couple of years apart. They'd grown up as more than brothers. They were best friends. No one knew Spencer better than Wyatt.

So Spencer's answer was, apparently, good enough for Wyatt. "Okay, let's go."

"You just gonna *leave*?" This came from Zeke, one of their many cousins.

"Gotta make sure the girl's okay," Wyatt said with a shrug as if that should be explanation enough.

And really, it should be.

"Do you want me to come?" This came from Caroline, Max's best friend.

"No, I've got it," he said.

"Did you upset her?" Caroline asked.

Spencer opened his mouth to reply and then thought about the question. Had he upset her? Yeah, maybe a little. But he didn't think that's why she left. That was more about the *attitude* with which she'd left.

"I've got it, Caroline," he said, rather than answering her question directly.

He felt protective of Max, and he had no idea why. She had never given any indication that she needed protection. She was incredibly intelligent, very good at her job, and completely confident in everything she did, including putting him in his place.

"Do you know where she's going?" Wyatt asked as he started his truck.

"I know where she lives." And now he was really hoping that

she wasn't heading to meet friends at a bar or to someone's place for a booty call.

Especially that last one.

She's not your type. You don't want to date her.

Yeah, that's what he'd thought. Until he thought about her heading to the city at midnight to meet someone else.

Wyatt waited until they got on the main highway before he said, "So this girl got under your skin quick."

Spencer had known his brother would not just let this go.

The thing was, it didn't seem *quick*. Max Keller had been niggling at the corners of Spencer's consciousness ever since he'd met her.

"You ever kissed a woman and thought, *oh, shit, I shouldn't have done that*, but at the same time known that you could never have lived a full life without having kissed her?"

Wyatt looked over at him. His eyes were wide. "I have not. Jesus, how much moonshine did you have tonight?"

Spencer stared at the dark highway in front of them. "I'm guessing you'll kiss a woman like that someday. You come back and tell me how crazy I am when that happens."

Wyatt chuckled. "You'll be my first call, brother."

Spencer couldn't wait.

Wyatt glanced at him again. "This is interesting."

"What is?"

"Seeing you all worked up over a woman. I've never seen this before."

"It's an ego thing," Spencer informed him. "I'm not used to women who can resist me. I just want the one I can't have."

He really wished all of that was true. He wanted Max Keller to be intriguing just because she was the un-gettable girl. Maybe that was part of it. Impressing a woman like Max seemed to be a feat. A worthy one, no doubt. But where did this desire to take care of her come from?

He suddenly had a vision of her propped up against the pillows in bed—his bed—but in pajamas, an oversized comfy shirt and pants, nothing skimpy or silky, with a book propped on her knees. She looked up at him as he came into the room and gave him a sweet, slightly sleepy smile. And his heart felt full.

That was what he wanted. Her, safe and happy, at home.

Jesus. He scrubbed a hand over his face.

He knew where that whole image and desire came from. He needed his home life to balance out the darkness he saw at work. It was as simple and as complicated as that. He was just surprised that it was such a big deal with *this woman*.

A woman who didn't even want a dog.

The dog—or lack thereof—was symbolic. And he needed to keep that in mind.

"Sure, it's an ego thing," Wyatt said, clearly not buying it.

"You don't think I have an ego?"

Wyatt laughed. "Sure you do. But this seems…not that."

Spencer was done talking about this. "Shut up. Turn here."

He directed Wyatt to Max's townhouse, and he parked down the block in the shadows of the other buildings.

There were lights on in the windows, and Spencer realized that he might have to just assume she was here. If she was here, she'd arrived several minutes ago.

"I'm going to go in."

"In?" Wyatt asked. "Like *in* her house?"

"Yeah. I have to be sure she's there. And maybe say I'm sorry."

"Sorry for stalking her, or did you do something before this?"

"I told her she wasn't my type." He frowned at his brother. "I'm not stalking her."

"You followed her home even after she told you she was fine without you," Wyatt pointed out. "Wait, you *told her* she wasn't your type?"

Spencer ran a hand through his hair. "Yeah."

"No wonder she didn't want you to come home with her." Wyatt shook his head. "So, is it true?"

"Yeah."

"Then why are we here stalking her?"

"I'm not *stalking* her." He moved to open his door. "I'm going up there to make sure she's okay."

"No, you're not," Wyatt said firmly. He pulled his phone out and dialed. "Zander, have Caroline call Max and see if she's home." He paused. Then sighed. "Because we're at her house but Spencer's too drunk to go talk to her. Just call and be sure she's here and okay so he'll go home."

Spencer knew that was a better idea than him going up to her door.

He still wanted to go up to her door.

Two minutes later, Wyatt said, "Thanks. Yeah, he's fine too." He glanced at Spencer. "Well, kind of fine. His head is gonna hurt like a bitch in the morning, but I think maybe he'll deserve it."

Spencer sighed. His brother's lack of sympathy was not appreciated.

But Wyatt was probably right on all accounts.

"She's home, and she's fine," Wyatt reported as he disconnected.

Spencer's eyes were on her townhouse and the light in the window he assumed was her bedroom. She was home. Safe.

Of course, she wasn't propped up against the pillows in his bed, and there wasn't a dog greeting her on the other side of the door—and he knew with one hundred percent certainty that her place did not smell like enchiladas—but at least she was home.

"Can I take you home now?" Wyatt was already shifting the truck into drive.

"Yeah. Okay."

The thing was, he wasn't going to be greeted at the door by a dog either. And his apartment wasn't going to smell like enchiladas.

And Max Keller living there would only make those things less likely.

Still, he couldn't shake that image of her propped up in his bed in pink pajamas and a sweet, happy-to-see-him smile on her face.

And worse, he was sobering up, so he couldn't even blame that image or his feelings entirely on the moonshine.

———

"I KNEW I shouldn't have kissed you last night."

Max propped her shoulder against the doorjamb of her townhouse and folded her arms.

"You had no complaints about the kissing," Spencer replied from her front step the next evening. "During or after."

Yes, he'd awakened that morning with the hangover from hell.

Yes, he'd immediately felt like a dumbass for the things he'd said to Max.

But no, he hadn't been sorry about the kissing.

And no, he hadn't gotten over the urge to see her again.

"I did not complain about the kissing," she agreed. "But it's like feeding a stray cat. You give in once, and it keeps showing up wanting more." Her gaze roamed over him from head to toe. "And here you are."

He felt his mouth kick up at one corner. Dammit, that mouth of hers was definitely part of why he could not get over her. The sassiness that came from it and the dirty dreams he'd had last night because of it.

And would he like another taste? For sure. But that wasn't the main reason he was here tonight.

He was here to apologize.

Max was Caroline's best friend. Caroline was Zander's fiancée. Zander was Spencer's cousin and one of *his* best friends. The chances of him and Max running into each other, repeatedly, in the future were very good. It would be great if she didn't think he was an asshole. And it would be great if he didn't want to get her naked every second they were together.

So tonight was about them trying to be friends.

"I'm here to say I'm sorry."

Her eyes went wide. "Really?"

"Yes."

"About what?"

"Being so drunk last night. Sounding like an idiot." He winced. "Being pretty insulting and stupid in general."

She seemed to consider all of that. "I forgive you."

"You do?"

"Sure. We obviously don't have much in common, which is no one's fault."

He frowned. They didn't? Maybe not, but it seemed she was on the verge of saying "see ya' later," and he really wanted to stay. "We had some pretty great kissing in common."

She smiled. "We did."

That smile made him want more of that kissing.

Okay, just her standing there made him want more of that kissing.

"And we've got a few similar interests." He lifted a thick manila folder.

"What's that?"

"You don't seem the flowers type of girl, and I have no idea what kind of food you like, only that it's *not* enchiladas, so I brought something else as a peace offering."

"I mostly feast on the pain and suffering of my enemies," she told him. "And you *should* have a plentiful supply of those. If you're any good at your job."

An investigative journalist and an FBI agent definitely had some enemies in common. And yeah, he'd locked up a few of those. As she very well knew.

"Kind of what I was thinking." He wiggled the folder.

She pulled her bottom lip between her teeth.

She was intrigued.

He grinned.

"What is it?" she finally asked.

"Cold case. Wanted to get some thoughts."

Max was gorgeous, but she was also brilliant, very nerdy—she competed in crossword puzzle tournaments, for God's sake—and incredibly good at her job. She mainly investigated and exposed white-collar crime, but there was a definite overlap between the people she kept on her radar and the darker underbelly of the criminal world. And she didn't shy away from it.

If a story she was working on uncovered something more sinister, she exposed it. She'd helped take down some major criminals, in New Orleans and around the state of Louisiana, with her journalism. He'd also recently learned that she'd assisted the FBI in Texas multiple times and that her research skills and networking had been crucial in a multi-state operation last year.

She was definitely interested in the folder he was holding right now.

And he was, despite himself, still interested in her. Even when their lips weren't glued together, and he didn't have a quart of Leo's moonshine coursing through his veins.

Max moved her gaze from the folder to his face. She narrowed her eyes. "You're not here for a hook-up?"

"I didn't say that."

Would he say yes to more kissing and *not* pulling back because they were both too drunk to take it any further? Abso-fuckin-lutely.

He couldn't get her out of his mind.

Despite the fact he didn't go for dark and sarcastic.

He liked bubbly and sweet.

But looking at the feisty redhead in front of him right now, he couldn't even remember the name of the perky, happy, blond pediatric nurse he'd dated a month ago.

The corner of Max's mouth curled up.

"Do I get to see your stuff"—her gaze flicked to the folder, then back to his—"before you see my stuff?"

He leaned in, propping his shoulder next to hers. Very much in her personal space. "Negotiable."

She didn't move back even a millimeter. "You're not using that folder as a bargaining chip?"

"Do I need a bargaining chip?" He watched her eyes intently.

Max Keller was a lot of things. Fascinating was one of them. Delicious was another. An excellent liar was another.

He didn't care that Max lied to her targets.

He did care that she might lie to him.

But when it came to their chemistry, there was no way she was faking that.

Hell, *he* might be the one that would like to pretend it was something less than it was. He might very well be tempted to lie about her effect on him.

"No," she finally answered, meeting his gaze directly. "I don't think you'll need a bargaining chip."

"Good."

Spencer stretched away from the doorframe and crowded close to her. She backed up rather than get plowed over as he stepped into her house.

"So, have a seat and tell me about this case." She gestured to the couch. "You want something to drink?"

He lifted a brow. "You wanna see mine first, huh?"

She gave him a smile over her shoulder on the way to the kitchen. "I think you already know I'm a woman with high standards. I'm *very* interested in seeing what you've got before I give you much of mine."

He chuckled softly, and as Max left the room, Spencer studied her townhouse.

It was very typical of most of the architecture in New Orleans. Her walls were exposed brick, the floor was hardwood, and the ceiling was high with exposed beams and ducts. French doors opened onto a balcony, and he could see the legs of patio furniture just to one side of the doors. She didn't have much on the walls inside, but she had a big TV mounted across from the couch and several framed black-and-white photos, mostly city skylines and landscapes.

Her furniture was nice, but nothing elaborate. There were no shelves, extra decorative tables, or curio cabinets full of knick-knacks. She had a couch, another armchair with a throw draped over the back, a coffee table, and a couple of tall floor lamps. She did, however, have a tall bookcase, filled to the brim, that sat next to a very interesting desk.

The desk was clearly an antique, with a roll-top, several little cubbies, and an actual typewriter sitting next to her laptop. The desk was cluttered and stacked with papers and books, and Spencer wanted nothing more than to cross the room and rifle through everything on and in it. He just knew that of all the spaces in her home, that desk would tell him the most about Max.

He turned away from greedily taking in details of her home and greedily took in details of *her* as she returned from the kitchen and crossed the room. She was dressed all in black. Her pants were a silky material that hugged her waist and hips but flared at the bottom. With them, she wore a fitted tank under a black zippered hoodie that was open at the moment, showing off how perfectly her breasts pressed against the cotton of her top.

Without a bra.

He swallowed hard.

She had been relaxing—okay, maybe she'd been working—at home and hadn't been expecting a guest, so she wasn't dressed for company.

Still, his cock seemed to think it was nice of her to have not put a bra on.

He cleared his throat and shifted on the couch, trying to make more room behind his fly.

Her feet were bare, but her toenails were painted black, and as she came to settle on the opposite end of the couch, tucking one foot under her butt, Spencer noted that even the scrunchy holding her hair in a loose ponytail at the back of her head was black.

Head to toe black. He rolled his eyes.

"What's with the eyeroll?" she asked, setting two glasses of iced tea on the coffee table.

He needed to remember that she was observant for a living. "Just tea?" he asked, eyeing the glasses. "Nothing stronger?"

"Thought maybe we should stay sober tonight."

He gave her a little smirk. "Just in case something happens later? You don't want to have to stop like we did last time?"

She picked up her glass and took a sip. "Something like that."

Of course, he was left to wonder what she meant by that. Did she hope something more would happen and she wouldn't be too drunk to keep going? Or was she afraid if she drank, something more would happen?

He hated the way he constantly felt off-kilter around this woman.

She glanced around. "Have you seen my phone?"

"Nope, don't see it." He pulled his from his pocket and held it out. "You can use mine."

"Maybe I left it out in the kitchen." She opened a browser screen on his phone and started typing.

"Anything I should be worried about you doing with my phone?"

She sent him a sly smile. "Now would be a good time for me to pull up some porn sites, wouldn't it?"

His body should not react to that. She was joking. For one thing. Also, he didn't want porn on his phone. "Honey, if you're in the mood for something like that, we don't need to go online."

Dammit, see, he shouldn't be saying things like that.

But she just gave a soft laugh. "I'm hungry. For food." Her thumbs flew over the keys. "You want a burger or something? Monte makes the best burgers and fries. He's only a few blocks away, so it should be quick."

"You're not going to make me dinner, huh?" Yeah, they'd been over this. Why had he said that?

She laughed. "Seriously, Spencer, you don't *want* me to make you dinner."

Yeah, well, he kind of did. But he was smart enough not to say that out loud.

"You really don't cook at all?"

"Very rarely. And when I do, it's super simple, boring stuff."

"So, what do you eat?"

"Grilled cheese and scrambled eggs and sandwiches." She tossed his phone back to him. "And takeout."

He wanted a really typical home life. His job showed him a lot of *not normal*, so he needed balance. He'd seen his dad's struggles and how much coming home to their family each night meant to him. Spencer understood how important that regular reminder of happiness was when his work was dark.

"Spencer, I think I need to reiterate something we talked about last night, but that I need to be sure you remember."

He met her gaze. "Okay."

"I am never going to bake you brownies."

Yeah, he definitely needed to stop seeing her.

"You actually said you were never going to make me enchiladas."

She nodded.

"*Actually*," he said, shifting to face her more fully. "You said that you had no intention of making enchiladas at any point in the future. It wasn't specifically about not making them for me."

"But I meant it specifically about you."

That almost made him smile. He nodded. "Thank you for being upfront about that."

"And yet, you still showed up here tonight."

He nodded again. "Weird, right?"

"Almost as weird as you caring that much about enchiladas."

"A lot of people like to cook. I was just making conversation."

She studied him for several seconds. "Okay, sure. And some people like to hack other people up into little pieces." Her gaze flicked to the folder on the coffee table. "We could make conversation about them."

God, he needed to date a woman who would be horrified to be talking about people hacking other people up.

The sunny pediatric nurse would have been.

He really wished he could remember her name right now.

"What makes you think somebody hacked someone up?" he asked.

"You said it's an old cold case."

"That automatically means hacking?"

"Most cold cases are violent crimes. There are occasionally disappearances. That'd be cool too. But if I had money on it, I'd guess murder."

"An unsolved disappearance would be cool?"

She gave him a little smile. "You know what I mean."

He did. She meant that she would find talking about an unsolved case fascinating. And the more violent and disturbing it was, the more excited she would be.

Yeah, this girl was not the sunshiny, happy brownie baker he was looking for.

"Fine. It's an unsolved murder."

"Yay!" She clapped her hands together quickly and bounced a little on her seat. Then she scooted closer to him. "Okay, fill me in."

"When you were a kid, did you ever *want* a pet?"

She looked at him, eyebrows arched. "Do *not* tell me this case involves hacked-up animals."

"That would be a line too far?"

"Well…" She looked back at the file again. "I just need to prepare myself for stuff like that."

Spencer huffed out a laugh. "Humans are fine? You don't need any prep for that? But animals, you need to brace yourself for?"

She looked at him and frowned. "Look, humans are complicated. I'm not saying innocent people don't get killed. Of course they do. I'm just saying, the animals are *always* innocent."

She was so… strange. "No animals in this case," he told her.

Max took a deep breath, a hand on her chest as if relieved. "Then why did you ask me that?"

Because he was stupidly interested in her. "Last night you said you never had pets growing up. I was just wondering if that was a you decision or your parents'. If you maybe wanted a pet, but they said no."

"Oh." She blinked at him. "You remember a lot from last night. I thought you were really drunk."

He remembered too fucking much. Like how silky her skin was along her neck just below her ear. And that damned moan she made when he kissed her collarbone. And the way her nipple felt against his tongue. He cleared his throat. "Yeah. Guess so."

"Okay, well, I guess it was… just never a subject we even talked about," she said. "We lived in an apartment and… pets just weren't an option I ever thought about."

He frowned. Didn't all kids want a puppy or kitten at *some* point?

He studied her. She'd paused right before "pets". He frowned.

She chewed on her bottom lip.

He wanted to kiss her so badly he almost leaned in, but he made himself focus.

"Did you have something that wasn't a real *pet*?" he asked.

"What do you mean?" Her gaze flickered to his earlobe, rather than holding his gaze.

Ah ha. "I'm a detective, remember?" Now he did lean in slightly. "You did have something. Did you sneak a stray cat into your closet that your mom didn't know about or something?"

"No. I didn't bring it inside. And it wasn't a cat." She paused. "Or a dog. Or a rabbit. Or anything like that."

That was a very specific, yet vague, answer.

"So what did you have?"

Jesus, she had a snake. The thought hit him a millisecond later. He was absolutely waiting for her to say that she had a snake. Or a tarantula or some other weird, creepy pet.

"I fed some…"

He leaned closer. "Some?"

She blew out a breath. "Rats."

He blinked. Then sat back. "What?"

"I fed some rats." She lifted a shoulder. "I saw them outside by the garbage cans one day. They were looking for food."

"Well… yeah."

She rolled her eyes. "I was a kid. I didn't know that's what they did. So I fed them."

"For… how long?" He worked on not grimacing.

"Until Phil, our neighbor, saw me one day and told me not to and why." She winced. "So probably two months or so."

Spencer shook his head. He'd been right. It had been weird.

"And now I have two crows."

He looked at her. "Sorry?"

"Now I have two crows," she repeated.

Crows. Okay. That wasn't so bad. But it was still… not a dog. Or something totally normal. "You said you didn't have any pets."

"Well, they're not pets. They don't live in my apartment. They visit my balcony. So they're not *mine*, but they've been coming around for a while, and they bring me presents." She paused and wrinkled her nose. "And actually, there's been four of them in the past couple of weeks, not just two."

"There are crows that visit your balcony and you think they're specifically here for you?"

She looked mildly offended that he'd even asked that. "Crows are incredibly intelligent. They'd fly down and sit on my balcony railing when I was out there reading or doing puzzles, so I started talking to them. They kept coming back. They especially liked it when I was playing music. After a couple of weeks, they'd come sit on the arm of my chair, and then, eventually, on my shoulder. That was even before I started feeding them."

He stared at her. Okay… that was definitely *not* a dog.

"Since I do feed them now, every once in a while, they bring me gifts. I have rocks and beads and shells and marbles. And something that I think is a fake ruby." She frowned and looked toward the balcony. "But I haven't had it appraised yet."

"You think there's a chance that one of these crows brought you a *real* ruby?"

She shrugged. "It's not impossible. It's not huge. They could have flown in through an open window in someone's house and lifted it. They love shiny things."

He studied her. She wasn't kidding. "And what will you do if you find out the ruby is real?"

"That's an excellent question," she told him, pointing her finger at him. "I've thought about it a lot. Because, of course, I should sell it and put the money in the bank to draw interest or, better yet, invest it in an IRA or something. But there's something cool about having a ruby a crow brought to me. The idea of telling that story to people when I'm ninety is tempting."

Again, for a few seconds, Spencer just studied her. And, again, he realized that she was not kidding.

Why did he have to want this very odd woman so damned much?

Because he was itching to kiss her right now. To touch her. To run his hand up the smooth column of her neck, and into that thick red hair, to the back of her head, so he could tip it just right before covering her lips with his.

"You could tell the cops. So they could try to return it to the rightful owner," he suggested.

She laughed. "Tell the cops that my not-really-a-pet crow stole a ruby for me? How would they track that down?"

"Someone might have reported it missing."

She scrunched up one eye as if pondering that. It was

adorable. "Would I be implicated? I mean, could they *prove* my crows did it?"

"That might be tough," he agreed.

"It's not very big. They probably haven't even noticed it's gone."

"What if it's an heirloom with sentimental value?"

"Then they should take better care of it than to leave it out where random crows could find it."

"I—"

A knock sounded on the door, and Max bounced up from the cushion, clearly oblivious to all of the feelings rioting through Spencer.

Because her having a possibly real, probably-stolen-by-crows-who-loved-her ruby and being utterly unapologetic about it made him want to kiss her even more.

That was *not* okay. He had been seconds away from complicating not just this night but possibly his life.

Which seemed like a hysterical statement.

But felt true.

Max returned to the couch and set two paper bags on the coffee table. She pushed one toward him, then reached for his phone.

"What's this?"

She was already tapping on the screen. "I have to leave a tip and a review."

That wasn't what he'd meant, but he said, "You put your credit card information in on my phone? You trust me with that?"

"I didn't put my credit card information in," she said, handing the phone back to him. "I am a little surprised an FBI agent saves his payment info in an app. You're the ones supposedly surveying all of us, though, right?"

"So I just bought you dinner?" he asked, unable to keep from smiling and not commenting on her poke at his profession.

"Well, I didn't invite you over, and you're crashing my

evening plans, so, yes. But you bought yourself dinner too." She gestured toward the second bag.

"I didn't give you my order."

She gave him a little wink. "Trust me."

He had to admit it all smelled amazing. But trusting her…

He wasn't so sure that was a good idea.

———

WHEN SPENCER LANDRY bit into his bacon bourbon blue burger from Monte's, Max was appalled at her nipples. They tightened right up as if he was moaning about something having to do with them.

Don't be ridiculous, girls. It's a burger with bacon, Monte's bourbon sauce, and blue cheese. Of course he's moaning. Only a vegetarian wouldn't moan over a Monte burger. And she'd bet even some of them could be won over if they'd give it a try.

Still, the sound of Spencer moaning should not be *that* sexy. He didn't know what he was doing to her.

Max pulled her hoodie together in front and hunched over to eat her food.

Oh, he knew she was attracted to him. That had been well established. Probably too well. She'd been all over him while they'd been dancing at the wedding and then when he'd pulled her toward the door of Ellie's with a simple "Come here," she'd gone along very willingly. And when he'd kissed her, there had been no mistaking that she was *into it*. But she couldn't just push bags of fries and burger wrappers out of the way, climb into his lap, and start licking him from head to toe.

Probably.

No matter how much she wanted to.

She didn't think he'd push her away. But it was a bad idea. She and Spencer were very different. She did not want to date a buttoned-up cop. Worse, an *FBI agent*. She was *not* turning her crow ruby in. She also wasn't going to overanalyze why this guy made her hot and needy in a way no man had in a *very* long time.

He, on the other hand, had not been able to shut up about *why do I feel this way about you when you're so not my type* last night.

Yeah, then there was the Spencer Landry's Perfect Woman Criteria.

No one liked enchiladas enough to use them to make important life decisions.

Or so she'd assumed.

There was just way too much overthinking and I'm-always-right going on inside that hot, broad-shouldered, charming-grin-giving guy on the other end of her couch.

He moaned again and she frowned.

He was also really bossy. Last night he hadn't even thought she should take an Uber back to New Orleans. She did not want to date a guy who thought she couldn't handle getting herself home.

She glanced over at Spencer. He clearly wasn't upset about her ordering food for him. Half his burger was gone, along with most of his fries. She grinned. She'd known he'd love Monte's. It was one of the neighborhood places she frequented, and she'd love to take him sometime…

She frowned and bit into her burger again. There wasn't going to be a "sometime" for her and Spencer.

He was a cop and not her type. But even more, *she* was not *his* type.

He thought that her not cooking or baking brownies was a flaw, and that her not having a normal pet was weird.

And maybe it was.

But it was ironic that her fascination with crime creeped him out, considering what he did for a living. Still, if Spencer wanted a girl who would like baking, and had a cat that would cuddle up in his lap, or a dog they could take for runs in the park, Max was not the girl for him.

Not just because of the dog. She did not run.

Max took another bite and thought about the pet thing. Her schedule was wacky, and it wasn't fair to leave an animal alone for hours and hours on end. She didn't cook or bake for similar reasons. She was either working or falling into bed exhausted from work when she was here. She was a workaholic and loved what she did.

So what if she wasn't making gourmet meals and hosting dinner parties?

Besides, as she'd pointed out, she lived in one of the greatest food cities in the world. She'd never out-cook or out-bake the people who did it for a living in New Orleans. She was supporting the local economy and allowing other people to live their dreams of making food for people like her.

Truthfully, that made her way more considerate and generous than any of the women Spencer dated who stayed at home and made him brownies, or whatever the fuck he thought was so sexy.

Max chewed with a scowl on her face. She did not care about Spencer Landry and the women he dated. She didn't even care what kind of cookies he liked best.

But she was hoping chocolate chip was on the list, considering she'd just ordered him some.

Okay, they weren't going to be homemade in her kitchen, and they weren't brownies, but they were from a local company that baked them fresh and brought them straight to her door. That was the best she could do tonight.

Besides, he'd showed up here unannounced. Even if she was so inclined to bake him brownies at any point, for any reason, she was utterly unprepared to do so tonight.

"So, tell me about who killed who," she said as she shoved three fries in her mouth.

Murder. That's what she wanted to talk about.

"You want to talk about this while we eat?"

"Why not?" She reached for her iced tea to wash down the spicy seasoning from the fries.

"There are photos in there. They're pretty gory."

"Well, I'd hope so. I can't give you all my thoughts on the case if I don't see the crime scene." Gory was good. It would take her mind off brownies, puppies, and Spencer's naked chest.

Not that she knew what his naked chest looked like. But she'd imagined it for months, felt it with only a thin dress shirt between her hands and all those glorious muscles last night, and it was now only a few inches away and covered with a single layer of blue cotton. Those buttons would take her no time.

"So eating a medium-rare burger while looking at human blood won't bother you?" he asked. He almost sounded annoyed.

"Just tell me about the case."

"Fine, I'll tell you before I show you."

She rolled her eyes. She did not have a weak stomach, but whatever.

He set up the case. A teenage party at the river. An argument between a guy and a girl. The girl left with the guy and his friend an hour later.

Max kept eating, taking in the details as Spencer spoke.

Or most of them anyway.

God, he had a great mouth.

Focus, Max.

"So the kid disappears for four days. The town is looking. All of his friends are looking. There is no physical evidence anywhere in or around the car. The two kids who were in the car with him are the last ones to see him."

Max frowned and shook her head. "Wait, which kid is missing?"

Spencer looked at her with one eyebrow arched. "Matthew."

"The friend?"

"The one who was arguing with the girl."

"Right."

"Are you okay?" Spencer asked, that eyebrow still up.

She scowled at him. "Fine. Just repeat it."

He'd doubtlessly covered this information, and she hated that she'd missed it. He was distracting as hell. And he didn't even like her. She was regretting ordering him cookies.

"Matthew drops Stephanie off at her house. Justin off at his. Their parents confirmed this. But Matthew never makes it home. Those two kids are the last ones to see him. Four days later, his body turns up by the side of a road leading from the party site back to town. A road that had been searched several times prior."

Okay, see, this was *interesting*. She was sorry she'd missed this information. It was really unfortunate that Spencer Landry was so hot. And that she already knew that kissing him was amazing. If they hadn't kissed, she could just pretend that he was an arrogant asshole who had nothing to offer.

"Do *you* have any pets?" she asked.

He blinked at her. "What?"

Yeah, okay, that was out of the blue. Or she was sure it *seemed* out of the blue.

She shrugged. "You just seemed overly interested in the fact that I don't have pets except for my crows. I'm just curious if you have pets."

He seemed like a dog guy. A big dog guy. As in, his dog would be big. Like a German Shepherd or a lab. Something that would like to run and play. Yeah, a lab. That fit. Spencer had grown up down on the bayou. She could just imagine that he would take his dog out running and swimming.

"No, I don't have a pet."

Oh. "Why not? You seem like a dog guy."

The corner of his mouth curled. "Do I?"

"You do."

"I'll take that as a compliment."

She lifted a shoulder. "So why don't you have a dog?"

"Crazy hours. I'm not home enough to take care of a dog. They need companionship and to go out and exercise. Doesn't seem fair."

She nodded. "That's why I don't have one."

He turned partially on the cushion to face her more fully. "But I *want* to have one someday. You know, when I get serious with someone. Get married. I'm hoping she'll have a normal job and be home regularly and can take care of the dog."

Right. That emphasis on "normal" did not slip past Max.

She was definitely not his type.

She nodded. "Good to have a plan."

He held her gaze for a moment, then nodded. "I think so too."

"So what condition was the body in?"

He blinked but was able to shift right back into their conversation about the cold case.

"Beaten badly. The coroner said he died of blunt force trauma to the back of the head."

"So, he possibly got into a fight with someone?"

"That angle was investigated. The coroner said that some of the blows were delivered by hand, but some had been delivered by an object. Likely a baseball bat. And some were inflicted nearly two days before he died."

Max bit into her burger as she thought. "Who were the main suspects?"

"The two kids who'd been with him were questioned. But Stephanie was way too small to have delivered the force needed to cause the injuries. Justin could've done it but really didn't have a motive. Plus, they both had alibis. They were dropped off by a car matching Matthew's car's description."

"The coroner's report says he died between thirty-six and forty-eight hours *after* the party," Max read. She looked up. "But that means he was killed up to two days before the body was discovered."

"Right."

Max finished her burger, chewing rapidly as her thoughts spun. "Which means the body was kept somewhere for two days before it was dumped. Wow."

Spencer finished his last fry, wadded up all the papers into one bag, crumpled it, and tossed it to the side. "There's no way those two teenagers could've kept a body hidden for two days without any trace evidence. Or without someone finding out, for that matter."

Max brushed her hands on her pants and reached for the folder. She started flipping through more reports and looking at all of the photos—and yeah, they were pretty gory. "I can't believe that there were no leads."

"Do you have scented candles or anything?"

She looked at Spencer. "What?" Did that have something to do with the case? Something else she was going to discover as she kept reading?

"I was just thinking… wondering… if you have any candles. You know, the kind that smell good."

"Is that about the case?"

"No."

"Does something smell bad in here?" she asked, wrinkling her nose.

"No. It's just…" He sighed. "I was noticing your shampoo."

Her eyes widened, and she became aware that they were sitting extremely close. They were both leaning over the file, looking at it together, and her ponytail had fallen forward over the shoulder closest to Spencer. She was sure he could smell her shampoo and probably her body spray.

"You don't like it?"

She tried to tell herself she was offended, but she could tell by the look on his face that he did not find the scent offensive. He wasn't leaning away from her, even now that she'd turned her head and their noses were mere inches apart. In fact, his gaze dropped to her mouth as she asked the question.

"No. It's… nice."

Was he looking for another scent to cover it up?

"It reminds me of… dryer sheets."

Max gave a soft snort. That wasn't exactly romantic.

His lips curled. "Well, it does. Fresh and light and sweet."

"Thanks." Hey, dryer sheets smelled nice.

"And it made me think of other… smells." He cleared his throat. "And I was just noticing that you don't have candles and potpourri and decorative things sitting around like a lot of women do."

Right. A lot of women. The little Susie Homemakers that turned his crank. Her house also didn't fucking smell like fresh-baked brownies.

"Only candles I have are those." She pointed to the candelabra on top of her bookshelf with five long, tapered candles.

"What do they smell like?"

"Nothing."

"That looks like something that would be sitting on top of the organ in a creepy castle in a horror movie."

She huffed out a small laugh. "It does?" She studied the black wrought iron candelabra with the maroon tapers with wax drips down the sides.

"Instead of blue pillar candles that smell like vanilla, that's what you go for?" he asked.

"I saw it in a window of an antique shop down in the Quarter and liked it. They're just candles to light the room if the power goes out or something. They don't have to smell like anything."

"A creepy, antique candelabra," he said almost to himself. "It's probably haunted."

She nodded. "There's a lot of that kind of stuff in New Orleans."

"That isn't a problem?"

"Well, I haven't seen any new apparitions since I've gotten it, but you never know. I have a gris-gris bag under my mattress, so I'll be okay."

His gaze snapped to hers. "Any *new* apparitions?"

She lifted a shoulder. "It's an old building. In New Orleans."

"You're telling me you have ghosts."

She really liked messing with him. "No, I'm not telling you that. But you're pretty funny when you're creeped out."

"But you do have gris-gris under your mattress, don't you?" he asked after looking at her for several seconds.

She nodded. She did. The Haitian woman who'd given it to her had promised it would protect her. Max figured it couldn't hurt.

Spencer sighed.

There was a knock on the door just then, and Spencer jumped. Max laughed and handed him the folder. "Be right back."

She retrieved the cookie delivery and returned to the sofa.

"What's this?" Spencer eyed the bag suspiciously.

Even though it *obviously* smelled like cookies.

She pulled the warm box out of the bag and held it out to him. "Cookies."

Spencer looked up at her with surprise. "You got me cookies?"

"They're fresh-baked. Homemade by someone. Not me. And they're not brownies. But I thought they might be an okay substitute."

He took the box from her, seemingly speechless for a moment. She liked that. He set them on the table.

"Thank you. I guess," he finally said.

She frowned. "You guess? I mean, you did pay for them, but I thought it was kind of a nice gesture."

"Well, yeah."

"You don't seem that enthusiastic. You don't like cookies?"

"I love cookies. But…"

Max propped a hand on her hip when he trailed off. "But what?"

"I don't want to fucking think about you every time I eat a chocolate chip cookie," he said with a scowl.

She scowled right back at him. "Excuse me?"

"You said last night that I'd laid out a bunch of reasons why we shouldn't date."

"I did say that," she agreed.

"And then I came over here to apologize."

"Right."

"But I thought maybe we could just be friends."

"Spit it out, Spencer," she said, exasperated.

He shoved a hand through his hair. "I don't think I can just be friends with you."

"We've been getting along fine!" She gestured at the table with the burger bags and the cold case files. "You think my crows and candles are weird, but that's okay. We can still spend time together."

"Not without me constantly thinking about how fucking amazing you smell and taste and *sound* when I kiss you!" He blew out a breath. "You're driving me nuts and I don't understand why."

Her eyes widened. She had, of course, known that he'd enjoyed the making out. She had not expected him to admit being so worked up over it though.

She also hadn't expected to be quite this delighted to know that it had been plaguing him too.

"It was *really* good kissing," she finally said.

He nodded. "It was. But we drive each other crazy. We were drunk. And it doesn't seem like something between us could work out."

She nodded. All of that was true.

"So why is it that ever since meeting you, my heart speeds up every time I see a woman with red hair? For almost a *year*, Max.

And why do I read your articles all the time now, when before I barely knew who you were? And *why* do I feel a little surge of admiration, maybe even pride, when I do? And why am I now afraid that even though you didn't make me those cookies, and have no intention of *ever* making me cookies, and would probably make terrible cookies if you tried, every time I smell chocolate chip cookies from now on I'm going to think about you?"

Max knew her eyes were as wide as they could go, and her breathing was faster than it should be for standing perfectly still next to her couch. But everything Spencer had just said had her heart racing and adrenaline pumping.

Several beats passed.

Finally, she said, "Well, maybe we should just stick to the part we know works."

"The part that works?" he asked.

But rather than explain, she simply stepped close, slid onto his lap, straddled his thighs, ran her hands over his shoulders to the back of his head and into his hair, and kissed him.

THE HEAT EXPLODED between them instantly.

Spencer's hands dropped to her hips, squeezing, then sliding lower to cup her ass, bringing her forward against his erection.

The thin material of her lounge pants allowed her to feel the steely ridge behind his fly, and her nipples rejoiced at being able to press into his hard chest.

She was right, too, that the buttons that held the blue cotton across that chest took her no time to unfasten, and soon she was running her palms over his hot bare skin and the hard planes of his shoulders, chest, and abs. She relished the way it made him shudder.

"So you do have tattoos," she said, running the pads of her fingers over the ink that decorated his left upper arm, shoulder, and shoulder blade.

"Yeah." His voice was husky.

"I like them. I like that I had to strip you out of your uptight button-down shirt to see them. I like that you don't seem like the tattoo type but—"

"God, I love your hands on me." He pulled her in, kissing her deeply. "Fuck," he groaned as he dragged his mouth from hers, along her jaw, and down her neck. He paused at her collarbone, breathing in deeply. "You feel so damned good. You smell so damned good. I was trying so hard not to do this."

"Well, stop trying not to do it," she told him breathlessly, tipping her head back so that he could drag his hot mouth up and down the front of her throat.

"Are you sure?"

"Yes. God, yes."

He pulled back just enough to look up at her. "This is probably a bad idea."

"Oh, it *is* a bad idea," she agreed.

"So, we're on the same page. Bad idea that we're going to do anyway."

"Same page," she said with a nod.

She knew they didn't belong together. But this felt good. There was no reason for them *not* to do this. Neither of them was attached. They both knew what this was. And yeah, if he loved chocolate chip cookies and would smell them in the future and think of her, a tiny part of her liked that idea.

Then she stopped having ideas. Because Spencer slipped his hands from her ass, up her back, and underneath her tank, drawing the material up and bunching it under her arms, exposing her breasts. He cupped her breasts as she shrugged out of her hoodie. Then he continued to strip the top over her head and toss it to the floor.

"You look a lot better in cream and pink than in black," he told her, his thumbs brushing over her nipples and making her whimper.

She smiled at him. "You don't even like the way I dress?"

"I prefer you undressed." He lowered his head and took one of the stiff peaks into his mouth, licking and then sucking.

She preferred herself undressed when Spencer was around, too, as it turned out.

She arched her back and ground her hips forward, pressing more insistently against his fly.

"More."

"This is foreplay," he teased, switching sides and swirling his tongue around that nipple before sucking hard.

She curled her fingers into his scalp, feeling her inner muscles clench hard.

"Don't need a lot of that. We already had burgers and crime scene photos."

He chuckled against her breast. "Of course you would consider that foreplay."

"Well, and a criminal investigation last year and a wedding reception."

"You think we've been working up to this all that time?" He lifted his gaze to hers.

She knew looking into those deep green eyes that the answer to that was absolutely yes.

"I think the first time I walked into Ellie's bar looking for Caroline and assumed that you were hiding her from me, I figured you'd end up taking your clothes off for me," Max told him. "So let's get on with it."

She reached between them for his fly, running her hand down his denim-encased cock.

He groaned, and the hands at her waist squeezed.

"Grab the condoms in my wallet."

She found them quickly and tossed the wallet onto the coffee table as she kept one of the foil packets in hand. He scooted her back on his lap, unbuttoning and unzipping, then working the denim and boxers over his hips to midthigh. That was all she needed. She reached for his impressive length, wrapping her hand around it and giving him a long stroke.

"Max," he said through gritted teeth.

"Just give me a second," she told him as she stroked again, watching his smooth, hard length slide through her fist.

"Before you go too far, you need to get rid of some clothes too," he told her, his voice tight.

Oh, yeah. She stood, quickly stripped off her pants and panties, and then returned to his lap.

"Fuck, woman. You're gonna kill me."

She arched a brow. "What am I doing?"

"Rushing. I'm not even getting a good look. Not to mention a good taste."

The next thing she knew, she was tipped onto her back on the sofa cushions next to her. Papers and photographs wrinkled underneath her, but she forgot all about them as soon as Spencer spread her knees and settled his big shoulders between her thighs.

The back of the couch kept her left knee propped up, but Spencer used an elbow to spread her right knee open until her foot slid to the floor. One big hand cupped her ass while the other splayed across her belly.

She was hot and so ready. She never in a million years would have imagined being in *this* position with *this* guy.

Max lifted up on her elbows. "Wow, this is first-time stuff for you?"

He looked up from where he had been carefully studying her pussy. She wasn't sure she'd even been so thoroughly examined at her last doctor's appointment.

He gave her a smug grin. "Does it surprise you that I'm thorough?"

No, it did not. "This just isn't common first-date treatment."

He shook his head. "The members of my gender can be so stupid."

She laughed lightly. "You don't have to, you know."

He kept his eyes on hers as he moved his hand from her ass to stroke up over her clit and then back down, sliding two fingers into her wet heat. She gasped. She felt the delicious tingles of the stroke, of course, but the way his eyes were locked on hers made it especially hot.

"Oh, I have to," he told her.

He stroked again, watching her face. She pulled her bottom lip between her teeth and worked to hold his gaze. This was as intimate as she'd been with anyone in a very long time. Not just having him down *there,* but Spencer made it seem like there was not a single thought or emotion that she could think or feel that he wouldn't know about.

She felt incredibly vulnerable. And strangely okay with it.

"I figure if I'm going to be thinking about you every time I smell a cookie," he said, his voice gravelly, "you can think about me every time you sit on this couch."

"I sit on the couch every single day." She couldn't hide the breathlessness as he moved his fingers in and out in a rhythm that made her toes literally curl.

"You have no idea how often I eat baked goods."

He picked up the pace slightly and added a thumb over her clit, and Max let her head fall back as the sensations rippled through her.

"You also clearly have no idea how much I love every fucking thing about seeing you like this," he said, his voice low and gruff.

She could only imagine how she looked. Completely wanton. At his mercy. Totally helpless.

The foot resting on the floor slid out, opening her even farther, and she whimpered. "Oh God, Spencer."

"Yeah, this is such a bad idea," he muttered.

Her head came up as he lowered his. His tongue replaced his thumb. He gave her clit a long lick as he continued to pump his fingers in and out. Then he sucked, and she gasped as an explosion of pleasure burst through her.

Of course he was good at this too. Spencer Landry had this air of competence about him. As if everything he did had to turn out perfectly, and he was personally offended when something didn't go according to plan.

If his goal had been to seduce her tonight, the project was going off without a hitch.

If his intent when he'd flipped her to her back was to make her lose her mind and have one of the hardest orgasms of her life, he was right on track to accomplish that objective.

His tongue moved over her clit in swirls that had her winding tighter with every pass until he finally sucked hard, and her orgasm crashed over her.

"Spencer!" Her back arched off the couch, and she reached for his head, her fingers clutching his hair as waves of pleasure coursed through her.

With a growl she couldn't completely decipher, he shifted away from her body. "Condom?" he asked tightly.

She became aware that she was gripping the foil packet in one hand. She uncurled her fingers and offered it up to him.

He took it, ripped it open, and rolled it on.

"You ready for me?"

She lifted her foot from the floor and wrapped it around his waist. "After that? I might just give you my crow ruby."

He was leaning above her, one hand braced on the back of the couch, one on the cushion beside her. She could feel his cock against her clit.

"How about enchiladas?" he asked.

"Well, let's not be ridiculous." She reached down and gripped his ass, pressing him closer.

"You drive me nuts," he muttered. But he followed that up with a nice, deep thrust.

On the heels of her intense orgasm, he slid home easily. There was a stretch, but it was delicious and welcome and caused tingles to dance through her body, from her scalp to the tips of her toes. He could do that again and again.

And he did. With a long groan, he pulled back and then sank deep again. Then again. And again.

Every time felt better than the last. Her already-delighted nerve endings welcomed the friction, and her brain synapses that had just enjoyed an amazing orgasm said *yes, more.*

"Goddamn, you feel good," he said in a near growl as he flexed forward and pulled back.

"God, same. Honestly, if you wanted to be incredibly cruel to me, you'd stop right now."

He thrust forward, deep and hard. "I couldn't stop right now if the entire nation's security depended on it."

For some reason, that was the hottest thing he could've said. Probably because she was weird. And because she knew this guy and his dedication to his job.

Still, she brought both legs tighter around him, pressing her heels into his ass and making him stay deep as she clenched around him.

"Dammit, Max."

"I know, this isn't a good idea."

"It's really not."

They might be very different people and never be able to work out as a couple, but at least they could agree that the sex was incredible and that this whole thing had been a mistake.

"Want to feel you come again. Around my cock, this time," he said roughly.

"Good," she said breathlessly. "I'm almost there."

That made him pick up the pace. He started thrusting faster, deeper, and harder.

"Yes, Spencer, just like that."

"Max," he said in a deep voice.

She loved that right-on-the-edge tone.

"You were not supposed to be this good."

She laughed softly. "Sorry."

He thrust again harder. "No, you're not."

"Not even one bit."

He moved harder and faster, and she couldn't get enough.

She felt the imminent orgasm, and she clutched his back. "Spencer, I'm so close."

"Come on, Max. Come on." It was clear he was speaking through gritted teeth.

She felt the beginning ripples.

"Of course fucking you is amazing," he said roughly.

It was probably the graphic language but also the fact that she was getting to him that sent her shooting over the peak. She cried out his name as her body clenched around him, and she came.

"Yes!" he hissed as he thrust into her relentlessly, as if he'd just been waiting for that moment to let it all go. Finally, roaring her name as well, he came hard.

He stayed braced above her for several seconds as they panted, trying to catch their breaths. Then he pushed himself up and headed into the bathroom.

Max covered her eyes with her hand and worked on pulling oxygen into her lungs. "Well, fuck."

"Just what I was thinking."

She peered at him through her fingers. "So, we did that."

He strode toward her, his pants pulled back up on his hips, but his zipper still open. "We sure fucking did."

She pushed herself up to sitting and reached for her hoodie, slipping into it but not bothering to zip it. The guy had seen everything she had to show.

"We wrinkled the crime scene photos," he said as he dropped onto the end of the couch.

She looked down. The crime scene photos were still under her butt, as a matter of fact.

"Oops." She shifted, pulling the folder from underneath her and tossing it on the coffee table.

He shook his head. "You know, most women wouldn't have been in the mood for that after looking at those photos, not to mention being nonchalant about being fucked on top of them."

"Then most women aren't properly caught up in the moment. So either you or they are doing something wrong."

He huffed out a breath. "Not that I've ever tried that with another woman and crime scene photos."

She lifted a shoulder. "Maybe you've been missing a key seduction technique."

He just sat looking at her for a moment. "I don't think so."

"Are you staying tonight?" she asked.

"I haven't been invited."

She tipped her head. "Me inviting you to spend the night and you saying yes would be a terrible idea."

"It certainly would."

"Do you want to spend the night, Spencer?"

"Yes, I do, Max."

———

THE NEXT MORNING, as he headed out of her bedroom, she sleepily called from the bed, "Don't forget to take the cookies."

"You don't want me to leave them for you?" he asked, turning back.

For fuck's sake, the woman was sexy as hell, even first thing in the morning.

She shook her head, her gorgeous hair moving like silk across the black—of course—pillowcase. "I don't like cookies that much."

"You don't like—" He cut himself off and shook his head. "Okay."

She didn't bake cookies, but she didn't even really *like* cookies? What the fuck was he doing here?

Having the best fucking sex of your life. Four times. And wanting more right this second.

Dammit.

He turned to head for the front door again, not wanting to say anything about seeing her again.

"You know, they never questioned Matthew's parents as suspects."

He stopped and looked back with a frown. She was thinking about the cold case from last night? First thing in the morning? After the night they'd had? "His parents?" Spencer asked, despite all the other questions.

She propped up on one elbow, the sheet *almost* falling away from her breasts.

Spencer felt his body tighten as if she was lying there bare naked. He wanted her again. Right now. Even after *having her,* very well, in multiple positions.

"Yeah. They asked them a few questions about what time he got home, his emotional state, appearance, stuff like that. But his parents should have been suspects."

And despite them talking about murder. And a pretty gruesome one at that.

"Why do you think that?"

"The file said he and the girl fought on the way to her house and that he slapped her. The other boy confirmed that and also reported Matthew was distraught after that. His parents confirmed that. Maybe he showed up at home upset. Maybe he told his parents he hit the girl. Maybe his stepdad hit *him* a couple of times. Maybe his stepdad was a drunk. Or an asshole child abuser. Or had stolen property. Who knows? No one ever looked at them as suspects. Maybe the stepdad was afraid the girl would tell someone Matthew hit her. Maybe his stepdad lost his cool and he beat the shit out of him because he'd done something foolish and was going to get cops poking around the house or cost them a bunch of legal fees. And maybe he beat him so badly that he ended up dying, and they had to dump his body."

Spencer stared at her. She said it all very matter-of-factly.

And it wasn't a crazy theory.

"You've been thinking about this? Between when we talked about the case and now? In spite of all the stuff we were doing?"

She grinned. "Well, I wasn't thinking about it *during* if that's what you're worried about."

He shook his head. He had actually been wondering about that. He sighed and focused on what she'd said. "So you think it was the kid's parents?"

"I'm just saying it's a possibility. Other than those first interviews, they weren't questioned again and no one else was questioned *about them*. I think the cops screwed up."

Spencer mulled that over. Fuck. It all made sense. It was horrific, of course. But people did terrible things to the people they were supposed to love and care for all the time. He knew that. "You got to that fast. And you were even a little… distracted…last night."

She shrugged. "I'm just really good."

He opened his mouth to respond, then closed it. He liked her. He *really* liked sleeping with her, but he also liked her. And she was weird and a little dark and didn't even like cookies.

All of this had been a terrible idea.

But at least he got to leave her in bed. Not his bed. And she wasn't propped up reading. But she *was* smiling. All in all, he could not be upset with how the night turned out.

"I'll see you, Max."

She frowned. "We're not dating now are we?"

He hesitated. Why did he hesitate? And why was she frowning? "No. We're…"

She lifted an eyebrow. And didn't even attempt to fill in that blank.

"Friends," he said weakly. "We'll probably run into each other once in a while."

She grinned. "Okay. Good luck with your cookie erections." Then she flopped back onto her back, pulled her comforter up to her chin, and closed her eyes.

He choked. "Uh, thanks." Dammit. This girl was just not what he'd expected.

He needed to avoid her. As much as possible. As in *not* seeing her again. Even at Zander and Caroline's future wedding. He needed to be sick that night.

He might also need to give up cookies. Forever.

But of course, at the last minute, he grabbed the bag of cookies on the way out the door, and stubbornly dug a chocolate chip out as he headed for his truck.

Maxine Keller was not going to ruin cookies for him.

And it took one bite to realize he was totally fucked. He was definitely going to think of her every time he ate one. And chocolate chip really were his favorite. Besides brownies, of course.

Two weeks later…

"THERE'S BEEN a bomb threat at the New Orleans News."

Spencer's partner, Chris Wilson, looked up. "I heard."

"Let's go."

"Where're we going?" But Chris was already on his feet.

"To her place."

"Whose place?" Chris followed Spencer's long strides down the hall.

"Max Keller."

So much for not seeing her again. He hadn't eaten a fucking chocolate chip cookie in two weeks. He hadn't talked to Zander in two weeks for fear he'd say something about Caroline, which would remind Spencer of Max. Spencer hadn't spoken to Wyatt in two weeks other than texts because he was afraid his brother would ask about her.

And he'd still fucking thought about her every damned day.

"Who's Max Keller?" Chris asked as Spencer hit the door

leading to the parking lot so hard it bounced off the bricks with a bang loud enough they probably heard it back in the main office.

"The reporter the threat was directed at. She's not at the office, no one's heard from her yet this morning, she's not answering her phone."

Spencer's gut was so tight he felt like he might be sick.

"This isn't our jurisdiction, is it?" Chris asked. "Local authorities will handle it."

"Just get in the truck," Spencer told his partner tightly.

Chris did.

Spencer left a black mark on the pavement as he peeled out of the parking lot.

CHAPTER ONE

"FBI! Open the door!"

There was no answer. Fuck, fuck, fuck.

He tried again, pounding louder. "FBI! Open up, or we're coming in!"

She has to be here. Her car's here. Her phone is here. No friends have seen her or spoken to her since early yesterday. She wasn't at work.

He looked at Lance. The detective nodded. They had to go in.

Spencer took a big step back. Lance took his place. Spencer lifted his foot and kicked the door open. Lance went through first, his gun drawn. He went left, and Spencer went right. Spencer's partner, Chris, and Lance's partner, Moreno, were right behind them.

And… nothing.

There was no one in the living room. Or the kitchen, which they could see across the island that separated the room from the main living space.

Well… hell.

Spencer started down the hallway toward the bedroom as Lance went for the balcony. Chris and Moreno headed for the other bedrooms.

"Clear!" Lance shouted from the balcony.

"Clear," Chris confirmed from the master bedroom.

"Clear," Moreno called from the guest room.

But Spencer had stopped outside the closed bathroom door. The shower was running. And a woman was singing along with music playing from, he'd guess, her phone.

Well… *fuck.*

He couldn't believe the relief that seeped through him. He braced a hand on the doorframe as his knees got weak.

"Okay?" Moreno asked.

"She's inside," Spencer said.

Moreno cocked his head toward the doorway. "Sounds okay."

"Kitchen is clear too," Lance said, holstering his weapon as he joined them in the hallway.

Spencer nodded and swallowed. Jesus. The adrenaline was still coursing, and he was having trouble getting his shit together.

"Damn, you okay, man?" Moreno clapped him on the shoulder. "You need me to go in?"

"Don't even fucking think about it." Spencer straightened and shoved the other man back.

"What the fu—" Chris came down the hall and stopped when he found the other three men gathered outside the bathroom. "What's goin' on?"

"We found her," Lance said with a grin, pointing at the door.

"She okay?" Chris asked.

"Not sure," Moreno said. "Haven't asked her yet. She's singing along to that new Hayden Ross song. She's pretty good. We probably shouldn't interrupt."

"For fuck's sake." Chris strode forward, and Spencer knew he was going to pound on the door if Spencer didn't move his ass.

Spencer put up a hand. "I've got this."

"We need to find out if she's all right. She's just taking a fucking shower? Not answering her phone or reporting in? You don't know what's going on in there. Does she even know what happened?"

Spencer was going to guess no. But he'd find out. Without these guys around.

"Just give me some space."

The three other men moved back, but not nearly far enough for Spencer's preference. He lifted a hand and knocked on the door.

He heard a scream on either side.

"Max, it's me!" Okay, she probably didn't know his voice *that* well. "Spencer. Landry." He felt like a dumbass.

"Spencer? Holy shit! What the fuck!"

He heard the sound of something that he hoped was only a shampoo bottle hitting the shower floor.

"What the hell are you doing?" she demanded.

"We need to talk."

"Did you *break into my apartment*?" she shouted.

"No! I…" Well, fuck. Yes, he had. "We have to talk!"

"That's what phones are for!"

"You're not answering your phone."

"So leave a message, and I'll call you back!"

He sighed and glanced at his three co-workers. They were all watching, with intrigued and amused expressions. He did not need this. He'd lost at least two years of his life this morning, worrying if Max was all right and where she was. And now she was going to give him a hard time. Of course she was.

"Something's happened, Max. We need to talk."

"Just get the fuck out of here, Spencer! I will call you later."

"I can't leave. Something's happened."

"Like what?"

"I'm…" He was not going to keep yelling this through a door. "I'm coming in."

"The *fuck* you are."

He heard the shower shut off and the sound of the rings of the shower curtain sliding along a metal rod.

He again looked at the three men accompanying him. So it was now *very* evident that he knew the woman they were here to check on. And that she wasn't happy to have him here. Great. He'd known all of that would be quite apparent to them at some point. But he hadn't cared when he hadn't known if she was dead or had been kidnapped or just what the hell was going on. Now he was so fucking relieved that she was all right that he couldn't work up much ire about her pissy mood.

He also had to make sure she stayed all right. That was probably going to take a little more talking and possibly more charm than he was capable of. So he needed at least Chris to stick around.

But this wasn't the FBI's jurisdiction. So as NOLA PD detectives, Peter Lance and Ricky Moreno had to be here. This was going to be their investigation.

Dammit.

He was *not* going to turn Max over to them right away. He just wasn't. Not until he had a moment—or forty-five—with her.

He heard the sound of footsteps approaching, and the door in front of him suddenly swung open, revealing a wet, mad redhead wrapped in only a single piece of light blue terrycloth.

His body reacted immediately. It didn't care that there'd been a bomb threat, that he'd spent the past nearly two hours wondering if she was dead or alive, that she was definitely *not* his type, that she thought he was kind of an asshole, or that they had an audience. He immediately flashed back to the last time he'd been in this apartment when she'd been wearing much less than that towel.

She stared up at him. "I cannot believe that you're here. What do you—" In the periphery of her vision, she apparently caught sight of the three other men. She turned toward them, frowning. "What in the hell is going on?"

She either noticed their badges or figured they could be trusted if they were with him.

He'd like to think it was the latter but was pretty sure it was the former.

"Guys, we need some space." No matter what else was going on, Spencer was very aware that the three other men were getting quite an eyeful.

Sure, she was basically covered. But the amount of skin she was showing—creamy, smooth, pale skin that he could personally attest had no freckles—was a much more significant percentage than the amount of skin she was covering.

Threat to her life or not, she looked hot as hell, and he stupidly didn't want any other guys seeing her like this.

"Ma'am, are you sure you want to deal with Agent Landry? One of us would be happy to help you instead," Moreno said with a shit-eating grin.

"We'll be in the living room." Chris grabbed each of the younger men by the collar and turned them before shoving them down the hallway.

Spencer listened to Moreno and Lance chuckle as they headed for Max's living room.

But his gaze was focused entirely on her.

She was in one piece. Alive and well. Seemingly oblivious to what had been going on that morning.

"Why aren't you at work?"

Her eyes widened. "I'm getting ready for work. I had a late night last night."

Do not ask about her late night.

She narrowed her eyes. "Do *not* ask me about my late night."

He sucked a breath in through his nose and let it out. "There was a bomb threat at the newsroom."

Her eyes widened again. "A *bomb threat*?"

"Yes. Considered credible enough to have us bring the bomb squad in. No one could find you. Hadn't heard from you. Caroline says she hasn't talked to you in over twenty-four hours. You weren't answering your phone. I was… *we*… were worried."

The hand clutching the towel against her breasts tightened slightly. "I… Thank you. I'm sorry I wasn't answering the phone. I woke up, went to work out—which makes it hard to hear my phone—and then came home and got in the shower. I wasn't expected at work until later today. I wasn't expecting anyone to call or text, so I wasn't looking."

"No one knew that you weren't coming in until late."

She frowned. "My editor, Paul, knew that."

"Paul wasn't in either. We haven't talked to him."

"Yeah, he's in Baton Rouge covering a story. But generally, the reporters don't report to one another. We don't worry about one another coming and going."

Spencer scrubbed a hand over his face. "Yeah, that's what they said. Doesn't make it easy for law enforcement when things like this happen, though."

"Sorry. I'm okay, though."

He studied her. She was okay. Fucking gorgeous, too. "You need to get dressed."

"Yeah. Okay."

"We have some questions. And… some more information."

She frowned. "Something else I need to know?"

"Yes. I assume you want more details about the threat."

Of course she would want more details. She was a reporter and one of the most curious women he knew. But there was more she *needed* to know as well.

"What are you not telling me?"

"I'm gonna tell you everything. Just put some clothes on."

"Spencer, tell me now. You're freaking me out."

"And you're standing in front of me dripping wet, in a towel. I'm having a little trouble being professional."

That seemed to stun her for a moment. She sucked in a little breath and just stared at him for three heartbeats. "That's a you problem. Tell me what you have to tell me."

She was so difficult. God, why did the sex with her have to be so good? Fuck, he was a professional. He was damned good at his job. He took what he did seriously. He could not be distracted by the fact that the sight of her bare skin, the smell of her, and the *memories* of her in this apartment were clawing through his brain and making his entire body tight and hard.

"The threat was directed at *you* specifically."

She didn't react to that. She just stared at him.

"Max? Did you hear me?"

He wasn't sure she had. She didn't say anything or even move.

Yeah, he didn't want to deal with her going into shock or having some kind of emotional reaction when she was wrapped in a towel. He wanted to be able to touch her, help her, and do whatever she needed him to do. But he really needed her to not be naked for that.

He took her by the upper arms. "Time to get dressed," he said firmly.

He turned her and nudged her down the hall. She took one hesitant step. Then stopped. He sighed. He nudged her again. She took two steps that time. Then stopped. And, with a deep breath, Spencer accepted his fate. He walked her into her bedroom and sat her on the edge of her bed. He crossed to her closet first.

She had dresses. He was actually surprised by that. But that was stupid. He thought of her as a black hoodie, sweatpants, and possibly a ripped black jeans kind of girl. But he'd seen her in more. When he first met her, she'd been wearing a skirt. The night they'd done their crazy stakeout of the guys who were illegally buying and selling big cats in a black-market scheme, she'd also worn a skirt. She looked fucking great in skirts.

He reached for a sundress that was bright yellow. If he had to put money on it, he'd guess she'd worn this thing about once. He turned toward her and tossed it on the bed next to her. She hadn't moved or said anything. She had her bottom lip pulled between her teeth and was staring at the floor.

Spencer knew the wheels in her head were turning fast. He didn't think she was actually in shock. No doubt she was going over a list of people who might have the motivation and means to bomb the building where she worked. At least he could count on her to take this seriously. She knew that people actually did build and deploy bombs.

He crossed to her dresser and went through her top two drawers, not bothering to feel creepy about it. Every single bra, however, was either black or tan. Not that he had a problem with either, but why did this woman have no other colors? Not even one? Sighing, he pulled out a flesh-colored bra—though, as he well knew, her skin tone was about two shades lighter than this—and opened her panty drawer. More black and tan. But wait, what was this?

With a grin, he pulled out a pair from the back right corner that was leopard print. Well, *that* was a little interesting, at least. Of course, the general black and tan were the same. But then something caught his eye. A flash of pink. Okay, *now* they were talking. He snagged the pair of hot pink bikini panties quickly and was pleased to find not just a pair of cherry red panties under it but a matching red bra.

Alrighty then.

He crossed to the bed with the panties and tan bra and held them out.

"Please tell me I get to help you put these on."

That seemed to snap her out of her daze. She looked at the hot pink silk, then up at him. "These?"

He grinned. "Oh yes, these."

She rolled her eyes, then over at the dress. "Not wearing that."

"It looks nice, and it's hot outside."

"I'm going to work, Spencer. I can't wear a sundress to work."

He scowled. "You're not going to work."

"Of course I am. What else am I going to do?"

"Max, a guy threatened to blow up the building where you work because of *you*. You are *not* going to work. In fact, you're not going anywhere until we get this straightened out."

She stood up from the bed and crossed her arms. The towel slipped a little, but she didn't seem to notice. Spencer did.

"What does 'straightened out' mean exactly?"

"It means finding out who did this."

"So I can't go *anywhere* until you find this guy? How long is that going to take?"

"You know I don't know that. Hopefully not long. But you're in danger."

Spencer was working on being professional here, but later, he might just admit how fucking scared he'd been that morning when he'd heard the call that the bomb threat had been at *New Orleans News*. He always worried, of course. He always got that dump of adrenaline when big stuff happened. And a bomb threat was always big stuff. But he didn't get *scared*. This was his job. He had to expect shit like this to happen. And then he went out and dealt with it.

When he'd thought about Max being the target today, he'd been scared.

Fuck.

She frowned, apparently processing that. "Was there any bomb found? Or was it just a threat?"

He knew where this was going. He propped his hands on both hips and gave her his menacing FBI-guy look. "No bomb. But that doesn't matter."

"Is everyone all right?"

"Yes. Basically. Shook up, as you can imagine."

She nodded. "So he doesn't know where I live. Or who I am."

He scowled. "You don't know that."

"If it was a personal attack, as you say, then why not threaten me at home? Put a note on my car. Email me or call me person-ally? The closest he could get was work."

"Maybe he wanted your boss to shut your stories and investi-gation down."

She nodded. "Yeah. Maybe."

"Which he's going to do."

She nodded again. She wasn't looking at him. And seemed oblivious to the fact she was mostly naked.

Spencer was able to admit he was struggling. This woman made him nuts, on many levels, and her standing there in only a towel, after having her life threatened, was stretching his very thin thread of patience to a near breaking point.

"So I need to let him know that I'm not at work," she said after a moment.

"You're *not* going to be at work."

She huffed out a breath. "But I need to let him *know* that. So if he tries again, he won't target the *News*."

Spencer closed his eyes and counted to ten. It wasn't her fault this had happened. It wasn't her fault that it was true that the guy might try again. It *was* her fault that she didn't seem rattled enough for Spencer.

How rattled would that be?

Yeah, well, launching herself into his arms and asking him to hold her would be a good start.

He shoved a hand through his hair. Max in his arms wasn't going to make anything easier. And now he had to think about how tiny the chances of her ever being in his arms again actually were.

Fuck.

"How are you going to do that?" Spencer managed to ask. He hated this plan, and he didn't even know what the plan was.

"Post about it." Her eyes came back to his. "Social media. My own. I mean, it's still my pen name, but I have accounts that are mine and not officially linked to the company. I'll post about the threat and that some coward decided to threaten all of my co-workers and bully me in an attempt to shut me up."

Spencer took a step forward. "You will *not* do that."

"Of course I will."

"You will not taunt and insult the man who threatened to blow you up this morning."

"I'm not going to let him think he scared me," she said with a lift of her chin. "I'll let him know that I won't be at work. But that if he wants to shut me up, it's not going to work."

"Max, Jesus." Spencer realized she was serious and a cold shiver went down his spine.

"I'm not going to stop. Guys like this think they can throw their power and money around and get away with *anything*. That's not how it works. But you're right. I can't put other people at risk. I'll do this on my own, away from the newsroom and everyone."

"So, just sitting here in your apartment?"

She shrugged. "I guess so."

"What if he knows where you live?"

"Why wouldn't the threat have come here?"

"Because threatening your co-workers is a bigger move than just threatening you."

She pulled her bottom lip between her teeth again, which Spencer found madly distracting. God, he loved her lips. He could remember everything about them, from the taste, to the feel of them under his, to the feel of them around his cock.

They'd definitely not gotten a lot of sleep the night he'd spent here.

In the bed right behind her.

"I'll stay at a hotel."

He blinked. For fuck's sake. He needed to *focus*. "No."

"Excuse me?"

"If he knows who you are, he'll follow you there. That could put a lot of people at risk."

"Then the people here in my building are at risk too," she pointed out.

He nodded. She lived in a townhouse with two more on one side and three on the other.

She broke eye contact, staring instead at the top button on his shirt. He could tell that her wheels were spinning again.

Then she dropped her towel, and *his* wheels completely stopped spinning.

She reached for the panties and started to pull them on.

He coughed. "Max."

She looked up at him, wiggling the pink silk into place. The move, of course, made her perfect tits bounce enticingly. "You've already seen it all. Up close. Repeatedly."

He sucked in a deep breath. "Does that make this appropriate?"

"You broke into my apartment while I was showering and are now telling me I can't go anywhere without putting everyone around me in danger. We're pretty far past me worrying if it's appropriate for you to see me naked, Spencer."

Well, that was a good point. He was pretty sure. He'd already forgotten what she'd said exactly.

She reached for her bra pulling it into place, and reaching behind to fasten the tiny hooks. Having her breasts covered with the bra cups should have been a relief. But it didn't seem to register with his body that she was covering up rather than undressing. What could he say? Women in underwear, especially *this* woman in her underwear, made him think of sex.

Was that a little caveman? Probably. But he'd just had a hell of a morning. He was beyond apologizing profusely for his natural physiologic responses.

"What was the guy pissed about?" she asked.

"The guy?"

"The guy who made the threat?" Her tone indicated she thought he was an idiot for not following the conversation.

The woman had no idea what she did to him. That was probably good.

"What makes you think it was a guy?"

She shrugged. "I mostly investigate men, so I tend to piss more men off than women."

Spencer couldn't help his short laugh at that.

She narrowed her eyes, then stomped around him toward her dresser. Her room was not huge, and she, of course, had to brush up against him to get there. Because the rest of his day hadn't been difficult enough.

Whether it was appropriate or not, he turned to watch her. "He didn't identify himself as a male, but you're probably right. He's pissed about the story on the chemical dumping."

She yanked open the third dresser drawer and pulled out a pair of jeans. She slammed it shut again, shook the jeans out, and started to step into them. Spencer didn't even try to avert his eyes from the sweet curve of her ass. In *hot pink*. He could still feel her bare ass in his palms, and honestly if she was just going to get dressed in front of him, who was he to argue? The chances of him ever seeing this woman naked again or even in panties were about a million to one.

"No. He's pissed about my *comments* about the article. And that other people read them and commented back."

Spencer frowned. "What do you mean? What comments?"

She pulled open the fourth drawer and withdrew a dark purple t-shirt. She pulled it over her head, then buttoned and zipped the jeans as she turned to face him, but she didn't meet his eyes.

Again, she was clearly lost in thought. "Our articles are published electronically."

Spencer nodded. *The New Orleans News* wasn't a print newspaper. There were no delivery people. It was an online news site that people could subscribe to for more in-depth articles, but they also published big headline stories and short highlight pieces to various social media sites and via text alerts.

"In the article, I didn't name any names other than the ones you guys had publicly released as suspects. And there were no threats after that. But in the *comments* on the article a few days later, I speculated that there were other people involved. The threat came after *that*."

Now that she was more covered, he was able to better focus on the conversation.

"Takes time to build a bomb."

"Was there actually a bomb?" she asked, running her fingers through her still-damp hair.

"The building was cleared."

"Exactly. It was a *threat*."

"It's still a big deal," Spencer insisted.

"Of course. It would have to be, right?"

He shook his head. "What do you mean?"

"The threat couldn't just be the usual, 'shut up, or you'll be sorry,' or 'you don't know who you're messing with.' It had to be something big and scary."

She still wasn't meeting his eyes, and Spencer could tell she was working this all out in her mind.

"He didn't get pissed until those comments started. So whoever it is was mentioned in those comments or is afraid *those* comments will link back to him. He maybe thought he was okay because the guys you picked up are small potatoes and can't be tied to him. But the stuff I put out there is different."

He frowned. "Who did you name?"

"I didn't outright name anyone. I just mentioned that a couple of the guys you picked up have worked with Pete Smith and Stephen White before. And that those guys have both worked with Gerald St. Denis and Antoine Moretti. Who, of course, have worked with Gordon Ridgewood."

Spencer was amazed she knew all those names. All of those names were on FBI watch lists. Including Gordon Ridgewood. Maybe especially Gordon Ridgewood, he supposed. Ridgewood was one of the wealthiest, most influential men in Louisiana.

Possibly the entire south. "You accused Gordon Ridgewood of being the man behind the dumping?"

"Of course not." She gave a little shake of her head, then turned back to her dresser. "I don't have any proof of that. And I understand libel." She plucked a ponytail holder from a cup on the dresser and reached back to gather her hair together. "I never said that Gordon Ridgewood did anything. I just put some strings out there. I can't prevent people from tying them together. But there is nothing prosecutable about what I said."

Ignoring the way her breasts pressed against the v-neck tee and the way his cock responded to that, Spencer scowled. "But you know about Ridgewood."

"Of course. And I'm convinced he's behind this." Her hair satisfactorily secured, she dropped her arms. "And I hate him."

"You hate Gordon Ridgewood?" Spencer asked. Ridgewood was not a good guy. But most people didn't know that. He came off as charming and magnanimous. He was a well-known public figure in New Orleans. If he were to run for mayor, he'd very likely win. Spencer also believed the guy was behind some shady shit, but he was brilliant, and powerful, and had money. That made it nearly impossible to prove it.

"Yes," Max said simply.

"Hate is a very personal emotion."

"Yes, it is."

"I don't like Ridgewood," Spencer said. "I don't trust him. I don't respect him. I would never do business with him or vote for him. I wouldn't loan him so much as an umbrella in a hurricane and wouldn't shed a tear if a gator took his leg off, but *hate*… that sounds like you have a bit more invested here than just knowing he's a bad guy who gets away with a lot of bad stuff, like many people do."

Max stepped closer. "I. Hate. Him. And I'd adopt that alligator and love it, make it a soft, comfy bed, and hand-feed it for the rest of its life if it caused horrible pain and suffering to Gordon Ridgewood."

Spencer shook his head. Wow. He knew she didn't like brownies, she loved the color black, and now he knew she had a deep and abiding hatred in her soul. Sure, it was for a pretty terrible person, but still… He was definitely looking for a sweet, loving, kumbaya type. He needed that. He had to fight the he-deserves-to-suffer urges *he* felt *a lot* in his line of work. He needed some sunny, sweet balance in his life.

"Why?" he couldn't help but ask.

He didn't need to know. Did he?

"He put someone I love very much in a wheelchair."

Well, fuck. Yeah, now he wanted to know more. And he hated Ridgewood now too.

"Who?"

She shook her head and stepped around him, going to her closet. "Doesn't matter. I have some history with Ridgewood. Just leave it at that. I'm sure he's behind this. He didn't care that the peons you arrested got caught, but he cares that people might start seeing his name pop up in connection. So he made a threat."

She bent and started rummaging in the bottom of her closet, and Spencer focused on the ceiling.

He was *not* a fifteen-year-old kid who couldn't handle his hormones. Just having a beautiful woman bend over in front of him should *not* produce a hard-on.

But it did. This woman anyway.

He chalked it up to the fact that she was bending over in *this* particular bedroom, only a few feet from the bed where she'd bent over for him just a few weeks ago.

Yeah, they *really* hadn't slept much that night.

He took a deep breath. "Bomb threat seems… out of character for Ridgewood."

For all of his flaws, Gordon Ridgewood was more subtle. More classy, for lack of a better word. He used his money and power to threaten people with things in the form of bribery and extortion versus flat-out I'll-blow-up-a-building-with-you-inside-it.

"Yeah. But he's pissed. The dumbasses got caught before they could dump the chemicals. So he not only has chemicals that *could* be traced back to him. But he also still has the problem of getting rid of them." She pulled on a pair of black boots. "I'm not saying *he* sent the bomb threat. I'm not even saying he's behind most of the threats I get. But this time, I poked the bear."

Spencer frowned. "Most of the threats you get? You get threats?"

She stood and faced him. "This is my first bomb threat."

"But other kinds?"

She lifted a shoulder. "Sure."

"Max." Spencer took a step toward her. "What kind of threats?"

"Okay, so some of them are really more insults. 'You're a stupid cunt', 'This is why no real men will fuck you', which is super presumptuous and"—She tipped her head—"*you* should probably be insulted by that."

Spencer just clenched his jaw.

"Others are things like, 'Why don't you stick to writing about shoes and makeup like a good little girl', 'You're in over your head', 'If I ever meet you in person, I'm gonna make sure your big mouth is put to *good* use.'" She shrugged. "I took those last two as threats. But of course, there are the more straightforward, 'I'm going to kill you' and 'You should watch your back' types too."

Spencer took another step toward her. "Jesus, Max. And you've turned those all in?"

He knew the answer to that was no.

She put her hands on her hips and looked up at him. "I expose wealthy and powerful white-collar criminals. I get that shit every week, Spencer. I keep them, but no, I don't turn them all in. Do you really think the cops want me to call them every Friday with a run down?"

He absolutely hated the stab of apprehension and fear that went through him. He was a professional. He knew that people threatened other people. He knew that criminals, in particular, threatened other people. And yes, rich, powerful men who dined at fancy restaurants, wore nice-looking suits, had lovely families, and even put on fundraisers for admirable charities threatened other people. They had more secrets to protect. Power and money made people defensive and eager to guard and keep what they had.

But the idea that there were people out there doing this shit *to Max* made him incredibly angry. Which meant he was compromised. He wasn't objective about this case and probably couldn't directly be a part of finding this guy. Because God help the man if Spencer did.

Before he could think about it too hard, he stepped forward, wrapped his arms around her, and pulled her in for a hug.

He knew he'd surprised her. Her body went rigid. And she did not relax into his embrace.

He squeezed her anyway.

He also worked on breathing. She was okay. And now he was here and could keep her that way.

She never leaned into the hug, but she also didn't try to pull away. Another fact he filed away.

When he finally leaned back, she looked up at him with wide eyes.

"I was really worried about you today," he said, also noting how gruff his voice was.

"You were?" Her voice was unusually soft.

"Yeah. I…freaked out a little when I heard where the threat was."

"Oh." She didn't seem to know what to do with that. "I'm okay."

"Yeah. For now. But I need to get you out of here."

Her eyes got even wider. "Out of here? Like out of this apartment?"

"Yes. And out of this city."

Now she pushed back from him. "Spencer, I can't just *leave.*"

He let her go, but he also made note of how much he hated that. He wanted to hold her. He wanted to run his hands all over her. Not in a sexual way, but in a reassure-himself-she-was-all-in-one-piece way. As soon as he'd touched her, he'd realized just how shaken he'd been.

Yeah, compromised was one word for what he was right now.

Totally fucked was another.

And that pissed him off. He was here in a *professional* capacity.

Sure. Even his subconscious didn't believe that.

This was a local investigation. But he'd insisted on coming to her apartment when he'd heard she couldn't be located. He'd made his partner accompany him and had forced the two detectives to put up with it.

She didn't like brownies or hugs, yet he was letting himself get professionally muddled?

This was so bad.

"Yeah, well, at the moment, I need to get you out of this damned bedroom," he said. He turned toward the doorway. He yanked the door open and bellowed down the hall. "Vacate the apartment!"

"What's your problem?" Max asked, hands planted on her hips again.

"I can't talk to you rationally in here," he said, not looking back at her.

The last two words might not have been necessary. He wasn't sure he could talk to her rationally, period. But certainly not in this room.

"Why not?"

"What's going on?" Chris yelled back.

"Just get out!"

"Why are you kicking the other agents out?" Max asked.

Spencer swung around. "Because now that I've felt you again, and seen you naked again, and smelled you again, and now that I know you have pink panties—"

"*You* picked those out!" she interrupted.

He glowered. Who interrupted a guy who was clearly ranting in frustration like this? This was why he couldn't leave her alone to keep poking at whoever had *threatened to blow up her building*. "But now I know you *have them* and I can't stop thinking about how you sounded and tasted the last time we were in here," he shot back. "Because I'm losing my mind between seeing you again and knowing that someone made a threat on your *life* this morning and the fact that when I came through that door a little bit ago, I didn't know if I was going to find you dead or kidnapped or beat up or raped and instead I found you *naked* and full of *attitude* and telling me that people threaten you regularly!" He was shouting now, and he didn't care. "So I need to talk to you *out there*, and I don't want an audience for this!"

Max certainly didn't seem concerned. Surprised maybe, but she was watching him with what could only be described as fascination rather than fear.

"Strange that you'd have the other agents leave when you're so concerned about safety, though," she pointed out mildly.

Yeah, she was clearly not upset about his yelling.

"They'll stay out front. They're not idiots."

"Ah, the irrational one is staying in here with me. That's comforting."

She wasn't entirely wrong. Spencer sucked in a long breath through his nose, then said, "You're going to need to move your fine ass *out* of this room before I do something *really* stupid."

He pointed down the hallway toward her living room and just prayed that either the other agents had already moved out or could be convinced not to say anything about any of this.

Chris would be good, he knew. The other two were the potential problem. But in their line of work, they would learn eventually that there were just days and situations that pushed a man to his very fucking limit.

Finally, blessedly, Max lifted her chin and marched past him.

He counted to ten, then followed her into the living room.

Out of the bedroom helped. A little.

Chris, Moreno, and Lance were gone. Spencer pulled in another long, deep breath.

Max had stopped on the other side of the living room, near the kitchen island. There was a coffee table and a chair between them. Not to mention the you're-not-the-boss-of-me attitude that was coming off her in waves.

He still wanted to hold her. And he *was* going to be the boss of her. When it came to keeping her safe anyway. No one else would do it well enough for his taste. And they were both just going to have to accept that and all the complications it was going to bring.

"You're not going to work," he said firmly. "We need to find out who did this."

"So, what's your solution? I just hide out?" Her tone indicated exactly how she felt about that.

He wanted to say yes. He wanted to hide her away. Forever. But at least until this asshole was found and locked up.

He also knew that was irrational. And that she was never going to go for it.

"Can you work remotely?"

"To an extent. But I need to meet with people to really do my job."

"You understand, meeting with people could be dangerous. Any of those people could be the person who threatened you. Or could be informing on you."

That made her hesitate. And blink.

Spencer knew that Max Keller didn't blink very often.

"Fine," she finally said.

Spencer felt a rush of relief so intense that he thought he needed to clarify. "Are you saying okay, that you'll lay low?"

She nodded. "Yes. At least for a time. But you can't expect me to do *nothing*. I won't let him think he's won."

She was a workaholic. And her job was exciting. There was no way that this woman would just sit around. It was something they had in common. It was another reason that he knew she was not his type. Yes, chasing criminals was what he did for a living, but he wanted someone at home at the end of the day who wanted to have quiet evenings on the couch. Lazy weekends by the pool or at a farmer's market. Long walks, late brunches, star gazing. Maybe even a nap once in a while.

He somehow knew that Max didn't do… any of that.

He'd even told her she wasn't his type at the wedding. He'd been drunk and rambling about what he wanted in a woman, that he needed some lightness and sunshine because his job was so dark…

Okay, he hadn't said it exactly like that, and yes there had been moonshine, but it was still true.

"I have one more thing to tell you that you're not going to like," he informed her.

"Other than that someone threatened to kill my co-workers and me and that you broke down my front door today and that you are *way* bossier than I expected?"

"Yep. And this one might even be worse."

Her eyebrows climbed nearly to her hairline. "Okay."

"I'm going to be staying with you until we find this guy."

CHAPTER TWO

Spencer staying with her. For a week. Or more.

That was… not a good idea. Max had so many conflicting emotions coursing through her since seeing him again that she, a woman of words, actually didn't know what to say.

Spencer Landry was a lot of things. But simple wasn't one of them. He wasn't easy to define in any way. He had come into her life very unconventionally as the friend and cousin of her best friend's boyfriend. Max and Spencer had had immediate chemistry and a definite flirtation when they'd worked together.

Then they'd gone months before seeing each other again at Charlie and Griffin's wedding. Where they'd flirted again. There'd been a kiss, and a hot make-out session that probably would've turned into more if he hadn't been too drunk.

Then he'd showed up on her doorstep the next day to apologize for being a cocky asshole. And had further cemented the fact that he was a cocky asshole.

But a cocky asshole who was *really* good in bed.

And now he was here. Not just here—and not here trying to win her over, or even try to get her into bed again—but he was here *caring*.

Yes, a bomb threat was kind of a big deal. But there was definitely something about him that seemed… wound up. More than she would expect a typical FBI agent to be at a potential victim's house. Especially when all was well. She'd like to think that all law enforcement cared about all victims, but she knew better. If nothing else, they were objective. Spencer Landry did *not* seem objective right now.

And it was making her heart beat fast.

He seemed legitimately freaked out. He'd used those words. And that was doing something to her. Something stupid.

It was softening her up.

"You're going to stay with me until we find this guy?" She took a deep breath. "This seems like a terrible idea." An idea that she kind of liked. Which made it a *really* terrible idea.

"It makes a lot of sense. You are a target, and the guy is still out there walking around. Until we find him, it makes sense for you to have someone protecting you."

"Is this standard operating procedure?"

"I would prefer if you didn't ask me questions like that."

Well, *that* wasn't an answer. "Because it's a secret operating procedure?"

"Because I don't want to answer the question."

Ah. She had no idea what standard operating procedure for the FBI was in cases like this, but she was not that interested in delving into the details, maybe for the first time in her life. Maybe because she would find out that it *was* standard procedure. Which would take some of the stomach-flipping-this-is-kind-of-exciting-that-Spencer-wants-to-protect-me stuff away. Or maybe she would find out that it was *not* standard procedure, which would make things more confusing.

One of the reasons Max was an outstanding investigative journalist was because details were her catnip. She always wanted to know more about every situation. Who, what, when, where, and why were how she lived her life. But she was going to let this one go. That told her a lot about how she felt about Spencer.

"Well, you seem to have a hard time with how I *smell* and being close to my bedroom and seeing me in a towel." She liked all of that. Maybe because seeing Spencer tortured was fun. Maybe because it had been a long time since she'd affected a man who affected her right back. But probably because torturing Spencer was fun. "So this could be awkward," she pointed out.

"We're going to Autre," he said simply.

She frowned and processed his answer. "Autre? Why?"

"Because you don't live there. You're not from there. It would be hard for someone who doesn't know you well to trace you to that town. And because you'll be surrounded by people I trust implicitly who can help watch your back."

"I need a whole army of people watching my back?"

"It won't hurt."

Autre, Louisiana, was a little town down by the bayou. Spencer's family was from there. She wasn't completely clear on his direct tie to the town, but she knew some of his cousins lived there. She'd met them at the wedding where Spencer had kissed the hell out of her and they'd barely kept their clothes on.

It was only about a twenty-five-minute drive from New Orleans. It was a charming little town, and the people there, especially the Landry family, were an interesting, rowdy, fun, and loving bunch.

Max's best friend, Caroline, had fallen in love with one of them. And honestly, Zander Landry and his family were some of the best people Max had ever met. Caroline was deliriously happy, and Max was thrilled for her friend. And definitely felt like Caroline was wholly supported and safe. She knew that Zander, the town cop and parish's Sheriff, had a lot of friends, including the fire chief and the local game warden, to help him keep the area safe. Even when she'd been there helping Caroline with the case that had taken Caroline to Autre in the first place, Max had sensed that there was a brotherhood amongst the men who wore badges, and they took their jobs protecting the area incredibly seriously.

Would she feel safe there? Absolutely.

Was this a complete overreaction on Spencer's part? Definitely.

What did it mean that Spencer was overreacting about her safety? She had no idea.

"So we're going to go to Autre together? Because you think that's the safest place for me to be so that you have help protecting me. And you're going to stay there with me?"

Spencer nodded. "Pretty much."

"How are you going to work on this case while we're there?"

"I won't be working on this case. Conflict of interest."

She frowned. "How is it a conflict of interest?"

"I'm sleeping with the target."

She ignored the way her *pink* panties said *whoo hoo!* "You are not. You have in the past, but that was before she was a target."

"I'm going to be staying in very close confines with her."

"I'm adding *presumptuous* to your list of character flaws," Max said dryly.

"I'm too close to the case, Max," Spencer said, seeming exasperated. "I'm not objective at all. The idea that someone made a threat against you, and my reaction to not being able to get a hold of you or find you immediately this morning, tells me that there's no way I can conduct an objective investigation and deal with any suspects in a fair way when we find them."

Her eyebrows rose. "You're that worked up about this?"

He simply nodded.

That did something to Max. She wasn't proud of it. But for a woman who had been on her own a lot from the time she was a little girl, she liked the idea that someone could be that concerned about her. She'd been independent from a very young age and generally took quite a lot of pride in that. But there was some little corner of her psyche, some little piece of her heart, that loved having someone worry about her.

She knew it was normal to want to have people who cared. And it wasn't like she'd been neglected or unloved. She had two loving parents who just happened to think that they'd done her a huge favor by raising her to depend on herself and know how to handle any situation life threw at her.

Hungry? Get yourself some food. Don't know how to do that school assignment? Find someone to help you. Your stomach hurts? Find something to settle it. Monsters under the bed? Vanquish those assholes.

Most people saw her as incredibly competent, and she was. She didn't need caretaking. A lot of it annoyed her, in fact. She didn't want or need people fussing over her. She didn't like people insisting that she do things in certain ways or change her habits or lifestyle. Clingy boyfriends lasted about two weeks.

But she didn't mind having a big, hot, sexy man be a little worried about her when the concern was legit, and he had a reasonable solution.

"Also, the FBI won't be investigating. The local cops will handle it," he said.

Oh. She rolled her eyes. Still, he was worried enough to stay with her. "It will be really hard for me to meet with my informants when I'm in Autre, though," she said. "I can't stop working. He'll think he's won. If his goal was to frighten us all and shut the *News* down, and then I stop putting out stories, he'll have gotten his way. That's *not* how we should handle this."

"You can keep working from Autre. But you'll have to get in touch with your informants another way for now."

"I can't call or email them, Spencer. That's traceable. We meet up. We pass notes like in eighth grade. We meet at seedy bars or run into each other at the park. It has to be done that way so that it can't be tracked."

"Then you'll have to take a week or two off." He said it firmly.

She frowned. Now he was stepping on her toes. "I don't want to."

Spencer rolled his eyes. "People take vacations, Max."

"I don't."

Spencer gave her a "come on" look. "Ever?"

She lifted a shoulder. "No."

"You *never* take a vacation?"

"I live in one of the greatest cities in the world. Why would I need to take time off and go somewhere else?"

"Well, how about just taking time off to kick back and relax here? Sleep late? Catch up on hobbies? What about when you go to your crossword puzzle tournament thingies?"

She frowned. "I don't need time off for that stuff."

Spencer sighed and shook his head. "Well, now you're going to find out what it's about."

"What about getting paid? I need a paycheck." He was going to bring up paid time off, of course.

Instead, he said, "Don't tell me you don't have savings. If you never take time off, I'm pretty sure you have some money in the bank."

"You don't know that."

He looked around. "What do you possibly spend money on?"

She gasped. "Hey." But he wasn't wrong. She lived very simply. She didn't need a lot. She also didn't have any dependents to speak of. So yeah, her bank account was healthy.

"You know I could find out how much you have in the bank if I wanted to."

She tipped her head. "I'm pretty sure it's illegal for you to poke into my financials without cause."

"Bet I can come up with cause."

"You're giving me an idea for a new story about local FBI agents making up cause for things," she warned.

"Come on, Max. It's one week off. Maybe two. Come to Autre, take a little time off, and hang out with the Landrys. Take a swamp boat tour. Go to the petting zoo. Eat some of the best gumbo you've ever had in your life. Hang out with Caroline. I promise it will be fun."

She doubted that. She didn't do well with downtime. Not

that the Landrys and their swamp boat tours and their petting zoo and their grandma's gumbo and Caroline weren't all lovely. And for a couple of days, Max would probably enjoy it a lot. But a week? Or *two*?

"I can find your parents' phone number and get a hold of them and tell them what's going on and have *them* convince you," Spencer said.

Max laughed lightly. He could. He would. "That won't work. My parents are some of the hardest working people you'll ever meet. To them, you always work. You always do whatever you need to do for the job."

"Even if it's risking your life?"

Max studied him for a moment, debating how much to share with him. But this was one of the most stubborn men she'd ever met. If she was going to win debates, she had to lay it all out there.

She lifted her chin and crossed her arms. "My mother is an ER nurse. Between communicable diseases, combative and aggressive patients, gang violence, and guns, she basically risks her life every time she works. She's had several close calls, and she goes back in every time. She works very long shifts and picks up extra.

"My stepdad is a lineman. His job is rated one of the most dangerous in the country. He's always one of the first guys out after a power outage and natural disasters. He had a terrible accident after Hurricane Irma.

"So yeah, my parents understand putting their lives on the line to go out and do vital work. I don't think you're going to appeal to them. No matter how charming you might be. And I don't think your cute smile and hard abs are going to work on them."

Spencer didn't seem to know how to process all of that information exactly. Finally, he said, "I'll call Caroline and tell her. Or Ellie Landry."

Max shook her head. "Caroline *might* work, because she'd be worried about me. But she's put up with a lot of bullshit to do the right thing in the end. And I have a feeling that Ellie Landry knows all about doing what needs to be done."

Ellie was the matriarch of the Landry family. She wasn't clear how Ellie was related to Spencer, but she'd witnessed the easy relationship between Spencer and the older woman on both occasions Max had been in Autre. Ellie was warm and welcoming but also told it like it was. She had a huge brood with *many* handsome, cocky, stubborn men in it, and she seemed to keep them all in line.

Spencer blew out a breath and nodded. "You're right. And you figured that out even in just the small amount of time you've known her."

"I've gotten pretty good at reading people."

"Okay, but I've still got Caroline and Zander. They'll both be horrified about what happened this morning. Hell, maybe Zander even more than Caroline. Caroline knows the kind of people you write about. On the other hand, Zander might come up here, throw you over his shoulder, and carry you to Autre."

Max felt a little different stomach swoop at that idea. It wasn't the heated, sexy swoop that Spencer produced. It was a softer, warmer curl through her belly and chest. Not that Zander Landry wasn't hot, but she wasn't attracted to him. The idea that someone could care about her to the extent that he would drive up to New Orleans and physically take her to Autre to keep her safe was just… nice.

She loved her parents and knew they loved her, and they would *absolutely* be upset over the bomb threat if they knew about it. However, she had no intention of telling them. But if she also told them that she was going right back to work and why, they would understand and support that. They had always understood hard work and sacrifice for what they did for a living, and, more, they gave her all the space she wanted to make her own choices. Always had.

But she hadn't *told* Spencer about the threat, and if *he* told

Caroline and Zander and they got upset and wanted to worry and protect her well… that might feel good.

And studying the tall, broad, muscled man standing across the room from her, insisting that he wanted to take care of her and make sure she was okay, and admitting just a little bit ago, that even being in that same bedroom with her had him wound up to the point that he couldn't think straight, definitely weakened her resolve.

"Okay, fine. Autre. No more than one week."

"Maybe *two*. I can't guarantee how long this will take. You know that."

"Fine. I'll be nice about it for *one* week. No guarantees what kind of roommate I'll be after two."

One corner of his mouth kicked up, and dammit, it made heat swirl through her stomach.

"Deal," Spencer told her.

"So… I guess I need to pack."

She moved past him on her way back to the bedroom, suddenly very aware that her panties were pink. She didn't even remember buying these. Pink was really not her color. But the fact that Spencer had seen them and specifically picked them out for her to wear suddenly made her body feel hot. Some areas more than others.

"You don't have to pack for two weeks, by the way. We're staying at the bed and breakfast, so we'll have laundry facilities."

Well, that was good to know. Also good to know because the bed-and-breakfast would include some meals. As Spencer already knew, she was definitely not a big cook, and she doubted that Autre had quite the carryout and delivery selection that New Orleans did.

"But don't just pack tan and black. You might as well throw those red ones in."

They had to be talking about underwear because she didn't have any red shirts or pants.

"I've never worn that red bra and panty set," she said, pausing at the entry to the hallway.

"No? Why'd you get them?"

"They were a gift from a boyfriend. Guy seemed to think that I needed more than tan and black in my life." Not a lie. Grant had lasted about a month. He'd also wanted her to take a vacation.

Spencer's eyes narrowed, and a tiny piece of Max enjoyed the idea that he might be a little jealous.

"What happened to that guy?"

"He didn't last long. I don't really like being told what to do." She paused. "And I'm not very good at forgiving people for things." Grant had bought them non-refundable plane tickets. To Scotland. Without asking her.

Spencer didn't say anything to that. So, she turned on her heel and started down the hall, but before she hit her bedroom, she heard him call, "Max?"

She turned back. She couldn't see him, but she asked, "Yeah?"

"Leave the red ones here."

She grinned.

———

"SO REMIND me about your connection to Autre. Your cousins just live there?"

Spencer looked over at her, then back to the road. "I spent a lot of time there as a kid. My grandparents lived there."

"Oh. That's nice." She'd visited her grandparents about once a year each. "Holidays and stuff like that?"

He nodded. "Weekends and summers too. We'd go as soon as school got out and stay with Grandma and Grandpa almost until it was time to go back to school in the fall."

Max blinked at him. "Seriously?"

He shot her a grin. "Yep. Autre was our second home."

"You and your brother Wyatt, right? Are there other kids?"

"No, just the two of us. Though all the cousins seemed like siblings at times. Zander and those guys are actually our second cousins. Our grandpas are brothers."

Max marveled at a family where second cousins could feel nearly as close as brothers.

"Do you have siblings?"

Max shook her head. "Only child. And I was an accident. My parents didn't intend to have kids at all."

Spencer frowned. "I can't even imagine that. Even though it was just Wyatt and me, we have a huge family on both sides. Did you at least have cousins and stuff?"

"No one close." She'd met a few of her cousins, but the last time she'd seen them had been at her grandfather's funeral. Six years ago. "My parents grew up in Oklahoma. They were both ready to get away from home, so they finished high school on a Friday, packed up my dad's truck, and drove to New Orleans that weekend. They got married by the Justice of the Peace on Monday. They were married for about three years. They got divorced, and my dad moved to Amarillo, so I didn't see him much. My mom met my stepdad, who is awesome. He's really more of a dad than my biological dad is. But he doesn't have a big family either. We didn't go back to Oklahoma much and I always felt like an add-on with my stepdad's family."

"Sounds lonely."

Max didn't comment. It had been very fucking lonely. Not that she'd known that until she'd gotten older. She wasn't sure that kids understood loneliness when it was all they ever knew. It was just… normal.

Sure, she'd been aware that other kids at school had siblings, but she also knew other only children. She hadn't understood how her home life was different from other kids' until she got older and went to Caroline's house for the first time. Caroline had been the first friend to invite Max over to her house, where Max could see a family interacting and routines like dinner together as a family around the same table all at once in real life. She'd read about movie nights and bedtime stories and morning swimming lessons and things like that but had never done any of it herself.

Those visits to Caroline's house had been like going to Disney World. And she'd been devastated when it had been taken away.

As soon as Caroline's dad had inherited his company, he'd bought a big house in the nice part of town, moved Caroline to her new private school, and cut off most of their old life. Max and Caroline had stayed in touch, but her father hadn't approved. He'd wanted her to make friends with the kids in "their circle" so the girls had kept their continued friendship a secret.

That's what had taught Max that there was no such thing as the perfect dad or mom or family or home, and what you saw on the surface could often just be window dressing.

"What are you thinking about so hard over there?" Spencer asked, breaking into her thoughts

"Just how Caroline was probably the closest thing I had to a sibling."

Now, why had she said that? Spencer was a cop. He was an FBI agent specifically. He wasn't a casual conversation kind of guy. He was going to want to delve into details the way she did. How close did she want to let him get? This was all temporary— Lord help her if it went past a week—and he'd made it very clear that she was not his type the last time they'd been together.

He'd kissed her, then flat-out told her that he had a list of qualifications for a girlfriend, including fresh-baked brownies, casseroles—enchiladas in particular—and a dog. Spencer was looking for a woman who would greet him at the door at the end of the day with a smile, a kiss, and dinner, probably with her freaking apron still on. The two kids would be sitting at the table —one boy and one girl, of course—and would be just as bright and sunny as the wife was.

Spencer basically wanted a look-a-like family to the Hollands, Caroline's family.

That wasn't Max's style. In fact, she firmly rejected all of that now. Now, the more perfect things or people looked, the more suspicious Max was.

Plus, she didn't know the first fucking thing about baking, and she didn't want to learn. So how close did she want Spencer to get? Not very.

Unless he was naked.

There was no freaking way Caroline's perfect socialite parents had ever used their expensive leather Camelback sofa the way she and Spencer had used her couch. No matter how perfect Gretchen Holland's smile, apron, and brownies were. Not that Max spent a lot of time thinking about Caroline's parents and their sex life. In fact, she needed to shut that down *right now*. She gave a little shudder.

"What was that for?" Spencer asked.

Really? She couldn't even shudder? "Nothing."

"Seriously, what are you thinking about?"

"I'm trying *not* to think about Caroline's parents' sex life."

Spencer let out a surprised chuckle. "That's probably a good idea."

"Caroline's parents always seemed like the perfect example of a married couple and family. I found out differently, of course, later. So now they're on my don't-be-like-that list. And I was just thinking how I can't imagine Charles going down on Gretchen on their fancy couch."

Spencer gave a little cough and shifted on his seat. "Any reason you're thinking about guys going down on girls on couches?"

She slid him a sly little grin. "None whatsoever." But now *he* was thinking about guys and girls and oral sex on couches.

"Good."

"So what's our situation going to be at the bed and breakfast?" she asked. Because now *she* was also thinking about guys and girls and oral sex on couches. And wondering what kind of furnishings her room in the B & B would have. And if she'd be able to walk past a couch with Spencer Landry and not get hot and bothered.

Dammit.

She should not sleep with Spencer Landry again. But it was a lot nicer thing to think about than all the ways the perfect-seeming Holland family had disappointed her and her best friend.

And hey, if she was stuck with the guy for a week, it wouldn't be so bad to have a few more run-ins with his tongue and the other parts of him that he used very well.

I thought you thought he was a cocky asshole.

Well sure, but the thing was, she was extremely good at being annoyed at *bad* guys. The problem was, no matter what had happened between them, Spencer Landry was not a bad guy. Max knew bad guys. She actually made a living off of knowing, following, studying, and writing about bad guys.

Spencer exasperated her, but in the overall scheme of things, he barely registered on the bad guy meter in her opinion. So it was going to be very hard to keep up her grudge against him. Especially if they were stuck together and he was acting all protective and making her feel warm and gooey by wanting to keep her safe.

He cleared his throat. "The woman who owns the bed and breakfast, Heather Hebert, is my cousins' aunt. On the other side."

Max laughed. "Is everyone in Autre related to one another?"

"Pretty much. It's why they have to keep importing girls to fall in love with." He gave her a grin.

Yeah, see that grin was going to make it really hard not to sleep with him again too. He was cute. He was definitely hot. But there were moments when he was just *cute*. "So, will we have adjoining rooms or rooms right across the hall from one another, or what?"

"Actually we'll be sharing a cottage. There's the main bed and breakfast with a few rooms, but there are also six cottages out behind the property. They're self-contained and I figured it would be easier to not only secure the entire perimeter of a cottage versus the main house, but it also keeps the rest of the guests from being in any kind of danger."

Max's eyes got wide. "They won't be in danger if this person has no idea where I am."

"I don't want to take any chances."

Any light teasing that had been present suddenly evaporated. "So you want me off by myself where you don't have to worry about anyone else being hurt if I'm targeted."

"Another reason to have you away from New Orleans and the other people who live near you."

Well, she appreciated that he wasn't trying to sugarcoat anything she supposed. "Are you overreacting a little?"

He glanced at her. "Possibly. Probably." He blew out a breath. "I don't even know. With you, I feel all jumbled up. I'm definitely not coming at this as professionally as I usually do."

"I feel like I should apologize for that."

He shrugged. "It's not really your fault. Or I guess it is, but you're not doing it on purpose."

"So you feel a weird connection to me that you didn't expect or intend."

"Yes."

"And it's bugging you."

"Yes."

"But you're not running as fast as you can in the opposite direction."

He looked over at her. "If I run in the opposite direction, someone else will need to make sure you're safe. Whether or not it's rational, I'm worried about you. Someone else could take care of you, but for whatever reason, I want it to be me."

She studied his profile as his eyes went back to the road. "I'm not your type."

"I know."

"I don't think you're my type, either."

His jaw tensed. "You're probably right." He waited for a beat, then looked over at her. "Why is that exactly? The bossy thing?"

"Oh, it's definitely partly the bossy thing." For sure. Her parents hadn't even bossed her when she'd been a kid. She definitely wasn't going to let grown-ups do it now. Especially men she dated. Or slept with but didn't date.

"What else is it?"

"Well, the fact that I'm not *your* type doesn't endear you to me."

He huffed out a little laugh. "Fair enough."

The night he'd been at her place, he'd made no secret of the fact that he didn't like her clothes, thought having a relationship with crows was strange, and found her fascination with murder creepy.

"I like my life," she said. "I like my lifestyle. I don't think there's anything particularly weird about the way I live. Or conduct myself. So the fact that you do kind of bugs me."

"That is all really fair."

"I appreciate you acknowledging that."

They were quiet for a long moment.

Then Spencer asked, "You want to get married?"

She snapped her head to look at him. "*What?*"

"Not to me specifically," he said quickly. "I mean, in general."

For just a second, she paused. She had to wait for her heart to flip back over. "I really like my alone time and my space and being able to do whatever I want, whenever I want. I've been doing that for a very long time. It's hard for me to imagine blending my life with another person's. Not sure I'm really cut out for it."

He nodded, as if not surprised by her answer. "I, on the other hand, very much want to get married. I want someone who can help me balance things out. What I do for a living is really intense.

I want someone who can ground me. Remind me that what I do, and the people I run into every day and the things *they* do, are not normal. And that there's a whole big world full of perfectly good, happy people who are living good, happy lives where they take care of one another and want to do the right thing."

She'd had no idea that a twenty-five-minute drive between New Orleans and Autre would be so enlightening. But she liked that Spencer was such an open book. He seemed to know himself well and was in touch with what he wanted and why. She respected that.

"Seeing how we tend to interact with a lot of the same types of people, I get what you're saying. When you spend all day, every day with bad guys and what they do, it's good to be reminded that there are good guys."

He just nodded.

"Of course, *you* are one of the good guys. And your partner and the other men and women you work with are too. I like to think I'm one of the good guys, too."

He looked over. "But I don't want to spend every evening after all day at work talking about cold cases and Gordon Ridgewood and the many ways he continues to slip through our fingers."

She lifted both brows. "Is that a warning? You don't want to spend our evenings together over the next week rehashing cases and listening to me rant about how much I hate that fucking guy?"

"I'm just thinking that maybe this next week we can find something else to do and you'll find that you enjoy *not* dwelling on those things for a while."

She resolutely kept from saying *well, we sure found some great common ground last time you were at my place.*

That would not be helpful.

"I'm not taking cooking lessons or fostering a dog or something," she said.

His hands tightened on the steering wheel and his jaw clenched again. Max found that fascinating.

Finally, he looked over at her. "Those would be so terrible?"

"If we can't do what I like, we can't do what you like. We have to do stuff we both like."

Well, crap. It was *right there* hanging in the air between them. They both knew what "stuff" they both liked.

A glance into his heated gaze told her he was thinking the same thing.

Max really did enjoy the idea that she affected the guy.

Spencer Landry was an in-control, incredibly intelligent, could-probably-have-any-woman-he-wanted guy. The idea that even in all her not-his-type glory he couldn't resist her gave Max a little thrill.

"So murder and plotting the demise of the rich and criminal, or brownies and puppies. That's all we've got to choose from, huh?"

She lifted a shoulder. "Or we just leave each other alone and do our own thing."

She wasn't exaggerating about not enjoying sharing her time and space with other people. She was a loner and had been from a young age. She was very used to keeping track of herself and not worrying about other people too much. She always figured if she could take care of herself at age ten, then people older than her, with much more support and many more resources, definitely could.

Spencer Landry could definitely take care of himself.

Spencer shifted on his seat and shot her a glance. "I can't leave you alone. I'm supposed to be protecting you."

"But it's not officially a job you've been assigned, right?" She knew it wasn't. He admitted that he wasn't a part of this investigation because of a conflict of interest.

"No. This is very… personal."

She ignored the warm swirl in her belly that dipped low and made her tingly. "Sounds like a you problem then."

"Oh, it's definitely a me problem," he muttered.

She rolled her eyes. He was so dramatic. "Really, you're just kind of a self-appointed, glorified babysitter. As long as I'm alive when the gig ends, you're good. We don't have to be best friends and you don't have to be on top of me every second."

There was a long moment of silence where they both, clearly, realized how that sounded.

She cleared her throat. "What I mean is, all you have to do is what the people who took care of me as a kid did."

"And what's that?"

"Tell me not to burn the place down or need the ER and then let me do whatever I want."

Spencer just sighed.

CHAPTER THREE

THE BED and breakfast sat on the edge of Autre, and it was adorable. The house was a huge, brick two-story home with an enormous front porch that wrapped around two sides of the house. There were flowers of all colors and kinds spilling from planters, hanging baskets, pots of various shapes and sizes, and beds that ran along the front of the porch and the edge of the stone pathway that connected the driveway to the base of the porch steps.

"Wow, she's got more flowers this time than I remember," Max commented.

Several months ago, she'd been here when she'd come to town looking for Caroline.

Caroline had been staying at the B & B, and this had been Max's first stop.

"The only thing Heather does better than grow flowers is bake," Spencer said as he pulled the truck into the drive and shut it off.

Max rolled her eyes. "No wonder you want to stay here."

"What's that mean?"

"You're *obsessed* with baked goods. Are you aware of that?"

He chuckled. "Of course I'm aware of that. But it's hardly a coincidence that a bed and breakfast would have baked goods. You know that, right?"

Actually, not really. She'd never stayed at a bed and breakfast in her life. "We could stay at a hotel or with any of the million relatives you have here in town, couldn't we?"

He sighed. "I'd rather not have my relatives' homes potentially blown up. And this has a detached cottage, so we're not endangering other people in a *motel*."

She sighed. Right. She was a potential danger to others.

Heather Hebert, a woman in her mid-fifties with shoulder-length blond hair and a bright smile, appeared on the porch. She waved. Max had, of course, met Heather when she'd been in Autre previously.

"Hey, Heather!" Spencer called as he got out and came around the front of the truck to open Max's door.

Dang, even things like that were completely foreign in her world. Not only was she almost always in the driver's seat when she went anywhere, but she definitely opened her own doors.

Spencer offered her a hand down from the truck seat.

She looked from it to him. He lifted a brow. She didn't need the help, but she wasn't sure what else to do at the moment, so she slipped her hand into his.

"Hi, you guys!" Heather greeted from the porch. "So glad you're here!"

"Hi," Max returned with a smile, trying to ignore how much she liked holding Spencer's hand.

His hand was big and warm and engulfed hers almost entirely. Liking his hands and his touch was hardly a surprise or something new. They'd been there, done that. But liking something this simple was... both. She wasn't a hand holder. But in the time it took to walk from the truck to the Hebert Bed and Breakfast front steps, she was pretty sure she'd become one.

Well... damn.

"So good to see you, Heather," Spencer returned charmingly.

Was it just her, or was Spencer actually this charming?

Judging from the smile on Heather's face, it wasn't just Max. That made her feel a little better. She'd like to think that she wasn't quite so easily won over.

True, she did try to date men who were equally independent and respected her space. That didn't automatically mean that they were not gentlemen, but between Spencer's door opening and hand-holding and his murmured, "I'll get your bags later," Max wondered if she'd been dating jerks.

You're not dating Spencer, her inner voice reminded her.

Right. Thank God for inner voices.

Twenty-four hours ago, if someone had asked her how she felt about Spencer Landry, she would have said *he* was a jerk.

Of course, her body would've heated, and her cheeks probably would've flushed, remembering how she'd climbed into his lap anyway. And she would've felt slightly mortified by the sounds he'd elicited from her. But dammit, they'd had fun that night. Or she had anyway. The cold case had been interesting. And even though he'd thought she was a little too interested in murder and mayhem, he had readily engaged in the conversation. And dammit, he'd liked that burger.

"Thanks for making room for us last minute," Spencer said as they climbed the porch to join Heather.

Spencer's hand was now on Max's lower back.

Which she liked too. Ugh.

"It was no problem. I had an opening. But even if I hadn't, I would've juggled things. You know that."

Spencer leaned in to kiss Heather's cheek, and again Max was struck by the fact that he had a sweet side.

It wasn't that he had been a raging asshole any of the times she'd been around him. But he'd been cocky every time and gruff several times, and things like opening doors and kissing women on the cheek didn't fit her image of him.

Of course, most of her mental picture of him involved his crooked grin, bulging biceps, and well-fitted jeans.

Okay, so she'd objectified him a bit. So what? It wasn't like she'd been expecting to move into a quaint little bed-and-breakfast bungalow with him for a week so he could protect her from some big, bad nameless threat. She definitely hadn't been expecting him to go all growly protective and make her stupid primal brain suddenly think I-shouldn't-want-that-but-ooh-that's-hot.

"Well, I appreciate it. We're gonna hang out in Autre for about a week, and a cottage would be a perfect place for us to have a little privacy," Spencer told Heather.

Um, privacy? Max looked up at him quickly. That sounded very… intimate. He made that seem like they were here for a romantic getaway. She quickly looked back at Heather. Yeah, that knowing smile and aw-aren't-they-cute expression said Heather thought the same thing.

"Absolutely. I put you in the bungalow at the end of the property. You'll have plenty of privacy. I can even bring breakfast down to you if you'd like." She gave them a wink.

A wink.

Max felt her eyes widen. Spencer needed to tell her that was *not* necessary.

"That's perfect," he said.

Then, to Max's… okay, she'd call it horror… Spencer's arm slid around her waist and tucked her up against his side. Like a boyfriend would. Then his big hand slid down and cupped her ass as if to *really* make the point.

Well, horror might've been extreme because she liked his hand there. At least certain parts of her body did. But what the hell was going on?

She was here because a guy had threatened to blow up the building where she worked. And because Spencer was overreacting. He wanted her here in this little town so the guy couldn't find her. And so that the rest of his badge brothers could help protect her. He hadn't mentioned that he was going to tell anyone that they were getting all lovey-dovey in the bungalow.

Of course, a bed-and-breakfast bungalow did have an automatic lovey-dovey sound, didn't it?

"It's so nice to have you back, Max. Autre does have a way of drawing people in and giving them reasons to keep coming back." Heather glanced up at Spencer, then back to Max as if the two women were sharing a secret.

Yeah, it was *not* a secret what Heather meant.

Max forced herself to smile.

Fine. She got it. After all, what were they supposed to tell people? That there might be a bomber coming after her?

She pasted on a smile and slid her arm around Spencer's waist, cuddling close to his big, hot, hard body. Hey, there could be some perks to this. "Well, you're right about that. Seems like I just can't get away from this town, or this guy, for good."

She felt Spencer tense slightly against her, and she smiled inwardly. Yeah, *he* kept showing up on *her* doorstep. He should remember that when he insisted on counting all the ways she was not Spencer Landry Girlfriend Material.

But she knew he'd also thought she would blow his little romantic-getaway story.

He didn't understand that she hung out and played parts all the time. She'd pretended to be a waitress, a blackjack dealer, a convenience store clerk, a bartender, and even a palm reader just to get a story.

Playing Spencer Landry's new girlfriend for Heather so that she could hole up in the cute little cottage behind this bed-and-breakfast for a week?

Piece of cake.

"Well, come on in. I have dessert waiting for you, and we can chat for just a little bit before I take you back to the cottage. Beau is just finishing up with installing new locks on the door."

New locks on the door? Max looked up at Spencer with suspicion as Heather turned to lead them into the house and toward the kitchen.

Spencer's arm was still around her. He met her gaze, one eyebrow up as if to say *what?*

She frowned.

He nodded.

So he had asked for new locks. Had he told Beau why? Did that mean that more than just his friends with badges would be in on the true story?

"I hope you like apple crisp," Heather said.

Spencer helped Max up onto one of the stools at the long, expansive breakfast bar in the kitchen before taking a seat next to her. She rolled her eyes. She could get onto a stool by herself. But dammit, she liked his hands on her waist and these little gestures of attention.

Ugh, she was pathetic.

Once he stepped away, she took a deep breath. That was when she finally noticed something other than Spencer. The kitchen smelled amazing. Sugar and cinnamon seemed to hang in the air. It was warmer in here, surely from the use of the oven, but the windows were open, and a breeze ruffled the gauzy curtains keeping the room from being hot. The kitchen was painted yellow and cream, a cheery and warm combination. The cabinets were oak, and the countertops were cream-colored marble.

Max felt her shoulders relax as the comforting, happy scents and colors surrounded her.

Spencer had one arm resting on the breakfast bar, and he leaned to drape the other over the back of her chair, practically caging her in. Of course, she could have slipped off the other side of the stool, but she couldn't imagine why she'd want to put more space between them.

That was probably a bad instinct.

He took a deep breath too. "Man, it smells incredible in here. That's not just apple crisp."

Heather turned from where she was dishing up three plates. "Wow, very good. What else do you think I made?"

He closed his eyes and sniffed. Max watched him.

"I think there's another pie. Maybe peach? And shortbread cookies. Or sugar. It's hard to tell between the two."

Heather laughed and crossed to them with plates laden with apples and sugary brown crumbles. "Very good," she praised as she set the dishes in front of them. "Peach pie and butter cookies, actually. Very similar to shortbread. But better," she added with a wink.

Heather was very winky.

"Ah, I do love it here," Spencer said, picking up his fork and digging into the apple crisp.

Max watched in wonder as he devoured half of it in less than a minute.

He realized she was staring at him and looked up. "What?"

"What *is* it with you and dessert?" she asked. "You can *smell* different desserts in the air after they're done baking?"

He swallowed. "Well, sure. I mean, obviously, it wasn't anything chocolate. And cherry and strawberry smell different from apple and—"

Max lifted a hand. "Never mind."

He lifted his fork and licked it.

Her body clenched. Holy crap.

"It's very normal for someone to enjoy desserts, you know," he said. "Lots of people do. Probably *most* people."

"Oh, do you not like sweets?" Heather asked Max. It was clear that possibility had only just occurred to her.

Max looked at the apple crisp she hadn't even tasted. She'd had every intention of taking a few bites, but she'd been too distracted by Spencer. "I'm just not that into them in general. I didn't grow up with many sweets or baked goods."

"That's just fucking sad," Spencer told her around a mouthful of apples and crumble topping.

Yeah, maybe it was kind of sad. In her childhood, there had been times when she'd thought it was sad. Lots of her friends had cookies in their lunch boxes, and their moms brought treats to school for holiday parties. The elaborate cakes that Caroline had had for her birthday parties had been the things of little girl dreams.

Max had been aware by fifth or sixth grade that a few of her teachers had believed that she was very poor and her parents couldn't afford to contribute to the class parties. The truth was, they just didn't have the time to bake at home and often forgot to buy anything from the bakery. They'd given her money a few times, and she'd stopped at the store on her way to school. One time Phil and Steph, the neighbors in the apartment next door, had provided a pan of bars for her. She'd never had a better school party than that Halloween party.

"I had Ho Hos a few times. And Oreos," Max said.

Spencer paused with his fork halfway to his mouth. He looked personally offended. "That is *not* what I'm talking about," he said.

"Well, my parents worked a lot," she said, lifting her chin. "Long hours. They didn't have time to bake."

And she'd told him that she hadn't seen her grandparents much.

He looked slightly chagrined. "Still, you eating Ho Hos and thinking you had *dessert* is sad. We need to do something about that." He said that last part to Heather.

"He's just using that as an excuse to get more dessert himself while we're here," Max said. "I don't have a big sweet tooth."

Spencer mumbled something under his breath that Max didn't quite catch. But she assumed it was something like *one more reason never to kiss her again.*

"Well, we'll see what we can do," Heather said. With another wink.

About the dessert or the kissing? Max wondered.

She didn't want either.

Much.

Okay, she was lying. About one of those things.

It was going to be a very long week.

———

AFTER SPENCER FINISHED his apple crisp *and* Max's, Heather escorted them to the bungalow.

The cottage was one of six along a walking path that ran from the back of the house and around the edge of a vast flower garden—complete with trellises, small benches, and even a fountain. According to Heather, the property also included a stable with horses for trail rides, a chicken coop that supplied fresh eggs, a huge vegetable garden, and even a few fruit trees that produced fresh fruit used in the B & B's kitchen. Including the apples Spencer had enjoyed so much.

Their cottage was at the far end and behind it was a wide-open field that Heather explained was approximately a mile from the bayou's edge. Consequently, there was only about half a mile of solid ground before things got soft and marshy.

Max cast a glance at Spencer. He seemed pleased. She supposed that terrain would make it more difficult for anyone to sneak up on them from behind the cottage. Trucks obviously wouldn't be able to drive over the marshy swampland, and someone coming from that direction would likely need a boat to get through the bayou waters and would then have to come the rest of the way on foot.

The cottage was adorable. That was the best word. The front porch had two wooden rocking chairs and a porch swing on the other end because of course it did. It looked out over the flower garden.

Heather proudly pushed the door to the cottage open, gesturing for them to cross the threshold ahead of her.

Max went in first. Looking around, she was pretty much delighted. She could so spend a week here.

It was one big room with living room furniture gathered on one side and the kitchen on the other. The ceiling was vaulted with exposed wooden beams and a slowly rotating ceiling fan in the center. The windows were large, covered by gauzy curtains with heavier curtains that could be pulled for privacy.

The floor of the entire cottage was wood, and an oversized couch, a side chair, and a coffee table were arranged on top of a large, colorful woven rug facing a television mounted on the wall.

Just beyond the television was a doorway, and Max could just see the foot of a bed and, she assumed, the bathroom was through the bedroom.

The kitchen area was separated from the rest of the room by a short bar. On top was a glass jar full of flowers, and underneath were cabinets that Heather happily showed them were stocked with dishes for four, including plates, bowls, glasses, and mugs, as well as a few pots and pans.

There was another cute rug, and a wooden table and four chairs with colorful cushions filled the general kitchen space, along with essential appliances—a stove and fridge and smaller essentials like a microwave, toaster, and coffee pot.

More cabinets were stocked with ground coffee, microwave popcorn, and bottled water, and there was a jug of tea in the fridge.

"We offer breakfast, of course, but most people like to go out and sample the local restaurants or head to New Orleans for dinner. Of course, you two have dinner in the city every night," Heather said with a smile. "You'll probably spend a lot of time over at Ellie's, though, I'd imagine."

"I think we'll be spending a lot of time just the two of us, actually," Spencer said.

Max swallowed her first reaction to that. *The fuck if we will.* She couldn't be cooped up in this cottage, just her and Spencer, for *a week.*

"Oh," Heather said with a touch of surprise.

And yeah, what was he doing? Announcing to a relative… or was she a relative? She was the relative of a relative, right? Or she was married to an uncle of a… Max sighed. She had no idea anymore. But she did know from her previous trips to Autre that everyone was pretty much family down here, blood or not.

So Spencer was announcing to *someone who was pretty much family* that he and Max were going to just be shacking up in here fucking their brains out for the next week and not even able to come out to eat?

Max had noticed that there was only *one* bedroom and felt a flutter in her belly. Had Spencer known that? It wasn't like *now* he could say, "Oh hey, can we have a two-bedroom unit, by the way?"

So what exactly did that mean for the week they would spend here together playing at being a couple? Max hadn't even peeked inside that room, but she knew that there probably weren't bunk beds in there.

"Well, someone from Ellie's would probably bring some food over for you," Heather said. With a smirk.

"Um, no, thank you very much," Spencer returned with a grin. He glanced at Max. "We'd end up with no fewer than a dozen Landrys, food for twice that many, drink for three times that many, and a party on our front porch." He took a step closer to her and slipped his arm around her. "And they won't leave for a very long time. Which is not… a part of my plan."

Max felt herself blushing.

He was *pretending,* and she was freaking blushing.

It was definitely going to be a long week.

"Well, there's a back porch too, but you can find that on your own, I'm guessing. Great view of lots of lightning bugs and sunsets," Heather said with a grin, moving toward the door. "I'll just leave you two alone. But if you're not feeling like going out for dinner, feel free to come up and raid my pantry. Wouldn't want you goin' too long without sustenance."

She gave them a little wave and disappeared through the door before Max realized she should be blushing *again.*

Max waited only long enough to ensure Heather was several

yards from the cottage before she stepped out of Spencer's hold and whirled on him.

"Oh my God! She thinks we're going to be fucking nonstop and need peanut butter sandwiches to keep ourselves going because we can't even make it up to Ellie's!"

He grinned. "Perfect, right?"

"How is that perfect?"

"It will explain why we're in town but not out and about."

"So you don't care that your *family* thinks we're *together*?"

He frowned. "Why would I care if they thought that? They saw us at the wedding. They saw us dancing, they saw us go outside together, they saw me…"

She planted her hands on her hips and narrowed her eyes when he failed to finish that sentence. "They saw you what?"

His gaze was now on her shoulder and not on her eyes.

He tucked his hands into his back pockets. "They, um, saw me after you left."

"And?"

"They realized I was… upset… about how things were… between us then." He frowned as if that hadn't come out exactly right

"How were things between us then?" She was watching him closely. He seemed uncomfortable. Spencer Landry was cocky and too sure of himself ninety-eight percent of the time, so this was interesting.

"They realized I wished I had been going home with you," he said.

She studied him. That didn't sound completely legit.

"And I told Wyatt that you were upset with me when you left," he added.

"I was. That stupid list of girlfriend requirements," she muttered.

"Right."

Max blew out a breath.

"We have to have a reason for being here," Spencer said. "I don't want them to know the truth because it will worry them."

"They'll think that someone might come and blow up a building here?"

"They'll be worried about *you*, Max."

She met his eyes. And blinked. "They will?"

"Of course. If any of them finds out what happened this morning, they'll be all over you. Wrapping you in blankets and spoon-feeding you gumbo, and setting up a twenty-four-seven watch around you. They might even bring their dogs over to sleep with you for protection," he said with a curl to his lips. "And they'll *definitely* bring baked goods."

She took that all in. They would all worry about her. She knew he was kidding about the dogs and twenty-four-seven watch… Then she looked at his face again. Or maybe he wasn't.

And damn if some of that didn't sound nice.

"So, we're just hiding out in here, though?" she asked, feeling a stupid jab of disappointment that she stubbornly blocked. "They'll all think we're here together as a couple, but if we don't go out anywhere, we won't have to *pretend*."

He nodded as if thinking that over. "That's true."

"So… that's good."

He frowned. "Yeah." He didn't look like he thought that was good.

What was he thinking?

"So now what?" she asked.

"I thought we'd have dinner. Maybe watch some TV."

She rolled her eyes. They'd been over this. Fortunately, she'd thought to pack crossword puzzle books, and her phone was loaded with tons of books to read. She supposed she could sit on one end of the couch while he watched TV for a bit. What else was she going to do?

"And since we're not going out, who's making dinner?" She already knew the answer to this and an idea popped into her head.

Spencer wanted to play house? Okay. They could play house. But this was going to be half her house. And her house did not have a gourmet chef. Or a picky eater.

"I realize the answer will not be lasagna, but what would you normally be eating tonight?" he asked casually.

"I guess I could throw together one of my usual go-to meals," she said, also casually, as if this was just occurring to her.

He perked up. "Yeah?"

She lifted a shoulder. "Sure. I'll have to go up to Heather's pantry like she offered, though."

"I'll go." He took a step toward the door. "Just tell me what you need."

"Nah, it's just easier if I go." She was already halfway across the room. "You know, in case I need to make a substitution in the recipe or something."

How she said that with a straight face, she wasn't sure. There was no way Heather wouldn't have these three, yes three, ingredients. Though she might grab a can of vegetables. Just to be well balanced. She almost snorted.

"Well, if you're sure."

"Yep." She pulled the door open and glanced back. "Just settle in. Relax. I'll be back in a minute."

CHAPTER FOUR

The door shut behind Max, and Spencer stood staring at it for several seconds.

Maxine Keller was going to make him dinner.

He felt strangely triumphant about that.

She wouldn't try to poison him on their first night, would she?

She was annoyed by him, but that was only fair. He felt perpetually annoyed around her.

Annoyed by his attraction to her. Annoyed by the fact that he couldn't stop thinking about her. Annoyed that whenever she was even within ten feet of him, he wanted to touch her.

It was partly why this pretend relationship was a great idea.

One, he could touch her. Not in a creepy way, but in a hold-her-hand-put-his-hand-on-her-back-brush-her-hair-away-from-her-face way that would be part of the image they'd be portraying. And all things he'd been itching to do since her bedroom in New Orleans. Among other lots-more-touching-lots-more-skin things.

Even helping her up and down off the stools in Heather's kitchen had felt natural and irresistible. Yes, he held doors and pulled out chairs for other women, but that was out of bred-into-him manners. With Max, it was just instinct. He wanted to touch her, help her, *be there.*

Spencer thrust a hand through his hair. Was this all because they'd slept together? Because of the threat that morning? Possibly. Probably. Maybe.

But damn, he just wasn't sure.

In any case, his constant need to be right beside her would help sell their story to everyone around them. And maybe it would help him quell some of these urges and instincts. He could stay close to her to keep her safe, he could run his hands through her hair whenever he wanted to, and maybe that would be enough to get over this… whatever it was. This inexplicable draw to her was probably just a matter of wanting what he couldn't have. So maybe kind of having it would help him get over it.

The second good thing about this pretend relationship was that it would annoy Max.

If he was going to be annoyed, she could be too.

Of course, as she'd pointed out, if they were mainly staying at the cabin, there would be less reason for them to pretend to be a couple. Including for him to run his hand through her hair, pull her into spontaneous embraces, and lay kisses on her for no apparent reason.

If he tried to do that when it was just the two of them in this little cottage together, it was possible he'd end up with a knee to the nuts.

Not that she wouldn't enjoy the kissing. But it was clear that she didn't like having her routine dictated, people insinuating themselves into her life, or people surprising her. She was smart enough to realize this plan was the safest thing to do right now, but she was damned stubborn and incredibly independent. She wasn't going to go along with just hanging out in Autre with him for too long.

But she *was* making him dinner. And Spencer couldn't help

but like the idea of spending a quiet evening in this adorable little cabin, just the two of them.

He headed for his truck to retrieve their belongings, resisting the urge to cut through the house. If she wanted to surprise him with whatever concoction she was coming up with, he'd let her. He did know what it would *not* be. Lasagna, enchiladas, chicken and broccoli casserole, or a bacon bourbon blue burger from the place down the street from her townhouse. He still thought about that burger. And the night he'd eaten it with Max. A lot.

He was going to find out what kind of cook Max really was. If nothing else, they'd get to know each other better over this next week, and while it was probably stupid, he wanted that.

Back in the cabin, he stored her bag in the bedroom, purposefully ignoring the bed. He wasn't making any assumptions about what was going to happen between them regarding any naked time or that bed. He wasn't going to be sleeping with her. Not all night. He needed to be out on the couch where he could keep the doors covered.

He tossed his bag in the living room corner and looked around. There wasn't anything else for him to do at the moment, so he sank onto the couch and propped his feet on the coffee table.

He pulled out his phone and opened his text messages.

Chris had promised he would check in with Lance and Moreno about the local investigation and keep Spencer updated, but there was nothing new yet from his partner.

He did, however, have several messages from Zander.

You're in town?

Heather says you're in cabin six.

What am I supposed to tell everyone?

Everyone is going to think that you're a couple.

Caroline is driving me crazy with questions. What can I tell her?

Spencer grinned. He should let Zander deal with the torture of his fiancée peppering him with questions. But sooner or later, Caroline would take it upon herself to show up in cabin six, demanding to know what was going on with him and Max. He honestly didn't want anyone around. Sure, part of it was because he wanted to keep them safe, and the less they knew, the better. Some of it was because he didn't want to make Max lie to her best friend or anyone else if he could avoid it.

And some of it was because he liked the idea of having her to himself. Sure, maybe it was a little forced. But come on, time alone with him wouldn't be that miserable for her, would it?

You cannot sleep with the woman you're supposed to be protecting, the voice in his head reminded him.

But I'm here voluntarily. It's not a job.

The reason it's not a job is that you're already compromised in your feelings for her.

He sighed. That much he wouldn't deny. His feelings for her weren't clear or simple, but some of those feelings kept him from being objective.

You need to be as objective as you can to keep her safe.

But if I'm already compromised in my feelings, I can't help if those turn into something more.

Something more like what?

Like falling in love with her or something.

The door opened just then.

Thank God.

He'd already been alone with his own thoughts for way too long.

Max strode toward the kitchen with a handful of ingredients.

Literally. She carried everything she needed in two hands.

"Is there more on the porch you need help with?" he asked, pushing up from the couch.

She glanced over. "No."

"You got everything you needed?"

"Yep."

Oh boy, this was going to be interesting.

"Need any help?" he asked dryly.

"Oh, I've got this," she said, giving him a little smirk that said she noticed his tone. "Though I'm used to only cooking for one, so I hope I make enough."

Spencer knew he could always sneak up to the main house and raid Heather's fridge and cupboards, so he wasn't too worried, but rather than poisoning him, maybe Max was just going to starve him.

"Well, if you got everything handled in here, I'm gonna return a couple of phone calls," he said.

She nodded. "It won't take long, though, so hurry back." She busied herself at the stove. "And make one of those calls to Zander. Tell him whatever you need to so he can reassure Caroline I'm fine. She's blowing up my phone."

"I figured. He said she's going a little crazy thinking that we're down here in cabin six, just the two of us, and she doesn't know anything about it."

That brought Max's head up. "Yeah, who knows what, by the way?"

Fuck. If he wasn't careful, it would be surprisingly easy to forget why they were actually here. Yes, he had this general sensation of needing to keep her safe, but he didn't think that would be any different if there was not someone threatening her. Something about her made him want to take care of her no matter what.

Her question was fair. "Zander knows the whole story. He's filled Michael and Theo in. I wanted to have them all on alert in case anybody shows up and starts asking about you. I'll fill Wyatt in too, and he might head down here if he can get away."

That made her grimace slightly. But she nodded.

"What do you think about letting Caroline in on it all?"

Max nodded as she stirred things together on the stove. He could hear the sound of meat sizzling in the skillet, and he was pretty sure it was ground beef.

"Yeah, I think we tell her. I mean, she's applying to the FBI. She and I've handled a lot of bullshit in the past. She'll be worried, but—" Max blew out a breath.

"But?" Spencer prodded.

Max looked over and met his gaze. "If I'm here with you, I'm sure she'll feel like I'm totally safe and won't be too concerned. She'll like that I'm here in Autre. And she'll trust that you'll keep me safe."

That made a surge of something like pride, but stronger and deeper, go through him. He was good at his job. He knew that, definitely took pride in it, and knew that most people around him felt the same way Max said Caroline felt. But hearing that Caroline would trust him with her best friend meant a lot. Especially now that he knew just how close the women were and why. Caroline was getting ready to apply to the FBI and she'd been an instrumental consultant on a few white-collar cases Spencer had been involved with in the past year. He admired, liked, and trusted her as well. She was going to be an excellent agent.

Caroline didn't know everything Spencer felt for Max, though. Hell, *Spencer* didn't even know everything he felt for Max exactly.

Max was more than a typical job, and the people who loved her needed to trust him. He hadn't realized it until now, but it was true. Maybe because he was getting the sense that there weren't many people super close to this woman. And so the ones there were really mattered. He needed to be sure they understood that she mattered to him.

"Okay, I'm going to make that call. I'll have Zander fill her in and reassure her. But sometime while we're here, you'll see her."

Max looked at him again. "Okay. I'd like that."

Fuck. He wanted her to see a number of people. Caroline, because she was already important to Max, but he wanted Max to feel the support she had here. She didn't even realize the way the Landrys would rally around her.

They wouldn't even have to know that there was a threat to her. All he had to do was show up with her at Ellie's, and they would all welcome her like family. She was already a friend of

Caroline's. That would be enough for them to surround her with love and laughter. But if the family thought he and Max were in a relationship, it would be even more intense.

He wanted her to feel that.

It was a strange impulse and he wasn't entirely sure where it came from, but he suddenly knew he had to make it happen.

"You better hurry up. This is almost done," she said.

In five minutes? Dinner was going to be ready in less than ten minutes total?

Yeah, he wasn't taking her anywhere to be with anyone else tonight. He wanted this evening with her alone. With whatever weird thing she was cooking on the stove and whatever the rest of the evening would bring.

But that does not include the bedroom.

His stupid inner voice and he were going to have to agree on what kind of advice that inner voice could be giving.

HE DIDN'T HAVE much to say to Chris and knew his partner would keep him updated, so he only called Zander. It was a quick call. Zander already knew most of the details, and Spencer just wanted to inform his cousin that he needed to tread carefully when he filled Caroline in on what was going on.

"I've got her," Zander promised. "And I'll keep her away from the cabin for as long as possible. But that's probably not indefinite."

Spencer chuckled. "I wouldn't expect it to be. And Max will go crazy if we don't see anyone else."

"We'll need to get together with the guys at some point. We want to give them as much information as possible so they can be on the lookout for anyone poking around town."

"Yeah, maybe we can all get together in the next day or two."

"Don't you think the sooner, the better?" Zander asked.

"Yeah, tomorrow." Spencer glanced into the cottage through the huge back windows. Max was dishing something from the skillet onto plates. "Not tonight. Need to get her settled here. But yeah, I want to fill everybody in."

They could help him keep her safe.

And they'd tell him if he was overreacting by bringing Max here.

If anyone would tell him the unvarnished truth about… well, anything… it was these guys.

The group of guys Spencer counted as his best friends had all chosen jobs where they could take care of their families and the town they loved by directly keeping everyone safe.

Zander and Michael and Theo had stayed right here in Autre. Spencer and Wyatt had gone a little bigger and wider, with a broader network of resources and a larger perimeter around Autre.

Still, this town was truly home in their hearts, and if anyone here needed anything, both of them would pull out all the stops and use all their resources to help.

"I'll tell everyone to meet at the cabin tomorrow night. Caroline can keep Max company," Zander said.

"Sounds good."

The cabin was a fishing cabin deep in the bayou. On the outside, it didn't look like much. On purpose. It looked like a rundown fishing cabin that hadn't been used in a while. However, it was a modern, high-tech base the guys used as a type of headquarters on the inside.

These same guys—Spencer, Wyatt, Theo, and Michael—had grown up goofing around on the bayou together as kids. Instead of a treehouse, they'd had an abandoned fishing cabin to play in. They'd pretended to be pirates and explorers out there as soon as they'd been old enough to drive an airboat.

Then, ten years ago, they'd been bonded even deeper by tragedy.

Autre's Community Center had been leveled by a gas explosion that had killed and injured several. Spencer and Wyatt had lost their grandmother. Michael had lost his son's mother. Theo had lost his brother, Wade. Theo and Zander had been best friends since kindergarten, and watching Theo go through that had profoundly affected Zander.

All of them had been drawn into protective fields after that. Zander, Spencer, and Theo went into law enforcement, Michael became a firefighter and paramedic, and Wyatt went into the Coast Guard.

Now the fishing cabin where they congregated was a place where they could share the pressures of their jobs, their worries, and frustrations with people who understood their motivations and passion for the work of protecting.

They also played a lot of poker out there.

And drank a lot of beer.

"Okay, gotta go," Spencer told him. "We'll talk tomorrow."

"But… you're good, right?" Zander asked.

Spencer understood his cousin's question. He wasn't asking if Spencer needed any provisions from the store or food delivery from Ellie's. He wanted to know Spencer's emotional state.

He just wasn't sure if Zander was asking because of the bomb threat or because Spencer was now bunking with Max.

And it was a good question either way.

"Yeah. I think so. I'll let you tell me tomorrow night for sure."

There was a pause on Zander's end and then a chuckle. "Got it."

They disconnected, and Spencer headed back inside.

"Just in time," Max said.

Her cheerfulness surrounding making dinner for him should've made Spencer suspicious. Instead, it made him grin.

He joined her at the table and looked at the plates.

The plate was covered with brown. That was it. Everything on the plate was brown.

He'd been right about the ground beef. That he could identify, at least.

"Okay, what the hell is this?"

"You asked me for something I might be eating tonight if I

was alone. This is something I make a lot of." She pulled her chair out and sat. "Been eating it since I was a kid."

Max tucked one foot up underneath her butt on the chair and picked up her fork.

She'd set the table so that he was seated directly across from her rather than next to her. He dragged his chair out and sat. He watched her take a bite. He scooped up a forkful and sniffed it. "It looks like ground beef and baked beans."

She swallowed and nodded. "Exactly. With barbecue sauce."

He stared at her. "This is really just ground beef and baked beans?"

"Yeah. It's good. Super easy. Super cheap. Takes no time to make."

"You do not eat this a lot."

She laughed. "I do. I told you I'm no gourmet. I do takeout and delivery a lot. But when I cook at home, this is one of the things I make. I'm serious," she added when he gave her a skeptical look. "Here. Veggies too." She handed him a bowl of sliced tomatoes. "Heather caught me in the kitchen and insisted I bring these down."

"How did you… come up with this?" Spencer took a tentative bite. Okay, it wasn't *bad*. It tasted exactly the way he'd expected it to. Like baked beans with ground beef and barbecue sauce in it.

"I had to cook for myself a lot as a kid, and this is one of the things I made because it was super simple, and we always had the ingredients."

"Your childhood sounds… interesting."

She took another bite and nodded. "I suppose that's one word."

"Tell me something else you made a lot."

"Well, not lasagna, but I would make spaghetti. Ground beef, spaghetti sauce from a jar, and noodles."

Spencer rolled his eyes. "At least that's normal."

She laughed softly, and the sound swirled through his chest.

He liked when she laughed. This wasn't the first time she had. They'd had fun at the wedding. They'd had fun the night he'd been at her apartment. He shifted on his chair with even the barest flicker of a thought of *that* night. But yeah, it really hit him just now how much he liked hearing her laugh.

He took another bite, chewed, swallowed, then shoved his chair back. "I'll be right back."

"Where are—"

He was across the room and out the door before she could ask.

He jogged up the path to Heather's back door. He let himself into the kitchen. It was empty, but there was a soft light glowing above the sink, and the room's aroma hit him, making him smile and think, *this is what I want.*

The kitchen smelled like a home should. Cinnamon and sugar lingered from earlier, combined with something that just smelled like "dinner." He couldn't place it any more specifically than that, but he didn't need to. This was what he wanted when he walked in the door at the end of the day. The aroma of a home-cooked meal made with love in a place that made him feel at peace.

He headed into the pantry and rummaged for only a minute before finding what he needed. Tucking the bag under his arm, he headed for the fridge next. Again, he found what he needed easily. He wasn't going for gourmet here either.

"Ta-da," he said, holding up the two items he'd retrieved as he came back through the cottage's door.

"Frito corn chips and cheddar cheese?" Max said.

He pulled his chair out again and dropped into the seat. He opened the bag of chips and dug in, grabbing a handful and sprinkling them over the top of his meat and beans. On top of that, he added a healthy handful of shredded cheddar cheese. He stirred it all together, then took a big bite. Chewing, he nodded. He swallowed and said, "Yep. Better."

She narrowed her eyes.

"Come on." He reached for her plate and added chips and cheese. "You have to try it."

She took a tentative bite. Which made him laugh. "You're the one who just mixed up beans and hamburger. Don't even give me that I-don't-know-about-this look."

She smiled. "Yeah, it's okay," she commented. "But, in all fairness, cheese can make anything better."

He grinned, and they continued eating.

"Okay, so you made this whatever-this-is and spaghetti. What else do you make for dinner?"

"Macaroni and cheese and hot dogs."

He paused and looked at her. "No."

"Yes. Of course."

He groaned. "That physically pains me, Max."

She laughed. "And yet I'm alive and well. Seems like it's working out."

"Anything else?"

"I told you before—grilled cheese, scrambled eggs, peanut butter and jelly, of course. Lots of canned soup."

He took another bite as he studied her. "That sound like a menu a kid would make for themselves all the time."

She nodded. "That's what it was. And that's all I ever really learned to cook. And I like it all. So that's what I still make. My work schedule is nuts, so I never know when I'll be home. I need easy things with ingredients that don't go bad too quickly."

That made sense. But there was something here that was bugging him. "Why didn't your parents cook for you more often?"

She lifted a napkin and wiped her mouth. Then she pushed her plate back, rested her forearms on the table, and regarded him. "I told you my mom is an ER nurse."

"Right."

"She has always worked long hours and is almost always the first person they call if they need extra help because she's amazing. And because she rarely says no. It used to be because of the money, partly, but it's also always been because she just really lives for her work. She also does a lot of teaching. Night classes and stuff like that."

Max took a breath. "And my dad was a lineman. Also a super hard worker, really smart, and motivated. Moved quickly into management, so he oversees a huge team. But he's one of those guys who would never ask someone to do something he's not willing to do. So he's always out on calls with his guys. Again, he's always worked long, strange hours and was on call a lot."

"So, where were you when they were at work?"

"Home. In our apartment. When I was little, they alternated shifts, so the other was at home with me when one was at work. But even after I got older and could stay home alone, it wasn't like they were gone *every* night. Mom would cook so I'd have leftovers to eat. We'd freeze stuff. But… it was great for them that I was smart and capable and independent, so they didn't have to worry about me coming home after school and staying alone and taking care of myself until eight or nine at night. It saved us childcare money and saved them from having to stop somewhere on their way home after a long shift to pick me up."

Spencer felt how tight his body was. From his gut to his spine to the fist around his fork. He willed himself to relax. "They told you that?"

"Sure. And I overheard them talk about it a lot."

He nodded, trying to unclench his jaw. "How old were you when you started staying alone?"

She shrugged. "Maybe nine or ten. By the time I was eleven for sure. I don't remember the first few times. We had neighbors, Phil and Steph, who were there if I needed anything and who would look in on me."

Jesus. Nine or ten? She'd been alone in an apartment until eight or nine at night? Making herself dinner? What if she'd gotten hurt? What if she was sick? What if…

Spencer shut down the thoughts. It was in the past, and she was fine.

But… was she?

He studied the woman across from him. She was playing with the edge of the woven placemat that matched the cushion they sat on.

She'd made him dinner in part to prove to him that what she was saying about you're-not-getting-lasagna-from-me-no-matter-how-many-orgasms-you-give-me-and-how-many-bad-guys-you-save-me-from was true. But… this was what she ate all the time. This was what she was used to.

Being on her own. Taking care of herself. In the most basic, simple way.

Without even extra cheese on top.

Now it made a hell of a lot more sense why she was so determined to do things on her own. And more, why she always seemed just a little puzzled when he helped her.

"I learned to be independent early on," she said after a moment. "And I honestly didn't mind. No one told me I had to sit down and do my homework the minute I walked in the door. I could eat whenever I got hungry instead of just when it was dinner time. If I was in the mood for macaroni, I had macaroni. Even if it was three nights in a row. It was pretty great, really. And I got good at taking care of myself. It was a lot of help to my parents. And I think it made the time I did have with them even better."

She still wasn't looking at him. She was staring at the table, but clearly not seeing the placemat or the edge of her plate. He wondered what she *was* seeing. Their old apartment? Her mom and dad's faces?

Spencer's chest felt tight, and he scrubbed a hand over his breastbone.

He saw a little redheaded girl with bright green eyes standing on tiptoes so that she could reach the top of the stove, stirring a pot of macaroni and cheese because her mom and dad were both still at work.

"And that's why you didn't have very many baked goods?"

His voice sounded sandpaper rough.

She nodded. "And we didn't have ingredients for stuff like that. My mom didn't bake because she didn't have the time. I just didn't get used to that stuff."

"Sounds lonely."

She finally looked up at him. "Yeah, in retrospect, I guess it probably was. But I didn't know that. I just thought that was how it was supposed to be."

"Until?" Somehow he knew there was a point when she'd figured out that other kids had moms that made them dinner every night.

"Caroline," she said softly. "Caroline and I became friends in first grade. But I didn't go to her house to visit until we were in fifth grade. And that was when I realized that some parents were home at the end of the day. Sometimes moms met their kids at the door after school. And families sat around the table all together at the same time. Sometimes moms and dads were both around for bedtime. I was so amazed by it all, but Caroline was the one who told me that what she had was more common than what I had."

"I see." He completely understood her independent streak now. She had always been on her own, to an extent. No wonder she didn't like being told what to do.

"I'm guessing your home life was a lot like Caroline's," she said, meeting his gaze directly now.

He nodded. "Yeah. Minus the tons of money, of course."

"They didn't always have money," Max muttered.

He frowned.

"Caroline's dad got rich overnight," Max said. "The owner of the company found out he had cancer and decided to give it all to Caroline's dad. He was just a manager who had been working his way up. Then one day, bam, he was CEO. And crazy rich."

Spencer had known that, of course. The story of Charles Holland's "inheritance" from a man who wasn't any kind of blood relative was legendary. But he had never really thought about it much, he supposed.

"So you knew them before they were rich," he commented. Stupidly. Of course, she had. But that was interesting.

"I did. Visited their house, spent the night, the whole thing. Caroline and I were tight for years before they became *The Hollands.*" She said The Hollands with extra emphasis. "After that, Caroline's dad had a very specific idea of the types of people he wanted Caroline—well, all of them—spending time with and getting close to. I didn't make the cut."

Spencer couldn't argue that everyone in New Orleans and probably most of Louisiana, hell most of the *south*, knew of Caroline's family. But it was clear that Caroline's family had been assholes to Max. He was glad he knew Caroline personally and had gotten to know her before Max told him this story. He would have hated her right along with the rest of her family for no other reason than the sad look just talking about them put on Max's face.

"Anyway, you had the perfect family life too, huh?" Max prodded.

Spencer couldn't deny it. "My mom was home when we got home from school. Often with fresh baked cookies or brownies."

Max rolled her eyes, but the corner of her mouth tipped up. "Shocker."

"So okay, it wasn't just about cookies and brownies. My dad is a medical examiner. So his job was pretty rough at times."

Her eyes widened, and Spencer couldn't help but smile and shake his head. "Your morbid fascination with dead bodies never ceases to amaze me."

She looked slightly chagrined. "I just bet he has some fascinating stories."

"I'm sure he does. I'm sure he'd love to sit and tell you about some of them too."

Hold up, had he just essentially said that he would introduce Max to his father sometime? But yes. Looking at the woman across the table from him, he thought there was a very good possibility that Sam and Mary Jo Landry would meet Max. His dad would really like her. They could talk cold cases all day long.

And there was no way in hell that Maxine Keller could walk away from his mother's kitchen without liking baked goods at least *a little*.

"So your mom baked cookies to make your dad feel better at the end of a rough day at work?"

Spencer found that he wanted to explain this to her. She'd opened up to him about her childhood, which had definitely helped him understand her better. Even though it broke his heart, he liked the little glimpse into past Max. And he knew that his insistence on what he was looking for in a girlfriend seemed perfectionistic and sexist. He wanted to help her understand where that was coming from.

"Kind of. But it wasn't the food. It was the normalcy that it helped establish. He needed that. He valued it. He did autopsies all day and saw some pretty bad things. And he battled depression."

Max was listening intently. He could tell she was interested in what he was saying, and that made the tightness he usually felt in his gut when he talked about depression, and its impact on his family, loosen.

"His job made his depression worse. For a while, when I was about six to eight or so, he turned to alcohol to help deal with all the stuff he saw. But when I was in third grade, he and my mom split up for a little while, and he went to AA and got cleaned up and got help dealing with it all in better ways. One of those ways was to compartmentalize. When he was done with work, he shut it off and left it at the office. He came home, and he reveled in his home life. He wanted as much normalcy as possible and cele-brated all of the good things about life. Having two healthy kids, a loving wife, and a house where he could provide for all of us. And my mom took that seriously too. She wanted to make our home a really happy, comforting place for him to be. And I guess that rubbed off."

Max nodded. "I can understand that. Though it feels like there's a lot of pressure with that. The idea that everything has to be perfect in a certain way or somebody might fall off the wagon or get depressed and that you would feel at fault."

He nodded. "Yeah, there was some of that. I'll admit that there were times when it felt like we had to make things seem good even when maybe they weren't. There was a time in high school when Wyatt got into a car accident. He had a few cuts and bruises. The car was banged up. My mom called in every favor and friend she had to get all of that taken care of without telling my dad. Not because he'd be angry, but because she just always wanted everything to be perfect for him."

Max frowned. "Yikes."

Spencer nodded. "I'm not *that* bad."

"You sure?" she asked. "I mean, you were *very* specific about the lasagna."

"Fucking moonshine," he muttered. "Yes. I'm sure. Things don't have to be perfect. I just really value having things around me that remind me of happiness and light and good things."

"Okay." She was watching him closely.

Spencer took a deep breath and blew it out. "In high school, I became aware that I was dealing with some depression too. We went to talk to the doctor, and he diagnosed me. It commonly runs in families."

Max seemed to lean in slightly. She was frowning now, seeming concerned.

"They gave me some meds that I tried, but I hated how they made me feel. And I handled a lot of it mostly just by being aware of it. And my mom took it very seriously and really devoted herself to supporting me, and Wyatt, the way she did my dad. Making sure our home was happy and comforting and a safe haven. And…" He gave her a look.

"What?" she asked, eyes wide.

"We got a dog."

"You've got to be kidding."

"Nope. Roscoe was amazing. I could tell him anything. He was a comfort dog before I even knew that was a thing."

She just motioned for him to go on.

"But then, I went to college. Left home, left Roscoe, my mom… the brownies." He gave her a little grin, but he felt that tightness knotting his stomach. "And then my grandmother died. Here in Autre, there was a huge explosion at the community center that killed a bunch of people. My grandma was one of them."

Max frowned and leaned in now as if not wanting to miss a word.

"So it was traumatic and very sudden. Wyatt was here in Autre when it happened, and he dealt with a lot of emotions after it. Some of my best friends in the world, Michael, Theo, and Zander, also lost people in the explosion, and watching them go through their grief was hard on me. So my depression got a lot worse, and it was the first time that I felt like it was out of my control."

"Well, shit, Spencer," Max said.

He gave a soft chuckle. It was such a Max reaction.

"Being away at college in Texas didn't help. I was away from home, away from family, out of my normal surroundings and routine. So I ended up dropping out for the semester. I didn't even really want to go back at all, but I re-enrolled at Loyola to be close to home. I did finish, and I realized that being close to home and around the people I love and doing what my dad always did—reveling in those good, simple things that make me happy—were essential to my mental health.

"So when I decided to go into law enforcement, I did it knowing that my job would be tough. That I was going to see stuff every single day and deal with people all the time who were going to remind me that there was terrible shit out there, and I was going to have to confront the fact that there was darkness around me and I was going to have to battle that."

Max wet her lips. "And you think that brownies and puppies will do that?"

"They're symbolic. They are things that I could have in my life that would remind me that I need to focus on good things. Every day, I need to have happy things in my life to remember that the bad stuff isn't normal and isn't everything."

She studied him for a very long time. Finally, she nodded. "I understand how you feel now."

"Yeah?"

"Well, brownies and puppies are better than turning to alcohol and drugs. That's why people do that, right? To feel better when things are shitty. We all need those hits of dopamine. We all need to be reminded of the things that make us happy. Of course, that makes sense."

"So you don't think I'm an asshole for wanting to date a woman who can bake and wants to have a dog?"

"Well, I think that's still extremely specific, and you are potentially setting yourself up for some disappointment. If, for instance, she makes amazing brownies and has the cutest dog in the world but is a raging bitch, you could find yourself in trouble," Max said. "But, it's good that you know what you need to be happy. And that you are consciously seeking that out. Everybody deserves to be happy. And it's worth seeking out, and not just hoping it comes along."

Spencer was shocked by how much it meant that she understood and accepted all of that.

Max Keller was someone whose opinion mattered to him.

"So growing up, I didn't get a lot of practice in cooking or baking. Mom did all of that." He gave her a wry smile. "Still does for me whenever she has the chance."

Max gave him a little eyeroll but smiled back.

"But I did get a lot of practice doing dishes," he said, pushing his chair back and picking up his plate.

He reached out, and she handed him her plate. "Thanks."

"I'm going to ask a question that I already know the answer to."

She lifted an eyebrow. "Okay."

"Have you ever watched the TV show *Schitt's Creek*?"

She shook her head. "I have not."

Dammit. She really was not his type. But he wanted her more every minute he was with her.

"I would love to be the person who introduces you to that show."

She gave him a little smile. "You would, huh?"

"It's one of my favorites. It's funny. You can easily catch on even if you've never seen it before. And it's very much part of my normal routine."

"Are you feeling like you need reminding of the good things today?" she asked.

The way she looked at him made Spencer feel like his answer was very important to her.

He thought about the question. And decided to be completely honest. "Well, my day started with a *bomb threat* against someone I care about—"

Emotion flickered in her eyes.

"—but I have to say I feel like I've had a pretty great day despite that," Spencer finished.

That seemed to please her. She pushed back from the table. "Okay. I will sit on the couch with you while you do that."

He actually let out a relieved breath. He hadn't realized how much he wanted her to do that. It was, at least in part, the reminder that there had been a bomb threat against her that morning. It felt like weeks ago in some ways. But he'd love to have her sitting next to him, relaxed, comfortable, and *safe*. Where he could just glance over and see her. Maybe even reach out and touch her. Like on the foot or something else completely innocent.

It reminded him of how he'd pictured her propped up in bed in pajamas, reading.

Yeah, he really wanted her on that couch with him.

"But I'm going to do something that's very much a part of *my* normal routine," she added as she stood.

"What's that?"

Maybe naked yoga in the living room was a normal part of her end-of-day routine.

"Crossword puzzles."

Okay. Probably not naked crossword puzzles either.

But he grinned. "Had almost forgotten that you are crossword puzzle champion of New Orleans."

She put a hand to her chest. "Excuse me, Agent Landry. I am the champion of the *Louisiana* crossword puzzle league. Five years in a row. *And* I won the American Crossword Puzzle Tournament two years ago."

He chuckled and carried their dishes to the sink. "I'm so sorry. I stand corrected." But that was pretty impressive when he thought about it. She was probably dumbing down her vocabulary when she spoke to him.

"I do always put my pajamas on this time of night, though," she said, starting for the bedroom. "So, I'll be right back."

Spencer froze. Pajamas. On the couch. *Yes.* Just what he'd wanted. A comfortable, cozy night at home.

But it suddenly hit him that the last time they'd been on a couch together, they'd done very dirty things to one another. He wasn't sure why that was just occurring to him *now*. It seemed those memories were *never* far from his mind.

Could he sit on the couch with her in her pajamas and focus on anything other than flashbacks of that night?

Of course. He was a grown man. They were not here because they were dating. Or even because they were *pretending* since they were alone.

They could just be exactly what they were—two people who weren't really sure how they felt about one another, sharing a space because one of them might have someone trying to kill her.

In pajamas.

"Yeah. Okay. Sounds good." He focused on the dishes.

"Meet you on the couch in a few minutes."

Max disappeared into the bedroom, shutting the door behind her, and Spencer blew out a breath.

This all felt very domestic. Intimate even. And pretty damn *normal*. There were probably millions of couples across the country right now changing into comfortable clothes before they settled on the couch to watch television. A few of those were maybe even doing crossword puzzles too.

But he was wound up, and his nerve endings were humming as if he was getting ready to run a 5K.

Was *this* going to be his *normal* for the next week?

What had he been thinking?

CHAPTER FIVE

SHE'D FALLEN asleep on him.

Literally.

Well, her feet were on him anyway. Actually, her legs from the knees down.

She'd started just propped against the opposite end of the couch, with her crossword puzzle book open on the arm. She'd mostly focused on the puzzle, but he'd noticed her smiling and even laughing a couple of times at the TV.

Eventually, she'd propped her head on her hand and just watched. Then her eyes started drifting shut. Then her head was on the arm of the couch.

But when she wanted to get comfortable, she got comfortable.

She'd scooted down to rest her head on the couch cushion and stretched out. Including putting her feet in Spencer's lap.

He'd had to catch her heels in his hands to keep her from kicking him in the balls.

And then he'd just held her feet, rubbing his thumbs along the arches of her feet, and absorbing the sound of her contented sigh and loving the way she cuddled deeper into the couch.

He'd wanted her to feel safe and be comfortable and relaxed.

Mission accomplished.

The woman was sound asleep.

At 8:30 p.m.

Spencer smiled even as he shook his head. She'd had a big day. Maybe it was all the emotion and activity.

The episode ended and Spencer realized he didn't remember a thing from what he'd watched. He'd been paying attention to Max.

Of course he'd started with the way her soft cotton shorts molded to the curve of her hips and ass. The way the matching tank hugged her waist and breasts. There was no way he could have ignored that. He was drawn to this woman and the part that *didn't* confuse him was his attraction to her body. She was petite, but had great curves in all the right places and he'd enjoyed every one of them up close and personal.

Now, having those sweet curves within touching distance again and barely covered, absolutely drew his attention. But with her asleep, and him unable to really *do* anything, he also had the chance to simply study her up close.

What he'd thought was black polish on her toenails was actually a very deep purple. It even had a bit of a sparkle to it. It turned out that she did have an extremely light dusting of freckles over the top curve of her shoulder. He assumed it was from wearing sleeveless tops in the Louisiana summer heat. He wondered if she burned easily and if she used sunscreen. He wanted to kiss those freckles desperately.

Her lips were the same color as her nipples and he wanted her to never wear lipstick.

Her eyelashes were pale and had a reddish hue. As did her eyebrows. And the fine hair on her arms. Of course they all did. She was a redhead. But he'd never thought about the color of a woman's eyelashes before. Now he was fascinated. Did she wear mascara? Now he was going to have to pay attention to see the next time she was awake.

The color of her hair mesmerized him. He wanted to run his

fingers through it in the sunlight and just study all the different shades of red and gold. Truthfully, he wanted to run his hands over every inch of her in full sunlight so he could study every single thing about her.

She stirred, shifting, moving her feet against his hands and he stroked a hand up one calf. It wasn't perfectly smooth. There was just a slight prickle, but he didn't mind at all. In fact, he wanted to feel that against his thighs and hips as she wrapped her legs around him. It was real and he wanted to feel her legs in every stage from freshly shaved to haven't-had-a-chance-for-days.

Wow, she was truly *asleep*. He should make her go to bed.

"Max?" he asked softly.

She didn't even wiggle.

"Max?" he asked a little louder, squeezing her foot gently.

She just breathed in deeply, then out.

He should just carry her into bed. She was in her pajamas, after all. He could just scoop her up and take her into the bedroom.

Spencer shifted her legs so he could stand. Then he leaned over. She was on her side, so he pushed gently against her shoulder, rolling her to her back. She went with a sigh, one hand moving to rest on her chest. Perfect. Spencer slid an arm under her knees and one behind her back.

And everything was great until he started to lift.

She came awake suddenly. She kicked her legs, flailed her arms, and her head lifted instinctively to look around. Her forehead hit Spencer in the chin. Hard.

His head snapped back and his teeth clamped down on his tongue.

"Fuck!" he swore in surprised pain.

"Ahhh!" she yelled.

She was still kicking and waving her arms and he unceremoniously dropped her the one foot back onto the couch cushions.

"Max! It's me!"

She kicked out, her shin connecting with his thigh.

That fucking hurt too.

"Max!" He pinned her arms down against the couch. "Max! It's Spencer!"

Her eyes were wide and not fully focused.

She just yelled again. "*Ahhhhh!*"

Jesus. The cottage next door was going to think they needed to call the cops.

Which was Zander.

Spencer did *not* want Zander showing up here, grinning and smirking and writing up a report about how Spencer had tried to sweetly carry Max to bed and she'd thought he was attacking her.

"Maxine!" he said sharply, putting a leg across hers to keep her from kicking and, against his better judgement, placing a hand over her mouth. "Stop it. It's me."

Her eyes flew to his as he put his face directly in front of hers.

"It's *Spencer*. Calm the fuck down!"

She suddenly went still. Her gaze focused and she stopped moving and he felt her pull in a long breath.

He waited another few seconds, making sure that she realized who was holding her down.

Slowly he removed his hand. "Okay?" he asked.

She drew in another long breath and blew it out. She nodded. "Yeah."

"Holy shit, Max."

"What happened?"

"You were sleeping like the dead, so I decided to carry you into the bedroom. And you turned into the Tasmanian devil."

"Well, I'm not used to people picking me up in the middle of the night."

That made him chuckle. "It's not even 9 p.m."

"Well… still."

He liked that she was at a loss for words. That was unusual.

Slowly, he became aware of the fact that he was pinning her to the couch. With almost his entire body.

In spite of the fact that she'd been fighting off an intruder in her imagination and he'd been fearing for his manhood, his eyes, nose, and jaw, it didn't take long for his body to register that this felt really nice.

The couch was big enough for the two of them to lie together. He wasn't entirely on top of her, but almost half of him was pinning more than half of her to the cushions.

"I, um… didn't mean to squash you. Self-preservation instinct."

She smiled. "You're not squashing me." Her voice was soft and a little breathless.

Their gazes locked. "I did this, honestly, to keep you from hurting me or yourself. But mostly me."

She wet her lips and nodded. "I believe you."

"So, I could probably get up now. You seem a lot more calm."

"Funny, I don't exactly feel *calm*."

His heart kicked against his rib cage. A moment ago she'd been ready to claw his eyes out. The moment before that she'd been so deeply asleep that she hadn't realized he was even there. But now, her gaze was hot and she was breathing fast, and she was definitely not wearing a bra with this pajama set. The breast that was not underneath his chest was pressed against the front of the soft cotton and the nipple was clearly hard.

Spencer's entire body responded. "You fell asleep really fast. And very deep," he said, his voice husky.

"I often fall asleep on the couch. Never that deeply, though. I guess I felt really safe with you."

Damn, he liked that. He felt the corner of his mouth curl. "Until I tried to pick you up."

"Sorry. Instinct."

"Honestly the cop part of me is very glad that your instinct is to fight hard when someone does something unexpected."

"Good." She gave a little nod. "I guess that means you just need to be sure I'm expecting anything you do."

He nodded slowly and his gaze dropped to her mouth. "Good idea. For instance, if I was going to kiss you, I should make sure that you knew that."

She nodded. "Right."

"Max."

"Yeah?"

"I'm going to kiss you."

"Good."

He lowered his head. He'd kissed this woman several times. But somehow this felt different. It was, for one thing, completely sober. Unlike the first time. It was also a lot more intentional than the second time. She'd been the initiator that night. Something he'd repeatedly told himself over the last few days whenever he'd started to feel slightly guilty about the entire situation. She'd been the one to climb into his lap and kiss him.

This time he very much kissed her.

Their mouths touched and immediately the heat flared. He gave into the instinct to sink his fingers deep into her thick, silky hair and pull them through the long tresses. But he didn't have a chance to study the colors up close the way he'd thought about earlier. That would have to wait for another time. Now he was very busy tasting her mouth fully.

He licked along her bottom lip, swallowed her soft sigh, then met the stroke of her tongue. She fisted the front of his shirt and arched against him and he gratefully pressed closer.

His free hand ran from her hip, up the side of her body to her shoulder. He stroked up and down the bare arm he'd been studying earlier. Her skin was soft and he wanted to kiss the entire length from her shoulder to the tip of her middle finger and back. He moved his hand to cup the breast that seemed to be begging for his touch, the hard center pressing into his palm. The resulting moan told him she welcomed the move.

"Spencer," she gasped against his mouth.

He moved his lips along her jaw and down her throat, then across her collarbone to her shoulder, giving in to the impulse to kiss and then lick over the freckles he'd discovered earlier.

Spencer felt her hands slip under the edge of his t-shirt and slide up his back. God, he loved the feel of her hands on his skin. He pressed closer, grinding his cock against her thigh. She arched her back, and he returned his mouth to hers, kissing her hungrily. He felt her hands drop to his ass, squeezing as she lifted one leg and hooked her heel around the back of his thigh.

His hand skimmed down to her ass to return the favor. He didn't feel the edge of any panties, and he groaned, thinking about her bare underneath the thin shorts.

She must have had a similar thought. She slipped her hands into his pants and clutched his bare ass before sliding to the front and wrapping her hands around his cock.

He groaned, unable to keep from thrusting into her grip.

"No underwear," she murmured against his mouth.

"I sleep naked."

"What if there's a fire, or you have to get up quickly?"

"Keep these pants on the floor next to me."

"Well, I'm a fan." She stroked him, and a shudder of lust went through him.

"Max—"

A loud bang like a door slamming came from next door, followed by loud laughter.

They both froze. Well, fuck.

Or… not.

Spencer rested his forehead against hers, sucking in a deep breath.

Right. They were at Heather's bed and breakfast. There were other people around. And this place had huge front windows, and they had several lights on. Whatever they'd been about to do would have been on full display for their neighbors.

"We probably shouldn't do this," he told her as common

sense started to surface through the lusty haze she so easily stirred up in him.

"We're not drunk," she commented.

He lifted his head and looked down at her. "No. But it's been a crazy day. And you're obviously tired."

"I'm feeling a lot more awake now."

He grinned. "Still. There's been a lot of emotions swirling today. You were less than thrilled to see me this morning when I first showed up."

She pulled her hands from his pants, the glide of her skin over his even as she was extricating herself delicious and causing a shiver of desire.

He moved his hands from her clothes and rolled to his side. He rested his hand on her hip, on *top* of her clothes. Her hands rested on her stomach, one on top of the other.

"I can't believe that was just this morning. But truthfully, I was mad at you, but I was happy to see you. Especially after I found out what was going on. You make me feel safe."

No matter what amazing, pleasurable sensations had just been coursing through him, nothing could have been as satisfying as hearing that from her. He was a protector. His life was about keeping people safe. Especially the people he loved. And no matter what his exact emotions were for Maxine Keller, her feeling safe with him was better than anything else she could have said or done to him.

"That matters a lot to me, Max. Seriously. More than anything. Which is probably another reason we shouldn't sleep together tonight. I want you to know that I'm here first and foremost to protect you."

She nodded. "I understand. I mean, I believe that no matter what happens between us physically, but I appreciate that this first night together, we just make it about you bringing me here to keep me safe."

He didn't have anything else to say, and he wanted desperately to kiss her again. So he pushed himself up from the couch.

He held out a hand, and she let him tug her up. Then before he could think better of it or say anything to ruin the moment, he pulled her into his arms and gave her a tight hug.

It wasn't sexual, and the fact that he could follow up what had just been happening on the couch with a hug that was truly about his gratefulness that she felt safe with him no matter what was a testament to their strange but more-wonderful-all-the-time relationship.

Unlike at her apartment earlier, this time, she relaxed into him and even wrapped her arms around him.

They stayed like that for a minute, and then he let her go.

"Bed. Now."

She looked up at him and wet her lips. "Alone?"

"I'm not going to lie and tell you that it wouldn't take much for you to talk me into joining you. But alone tonight, I think would be best."

"But there's only one bed. Where will you sleep?"

He inclined his head toward the couch.

She frowned. "Spencer, that's silly. We've already slept together. Even if you don't think we should have sex tonight, you can sleep in the bed with me."

"I don't think I can, actually," he told her, giving her a meaningful look. "If I'm in there with you, we will have sex. And the whole point of being here is for me to keep you safe. I'm sleeping on the couch because it is the easiest way to protect both doors."

Her eyes widened. "You think someone is going to come here and come through one of the doors?"

"Until I can get a little more information about what happened in New Orleans and until I can get the other guys on board down here, I think I'll just feel better if I'm out here just in case."

"You know you're still overreacting, right?"

"Maybe. But I'd rather overreact than completely lose myself in you tonight in that bedroom and have something happen."

"Is that what would happen?" Her voice was a little huskier now.

"It's what happened the last time I spent the night in your bed. I can't imagine it wouldn't be the same this time. Maybe even more so."

Truthfully, the last time he'd been in her bed, he'd liked her. But he hadn't liked her as much as he did now. And the protectiveness he felt toward her had only grown stronger.

"Really? You lost yourself?"

He lifted a hand and brushed his thumb over her cheek. "Max, last time I was with you, nothing else mattered. I wasn't thinking about a single thing other than you."

He let that sink in. He'd been there that night to apologize. To try to convince them both he wasn't crazy. But once she'd taken her clothes off, that had all been forgotten. And once he was across the threshold of her bedroom, Max had consumed him.

He wasn't sure he had been aware of it at the time, but thinking back on it the day after and since, he realized just how true that was.

"Okay. I believe you."

Just like having her trust him and feel safe with him, the way Max believed the things he told her without question made his chest feel tight as his heart swelled. Having this woman accept him mattered. She'd been on her own a lot, and he understood that now, and every day she also saw a lot of the darkness and terrible stuff people did. He had to imagine that it was hard for her to trust. But she gave it to him fairly easily. Even after he'd trampled on it the last time they'd been together.

He ran his thumb over her cheek again and then let his hand drop.

"Bed. Now."

She pressed her lips together and nodded. "Goodnight, Spencer."

"Night, Max."

He watched her walk to the bedroom, and she didn't look

back. Once the door shut between them, he let out a long breath that he didn't even realize he'd been holding.

He wasn't sure how many more times he could send her into the bedroom by herself. So he needed to figure out what the hell had happened in New Orleans with the bomb threats, who had been behind it, and he needed to make sure that this cottage in this town with these people was absolutely the best place for Max to be.

———

MAX WOKE AT 5 A.M.

She always woke up at 5 a.m. She'd been doing it since she was ten. And even as an adult, when she had been out late the night before, even when she'd had too much to drink, she could rarely sleep past six.

Despite being awakened by Spencer partway through her REM cycle the night before, she'd gotten her eight-plus hours of sleep, and now she lay in the cottage bedroom, staring at the ceiling, wondering what she should do.

Five a.m. was early for a lot of people. Like maybe Spencer.

She listened intently and didn't hear a sound from around the living room. She assumed Spencer was still asleep on the couch.

She knew he hadn't gone to sleep when she had. Most adults didn't go to sleep at eight-thirty at night.

She'd listened to the sound of the television on the other side of the wall for several minutes when she'd first gone to bed. She drifted off reasonably quickly, but part of that was due to that television sound.

She smiled and stretched. She knew that Spencer didn't realize how comforting that sound was to her. She'd always gone to sleep with the sound of the neighbor's television when she was home alone as a kid. Even now, she listened to Hulu or Netflix on her phone on her bedside table.

It didn't matter what was on TV, just that there was the low hum of television conversation as she drifted off.

But now, everything was totally quiet, and she could only assume that Spencer still needed a couple of hours of sleep.

She sat up and blew out a breath. There was no way she could stay in bed for the next couple of hours. She knew she couldn't make coffee or anything that she usually did, but she could at least take her phone and computer out to the porch.

The back porch was probably safer. The front porch would be more on display, and she knew Spencer would be annoyed if he thought people coming and going would notice her. She didn't think there was any chance that whoever had sent the threat in New Orleans would know that she was in Autre, but she respected Spencer's caution and wanted to make sure he understood that she was taking this seriously.

She rummaged in her bag for a sweatshirt, slipping it on and zipping it over her pajamas. Then she grabbed her phone and laptop from the bag that Spencer had brought in yesterday. She tiptoed to the door and cracked it open.

The dim morning light was just starting to touch the living room, and sure enough, Spencer's form was still lying on the couch. She swung the door open carefully, praying it wouldn't creak. But Beau Hebert apparently kept the hinges well-oiled because the door swung open quietly.

She crept across the cottage floor, also hoping for no squeaky floorboards. She made it to the French doors leading out to the back porch without a single sound. She turned the lock and held her breath as a slight click sounded.

It wouldn't surprise her if FBI Agent Landry heard the tiniest noise and bounded off the couch.

But she heard only a soft snore from that direction.

She was proud of herself for not stopping by the couch and checking out his sleeping form.

He said he slept naked. She wondered if that included on

couches when he was on patrol protecting an investigative journalist from a would-be bomber.

But she'd mustered her willpower and not taken a peek.

She slipped out onto the back porch, pulling the door shut softly behind her, and settled into one of the surprisingly comfortable deck chairs.

She was facing southwest, so she would not be able to watch the sunrise directly, but she could watch the sky lighten as the sun came up, catch up on emails, and see what was happening online. She was particularly interested in knowing if any information had leaked about the bomb threat at the *New Orleans News*.

It only took her a few minutes to realize that the bomb threat had apparently been kept quiet. There were no news headlines, or social media posts, or comments related to the threat.

That was probably a good thing.

But she rested her head back on the chair, pondering her next move.

She wanted to post something on Facebook or Twitter.

Not officially from the *New Orleans News* but under her pen name's profile. She could call out the coward for the anonymous threat and see what kind of response she got. It could be telling. Was it someone who followed *her* online or only the *News*?

Suddenly a man came around the corner of the cottage.

Max screamed and bolted out of the chair.

She'd never considered herself a screamer before, but last night when Spencer had tried to pick her up from the couch, she had, and now as a man in blue jeans, a black t-shirt, and a black ball cap stepped out from the side of the cabin where no one else was supposed to be, she did.

"Jesus! You scared the hell out of me," the man snapped.

He spoke with an Irish accent, and Max frowned. "*I* scared *you*?" She was backing toward the door. Spencer was just inside. "Who are you?"

"I'm here to—"

The door behind her swung inward, and she felt a strong arm wrap around her waist, picking her up and pulling her back against a hard chest.

A gun lifted in front of her.

He swung her around to set her behind him and stepped in front of her. It wasn't until then that she realized he had a gun drawn.

The man came up onto the porch with his hands up. "Take it easy, now."

"Fucking hell, Colin." Spencer dropped his arm with the gun. "What are you doing?"

"Perimeter check. Just checking to see what we might need out here in case you wanted alarms or anything, and just generally checking the setup."

Spencer spun on Max. "Are you all right?"

Okay, so Spencer knew the guy. "He startled me. I had no idea some guy would be creeping around the cottage this early in the morning."

Spencer's gaze tracked over her. "What were you doing out there?"

She crossed her arms, hugging them against her body. "Trying not to wake you up, ironically."

He did have pants on, but no shirt, and his big, broad body distracted her. In spite of the way her heart was still hammering.

Her brain was quickly processing the fact that this man was not a threat and had shifted into hot-half-naked-Spencer-is-nearby mode.

"You have a gun," she said stupidly.

He frowned at her. "Of course I have a gun."

She nodded. Of course he had a gun. He was an FBI agent. And he was here specifically protecting her. This was the entire reason they were in this cottage to start with. They were not on vacation. Were not cuddling up together in this cottage for a week of romance and sex. No matter how it looked to the outside world.

She was not a lover of guns, but she had to admit that Spencer looked badass with his and the fact that he had come to her defense was making her stupidly swoony.

"Get inside," he said, his big hand landing on her hip as he nudged her through the door.

She frowned. "Hey. I'm fine."

"I need to talk to Colin."

"About me," she pointed out. That much was obvious. "Why can't I listen?"

"Because you're half-naked," he growled.

She looked down. Sure, her pants were pajama pants, but they covered her fully and were not see-through. On top she had a sweatshirt over her tank. She was as not half-naked as she could possibly get. She glanced at Colin. He was clearly amused.

"If that's what you think is half-naked, I'm feeling really sorry for your lady friends. Of course, your sexual frustration makes a lot of sense," Colin said, his accent a little thicker.

"Fuck off."

"I'm just saying, her hair is all wild, she's got an old sweatshirt on covering up the good stuff, and the only bare skin I can see is on her feet."

Max's hand flew instinctively to her head and she combed her fingers through her hair.

"She looks like she just rolled out of bed." Colin tipped his head. "She's a bit of a mess, wouldn't you say?" He glanced at her. "No offense."

She gave him a wide-eyed look. "Seriously?"

Not that she cared what Colin Whoever thought of her, but she didn't really need him pointing out to Spencer how *not* sexy she was looking.

Colin gave her a grin that, she had to admit, was quite sexy. He had dark hair and a thick, short beard. He also had tattoos that ran from his left wrist up his arm to disappear under the sleeve of the black t-shirt he wore. He looked to be solid muscle, and that grin gave her a sense of mischief. Then he winked.

Max frowned. Then looked up at Spencer.

He looked pissed. "Go away," Spencer told Colin. "Come back at a decent hour. When she's not… looking… like that."

Max tipped her head, watching Spencer. "Looking like what?" she asked.

She was certain she did look messy. This was how she looked every morning at this hour. What did she care? She didn't see people at this time of day.

Usually.

Hell, she probably still had a crease on her cheek from the pillowcase.

Spencer glowered at Colin. "You look sexy and sweet and he fucking thinks so too. Go inside."

She did? That made no sense. But Spencer seemed ruffled and pissy.

She glanced at Colin. He wasn't rushing to deny what Spencer had just said, but he wasn't confirming it either.

Max didn't think she was a troll or anything. Though morning Max might be more troll-ish than dressed-up-for-a-friend's-wedding-Max. She knew there were a few guys besides Spencer who found her attractive even. But from the first time she'd met him, Spencer had made her feel gorgeous. Like he thought she was stunning and that all the men around her must be falling at her feet. And now he was acting like he couldn't stand the idea of another man seeing her even in baggy pajama pants.

The way that made heat swirl through her stomach was not okay.

She didn't need a caveman in her life. Especially a delusional one.

"Spence—" she started. Though she definitely didn't know where she was going with that.

But he was already frowning at Colin again. "You go away."

"I'm here to help. On direct orders." Colin spread his arms, clearly amused. "Zander filled me in and wants everything checked out before we meet tonight."

"Fine. Hurry up. And no, you can't come inside for coffee." Spencer turned and nudged Max into the cottage with his entire body now crowding close and moving forward until he could slam the door behind them on Colin. He turned the lock and frowned down at her. "The hell are you doing out there this early anyway?"

"I'm an early riser. I always get up around this time. I was trying to be quiet so I didn't wake you up. I went out there thinking I could check my phone and be on the computer for a little bit."

"You get up at 5 a.m. every morning?"

She nodded. "Sometimes four-thirty."

Spencer shoved a hand through his hair. Without a shirt, the move drew her attention to the broad expanse of his torso and the sexiness of seeing a man's naked underarm. She'd never really considered that part of the body especially sexy, but something about seeing Spencer with his arm up, his workout pants riding low on his hips, and the knowledge that he had no underwear underneath there, stirred her body to life.

She might not need caffeine early in the morning with Spencer Landry around.

"Why the fuck do you set your alarm for 4:30 in the morning?"

She shook her head. "I don't set my alarm. It's just what time I wake up."

"You only need, what, six hours of sleep?"

"I get eight, sometimes nine, by then."

He dropped his arm and planted his hands on his hips. He narrowed his eyes. It was clear he was still trying to think through his own early morning sleepiness. "You get eight or nine hours of sleep by 5 o'clock in the morning?"

She lifted a shoulder. "You saw me at eight-thirty last night."

"Yeah, but...you fall asleep that early every night?"

She nodded, pressing her lips together. Again she was tempted to tell Spencer this whole story. Why? She wasn't sure, but when she opened her mouth the words spilled out.

"I often went to sleep early when I was a kid because I didn't really like being alone when it got late and dark. I realized if I went to sleep, then I didn't have to think about the fact that I was in the apartment alone. I would then be up early in the morning and could do my homework then instead of at night. And I'd get to see one of my parents before they went into work if they had an early shift."

It took him a few seconds to go over her story in his mind. Then Spencer swore softly. "So you never were scared of the dark or monsters under the bed because you were just already asleep?"

She nodded. "Something like that. I would go to sleep with the lights on in the outer rooms because then the apartment was lit for my mom and dad when they got home from work. They would shut the lights off when they went to bed. I never really knew what it was like to fall asleep in the dark."

His expression gentled. "Do you still do that? Leave the living room lights on?"

She nodded. "I know it's bad for my electric bill. I usually keep it to just one lamp."

He took a deep breath. "No wonder you fell asleep so easily on the couch last night."

"Lights and TV on," she agreed. "That's like a lullaby. I could always hear the TV through my bedroom wall from the apartment next door. It's a familiar, comforting sound."

He shook his head, but she could have sworn she saw something that looked almost like affection in his eyes.

"And now you can't stay awake late?" he asked

"Only on special occasions. Like weddings. Or when someone comes over to… go over a cold case."

Yeah, they'd definitely stayed up late that night. And he'd awakened her multiple times in the night.

The air between them heated but when he blew out a breath and reached out, grasped her elbow, and pulled her in, Max knew it wasn't a seductive move.

She was already getting used to Spencer Landry.

His arms wrapped around her and she let him press her close. She lifted her arms around his waist as well. This was different than the two previous hugs, though. Because he was half-naked. Her cheek resting against his bare chest, and the hot skin and soft hair against her cheek, definitely made this different.

And then she felt him kiss the top of her head.

"I'm sorry that Colin scared you."

She took a deep breath and stepped back. "Who is he?"

"He has a private security company. He's friends with everybody down here. Good guy. I haven't worked with him before but Zander, Michael, and Theo trust him completely. He worked as a personal bodyguard for almost a decade so he knows what he's doing. I figured Zander would loop him in, but I had no idea he'd be over here this early."

"I'll be fine. It's nice to know that there are so many resources down here."

Spencer nodded. "It is. We just need to get coordinated." He finished that thought with a huge yawn.

"You need to get more sleep. If you want to take the bedroom for a few hours, I can sit out here. And make coffee." She cast a longing glance in the direction of the pot on the counter. "We obviously don't have anywhere we need to be today."

He nodded. "Maybe I'll give that a try." He yawned again.

"I'll feel bad if you don't," she said. "By the time you wake up, there will be coffee and Heather will probably have shown up with our breakfast." She gave him a grin.

He laughed. "Probably. If not, I'll sneak up there and grab something."

She nodded. "Sounds good. I'm just gonna get a little work done."

He frowned. "I don't want you on the internet. I don't want anyone tracing you."

She shook her head. "My friend Diego's already taken care of that. Unless this guy is working for the FBI or the KGB or something."

"Diego?"

"He's my computer hacker… um, expert… friend. And that is all I'm going to tell you about him."

"I remember you mentioned him when we worked the big cat case. He helped with that, right?"

She nodded. "He's amazing. But I am not going to give you any information that might help you find him."

"The less I know, the better. And if he's helping keep you safe, I'm more liable to look in the other direction. Which is going to make me uncomfortable."

"You mean wavering on your principles for a woman?"

He nodded, his gaze intent on hers. "Exactly."

"Especially a woman who doesn't bake and doesn't have a dog."

He didn't even bother to look chagrined. "Yeah. Exactly."

That seemed important. Maybe they were kind of kidding, but maybe they weren't. Maybe the fact that Spencer was willing to go outside of his comfort zone for her, even when she wasn't checklist perfect, meant something.

She didn't want to think about that. That was confusing and complicated and probably a pretty good way to end up disappointed.

"Bed. Now." She repeated his order with the same tone from last night.

His mouth quirked with a grin. "Yes, ma'am. See you in a bit."

CHAPTER SIX

HE ABSOLUTELY COULD NOT BE with a woman who woke up at 5 a.m.

That was the first thought on Spencer Landry's mind when he rolled over and woke up in the bed where Max had spent the night.

He breathed deep. The pillowcase and sheets smelled like her. It reminded him of waking up in her bed, and his body responded accordingly.

Dammit. He wanted her. He wanted to take care of her. And now, he knew she ate beans and beef for dinner some nights and got up before the fucking sun.

And it didn't make him want her less or want to take care of her any less.

It made him want to come up with all kinds of fun ways to keep her sweet ass in bed.

Though he'd have to be awake for those things, and he needed his damned sleep.

He lay staring at the ceiling for a moment. Then he glanced at the clock beside the bed. Roughly three hours ago, he'd heard her scream. He swore he'd lost two years off his life. He'd gone upright on the couch and been out the door with his gun drawn, his body wrapped around hers before he'd even thought about it.

Sure, some of that was cop instinct and training.

But it had felt like more.

It had felt like… someone had been threatening something that was *his,* and he was ready to battle to the death to save her.

It was accurate to say he was on edge.

He scrubbed a hand over his face. He couldn't believe he'd fallen back to sleep after that. But he'd slept deeply for the last couple of hours. The last time he'd slept that deeply had been in Max's bed the night he'd spent with her.

Sure, that night had been interrupted by bouts of the best sex of his life. But in between the ruin-him-for-sex-with-any-other-woman-ever fucking, he'd slept hard and deep.

Spencer rolled and swung his legs over the edge of the bed. Okay, now he had to face the day. A day with Max. A day of dealing with the fact that he was half in love with her. And a day in Autre with the Landrys, explaining why he was here in Autre with Max without letting any of them know that her life might be in danger.

Also, her life might not be in danger.

He needed to hear back from Chris about the bomb threat.

On edge was an understatement.

He was still in the sweatpants he had slept in, so he crossed to the door and stepped out into the living area.

Immediately he found Max sitting at the kitchen table with her laptop open.

"Hey."

She looked up. "Hey."

She smiled at him, and Spencer felt like he'd been punched in the gut.

That smile.

That was the one he'd been imagining when he thought about her sitting propped up in his bed at night reading, happy, safe, and taken care of. By him.

Well… fuck.

"You feel better?" she asked.

He cleared his throat and started for the coffee pot. "Yep. Much better. After waking up at a *normal* time of day."

He glanced at her and found her smiling, but her eyes were back on her computer. He reached for a cup, and when he looked again, he found her frowning at the screen.

Despite that, she looked sexy as fuck. Sitting at the kitchen table with a cup of coffee, still wearing what she'd slept in, her hair finger-combed, her sweatshirt falling off one shoulder… she looked exactly the way she would if they lived together and he'd awakened at his usual time, two to three hours after she'd gotten up.

"You okay?" he asked, pouring the coffee, then crossing to the table to refill her cup.

She looked up. "Um… just annoyed. But you're good? No guns needed?"

He returned the carafe to the machine, then propped his hip against the counter. "Instinct when I hear the woman I'm supposed to protect scream."

"Yeah. I guess the gun just made it real."

"Didn't mean to scare you."

She frowned. "You don't scare me, Spencer."

He took a deep breath but decided to take a sip of coffee to cover how that affected him. "Good," he finally said after he swallowed.

"So you slept well?" she asked.

"I did."

"The couch isn't good?"

"Couch is fine." The truth was, he didn't sleep well, no matter where he was. He had a fantastic bed and mattress in his apartment and was still up at least once at night. Every night.

He just couldn't quiet the voices in his head that said bad things were happening while he slept. Evil men were out there doing bad things to good people. It was hard for him ever to completely let that go. When he was awake, he could push it aside and tell himself that he needed to have a normal life and do normal things and that he deserved work-life balance. But when he was asleep, the thoughts got through.

"What's annoying you so early?" he asked.

Her gaze dropped back to her laptop. "My boss is benching me."

Spencer sipped again before responding. He was glad but didn't think Max would appreciate his agreement with her boss. "It's only been a day since everything happened."

"He's pulling my story that was going to run later this week."

"Did he say why?"

"Because it's about the chemical dumping again. He doesn't want to poke at these guys."

"Is it so bad to put it off a little bit? Let us find this guy. Once he's in custody, then you don't have to worry."

She pushed her laptop back and leaned her forearms on the table. "You're not going to get *the* guy. You might find the one who sent the threat, but you won't get the guy who wanted it sent."

"He might give the boss up."

"But whoever he gives up isn't *the* boss."

"Ridgewood?"

She nodded. "His strategy is money and lies. He gets the guys under him all riled up about how unfair the regulations are, how there are too many people poking their nose into other people's business, how someone is making money off of keeping *them* from making money, and how unfair it all is. Why do *they* have to have all these rules and 'the other guys' don't? That kind of bullshit. He planted the idea of threatening me to get me to back off so they can go back to quietly doing their thing. But he wanted the threat carried out."

It all made sense. Spencer knew that's how all of this worked too. The guys with the brains and strategy usually sat higher up and had the means to manipulate those under them.

"So even if we get the guy who sent the threat, you think there will be more?"

"If I keep informing the public about what this company, and the ones like it are doing, yes," she said. "Eventually if not right away. But this makes Ridgewood antsy. We finally have a governor and enough people in the legislature who care about environmental issues. With public pressure, they'll look into things. Maybe even change up some regulations and oversight."

"Which means you intend to keep writing about this no matter what," Spencer filled in.

"Of course," she said matter-of-factly. "This is one of those stories that covers everything. There's money exchanging hands under the table. There are rich assholes buying politicians. There are violations of all kinds of safety standards. There's racism and classism and exploitation of workers."

"And there's a chance to get at Gordon Ridgewood."

She nodded. "And there's a chance to get at Gordon Ridgewood."

Spencer blew out a breath. "Who are the other guys?"

"There are no other guys. Unless you count scientists and environmental groups and the government and law enforcement. The people who are saying that what these big companies are doing is wrong and they can't cut corners, and they can't pollute and endanger the environment and humans. But that's, of course, not an effective spin. Still, he needs someone to blame."

"He," Spencer repeated. "Ridgewood specifically?"

"He's not the only one, of course. Cancer Alley has been a thing for decades. People know about it, people *say* it's bad. People protest and politicians act sympathetic. But on some level, everyone has just almost written it off."

Spencer knew about Cancer Alley, of course. It was an eighty-five-mile stretch from Baton Rouge to New Orleans along the Mississippi where over a hundred and fifty oil and chemical plants and refineries occupied land in the river parishes. The pollution in the area was commonly blamed for the fact that the people living there had a much higher chance of developing cancer than the national average.

"Now, people like Ridgewood are trying to expand it. They are trying to build outside of that corridor and, when they run into pushback, they just illegally ship and store and dump their stuff."

Her tone and the expression on her face made Spencer brace a hand on the counter and lean toward her. Gordon Ridgewood wasn't just the subject of a story or even a series of stories. He wasn't just another criminal she wanted to expose. He'd hurt her.

And Spencer wanted every detail.

"Who did Gordon Ridgewood put in a wheelchair?" Spencer asked. She'd already confessed her hatred for the man was personal. Of course Spencer hadn't forgotten that.

She lifted her chin and met Spencer's gaze.

Spencer's chest tightened as she didn't even hesitate to share with him.

"Phillip Morel," she said. "He and his wife were the neighbors who checked on me when I was home alone as a kid."

"The one that told you rats weren't pets?" Spencer asked, feeling a stupid affection for this woman.

She nodded. "Phil worked for Ridgewood in one of his warehouses. There were multiple safety violations. Phil was a supervisor and would often do dangerous jobs instead of having one of his guys do it. One night he climbed up to fix something and fell forty feet. He's now paralyzed from the waist down."

Well, fuck. "And you blame Ridgewood."

"Oh, for sure. Not only because of the unaddressed safety concerns, but because of him squashing the unionization attempts four times, him paying high-cost lawyers to fight and defeat Phil's lawsuit against the company, him paying off the inspectors and supervisors who could have helped Phil's case, him firing the three employees who were witnesses at the trial, and, of course, all of the other immoral and criminal things I've dug up since I started looking into the man."

Spencer pushed off the counter and crossed to take the chair across from her. He swung the chair around and straddled it. "You've held this grudge since you were a kid?"

"The accident happened when I was fifteen," she said. "Phil was one of the few adults in my life who really cared about me and that I could count on, and by that time, I understood how much he'd done. He'd helped my parents out in so many ways. He and his wife, Steph, did more than just make sure they were home whenever my parents weren't. They were about ten years older than my parents and kind of…mentored them, I guess. They helped them through a tough spot in their marriage. They helped them with some financial stuff. They actually kept CPS from taking me because I was left alone so much. One of my teachers got suspicious and called them. Phil and Steph covered for my parents. I didn't know that until I was a teen."

She took a shaky breath and Spencer had to resist the urge to pull her into his lap and hold her. Phil and Steph might have been great, maybe they'd made Max feel safer and cared for, but for a little girl who hadn't had anything to compare it to, the bar had been low. And that hadn't been *enough*.

Max hadn't had anyone baking her brownies, had never come home to lasagna in the oven, had never had a pet curl up on the foot of her bed. She'd gone to bed by eight o'clock so she didn't have to face the dark night by herself, for fuck's sake.

In a wheelchair or not, Spencer would like to have a word with Phil Morel. Not to mention the conversation he'd love to have with her *parents*.

"By then, too, Caroline was immersed in that world of the rich and powerful," Max went on, oblivious to Spencer's spinning thoughts, the tightness in his gut, and how firmly he was gripping his coffee cup.

"And I'd had an inside look at the corruption and greed. I knew I had to dig into it more and try to help karma along somehow. Even if it takes me years, even if I can't help Phil directly, even if I can't totally take Ridgewood down, I can do what I can to make Gordon Ridgewood as miserable as he deserves to be."

Spencer bit back his first instinct to insist she stop, point out this was nuts, and tell her the chances of taking down a man like Ridgewood were tiny.

That was on the tip of his tongue because he wanted to keep her safe. Far, far away from a man like Ridgewood. Spencer knew Ridgewood and his cronies. He didn't want Max even in the same city block with that man.

But that wasn't how Spencer operated. He believed as Max did that the bad guys deserved to be miserable. That the fight was worth it. That the good guys couldn't just give up. Did he want to tuck Max away where no one could ever get to her and hurt her? Of course. Did he wish that her job would never put her in jeopardy? Yes. But did he also understand that part of his attraction to her was this passion, this shared desire for justice, her feistiness, and fight? Absolutely yes.

Especially in this moment when her emotions had her breathing a little harder, her cheeks pink, and her eyes flashing.

She was always beautiful, but when she was riled up and passionate, she was so fucking gorgeous it hurt.

"Is miserable enough?" he asked. "Even if he's out, walking around, free and living his life?"

She narrowed her eyes. "It's better than happy and oblivious."

Spencer nodded. "Okay. So what do you want to do?" he asked.

She frowned, as if puzzled. "Show him that I'm not going to back down. Continue to investigate all his criminal acts and tell people about them."

"What if he's never prosecuted? What if he doesn't lose his business? Or his friends?"

"I have to believe that at least a few people who read my

stories will at least doubt him. I'll plant seeds. And, if nothing else, he'll know someone is watching and knows the truth."

Spencer was proud of her, he realized. That was a strange emotion to feel for a woman he wanted to... well, that list was long and complicated too and he didn't have time to really delve into all of the things he wanted to do with Max Keller. Several sexual positions were on it, of course, but taking her for ice cream was on it, and buying her a birthday present that would make her eyes light up was as well, and that was mixing him up.

But yes, he was proud of her. She understood her work and why it was important. Whether she was driven by a vendetta or not.

"And right this minute, today, what do you want to do?" he asked. "This isn't going to be one grand sweep. If you're right and he's behind the threat, he's not going to suddenly come storming out of his office calling for your head on a platter or show up on your doorstep. Or on a backroad boat dock himself. But that doesn't mean you can't become a very present, very annoying, very effective thorn in his side."

She leaned in. "Are you suggesting I harass Gordon Ridgewood, Agent Landry? Or are you just trying to find a way to get me into handcuffs?"

Dammit. His body actually reacted to that. What the fuck was wrong with him? He pinned her with a serious look instead of letting on that her teasing words had worked. "You are *not* going to show up on his doorstep either. Or on any backroad boat docks," he added, his voice firm. "You're not going to threaten him. Or coerce him. You're not even going to make any implications. You're going to state facts and reveal that you have information. And make sure Ridgewood knows *what* information you have."

"What if some of my facts are more hearsay or rumor than concrete evidence? Things I've heard from sources but can't corroborate? Things that would require people to connect dots that might not be obvious? Things I can't really publish because it would require me reaching for connections I can't prove?" she asked. She looked crestfallen. Clearly, this was something she'd already discussed with her editor.

Spencer wanted to make it all okay.

"You're not trying to convince a judge and jury. Or even a law enforcement officer," Spencer said with a wry smile. "If he's guilty of something, *he'll* connect the dots himself. Hearsay isn't hearsay to someone who knows the truth. And it's enough to make a lot of criminals nervous. A slow leak of it over time will drive him nuts. He'll wonder what else you have. He'll wonder if he has a leak in his company. It will create distrust. He'll wonder when you'll expose it all. And to who."

Her brows were still pulled together, but she said, "Go on."

"You publish what you can. What's solid. But if you have other stuff, you can send it in an email to his business address that's publicly listed. You could put something in a letter, again addressed to his office. You could put something on social media where you carefully state it's not anything official or associated with the *News*."

"And if it's not public, it's not libel," Max said. "And even the pieces that I do make public… he'd have to *prove* they're untrue to sue for libel. If he can't do that, he won't yell about it. Probably."

"He'll threaten you privately," Spencer said, not thrilled with that option either. "But if you put little bits up, over a long period, in a variety of places, it will poke at him, needle him. If he is the big boss behind it all, he'll be concerned. If he's not, he won't care. But it might make him sloppy enough that he'll slip up in a way that gives us something more concrete to go on. Or, it might just make him miserable. Either way, Ridgewood has to think about you as much as you think about him. There's a certain satisfaction in that."

"You know personally?"

He lifted a shoulder, but gave her a half-smile. "There are a few guys I keep an eye on. And I make sure they know I'm keeping my eye on them."

"How?"

"Stop into their shops once in a while to buy a soda or get a beer. Show up to a restaurant for dinner when they're there. Just so they don't forget about me."

Max thought that over. "I want a big, splashy story that clearly implicates him in a number of crimes and makes everyone turn against him and ruins him professionally and personally. And I want that to happen tomorrow."

Spencer nodded. "I get it. I want that too. I want to catch every single criminal in the act and lock them up for the rest of their miserable lives. But sometimes we have to be happy with *something*.

"I have to be happy with Roger needing ibuprofen every time I stop into his liquor store for a six-pack, which just happens to be where he was illegally selling guns a year ago. Not as good as prosecuting him for the crime, but he gave up three bigger fish, so he's out, living his life. Still, I make sure he knows I haven't forgotten him.

"I have to be satisfied with Trish flubbing a song when she's on stage singing whenever I walk into *Old Timer's*. It's not as good as locking her up for recruiting college girls into a prostitution ring two years ago, but it's better than her thinking she got off scot-free and doing it again."

Max was scowling. "I hate when bad people get away with stuff."

He finally gave in and reached for her hand. "I know. Accountability and justice are what I get out of bed for."

She turned her hand over so they could link fingers. "And why you need brownies at the end of the day. Because you don't always get accountability and justice. The food and dog are the good stuff at home when you can't always get the good stuff at work, right?"

He swallowed hard. That sounded so simple. The food and

the dog and the cuddling on the couch signified his idea of normal after a day of trying to keep bad people from doing more bad things. They would be the proof that the dark hadn't crept into his life. That he could still be a normal guy and have a perfect life without the darkness touching it, the way his dad's work had seeped into his life. *Their* life.

But maybe they would just be comforting. Maybe the darkness would be there, but the dog and the brownies and... the girl... would make it not so bad.

He had to clear his throat before finally saying, "Yeah. Something like that."

She nodded. "I get that, I guess. It's why I work such long hours."

He squeezed her fingers, bringing her gaze back to his. "What do you mean?"

Her green eyes on his, Spencer felt himself getting sucked in deeper.

"I work hard so that at the end of the day, I can go to sleep knowing I really gave it all I've got. I think about Phil at night. How hearing his TV on the other side of my wall made me feel safer at night. And now how he needs help and special equipment to even get into bed. Every single night. Because of Gordon Ridgewood."

Her fingers were squeezing his harder, but Spencer didn't mind. If she needed someone to hold onto, he wanted it to be him.

Spencer studied her. He understood all of that so well. He *made* himself quit at the end of his shift. He went home and forced himself to maintain as normal a routine as possible, whenever possible. He knew how tempting it was to stay behind the desk for "just one more hour". He'd seen his dad pull all-nighters. He'd done it himself. It was so fucking easy to let the job become everything.

Maybe he wanted brownies and a dog and a gorgeous

woman with sweet smiles at home because he thought it would make him more willing to leave his desk.

Suddenly he wanted to get Max away from it all. He wanted to show her that not everything had to be a kick-down-doors-go-in-guns-blazing raid. More often than not, patience was the answer.

His work today was to keep her safe. And make her happy. And he could be patient in showing her that bright, sunny, happy things were worth taking time for.

"Can you put the story up another way? Separate from the *News*. Make it clear that it's just you?" he asked. "Then you don't have to worry about what your editor thinks or how it might affect your co-workers."

Max studied his face, clearly thinking that through. Finally, she nodded. "Yes."

"Do that. Then I'll alert Chris and the team that they need to diligently watch all the leads to see if there's any activity in response. I'm guessing that will piss somebody off. And I'll put someone on Ridgewood."

"You will? You believe me that he's behind it?"

"Why wouldn't I believe you?"

"Because it sounds like I just want revenge on this man who hurt someone I love. It sounds like I'm obsessed and would do anything to hurt him back."

"Max, you're an intelligent, talented journalist who I respect and trust. If you think Gordon Ridgewood is behind this, I believe you. And, if it turns out he's not, it's not like he's not a part of other terrible things. He doesn't deserve a restful night of sleep or a peaceful day that's headache-free. And hell, if he wants to come to me and *prove* that he's *not* involved in any of this so that I get the feisty, annoyingly determined journalist off his case, I'll listen."

She looked so relieved he almost reached over to kiss her.

"Thank you, Spencer."

"Of course."

She frowned. "I thought you'd want to keep me quiet too. That would be safer."

"It would," he agreed. "And part of me does want that. But that's not the… professional side of me."

Her voice got softer. "Which part is it that wants to keep me safe?"

"The part that thinks you look pretty damned adorable with your hair messed up and in PJ pants and a sweatshirt."

Her hand flew to her hair, and her cheeks got pink. But not in anger this time.

"Oh."

That one little word said a lot. It said she knew exactly what he meant by all of that. Which was probably good. And also dangerous. Because if she understood, and didn't tell him that was crazy, then maybe it was… not crazy.

There was a knock at the door, and Spencer was immediately on his feet. "Stay here," he ordered her as he moved quickly across the room.

He checked the window and saw Heather heading back up the path to the main house. Relief flooded through him, and he pulled the door open. He returned to the table with a basket of food that smelled amazing. His stomach growled loudly.

"Breakfast," he announced.

"Oh my God, that looks awesome," Max said as she took in the breakfast burritos and fresh fruit.

"It does."

He went to the cupboards for dishes, and Max dug into the basket, unpacking the food.

"How about after breakfast, we head out? We can go on a swamp boat tour and to the petting zoo?" he suggested, scooping fresh berries onto his plate.

Max paused with a burrito in front of her mouth. "Really?"

"You've been sitting out here by yourself stewing about all of this after the scare with Colin this morning. Let's go just have a nice, normal touristy day. Then, later, when you've been away from everything, if you still want to post the story, you can send a very reasonable email to your editor and then put it up."

She thought about it as she bit into the burrito and chewed. After she swallowed, she nodded. "Okay."

"Okay."

"But that means going out in public and being around other people."

"Yep. Probably some Landrys. We can even find Caroline and Zander for lunch."

She tipped her head. "But then we'll have to pretend to be boyfriend-girlfriend."

Yeah, that had occurred to him. And he liked the idea. Way too much. "Yup. I'll even put my hand on your ass if you're lucky."

That made her laugh, and Spencer felt a kick in his gut. God, he loved when she looked happy like that.

"They have penguins here, right?"

"They do. And I have an in. Bet I could get them to let you feed them."

Her eyes widened.

He laughed. "Penguins do it for you, huh?"

"Well, I mean… they're *penguins*, Spencer."

"I am *definitely* getting you in to feed them. I have a feeling I want every one of the extra good-guy points that's gonna get me."

She laughed again. "Okay, fine, but you're buying lunch. And you've already seen how many French fries I can eat. You have no idea how many fried *pickles* I can put away."

Feeding this woman fried pickles and cuddling up to her on a swamp boat and watching her feed penguins—and yeah, putting his hand on her ass—sounded like everything he'd ever wanted. And like no date he'd ever imagined taking a woman on in his life.

Because, of course, a day with Maxine Keller would be like no other day he'd ever spent with any other woman.

CHAPTER SEVEN

IT WAS a bit of a walk from the north side of town to the Boys of the Bayou Swamp Boat Tour Company, so they took Spencer's truck. They parked in the lot next to the bus that had a bright green cartoon alligator on the side.

"Leo drives the bus a lot of time. He takes it up to New Orleans and picks tourists up at the hotels to come down here for the tours." Spencer put the truck in park and turned off the engine.

"I bet he loves that. Meeting all those new people all the time," Max said. She'd only met the patriarch of the family a couple of times, but Leo Landry had a way of making a person feel immediately comfortable.

He had a short gray beard, nearly white hair, tanned skin that spoke to years out in the Louisiana sun, and blue eyes that absolutely twinkled. There was no other way to describe them. He smiled and laughed easily, made his own moonshine, and had been living along this bayou all his life. It was easy to see where all of his grandsons got their cocky charm from. Yet next to his wife, Ellie, Leo was almost an introvert. He came off as the steadier, quieter of the two elder Landrys who were the heart and soul of the family. Ellie was always in the middle of everything and always had something to say.

"Oh, absolutely. Along with the Cajun music he plays over the speakers, he loves introducing them to the bayou myths and tall tales from down here during the drive."

Max laughed and let herself out of the truck. "Is the other side of your family this interesting?"

Spencer joined her at the front bumper. "Oh, absolutely not. Then again, I'm not sure anybody could be as interesting as the Landrys."

They headed toward the tour company reservation office. The wooden structure sat up a little higher than the boat docks. There was the main office, a gift shop, the owners' office, and restrooms. The dock was currently filled with tourists waiting for the next tour. There were benches, but most stood along the railing looking out over the water.

Across the street sat Ellie's bar. Spencer's great aunt owned and operated the place with her best friend, Cora. It was where the wedding reception had been held. It was also the first place she'd stopped in Autre when she'd come looking for her friend Caroline. Max had not expected that she'd be back here this soon. Or maybe ever.

It was a nondescript building. There were no neon signs, and no music poured out from inside. It was a long rectangle surrounded by crushed gravel on all sides.

Even inside, it wasn't much to talk about. The tables and chairs were mostly mismatched, and the bar was worn and scarred. The walls were covered with various mementos, including posters, photographs, sports team banners, and anything else Ellie and Cora felt was important enough to display. There was one wall that stood out because it was painted another color and held only framed photographs. Those seemed to be the most important items, given a special place of honor. Every photo was of a person or group at different locations around Autre. They were all smiling, laughing, and living seemingly everyday moments, but they'd been captured for a reason. She'd been mesmerized by the display and had wanted to know every story behind every photograph. She suspected most people who took the time to study those framed images felt the same.

"Spencer!"

Spencer pivoted toward the greeting. His face broke into a grin, and Max couldn't help smiling. She recognized the man coming toward them. He was one of Spencer's cousins. At least she was ninety percent sure. That was a pretty good bet anyway. Most of the men walking around this town seemed to be a cousin or related one way or another.

"Hey, Josh!"

Josh. Right. Josh Landry was definitely a cousin.

"Hi, Max," Josh greeted.

"Hi." She appreciated Josh remembering her name, but she had to admit that her attention had snagged on the little girl toddling beside him. And the animal walking along beside her.

"Is that a… cow?" Max asked.

It looked like a cow. Except that it was the size of a dog.

"Moo," the little girl told her.

Josh laughed. "Yes, it is a cow. A miniature cow. He's Ella's newest adoption. His name is Moo."

Spencer chuckled. "Moo? You're gonna lose your free passes to the petting zoo with an obvious, boring name like that."

Yeah, even Max knew about the crazy, creative animal names here at the Boys of the Bayou Gone Wild. There was Sugar, the goat that had crashed Charlie and Griffin's wedding.

And then there were the otters who had been in attendance. The wedding had, after all, been *inside* their enclosure. Gus and Gertie and their kids Skittles, Rolo, Baby Ruth, and the others named after candy bars and cookies had joined them. Max had also briefly visited the alpaca pen where Alpacalypse, Al Pacacino, and Alpacapella all came over to have their noses stroked.

"Hey, Ella's not even two," Josh protested. "I'll admit her

uncle Owen was disappointed we didn't go with Cowabunga, but Ella didn't get it."

Spencer laughed.

"And he tried to sell her on Mootilda and Moolinda, but he couldn't convince her," Josh said. "But I have no doubt we'll have plenty of interesting animal names in our future." The look he gave his young daughter was so full of love that Max felt her heart flip over. She had never considered herself the nurturing, maternal type, but watching Josh Landry go gooey right in front of her over the tiny little girl standing next to a miniature cow made something happen in her chest.

Max crouched in front of Ella. "I like your cow."

Ella beamed at her. "Moo."

Max nodded. "Moo."

Ella even had a leash around the cow. Max looked up at Josh. "Will he get bigger than this?"

"Yeah, a little. This guy's a baby. And, of course, a runt. But they don't get much bigger than about four feet."

"Of course?" Max repeated.

Josh nodded. "We have an entire menagerie in our backyard. And not one of them is just a typical, straightforward animal without issues. Tori collects those with special needs."

Tori. Right. That was his wife's name. Max remembered her being very sweet at the wedding and her and Josh being clearly, madly in love.

Spencer clapped Josh on the shoulder. "And suddenly, that sweet, gorgeous woman falling in love with you makes sense."

Josh laughed. "F-U-C-K off."

They all looked down at the little girl.

"Oh my God, the Landrys are trying to watch their mouths?" Spencer hooted with laughter. "And how long will it be until Ella yells F-U-C-K across the boat dock?"

Josh shook his head. "It's already a lost cause. She heard the worst from the parrots over a year ago."

Max looked at Ella. "The *parrots*? As in actual parrots?"

"The parrots that live at the petting zoo swear," Josh explained.

"No way." Max laughed.

"Funny birds." The little girl giggled.

"Oh, yes," Josh said with a sigh. "Only when they're together and only when they have an audience. But it's graphic and…." He glanced at his daughter. "Hilarious," he admitted.

Max stretched to her feet, shaking her head. "This place is so interesting."

"What are you two doin' down here anyway? Don't tell me the FBI is looking into something down here?"

Spencer stepped close to Max and slipped an arm around her waist. He did it so smoothly that it was almost as if he had been doing it for days. And meant it. She leaned into his side. Again, there were perks to this whole scenario.

"Nope. Just down here for the week to kick back. We're staying over at the bed and breakfast," Spencer said.

Josh looked from one of them to the other, eyebrows up. "Is that right?"

"We had a really good time at the wedding." Max put her open palm on Spencer's stomach. It was a familiar, girlfriend-type gesture—or if it wasn't, it should be—and again, it was a very nice side effect of this set-up. She felt his abs jump under her touch, and she had to fight a triumphant grin. If she was going to be all worked up and physically aware of him every second he was in a room with her, then he could be a little tense too.

"So I guess heading to New Orleans after the reception turned out to be a good idea," Josh commented to Spencer.

Max felt Spencer stiffen against her, and she looked up at him.

"Oh, yeah. Definitely. So we should get a tour reservation. Are you taking a boat out today?" Spencer said, rushing past the subject of New Orleans.

Of course he'd gone back to New Orleans after the wedding.

But was his family under the impression that he'd returned to New Orleans *with her*? She assumed that he had gone back into Ellie's after she'd left the wedding that night. But maybe not. Wyatt had been planning to take him home, according to Spencer. But Spencer had been really drunk. Maybe he'd called an Uber right after she had.

"Not till this afternoon. I have Ella duty until then. Tori's doing some house calls."

Max remembered that Tori was a veterinarian. She worked with Griffin, the wildlife vet who'd come to Autre and taken over care of the animals in the petting zoo and animal park.

"But we'll get you on a boat with Owen." Josh grinned. "Or maybe Cian can take you out."

Spencer's brows rose. "Cian is taking tours out already?"

"The guy loves the swamp boats. And he's awesome with the tourists. We're happy he stuck around. It's giving me more time off, and now that Maddie and Owen have the foster kids, it's giving them a lot more time to spend with the boys. Owen's even teaching Landon the ropes. He's been co-piloting and learning all about boat maintenance and repair from Mitch." Josh pointed down the hill. Owen was at the end of one of the docks with a teenager who looked to be about fifteen.

"How's that going?" Spencer asked.

Josh got a soft, affectionate look on his face. "Owen and Maddie are amazing at this. Seriously, those boys are doing great. We're all thrilled to have them around. Hoping the adoption process is nice and smooth."

"Owen and Maddie are adopting?" Max asked.

"Yeah, they finally realized they couldn't get pregnant, so they looked into fostering. Those three boys are brothers and want to stay together, of course. They've bounced around a little bit in the foster system, so Maddie and Owen would like to make this time permanent."

Max shook her head. This family… was something. Every time she heard a story from Caroline or came down here to

Autre, she learned something new about them. They were a bois-terous bunch. And there were a lot of them. But they all had huge hearts and would do anything for one another. She had no doubt that those three kids had a lot more than just a foster mom and dad. They had a grandma and grandpa and tons of aunts, uncles, and cousins already built-in.

"And who's Cian?" Max asked.

"You remember Fiona?" Spencer asked.

"She's a wildlife expert or something, right?"

"She does a lot of animal rescues. She's the one who brought all of these exotic animals to the petting zoo and turned this place into a wildlife sanctuary. She owned a wildlife park in Florida before she moved here."

"Right, she's with Knox," Max said.

"Yep. And Cian is her younger brother. He came with her when she moved and stuck around."

"And His Highness has turned into a blue-collar bayou boy overnight, it seems," Josh said, starting toward the tour company office. Ella toddled along beside him, and Moo followed beside her like a trained dog.

But after a few steps, she stopped and squatted. Ella poked at the toad sitting at the edge of the grass. "Frog."

Josh squatted next to her. "You guys go on ahead. When you stop and look at every frog, caterpillar, and mosquito, it can take a while to get from one place to another."

When he turned his attention back to Ella, the look on his face made Max suck in a quick breath. That man was head over heels.

"She's definitely Tori's kid, huh?" Spencer said with a grin.

Max wondered if she would ever become immune to that grin. She loved seeing Spencer laid back and happy and joking. She wondered if he was only like this with his family. She real-ized she'd love to see him hanging out with his brother or his mom and dad.

Oh, you want to meet his family? Sure, that's a great idea. Totally gonna happen.

She and Spencer were pretending to be together for this week. So that he could keep her alive and find whoever Gordon Ridgewood had manipulated into trying to silence her. That was all this was. Well, and some explosive chemistry.

They started toward the office again. "What did Josh mean by His *Highness*? Is Cian full of himself?"

"Oh no, he's actually a prince."

Max tripped on something in the dirt, and Spencer's hold on her tightened. He chuckled.

"He's a *prince*? Come on."

"It's a long story. But short version—Fiona's family rules a small island country off the coast of Ireland or something. Her brother Torin will be taking the throne over from their grandfather. That makes her a princess and Cian a prince. But neither of them is interested in any of that. Still, it's pretty funny and an interesting story. If you have a chance to sit down with her, ask her about it."

"And I thought I would be asking her about raising giraffes." Max knew that Fiona Grady had a small herd of giraffes. She even knew a group of giraffes was called a tower. That had been a crossword puzzle clue more than once.

They stepped onto the deck surrounding the building that led to the docks. Spencer twisted the knob and pushed the door open. A little bell jingled, but no one inside could've heard it.

"I'll bet you twenty bucks that I get bigger tips than you do today."

This came from a very handsome dark-haired guy leaning on the front counter. He had tattoos down his left arm and over the top of his right shoulder and bicep. Both were fully on display in the tight black tank he wore with the Boys of the Bayou logo on the front. He had sunglasses on top of his head and a huge cocky grin stretching his mouth.

"You know that I don't worry about tips."

The big man standing next to him sounded bored. He had a jagged scar on one cheek, and Max knew this was another of Spencer's cousins she'd met at the wedding.

"You should. You're havin' a baby soon. Tips are more money, man. I'm hoping to turn up your energy a little bit with some friendly competition."

"Sawyer and Cian," Spencer said near her ear.

His low voice and warm breath on her neck made goose-bumps dance up and down that side of her body.

Right, Sawyer was the big guy. So the other one was Fiona's brother. He looked vaguely familiar as well. He'd probably been at the wedding. And he was a *prince*?

"Don't you worry about my energy," Sawyer told him. "Or anything else about me. Please. I don't want to be in your thoughts really at all."

Cian grinned. "I just care about the business. I want every tour to be the best it can be."

Sawyer didn't look impressed. Or worried. "Well, I have an advantage or two," Sawyer said. "One, I'm taking out a bunch of girls down here for a bachelorette party, and they're pre-programmed to have a good time. And two," he said over Cian's chuckle. "I'm actually good at my job."

Cian pushed up to standing. "Trust me, charm and humor go much further than expertise in this life."

"And you learned all this wisdom in your, what, twenty-two years of life?"

"Twenty-seven, thank you very much."

"I will say Cian has been bringing in a lot of tips lately," the very pretty blonde behind the front desk said. She was leaning onto the counter with her chin resting on her hand, watching the men as if very amused but not at all surprised by the exchange.

"And that's Paige," Spencer said.

Paige was one of Spencer's cousins' fiancées. Donovan's, maybe? No, Donovan wasn't a Landry. Maybe Paige was the one that was with Michael. But no, Michael was the good-looking

Black man. Naomi's brother. The hot fire chief. And Max was pretty sure he was single. Maybe Paige was with Mitch. Max was going to need flashcards.

"You can keep giving me the old, retired guys, but I'm still getting big tips," Cian said.

"Those old guys are gonna be a lot more forgiving when you get the boat stuck in the weeds," Sawyer said.

"The group didn't mind the other day when I had to get in the water and ended up shirtless and wet," Cian said, preening a bit.

"Right. Until you climbed back in the boat and tipped it and dumped two of *them* in the water too," Sawyer said with a frown.

Cian blew out a breath. "I still got one phone number from that."

"But," Sawyer went on. "You definitely need to work your ass off for tips. Because you owe me every one of those dollars until those eight refunds are paid back."

Spencer cleared his throat loudly, and all three turned to face them.

"Well, hey there, Spencer," Sawyer greeted with a genuine smile.

Max almost said the *wow* out loud.

"Welcome to Boys of the Bayou," Cian said, snapping into charming host mode.

His attention was directed exclusively at Max. And she had to admit that he succeeded in pulling her eyes away from Sawyer. Cian was equally good-looking but definitely had more of the laid-back, good-time air. Sawyer seemed a lot more serious and broody.

Spencer's arm tightened around her, and he leaned down. "You're taken," he said deep and low in her ear.

She shivered again, and she didn't think it was from the heat of his breath on her skin. It was the possessive note in his voice.

And that he'd said the words soft enough that they had to be for her ears only. That meant it wasn't a show for an audience. She swallowed hard. How was she supposed to react to that?

"Hey, we were hoping to get on the swamp boat tour. Any openings?" Spencer asked.

"Well, I think we can manage that," Paige said. Her gaze was predictably interested as well as friendly. "Surprised to see you again already, though."

"We had such a good time at the wedding, we decided to come right back," Spencer said. "We're saying at the bed and breakfast this week."

He kept adding that part, and Max realized that was more or less working as code for *we're sleeping together*.

Paige's eyes widened further. "Are you now? That's awesome. And of course, we'll squeeze you onto a tour."

"But we might need to split you up. I've only got room for one." Cian gave her a broad grin. "But it's plenty *big* enough for you, darlin'."

Wow, the prince had already learned how to drawl his *darlin*'s.

"I promise I know this bayou better than you do, and no one will ever find your body."

Spencer delivered the line without a change in tone of voice or body language, so it took a second for it to sink in.

Max looked up at him quickly when it did.

He was staring right at Cian.

Cian started laughing. "Well, that answers that question for me."

Spencer was still looking straight at him. "Good."

Sawyer and Paige exchanged a look, and Sawyer nodded. "Mine too."

"Mine too," Paige said.

If Spencer had intended to spread the news amongst the family that he and Max were here in town together and Spencer was staking his claim, it looked like he had just accomplished it with one stop and one sentence. Max was sure that both Sawyer and Paige would be on their phones spreading the word.

Was that why he'd brought her for a tour? There was no way he could have known that Cian and Sawyer would be in here joke-fighting about who was the better tour guide. Or that Cian would hit on her. It felt as if this was Spencer's honest reaction to another man offering her a ride on something big in a very innuendo-laced tone.

Huh.

They ended up booked on Cian's boat with the other retirees, and Sawyer's apologies ahead of time for the fact Spencer was probably going to end up in the bayou, helping push the boat out of the weeds.

Spencer laughed and assured him it was fine.

Max also thought it was fine. Spencer wet and shirtless? Yes, please. Throw in a side-show with a prince, and she wouldn't complain. She almost said as much out loud just to hear Spencer growl about it.

Even the thought of him saying something hot and possessive in her ear made her lower belly clench.

What was going on with her? She didn't want a possessive *you're mine* kind of guy. Even a pretend one.

But her body said differently. And a little daring portion of her brain that said, *oh, just tease him, see what he does.* Okay, and another naughty little part of her imagination that wondered if he'd throw her over his shoulder, carry her back to the cottage and do some handcuff-her-to-the-bed-stuff, and make her say *I'm yours* before he…

"Max?"

She looked up at Spencer and realized he was looking at her as if maybe he'd already said her name once. Or twice.

"Um, yeah?"

"You okay?"

She was sure her cheeks were pink. And that Spencer would

notice and wonder about that. But she nodded. "Yeah, sorry, thinking about something else."

"Paige said the tour isn't leaving for forty minutes. You want to go to the petting zoo or up to Ellie's for a drink?"

"Sure," Max said, probably too brightly. She needed to *not* go back to the cottage with Spencer evidently. Who knew what she might do back there? Or what she might ask him to do to her?

Or beg him to do…

He chuckled, and the sound tripped over her nerve endings, making them want more and more stimulation.

"Which one? Goats or Pimm's Cups?" he asked.

God only knew what she might say or do if she got tipsy at this point. "Goats."

Paige laughed. "Good. As soon as I send this text to everybody, Charlie will be looking for you anyway."

"Oh yeah, why is that?" Spencer asked, obviously playing dumb.

"Because she's gonna love that you two danced at her wedding and are now back only two weeks later."

"We already knew each other before the wedding," Spencer said. "She didn't play matchmaker."

"You know that's not how *she'll* see it," Paige said with a wink.

"Well, heaven forbid anybody have any privacy in this family," Spencer said with an eye roll.

Max also rolled her eyes. She barely knew the Landrys, and she knew *that* was ridiculous. He'd known exactly what would happen if they showed up here.

Paige laughed. "You brought her to Autre, Spencer. There's no way you wanted privacy."

Max thought about those words as they wandered outside and up the dock to the road again.

He had brought her here because he knew a bunch of guys who would help protect her. He knew the cottages and the area well enough to feel secure here.

But surely there were other places they could have gone. Here he had to pretend they were dating because every other person was a part of his big, over-involved, loving, and loud family.

"What will we tell them all when we break up?" she asked.

Spencer stopped at the bottom of the ramp that led to the deck around the building. "What?"

"Now that we're here and everyone thinks we're dating, what will we tell them when we're not anymore? I'm still going to be close to Caroline. I'll probably come down here occasionally to hang out with her. And you've got a million connections here. So… at some point, we'll have to tell them we broke up."

He stood just looking at her for several seconds. "Yeah, I guess you're right."

He hadn't thought that through.

They were going to have to break up officially. Come up with a story about why they didn't work out.

And then they would probably be the best man and maid of honor at Caroline and Zander's wedding.

And Spencer would bring a plus one. Because he'd need someone at home baking him brownies.

And Max would end up *very* drunk that night and very hungover the following day.

She could feel the headache already pounding.

"I guess we'll just say we were too different to make it last," he finally said.

Max swallowed and nodded. "That will be easy to believe."

He didn't nod. "At least Caroline and Zander will know the truth about what's happening."

Yeah, that they were too different to even give it a real try.

But he was right. The people closest to them wouldn't be upset by their break-up because they'd know it had never been a real relationship. That was good.

Without another word, he took her hand, linking their fingers, and started for the petting zoo. It was such a natural move she wondered if he'd done it instinctively or purposefully. She glanced around quickly and didn't notice anyone in the immediate vicinity for whom he would have to put on a show.

Interesting.

Almost as interesting as how much she enjoyed the contact.

She wasn't a hand-holder. At least, she hadn't been until Spencer. Then again, she wasn't much of a hugger either. Nor was she a take-off-an-entire-day-and-hang-out-on-a-swamp-boat-and-at-a-petting-zoo girl. She couldn't remember the last time she'd taken an entire day off.

Then again, she couldn't remember the last time someone had threatened to blow up her workplace.

They passed Josh and Ella on the path to the petting zoo. They were sitting in the grass, Ella in his lap. He pointed to two rabbits on the other side of the path. The rabbits were simply eating grass. As was Moo.

"Aren't there rabbits up at the petting zoo?" Spencer asked quietly. "That she can hold and pet and feed?"

Josh nodded. "But not *these* rabbits." He shrugged. "I'll hold her any time, any place. Right here is fine by me."

Max felt tears prick the backs of her eyes.

"Well, have fun," Spencer said softly.

"Always," Josh said, looking down at his daughter. Her attention was entirely on the rabbits.

Spencer and Max started up the path again. He glanced down at her. Then stopped and turned to face her, frowning. "What's wrong?"

She looked up, surprised. "Nothing."

"You look sad."

Damn the detective in him. "I'm just… Josh and Ella are so sweet."

Spencer narrowed his eyes. "They are. Why does that make you look sad?"

"I haven't been around many dads with young kids, I guess."

"Again, why does that make you look sad?"

She blew out a breath. "I don't know."

He waited a moment, then asked, "Do you want kids?"

Startled, her eyes went wide. "No. I don't… think so. I've never thought about it much."

"Really? Never?"

"I suppose you want eight." He seemed like a big family kind of guy.

His mouth curved. "Eight? That's a lot. But a couple. Sure."

She nodded. "That fits."

"Wanting to have kids is a pretty…" He trailed off.

"Normal thing to want," she filled in.

He shrugged. "It's not bad not to. I guess I've always just assumed I'd be a dad."

Yeah. "Cool." She turned to start up the path again.

But Spencer tugged on her hand. "Max."

She stopped and turned back with a sigh. "What?"

He looked frustrated. "I…" He blew out a breath. "I don't know. I just don't like that you're feeling bad. I wanted today to be fun and happy."

"It's not your fault. And I'm not *sad*. I just haven't really thought about having kids, and I don't think I'd be very good at it. And you want—"

She broke off as she realized that being upset that he wanted a woman who wanted kids and that she didn't fit another of his criteria was very close to admitting that she wanted him to want her. For real.

"Just because you didn't have the childhood you wanted and *should have had*, doesn't mean you can't give a loving, amazing childhood to someone else, Max," he said softly, tugging her closer. "That might make you even better at it. You could give someone the things you missed."

Her heart squeezed. How had he known that was her fear? That she didn't know how to parent because she hadn't been parented?

"I can't even have a dog or cat," she said, her voice unintentionally soft as well. "My schedule is crazy, I can't cook, and I have a deep, driving need to make grown men cry. Not very conducive to gentle mothering."

He just looked at her for several hard beats of her heart. Then he lifted a hand and brushed her hair back, tucking it behind her ear. "Teaching a little redhead with big green eyes to not take any shit and to hold people accountable for the bad stuff they do sounds like great mothering to me."

Her eyes widened.

"You just need to find a guy who has a normal schedule and can cook."

She swallowed. Right. Which was *not* him. She nodded. "And who likes crows."

"Right."

Max took a breath and started down the path again, pulling Spencer with her because he wouldn't let go of her hand.

The petting zoo started just to the east of the tour company. Caroline had told her the whole story on her first visit about how an otter named Gus had adopted the Landry family a few years ago. Then he'd gotten a girlfriend, Gertie. Then they'd had pups. The Landrys had built an enclosure right next door rather than letting them keep living out behind Leo's old trailer. The otters had entertained the tourists while waiting for their boat tours, and it seemed like the perfect set-up.

Then Charlie had come to town and immediately decided the whole thing should be a part of the bigger business plan. Including charging people to pet and play with the goats, pigs, and alpacas that Tori kept in the barn on the other side of the otters.

The rest was history. Griffin and Donovan Foster, Jill Morris, and Fiona Grady, all wildlife experts—vets, rehab specialists, and rescuers—had come to town, and the petting zoo had turned into an endangered animal park and then evolved into an animal sanctuary for abused animals. They now had everything from hedgehogs and alpacas to a colony of endangered Galapagos penguins and giraffes.

"Do you want to head up to the penguins first?" Spencer asked. "We can also come back after the boat tour and do that, so we have more time."

"After sounds good. I want more time there," she told him.

Spencer dug out his wallet to pay the fee to get into the barnyard and up to the alpaca pens.

"What do you want to see first?"

Max shook her head. She honestly had no preference here. "Up to you."

He grinned. "Okay, come on." He led her toward the little barn.

They were halfway across the barnyard when she heard, "Spencer! Max!"

They turned to see Charlie Landry coming toward them.

Correction, Charlie Landry Foster.

Charlie caught Spencer in a hug, squeezing him tightly, then turned a beaming smile on Max. "It's so great to see you guys again so soon."

"Paige texted already?" Spencer teased.

"Well, yes. But it would be nice to see you anyway."

"So, you know we're here for the week."

"I'm delighted by the news," Charlie said. "We'll have to get together at Ellie's later."

Spencer nodded. "Figured that would happen. Hoping there's a crawfish boil on Friday too."

Charlie laughed. "Of course there is."

Max felt her heart trip. She hadn't been to a crawfish boil in years. But she did love crawfish and cold beer. That would probably surprise Spencer.

Not that she'd ever *made* crawfish herself, of course. Which *wouldn't* surprise Spencer. But she'd been to two or three boils.

One memory rose up and engulfed her just then. A festival that Phil and Steph had taken her to one summer weekend when she'd been eleven. She'd seen a parade, sampled at least five different kinds of homemade pie, and had gone to a crawfish boil. She'd even danced. There had been a live band, and Phil had taught her how to do the Texas two-step on an outdoor dancefloor under twinkle lights.

It was a bittersweet memory. Phil was now in a wheelchair, living in an assisted living facility because Steph couldn't lift and transfer him on her own. Max visited a couple of times a month, and she thought they were generally happy. But she hated Gordon Ridgewood a little more every time she left the place.

Now she looked up at Spencer and realized she might just understand why brownies were important to him. They reminded him of coming home to a place that made him feel happy and safe. She hadn't had strawberry rhubarb pie since that festival, but she knew if she tasted it again, it would bring back happy memories of that summer day with Phil and Steph.

Spencer was watching her. "You okay?"

He must've picked up on the tension in her body. Or maybe he'd asked her a question she hadn't heard.

Was she okay? She wasn't sure.

She had *been* okay. Yesterday. Before he'd kicked down her door, told her she was in danger, swept her off to Autre, and started making her think and feel things that she hadn't in years. If ever.

She'd been okay before Spencer Landry had asked her to dance at the wedding. That's what had started all of this. All of this… delving into emotions and wondering and being *seen* and understood, dammit.

He hadn't blown her off earlier. He hadn't told her she was overreacting, assuming Ridgewood was behind all of this. He hadn't told her she was obsessed and that she had to let her grudge go. He'd understood. And he'd given her some ideas about how to move forward. No, it wouldn't take Gordon Ridgewood down in a blaze of defeat and humiliation that would ruin his life and make him rue the day he'd chosen money over humans. But it was something.

It was more than she had from anyone else in a very long time. Her editor had told her numerous times that he would not allow her to print anything that didn't have cold, hard facts. That was fair, of course.

Diego had also told her that she was barking up a tree that would never produce fruit. True, he had mixed a few metaphors there, but she understood his general message—she was hoping for an outcome that may never occur.

Even Caroline had cautioned her about giving too much time and effort to something that might never actually conclude satisfactorily.

Max understood what they were all saying. She knew they were right. But she couldn't drop it. Gordon Ridgewood was a bad man who was doing bad things to good people. How could she just go on with her everyday life knowing that? Even if she never brought him down, even if no one ever did, she couldn't just sit around and do nothing. She had to try at least.

Spencer understood that. He did the same thing.

But was she okay?

Was she okay with falling in love with Spencer Landry?

Because that's what was happening here, she was pretty sure.

No. Actually, she didn't think she was okay.

CHAPTER EIGHT

"Come on in. Look around and do whatever you want," Charlie told them brightly. "And then come back over after your swamp boat tour. There's so much to do, and I want you to see everything."

"What are the chances I can get this girl in to feed penguins?" Spencer asked.

Charlie's face lit up. "Whatever you guys want. You're family. Of course we'll get you into the penguins." Her phone chimed, and she looked down. "Oh, I have a call coming up in about five minutes. But you guys do whatever you want. I'll see you later."

She rushed off, and Spencer looked at Max. "You didn't answer my question."

"What question?"

"Are you okay?"

She wanted to kiss him. Right here in the middle of a petting zoo.

And that urge felt very real. Not at all pretend-you're-together-so-no-one-knows-you're-hiding-out-from-a-would-be-bomber.

Nope, she wasn't okay.

"Sure. I'm at a petting zoo and get to feed penguins later.

And I get to go on a swamp tour on a boat driven by a hot prince. How could I not be okay?"

Spencer gave a little growl and dropped his hand to her ass. He squeezed. "I will throw that prince overboard and leave him for gator bait. Do you want that on your conscience?"

She laughed, feeling some of the tension dissipate. "Okay, fine. I'll quit talking about how hot he is."

"You stop *thinking* about how hot he is."

"Then you're gonna have to distract me." She took the front of his t-shirt in her hand and stepped closer. "So my mind is on something else." Was she begging for a kiss?

Yep.

He leaned down and pressed his lips to hers. The kiss was short and sweet but hot. And again, it struck her that there was no one around to be an audience to this. This wasn't a part of their act. This wasn't pretending. And she'd initiated it.

He lifted his head. "Challenge accepted."

All she could do was smile at him. She was sure it looked goofy and dazed, and she was very afraid that he would start to notice that she had a big crush on him.

That might be a problem.

So she started for the barn again.

And realized that the universe was just really not on her side today the second they stepped inside.

"You've got to be kidding me," she groaned.

Spencer was right behind her. He laughed, the sound vibrating through her. Which she might have enjoyed. If not for what he was laughing about.

They were having a bake sale.

A *bake sale.*

And while there were frosted cookies shaped like alpacas, cupcakes with otter faces, and Oreos that had been turned into penguins, right there front and center, nestled next to gigantic chocolate chip cookies, were the brownies.

There was also a very pretty brunette behind the table. And she evidently knew Spencer.

"Spencer Landry? Oh my gosh!"

"Liv? Well, hi!" Spencer gave the woman a big grin and stepped closer to the table. "How are you?"

"I'm fine. I haven't seen you in forever," Liv gushed. "You look great." The woman's gaze tracked over Spencer, slowly, from head to toe.

She wasn't wrong. But Max suddenly had the crazy urge to throw a blanket over Spencer so the woman couldn't see so much as his pinky finger.

What the hell was that?

But she knew. She was jealous. Of an old friend of Spencer's.

"So do you, Liv. How long has it been?"

And Spencer thought Liv looked great. That certainly didn't quell any of Max's jealousy.

She stepped up next to him, and slipped her arm around him, tucking her thumb through the back belt loop of his jeans. He looked down at her. He didn't seem surprised, but he was clearly amused. He hooked his arm around her as well.

Liv's gaze went from Max to Spencer and then back. "Hi, I'm Liv."

"Liv, this is Max," Spencer said, making the introduction.

"Nice to meet you," Liv said. "Spencer and I've known each other for years."

"Hi," Max returned. "Spencer and I have been sleeping together for just a few weeks."

She heard Spencer's choked laugh. And noted the way Liv's eyes narrowed slightly. Well, good. That wasn't a lie. They weren't pretending right now. She and Spencer had slept together. And no matter what soft, mushy feelings he was stirring up inside her, or the confusing feelings she had whirling through her mind with his understanding and support, she had no doubt that they were going to end up sleeping together again at some point this week.

"Oh, well…" Clearly Liv didn't know how to respond to that.

Which was fair. That was not typical conversation when at a bake sale booth in a cute little petting zoo.

"Max, Liv went to high school with all my cousins and we used to hang out in the summers when I visited."

Max didn't care. But she did care that Liv was beautiful and was standing behind a table of baked goods and clearly thought Spencer was great. "Did you bake all of this?" Max asked.

Liv looked at the table. "Not all of it. But a lot."

Of course she had.

Max didn't like being jealous. Ugh. It caused stomach aches. Who knew?

"We're raising money for the little kids' baseball and softball programs." She glanced to her left and Spencer and Max followed her gaze. There was a little boy pushing trucks and cars around on the wooden floor.

"Yours?" Spencer asked.

"Yep." Liv's gaze was full of love. "That's Tyler. He's only five but he loves anything having to do with cars and balls."

"I didn't know you'd gotten married and had a baby," Spencer said.

Well, good, that meant they weren't on each other's Christmas card list or Facebook friends, Max thought. And yeah, maybe Liv was married—

"Not married," Liv said.

Well, damn.

"His dad was a lot of fun one weekend," Liv said, her cheeks getting pink. "He's stationed at Fort Bliss. He's helping out and visits when he can, but we're not in love or anything."

Spencer nodded. "Glad to know you've got support. I'm sure your mom and dad are great." He glanced at the little boy again. "He's adorable."

"Thanks. And yes, Mom and Dad are wonderful." Liv smiled up at him. "We're doing well."

"That's great."

"Do you want to get something?" Liv asked. "I made the chocolate chip cookies, the peanut butter cookies, and the brownies."

Of course, she had. Max's stomach felt even sicker.

Then Liv looked at Max. "What's your favorite?"

"I don't really like cookies," Max told her. Again, not a lie. Though she probably didn't need to say it smugly.

"Oh, we have apples and dip too," Liv said without blinking. "I wanted to be sure we had something healthier for anyone who didn't want too much sugar. And we have gluten-free bars over here."

"Apples would be great," Spencer said, reaching into his pocket and pulling out a few bills. He handed them over as Liv offered Max the apples.

She didn't want Liv's stupid apples, but what was she supposed to do? She took the sliced apples in the cute little container with the additional smaller container of fruit dip that she didn't want from the woman that Spencer should absolutely ask out on a date and tried to smile.

She was sure it came out as a weird grimace instead.

"Mom!"

Everyone looked toward Liv's son as the little boy called out. A goat was standing beside him, and the boy was cowering in fright.

"Oh, Tyler!" Liv gasped and crossed to him quickly.

Max thought the gasp was a bit of an overreaction. The goat was a baby, tiny, and it wasn't doing anything but watching the little boy.

Then Spencer stepped in that direction and knelt next to the boy. He held the goat by the shoulders with one big hand, stroking its head with the other, talking softly to either the animal or the kid.

That was *for sure* an overreaction. He hardly needed to charge in and intervene.

"Hi, Max."

Max glanced to her left. Jordan Landry had joined her. Jordan was married to another of Spencer's cousins, Fletcher. She was also very pregnant. She ran the petting zoo with Charlie, and Max remembered talking with her for several minutes during the wedding. She found the other woman laid back and friendly and was able to give Jordan a genuine smile.

"Hi, Jordan."

"I heard you and Spencer were in town."

"Wow, that Landry grapevine works fast."

Jordan laughed. "You have no idea."

Max looked back to where Spencer was now sitting on the barn floor with a baby goat in his lap.

Damn, that was cute.

She picked up one of her apples and took a bite, chewing as she took in the sight. The little boy was looking at Spencer as if he was Captain America. And Liv was looking at Spencer as if he was Chris Evans.

Max thought Spencer was better looking than Chris Evans.

But crap, they made a cute little family picture. Liv was smiling and laughing about something Spencer had said. Tyler was reaching out a hand to tentatively pet the goat, clearly brave now that Superhero Spencer was there. Even the goat seemed enamored with Spencer.

However, Max knew how good it felt to have the man's hand stroking over her body so she could cut the goat a little slack.

"What's going on over there?" Jordan asked.

"Spencer's dreams are all coming true," Max muttered.

"What?" Jordan asked.

Max shook her head. "Nothing. Forget it."

"Is everything okay?"

Not really at all, no. Max lifted another apple slice. "These apples are delicious." She dipped it in the little cup of white fluffy fruit dip. "Did Liv make the apples?"

Jordan's brows arched. "I don't think Liv made the apples, no. But she might've made the fruit dip."

Max sighed but still chewed. It was very good.

"Are those brownies pretty amazing?" Max asked.

Jordan nodded. "Liv is an amazing baker and cook."

She'd figured. "Does she have a dog?"

Jordan's eyes widened as if she didn't know what was going on exactly, but she knew it was something weird. "A sweet German Shepherd named Dixie."

"And Dixie is completely adorable?" Max asked. Though she already knew the answer was yes.

"Dixie's a great dog," Jordan said, a bemused smile tugging at the corner of her lips.

"And what does the amazing Liv do for a living?" Max asked, picking up another apple slice and this time scooping a massive dollop of dip out of the container. It was really, really good. She'd pay Liv for a bowl of just the dip and a spoon.

"Does she train seeing-eye dogs for the blind or something?"

"She's a third-grade teacher with Fletcher."

Max stopped chewing and stared at Jordan. Jordan's husband was a third-grade teacher at the school here in Autre. He'd been named teacher of the year four years in a row. She knew because the certificates were hanging on the wall at Ellie's bar.

"You've got to be kidding me," Max said.

Jordan finally laughed. "Why all the questions about Liv?"

Max glanced over at the other woman. Anyone walking into the barn would assume the three of them were a family. "Because she's perfect for Spencer."

Jordan frowned. "That's a strange comment from the woman he's dating."

"The one he's sleeping with," Max corrected. "We're just getting to know each other. And it's already obvious that we're not each other's type. Well, other than physically. That's been pretty good."

Jordan opened her mouth to respond, and Max had to admit that she would've loved to hear what the other woman had to say. Especially if it was in the form of advice. But just then, she felt something hard hit the side of her knee. She looked down. A goat was staring up at her. He'd head-butted her. "Hey! Ow."

Jordan shooed the goat back with her foot. "He thinks you're going to give him some of your apples," she explained.

Max frowned down at the animal. "These are mine. And the dip is excellent but not goat-appropriate, and you shouldn't eat the apples without it. And I'm grumpy. So I'm not sharing."

"*Beehh*!" he replied.

Max shrugged. "Not sorry."

"Jordan!" someone called from outside the barn door.

Jordan glanced in that direction. "Hang tight," she told Max. "Let me go check on that. I'll be right back."

"I'll be here." She wouldn't want to give up her front-row seat for Spencer falling in love with the perfect woman.

"*Beeehhh*!"

The goat bleated at her again, and she frowned down at him. "Seriously. I know you're very well fed. I saw the sign that says people can come in and pay for food to hand feed you. I'm guessing that happens like forty-seven times a day. You do not need my apples."

"*Beeehhh*!"

"No." She looked back at Spencer, Liv, Tyler, and their well-behaved goat.

Damn, Spencer looked cute holding that baby goat. And the way he was talking to the little boy was sweet. What was it about men and animals and little kids? Max wasn't even the nurturing type. She liked crows. But still, watching Spencer hold a baby goat, pet its little head, talk softly to it, and smile as if he'd never had more fun in his life, made her heart do a little pitter-patter that she did not appreciate. She did not need to be reinforcing her crush on him while he was at that very moment, right in front of her eyes, realizing all of the little checkmarks Liv could put in the boxes on his list of girlfriend criteria.

"Ow!" Max felt a sharp pain in her knee as the goat head-butted her again.

"*Beeehhh!*" Then he did it again, harder this time, and her knee buckled slightly. But in the wrong direction.

Pain shot from the joint up her leg, and she gasped.

Suddenly the goat reared up on its hind legs, propping its front hooves on her thigh, she assumed reaching for the apples. Trying to get away from the goat and some weight off of her sore knee, Max shifted. The goat didn't like that, and in the next second, she felt a sharp stabbing in her left hip.

The goat had bit her.

"What?" she gasped. "Ow!"

She shoved him away, spilling apples and dip all over the floor, and pressed a hand to the spot right below her hip bone and the curve of her butt. The goat leaped on the apples immediately, and Max took a deep breath. Just before she heard a low growling. She looked up to see a dog staring at her, growling low in its throat.

It was a German Shepherd. "Dixie?" she asked softly.

The dog barked, and the next thing Max knew, Spencer was practically on top of her.

"What happened?"

"The goat bit me!"

He looked confused. His gaze went to the goat happily chomping on apples at her feet. "You're kidding."

She scowled at him, then held up her blood-covered hand.

He grabbed it, turning it over and back, inspecting the alleged wound.

"Not my hand! My hip!"

Spencer muttered a curse and swept her up into his arms.

"Spencer!" Max started.

"My God, what happened?" Jordan exclaimed as she came back into the barn.

"A goat bit Max."

"A goat *bit her*?"

"Do you have bandages?" Spencer snapped, setting Max down on top of a stack of hay bales outside the barn door.

"Ow!" Max's hand flew to the bite that was now being poked by straw.

"Fuck, fuck, fuck," Spencer muttered, sweeping her back into his arms and looking around.

"My office is this way," Jordan said, starting to walk as she typed something into her phone.

They headed across the barnyard to a separate structure between the goat barn and the alpaca pens. Jordan let them in, and Spencer shifted Max to one side so he could use an arm to clear space on Jordan's desk.

"Hey!" Jordan protested. "I was going to do that."

"She's bleeding, Jordan," Spencer said.

"I don't think it's a major artery, Spencer. I think we have a few seconds," Jordan shot back. She restacked the papers and folders he had moved and put them on the other side of the desk. Spencer huffed out another frustrated breath.

"What's wrong now?" Jordan asked.

Max's hip throbbed, and her knee was aching, but she still felt herself smiling.

"Fuck, hell, damn," Spencer muttered without answering Jordan's question. He gingerly set Max down on her good foot, leaning her into him as if her left leg had been broken. She didn't need the support, but he seemed riled up enough that she decided not to argue. Plus, he felt good.

He stripped off his shirt and spread it on the desk over the space he'd cleared.

Jordan and Max both stared at him.

Max was fairly certain that Jordan was staring at him because she was afraid he'd lost his mind. Max was staring at him because she really liked Spencer Landry naked.

"What the hell, Spencer?" Jordan asked, her hands planted on her hips now.

"I can't set an open wound down with nothing between it and the desktop."

"But your sweaty shirt where you were just holding a goat and had a little boy's dirty hands is fine?" Jordan asked.

Spencer glowered at her but then looked at his shirt, swore again, and grabbed it back. He turned the shirt inside out and laid it back on the desk. Then he picked Max up by the waist and set her on top of it.

"Well, if she gets an infection and you have to amputate her leg, at least she'll know who to sue other than Boys of the Bayou Gone Wild," Jordan said cheerfully.

"It was your fucking goat," Spencer snapped.

"Maybe she antagonized him," Jordan said.

Max could tell Jordan was only poking at Spencer, and she waited for his reaction. It was fun to annoy him.

"What the fuck, Jordan? She wouldn't antagonize a goat. And even if she did, people should be safe to walk around the goat barn and not get bit." He focused on Max. "Then he head-butted you? Are you all right?"

"He head-butted me first. Then bit me." She lifted a shoulder. "And not really. I think he hyperextended my knee. There could be meniscal damage. I think my ACL is intact, but we might need an MRI. And seriously, the blood loss is becoming an issue." She lifted a hand and pressed it against her forehead as if she was getting faint.

"Jesus, Max."

He looked appalled, and she opened her mouth to reassure him she was kidding.

"What's going on?"

A deep voice from the doorway made them all turn.

Michael LeClaire stood there in his uniform, a first-aid kit in hand. "I got a call that there was a medical emergency here?"

"Max got bit by a goat," Jordan said simply.

"And she might have a ruptured ACL, and she's losing blood," Spencer said.

Michael's eyes went wide. "*What?*"

"No," Max interjected. She reached out and squeezed

Spencer's arm. "I'm sorry. I was messing with you. My knee is bruised, and I think I've already stopped bleeding."

Spencer frowned at her. "Not funny."

She looked over at Michael. "Sorry."

Michael's gaze went from Max's to Spencer's, then back. "I should probably take a look, though."

He was a paramedic and firefighter. Max was sure he could address her injuries fully. In fact, him being here was probably overkill.

"That'd be great," Max said. "Thank you."

Michael did not comment on Spencer being half-dressed. Jordan just crossed her arms and smirked.

"Do you need to be here?" Spencer asked his cousin's wife.

Jordan shook her head. "Probably not. But I haven't been this entertained in a while."

"You find people getting bit by your goats entertaining?"

"Oh no. I'm entirely entertained by *you*, Spencer."

"I think you need to go find Charlie and make sure your insurance is fully paid in case anyone decides to sue you." His voice was firm and low and very not-amused.

Jordan's smirk spread into a full-on grin. "Fine. But you know Michael gossips as much as the rest of us."

She disappeared through the door.

Spencer looked at Michael. "You do not gossip as much as everyone else around here."

"No, but if it's about you acting like a jackass over a woman —" Michael shot Max a wink. "I totally do."

"Just make sure she's okay," Spencer said.

Max noted that he didn't argue that he was overreacting. Again. He seemed to have a tendency to do that. At least with her.

And she tended to like it.

That was a problem.

So was the fact that she would happily suffer a goat bite to get Spencer away from the beautiful brownie-baking Liv.

Well, not *happily*, maybe, but she'd do it again.

Max blew out a breath.

Great. It'd taken Spencer Landry just a little over twenty-four hours to complicate her life completely.

———

SPENCER WATCHED as Max explained what happened in the barn to Michael.

He was overreacting. So what was new when it came to Max? It wasn't just that she was bleeding—though that was seriously an issue for his heart rate and blood pressure. It was also that he'd brought her up here today to make her happy, to give her a fun day away from work, to show her a little work-life balance. She'd even worn the sundress. The sweet yellow sundress he'd pulled out of her closet that she'd initially said no way to. She'd packed the damned thing and she was wearing it today.

And she looked gorgeous. So much like everything he'd ever wanted that he'd had a hard time taking a deep breath when she'd first stepped out of the bedroom.

He'd been so fucking happy bringing her here on this day date that hadn't felt fake for one damned second.

And she'd ended up with goat teeth marks and a sore knee.

And before that, she'd been confronted with an entire table full of cookies and brownies made by a sweet third-grade teacher with a dog and a little boy who had clearly made Max jealous.

And before *that,* she'd been hit by sad reminders of her parents being generally not very good at parenting.

His plan to show her a happy good time had blown up on him.

And he was now facing the fact that he was crazy about a woman who not only didn't bake but didn't know if she wanted to have kids.

Of course, he hadn't missed the contrast between her and Liv.

It was stark, and he wasn't stupid. He liked Liv. She was sweet, and funny, and she knew and liked all the same people and things he did. She had a kid, a dog, a table full of brownies, and a job that would ensure she would be home at the end of every day. She would be appalled at the cold case he'd shared with Max. She probably thought Gordon Ridgewood was nothing more than a successful businessman and a kind and generous donor to things like art programs and scholarships and children's hospital wings.

But instead of thinking about Liv, Tyler, and Dixie, all he could focus on was how much he hated Michael LeClaire's hands rubbing all over Max's knee.

It was just her knee. Michael was a paramedic. And he was probably doing more prodding than rubbing. Max was hurt, and Michael was here to help her.

Spencer still wanted to punch him.

"Okay, already. Does she need some ice or what?" Spencer asked.

Michael looked up at him. "Maybe also some ibuprofen. Some elevation and rest too."

"Great. How about the bite mark?"

"Let's see it," Michael said. He reached into his kit, pulled on some rubber gloves, and then opened a package of gauze in preparation.

"It isn't that deep. It just surprised me. But it does hurt." Max slipped off the desk and turned, bracing her hands on the desk.

And put her ass directly in front of Michael's face.

Then she hitched up the bottom of her dress, showing Michael her plain tan panties that Spencer suddenly didn't think were so boring after all.

"What the hell?" Spencer was next to her before he thought about it.

She looked up at him. "What?"

"He bit you on the ass?"

"Upper thigh." She angled her body so that Spencer could see.

The bite mark was an especially angry red on her creamy skin, and Spencer suddenly had the urge to make goat burgers for dinner.

He also had the urge to take his shirt off the desk and cover her backside with it.

Of course, then Michael wouldn't be able to see the injury, which would defeat the entire purpose of him being here.

"No, it's not too deep. You don't need stitches," Michael told her. His long, thick fingers ran over her skin and around the wound, brushing very close to the lower curve of her butt.

Spencer gritted his teeth.

"This is probably all going to bruise," Michael said as he glided his fingers over the area.

Max sucked in a little breath. "Yeah, that's tender."

"Cover it up and let's go," Spencer said firmly.

They both looked up at him.

"What? You're not doing brain surgery. This doesn't need to take this long. You've seen what you need to."

And then some. Like what a close shave Max got on her thighs. And those fucking panties. He'd actually thought those weren't sexy? That she should wear pink and cherry red instead? Spencer ran a hand over his face.

Michael snorted softly and ran *his* hand over Max's thigh again.

"LeClaire," Spencer bit out.

"Just bein' thorough." Michael was grinning.

"I'm going to thoroughly beat your ass."

"Spencer," Max admonished. "Maybe you should wait outside."

"No fucking way."

Michael would never make a move on Max. He'd never do anything unprofessional, for that matter. Spencer knew that. Why he was acting like a jackass he really couldn't say.

Or rather, he didn't *want* to say.

Finally, Michael reached into the first-aid kit and withdrew hydrogen peroxide, more gauze, and bandages. He handed the supplies to Spencer. "Help me out?"

"I could do all of this. I'm trained in first aid," Spencer said. Sure, it was basic and more triage stuff designed to keep a victim alive until they could get to someone like Michael. Still, it was a goat bite. *On Max.* Spencer needed the other man's face away from her panties ASAP.

"But I'm right here," Michael said, his eyes landing on Max's backside before returning to Spencer's.

He might punch Michael after all.

"You're getting on my nerves, LeClaire."

"I know." He wasn't a bit sorry either.

Finally, after what felt like a week, Michael had Max cleaned up and bandaged.

"Thanks," Spencer said shortly to his friend.

Michael chuckled. "Oh, it was my pleasure."

Spencer gave a soft growl and started packing Michael's stuff.

Michael just laughed louder. "Let me know if you need anything else, Max. I'm here for you anytime."

"Get out." Spencer shoved his friend toward the door.

"I'll see you tonight, though, right?" Michael asked.

Dammit. He had to meet with the guys tonight. Spencer nodded. "Yeah. Later."

"Bye, Max," Michael called as Spencer pushed him out the door.

"Bye, Michael. Thanks."

Spencer turned back. "We missed our boat tour."

She sighed. "Sorry."

"It's not your fault." He crossed to her. "Are you okay? Seriously now. I'm sure it hurts."

She lifted a shoulder. "A little."

"Let's head back to the cabin. Ice, rest, ibuprofen."

"I'm ruining our day."

He shook his head. "You're not ruining anything. But *I* feel like an ass. I tried to take you out for some fun, and I feel like everything fell apart."

"It's not your fault that I can't even get along with the goats. I probably should just stick to crows."

How did bringing her to a *petting zoo* turn out like this? Dammit. He'd just wanted her to have a good time. And now she was limping.

She made it two steps before he muttered a curse and swept her into his arms again.

"Spencer, you can't keep carrying me around."

"The fuck I can't."

CHAPTER NINE

He took her to his truck and deposited her in the passenger seat.

"Ow!"

He gritted his teeth. She was in pain, because he tried to bring her to a fucking petting zoo. Why couldn't things with Max just be straightforward?

He shut the door and rounded the front of the truck. He needed to breathe. Things were fine. They were here because he was keeping her *safe*. Chris and the guys were working to find the guy who'd threatened her. Spencer would fill the other badges in tonight and Max would *stay* safe.

Happy was just a nice perk if he could swing it.

Clearly, that was just going to be a little more difficult than he'd anticipated.

But as he started the truck, his jaw was still tight.

He wanted her to be happy, dammit. Safe, yes. For sure. But happy too. And he wanted that to be easy to accomplish.

The longer he spent with her, the more he wanted her happiness, in fact. Today he'd seen a peek at the vulnerable little girl who'd never had a pet but also hadn't even had a father who'd taken the time to stop and look at bunnies and frogs with her.

They were quiet on the drive back to the bed and breakfast,

and she shook off his attempt to try to carry her to the cottage from the parking area.

"Come on, Spencer, I can walk."

"At least let me hold your hand," he said crossly, taking her hand in his without waiting for permission.

She huffed out a breath, and he let her limp to the cottage, both of them equally grumpy with the situation. Once inside, he pointed to the couch. "Lie down. Prop your leg up."

Of course she didn't listen. She started for the bathroom. "I need to get some ibuprofen and ice first."

"Max," he said through gritted teeth. "Put your ass on the couch or I'll toss it there myself."

Max opened her mouth, to protest, Spencer was sure, but he took a step toward her and she snapped it shut and turned for the couch. She plopped down, wincing as she did, and he took a deep breath and bit back his words. He wanted to bitch at her to be careful. He wanted to hold her. He wanted to spank her.

And he wanted to make her dinner.

Of course, he didn't know how to do that.

He'd never felt so incompetent in his life as he did around Max Keller.

She needed him to do things he didn't know how to do. He could take down bad guys, figure out complex criminal cases, charm nearly anyone, make women fucking swoon… except this one.

This one needed him to be sweet and take care of her and he couldn't seem to fucking do that.

Spencer stomped into the bathroom. He rummaged through his travel bag and pulled out the ibuprofen. Then he stomped to the kitchen for water. He kind of liked the wooden floor of the cabin. It made his stomping extra loud.

He grabbed ice from the freezer and wrapped it in a towel, then returned to the couch with all the supplies. He handed them over without a word, balancing the ice on her sore knee.

Once she'd taken the glass and ibuprofen, he grabbed one of the throw pillows, lifted her leg, and tucked it under her knee.

After she'd swallowed the tablets, she looked up at him. "Thanks."

He huffed out a breath. "Sorry, you got hurt."

"I'm fine, Spencer. And it's not your fault."

"Maybe not. But my plan for the day didn't turn out. And I'm pissed about it."

She studied him for a moment, then slid over on the couch, making room next to her. "You know what might feel good?"

He sat and braced his elbow on the back of the couch, leaning over her. Maybe she'd say an orgasm. *That* was one thing he could do for this woman that worked. At least he had that. "What?"

"Will you massage my knee? I think it's swelling a little bit and that might help."

It wasn't an orgasm, but *yes*. Yes, he would massage her knee. He would *love* to massage her knee. To do *something* to make her feel better.

He slid back on the cushion so he could better reach, then ran a hand up the inside of the joint. "Where does it hurt the most?"

"On the outside where he hit me. I'm sure it will bruise."

"I can't believe the goat attacked you." He coasted his palms over both sides of her knee. His hands were big enough to encase her entire joint.

"You can push harder than that. I'll tell you if it hurts."

He met her eyes. "Promise?"

She nodded. "I will absolutely tell you if there's anything you're doing that makes me not feel good."

He paused for a moment as it hit him that he believed her. And that the promise extended to more than her knee. At least there was that. One thing about Max Keller he could count on was that she would let him know how she felt about… everything. Including him and the things he did and said. He pressed a little harder on her knee. "Okay."

She was watching his hands on her leg. "The goat was going for my apples. And I wasn't sharing, so he got mad."

"Still, those goats are around little kids all day, every day. I can't believe he decided to be mean to *you*."

Max lifted a shoulder. "Liv's dog didn't like me very well either it seemed."

Spencer didn't care about Liv. Or her dog. Hell, he hadn't even petted the dog.

He sighed. Dammit.

That told him everything he needed to know about his feelings for Max.

"Oh, you didn't get any brownies," Max said suddenly.

"What?" Spencer looked up from rubbing her knee and thinking about how much he liked German Shepherds.

"I wanted to distract you from Liv, but I didn't need to pull you away before you got cookies or brownies."

"You were trying to distract me from Liv?"

"Yes. Stupidly. You obviously know where she lives."

He chuckled and ran his hands over her knee again, stroking his thumb a little harder along the joint line where he could feel it getting puffy.

"I've known where Liv lives for a long time."

"Well, you should have at least... tasted her brownies, don't you think?"

He lifted his eyes to her at that little pause in her question. "I had no intention of *tasting her brownies*, Max." Literally or metaphorically, his answer was the same either way.

"Why not?" Then she shook her head. "Never mind. You like them fresh-baked and the house smelling like chocolate, right?"

If they were talking about *literal* brownies then yes. Though he could imagine enjoying a chocolate-scented body lotion. He cleared his throat. "I do. But I typically would have bought a brownie from a bake sale that was raising money for little kids."

"So why didn't you today?"

"I saw your reaction."

"My reaction?"

"You were uncomfortable. I wasn't flirting with Liv. At least not intentionally. But I could tell you were unhappy, so I didn't want to give any further indication that I was interested in anything—brownies or otherwise—from Liv. But then…" He lifted a hand and ran it through his hair.

She tipped her head. "What?"

He blew out a breath. "Then I went and helped Tyler and played with the goat and…" He shrugged. "That might have seemed like I was flirting or was acting interested or something. And then while I was doing that, you got *bit*. I feel like an asshole."

Max regarded him seriously. "So you were worried about what Jordan would think about you paying attention to Liv's son? Since we're pretending to be together?"

He frowned. "It had nothing to do with Jordan."

"Then what's it about?"

"You." His hand tightened on her knee.

"What about me? I shouldn't be jealous. And you shouldn't feel responsible for me. You and I are only here together for this week and it's because we have to be. We've already acknowledged, repeatedly, that we aren't a good fit. Liv seems perfect for you."

He hated the way she so matter-of-factly said *they* weren't a good fit. He nodded. "She really does, doesn't she?"

"Yup." Max didn't sound particularly happy about that.

"Fuck. I don't know, okay? I went over to help the kid out of instinct and I think baby goats are cute. But I'm not interested in Liv. She's beautiful and bakes and smells great and still, all I could think about was you. I wanted to make *you* happy." He frowned. She hadn't been ooh-ing and ahh-ing over the goats. She certainly hadn't wanted any cookies. He wasn't sure she'd even thought Tyler was all that cute. "You looked mad about the apples, even when you were eating them."

Max nodded. "I was mad. Because the apple dip was really good."

"Oh." He frowned. "I don't get it."

"Jordan said Liv probably made it. It was just one more reason that Liv seems perfect for you."

Oh. Well, he kind of liked *that*. "And you don't like the idea that Liv is a good fit for me?" he asked. His hand started stroking up the back of her leg again.

Max sighed. But not in pleasure. In resignation. "I don't. I know that's stupid. But I think your girlfriend criteria are bullshit and I think if you find someone who fits them all, you'll never realize just how much bullshit they really are."

He stopped the massage again and stared at her. "You think my criteria are bullshit?"

She lifted her chin. "I do."

"In what way?"

"You want a woman who does something for a living that's sweet and innocent and has nothing to do with crime and corruption. But I think you need someone you can talk to about your job. Someone who won't be shocked and appalled. Someone who can handle the weight of what you do. And who can remind you that it's important and who can be properly proud of you because they know everything you go through."

Spencer felt his chest tighten as he stared at her.

"You also want someone who will take care of you—cook and bake, give you this sense of normalcy, and this place of comfort, and feeling of home—and the thing is, *everyone* wants that. But what you do isn't *abnormal*. In fact, it's pretty fucking heroic and brave and amazing and important and if you go home at the end of the day and shut it all off and hide from it, I'm afraid you'll start believing it's strange and bad." She took a breath. "You can make your own comfort and home, Spencer. You're striving for this ideal that is what someone else has told you is right. But home doesn't have to look a certain way. It just has to be home for *you* and I think it means more when you make it your own." She paused, pressed her lips together, but then said, "And, dammit, Spencer, if you want brownies, you should learn to make your own fucking brownies."

He had no words.

He knew, again, they weren't just talking about literal brownies. Maybe that too, but brownies symbolized something to him and Max understood that.

And she was saying he needed to make that for himself.

That was… a lot.

More, her cheeks were pink and her eyes were flashing, just like they did when she talked about her work and how much she hated Gordon Ridgewood.

She really meant everything she'd just said.

"And for the record," she went on, her voice softer now. "Just you *wanting* to make me happy today makes me happy. And so did you listening to me about Ridgewood. And understanding about my parents. And caring so much about my injuries." She paused and one corner of her mouth tipped up. "And being willing to give up brownies for me."

Spencer's chest felt tight, and it took him a second to pull in a full breath. He wondered if she had *any* idea what all of that did to him. He was even shocked by how important that all was.

His hand went to the back of her head, and he pulled her in until his mouth touched hers. He kissed her softly. "Thank you for saying that."

"Thank you for making it true."

"MAX, I HAVE A PROBLEM," Spencer said gruffly against her mouth.

"What's that?"

"I hated having Michael's hands on you. Even though I knew he was helping you. Even though I *wanted* him to help you. I really hated having another man touching you. And I wasn't pretending."

Max felt her heart flip. She'd wondered if the over-the-top possessiveness had been part of the pretend-relationship act. Hearing him admit it was real heated her blood.

She lifted her arms and slipped them around his neck. "Well, I hate to break it to you, Spencer, but I think that means you like me."

He gave a soft laugh. "I think I more than like you, Max."

Well, now she had to kiss him. She pressed her mouth to his, and he quickly took over the kiss. His hand flexed in her hair, gripping the strands a little firmer, and she tipped her head to the side to fit their mouths more fully together.

His tongue licked along her bottom lip, and she happily sighed and opened. The kiss heated quickly as things always did between them. He moved closer, leaning her back against the pillows behind her. He moved carefully, gently shifting so that he could lie beside her. He was sweet.

In the time she'd known him, Max had thought a lot of things about Spencer Landry, but "sweet" was not a word she would have put in the top ten. Still, the way he treated her… it was the best descriptor. He was careful with her, wanted to keep her safe, and yet made her feel sexy and as if he could *not* resist her. He skimmed his hand down her side, over the curve of her breast to her hip, where he squeezed.

"I don't want to hurt you."

She arched against him. "You're always careful, and I promise I will tell you if there's anything you need to do differently."

That seemed to reassure him, and he returned his lips to the work of making her lose her mind.

His hand slipped one strap of her dress from her shoulder and then skimmed that side of the bodice down, taking the bra cup with it. She shivered under his touch as he palmed her breast, running his thumb over the stiffening peak. The sensations shot from her nipple through her belly to her clit. She wanted his touch there. She shifted again, arching against him.

He pressed his hips against her thigh, and she felt his cock hardening. This was the side where the goat had taken a chomp, and she realized that Spencer was trying not to press against her injury. He had a point. She felt an ache and shifted her knee slightly so that he had more room without crowding the sore joint.

He lifted his head and looked down at her. "Are you okay?"

She nodded. "I'm always okay when you're kissing me."

"But your knee."

She wasn't going to lie to him. "It's a little sore. But I want to keep doing this."

"We can't go too far."

"Why not?" She reached up and kissed him.

But he lifted his head after just a few seconds. "Because I don't want to hurt you, and some of the things I want to do might. They definitely involve you needing to bend your knees."

Even as heat swirled through her, she chuckled. "Knee bending is required?"

His gaze tracked down her body and then returned to hers. "Maybe not for everything."

"Let's do that then. Whatever that is."

He laughed softly. "I love how much you want this. Me."

She curled her fingers into his neck, then stroked up and down. "I am certain I am not the only woman who wants you, Spencer. And I'm also very certain that you know that."

He nodded. She appreciated that he wasn't going to try to pretend he didn't realize that.

"Maybe. But with you, it feels different."

"You don't have to say things like that to get into my pants."

He pinned her with a serious look. "I know. I mean it. I haven't been with anybody in a while. And a lot of that has to do with you."

She frowned. "What do you mean?"

"I mean, since we met, you've been challenging me. And now that I've given it some thought, I realize that you've made me think that maybe I wasn't with women who cared about the right things."

"The right things like what?"

"I've been dating women who think I'm good-looking, funny, charming, nice to their moms if I meet them. I can take them to nice restaurants. I appreciate their cooking," he said with a self-deprecating smile.

Max rolled her eyes.

"We go to movies. Concerts. Very typical date stuff."

Max nodded. "There's nothing wrong with any of those things." They sounded boring, but there was nothing *wrong* with them.

"No, and I specifically avoid talking about my work. We talk about very normal, safe topics."

Max thought about the mini-rant she'd had just a few minutes ago. She hadn't meant to go off on him, but... well, maybe she had. She did hate the idea that Spencer was trying to hide or at least separate what he did for a living from everything else. She also hated that he seemed to think he needed to rely on other people to give him normalcy and make him happy. And that he was kind of desperate in his quest to find The One who would make it all okay for him.

"Annnnnd?" she asked slowly.

"The first time I met you, you were spitting fire and about two seconds away from kneeing me in the balls. You were gorgeous. I knew I would never be able to just charm you. Then we met up for the stakeout, and I knew instantly that you would never be impressed with a normal, common date like dinner and a movie. At first, I thought that I should never ask you out for anything. But the longer I've known you, the more I realized that you might want more from me because you know I can give you more."

Max was stunned. She hadn't expected any of this. Of course, he was right, but she hadn't realized that *he* had realized any of it. And further, she'd had no idea that he might *appreciate* it. Spencer had made up his mind about what he wanted and why.

"So, how long has it been since you've been with anyone else?" she asked, suddenly needing that clarification.

"I've been on some dates but haven't slept with anyone since we met."

Her eyes widened. "You haven't had sex since we *met*? That was almost a *year ago*, Spencer."

He blew out a breath. "I'm aware."

"But you didn't even like me. And you were very determined *not* to date me."

He nodded again. "Also aware of that."

She was stunned by this.

She hadn't been with anyone else in that time either. But that wasn't a shock. She wasn't that big on dating. Or big on let's-have-hot-sex-and-not-date. But Spencer Landry hadn't slept with anyone in *a year*?

"You can stop staring at me like I've sprouted a second head," he commented dryly.

"I don't know if I can," she said truthfully.

He rolled his eyes. "I just haven't met anyone I wanted to sleep with. It's not that big a deal."

"Do you think this was all your subconscious or something?"

"Now that I've been with you, had sex with you, and spent these last couple of days with you? Yes. I think that you are the reason."

"Whoa."

He just smiled and shook his head at her somewhat under-whelming reaction.

Her thoughts were still spinning. She had never caused a reaction in another human like the ones she seemingly caused in Spencer Landry. And it was a powerful, if overwhelming, feeling. She didn't think she'd ever been this... important... to anyone before. "So now what?" she finally asked.

"I think I need to date you."

Her eyes widened again. Well, she hadn't been expecting that.

Dating her had been very specifically something Spencer was against.

She also hadn't been expecting her heart to flip over in her chest and her brain to say, *yes, yes, yes, let's date Spencer! Yay!*

She stared at him for nearly ten full seconds without saying a word. Then she gripped the front of his shirt, pulled him in, and kissed him. Then she said against his lips, "Yes. Please date me."

She felt him smile against her mouth. "Okay."

"And also," she said.

"Yes?"

"Please give me an orgasm."

He sucked in a little breath that was probably surprise combined with a shot of lust. At least judging by the heat that flared in his eyes.

"Max, I don't want to hurt you."

"You won't."

"The way I'm feeling? The things I want to do to you? Yeah, I might."

She gave a soft moan. That was hot. "Please, Spencer. Take care of me."

That was probably a low blow. She knew he wouldn't be able to resist that.

He groaned and rested his forehead against hers. "I can't say no to that."

"Yeah, I know." Her grin was probably wicked. But he was too close to see it.

He lifted his head, and she pressed her lips together quickly.

His gaze was hot on hers. "Okay, but we do this my way."

"I don't know what that means, but I'm in."

"You sure?" His hand was already moving. He skimmed the bodice to her waist, then unhooked her bra and tossed it.

She moaned. "Yes. So sure."

He hiked her skirt up as he lowered his mouth to one nipple, licking then sucking.

Her hand went to the back of his head, holding him close. If this was just the beginning of this idea, she was happy to agree to the whole thing.

As his mouth worked her nipple, his hand moved down to the front of her panties, cupping her through the thin cotton.

"And you didn't want to wear the sundress," he teased.

"You didn't like me having the sundress on earlier with Michael," she teased right back.

"No, I fucking didn't," he growled against her breast as he sucked her nipple harder then gave her a little nip.

Sensations shot to her clit, and she was suddenly aching for him.

"Touch me, Spencer," she said breathlessly.

"Oh, I'm going to touch you, Max."

His hand dipped into her panties, and he found her hot and wet already.

She completely lost her ability to be even slightly embarrassed about that as his middle finger slid over her clit and down to her entrance.

She bent her uninjured knee and lifted her hip. "*Please.*"

"I've got you."

He slid his thick middle finger into her, and she whimpered. He quickly added another, pumping twice before returning to the tiny bundle of nerves where she was aching. He circled and pressed, delicious sensations streaking through her body in all directions.

She was already winding tight. It was amazing what this man's touch could do and how quickly. She suspected it had something to do with the fact that she just really, really liked him.

She'd liked all the men she'd let do this to her, but Spencer was different. Liking him was a challenge. He tried her patience. He bossed her around. He paid attention and didn't let her hide things as she could with others. He made her feel things. Not just physical things, but emotional things. And she liked him anyway. And he liked her back. In a way that she wasn't sure other men had. Because he understood her and knew her in a way that other men hadn't.

"God, you feel good," he said gruffly, trailing his mouth up to her neck and placing a kiss and then a little nip there.

"So do you."

She reached for his fly, but he moved away, pulling his hand from her hair to grasp her wrist before she could unzip him.

"Nope. This is all about you."

"It doesn't have to be," she protested.

"Let it be. Let me take care of you."

Well, that was hot. Was she going to argue? A hot, protective guy, who seemed crazy about her for some reason, wanted to give her an orgasm and wanted nothing in return? Darn.

Spencer circled her clit faster, then slipped his fingers to dip inside, this time using three to fill her.

Max gasped. "Spencer!"

"God, I love that." His voice was rough. He lowered his mouth to kiss her, hot and deep, as his fingers thrust into her and his thumb circled over her clit.

She was already climbing closer to the climax, and her hips arched against him, grinding up into his hand.

"That's right, go for it. Whatever you want," he said against her mouth.

She grabbed onto his forearm, gripping it, and holding him close, then lifted her hips again. She pressed against his hand, and he rewarded her with a deep, full thrust and somehow the perfect pressure against her clit.

"Spencer! Yes!"

"Let go, Max. Let me feel and hear you come apart."

So she did. She wound tight and then completely broke apart under his hand. She cried out his name as her body clamped around his fingers.

He let her ride out the waves, slowing his strokes. He slowly eased his fingers from her when her body stopped rippling. He rested his hand possessively on her stomach as he gathered her close, hugging her against his chest.

She sucked in a deep breath. "Damn."

"Dating me is already pretty good, isn't it?"

She could hear the smile in his voice. But yeah, dating him was already pretty good.

"You sure you don't want to go into the bed? I'm sure we could find some other fun things to do."

At that, he rolled away, leaned down, and kissed her sweetly, then pushed himself up from the couch. He crossed to the sink and washed his hands as she straightened her clothes.

"Nope, I'm gonna go get some lunch."

She frowned at him. "What?"

"It's lunchtime. I'm going to grab us some food from Ellie's. Then we're both going to work for a while. I'm going to make sure your knee and hip are fine. And then I'm going out with the boys for a little while tonight, and Caroline is coming over to keep you company."

Max pushed up to sit and watched him. "You have this all planned out."

He gave her a satisfied smile. "I do."

"Okay, well, you might think you're all organized and in charge. But you realize that you accidentally got yourself a girl-friend, right?"

His grin grew. "I am aware of that."

"You can take it back, you know," she said. She wasn't sure where those words came from, but she felt the need to say them.

His grin died, and he stalked to the couch. He braced a hand on the back and the other on the cushion next to her and leaned in until their noses touched.

"Maxine, I don't want to take the words back. We're dating. It's official. If you want to end this, you'll have to break up with me. And I gotta say, I'm pretty crazy about you. So I think I might be hard to get rid of."

She sighed. "That should sound creepy."

He grinned. "Does it?"

"No. That was actually pretty hot."

He kissed her on the nose, then stood up. "Good. And brace yourself."

Her eyebrows rose. "For what?"

"I've had a realization."

"Oh, boy." She did feel a ripple of trepidation.

"Yeah. I realized I could be the delightful one who makes everything cozy, and cheery, and awesome."

Her eyebrows stayed up. "Delightful, cozy, and cheerful?"

He looked very proud of himself. "Yeah, I think I'm going to be the Stanley Sunshine of our relationship."

Max snorted. "The *who*?"

"They always call the happy, perky woman Susie Sunshine, right? Why is there no term for a happy and cheerful man?"

"Oh, I think there is," Max said. "I believe it's annoying and friendless."

He gave her another grin and turned toward the door. "I'll be back with lunch soon."

She watched him leave, then sank back onto the cushions.

"What the hell just happened?" she asked the empty cabin.

When they'd crossed the threshold, they had been two people who weren't sure how much they liked each other, pretending to be in a relationship.

Now they were officially dating, and Spencer had decided he was in charge of the "sunshine."

But as she thought about that, she couldn't help but be curious about how this would play out.

There was a chance she might end up with some home-baked brownies, and how could she be upset about that?

As long as she didn't end up wanting to stab cheerful Spencer with a fork.

CHAPTER TEN

"ARE you sure you don't want to make shrimp and grits, or maybe catfish or something?"

"I really need it to be enchiladas," Spencer told Cora Allain, Ellie Landry's business partner and best friend, as he leaned against her workstation in the middle of the kitchen at the bar.

He needed to make this symbolic. Max would love it.

He was ninety-five percent sure.

"Well, all right," Cora said. "I can help you with that. It's not a usual, but I should have everything we need."

He leaned in and kissed her on top of the head. "You're the best. Seriously."

"Do you want me to just make them for you, and you can bake them later?"

"Oh no, no, I want to make them myself."

Cora looked dubious, but she smiled and patted his cheek. "I'll write it all down and gather all the ingredients for you."

This was going to be great. Max was absolutely right. Not only should he make his own brownies, but he should make his own enchiladas too. *And* he should make enchiladas for Max.

"I'm going to order some lunch from Ellie, and then I'll be back to grab that."

"I'll bring it out to you. No worries. What are you and Max eating? I'll probably be making most of that too," Cora said with a wink.

He laughed and looked around the kitchen. This was Cora's domain. Ellie took care of everything up front, including the bar, but Cora was the genius behind ninety percent of the food. Though the gumbo recipe was Ellie's and it was a sworn secret. Ellie always told everyone she'd reveal the recipe at her funeral. But they'd have to roll her body over in the casket to get to it. So it would literally be over her dead body. He wondered if it was a secret from Cora and knew he wouldn't be a bit surprised to find out it was.

"Max is a burger girl. Medium rare. All the fixings," he said.

Cora nodded. "No problem. And I assume you're doing gumbo."

Spencer grinned. "Absolutely."

"Any desserts?"

Dessert. It seemed this was the new most important, talked about thing in his life. "No. I think I'm going to hold off on that right now."

Cora turned toward her stove. "Okay, I've got you covered."

"Thanks, Cora."

He pushed through the swinging doors that separated the kitchen from the front of the bar.

"Well, well, well, if it isn't lover boy."

Spencer gave Caroline Holland a huge grin as she met him at the end of the long stretch of scarred wood where Ellie Landry served up some of the best drinks, hilarious stories, and sage advice southern Louisiana had to offer.

Behind Caroline, he saw Zander, Michael, JD, another of the full-time firefighters and paramedics, and Theo all gathered around what was usually the Landry family table. This time of day, though, everyone was off at work. Feeding alpacas, giving otters check-ups, guiding swamp boat tours, conducting yoga classes, and seemingly a million other things.

"Hey, Caroline." He'd planned to call Caroline if he didn't run into her.

He wanted Max's best friend to hang out with her while he met with the guys. In part because she was, after all, one of the few people that seemed to have been granted admission to Max Keller's inner circle.

But Caroline was also training to join the FBI, and from what Zander had told him, Caroline was getting to be a very good shot. Colin would be meeting with the rest of the guys, so Spencer needed someone who was trained and naturally suspicious hanging out with Max tonight.

"Hey, Caroline? That's it? You bring my best friend to Autre and snuggle her up in a romantic cottage without letting her so much as *text* me the dirty details, and all I get is, 'Hey, Caroline?' As if you two being here together isn't huge news?"

"I didn't keep her from calling you. She's just been… distracted."

Caroline's brows rose. "Has she now? You're not denying that the details would be dirty."

He grinned. "No, I am not."

She narrowed her eyes now. Then she glanced around and moved in closer. "I know you're just faking it."

"But I'm not."

Caroline frowned. "What?"

"I'm in love."

Her frown deepened. "*Excuse me*?"

"I'm in love with Max."

"But…" Caroline looked over at Zander, then back to Spencer. "You're just playing this out because we're in public, right?"

"Nope. She makes me nuts. I can't stay away. So I've decided to quit fighting it."

"It's been a day and a half!" Caroline exclaimed.

"What can I say? I was halfway there already when I kicked

in her door yesterday morning. Spending this time, just the two of us, I fell the rest of the way."

"You're *seriously* in love with Max Keller?"

"Yes."

It felt so good to say it. He would've thought it would feel strange. Or that he would be still getting used to the idea, but it felt amazing to say those words. It felt *right*. It was true that he'd been fighting the idea. On paper, they didn't make sense. Hell, in his head, they didn't make sense.

But there was no other explanation for his feelings.

He wanted to protect her. He wanted to make her happy. He hated the idea that anything hurt her, made her feel insecure, or even made her sad. He would do anything to keep her happy and safe. And it was beyond anything he had ever felt for anyone else.

"Have you told Max this?" Caroline suddenly looked incredibly curious and slightly amused.

"I have." Spencer shook his head. "Okay, I haven't said *I love you*. But I told her that I thought we should date for real, and she agreed."

"Did she?" Caroline seemed surprised by that.

"I'll admit I've been turning on the charm and being extra sweet lately, but I think she knows I'm sincere, and I have to admit that the feelings seem genuinely mutual."

"Oh, I'm not worried about Max seeing through your charm and sweetness," Caroline said. "Max's bullshit meter is excellent."

Spencer nodded. "One of my favorite things about her."

"Same."

"She told me about her childhood and her parents. How she was on her own so much. The things that she thought were normal until she met your family."

Caroline winced. "Yeah. Well, it turned out my family was no epitome of normalcy."

Spencer had to agree. "But early on, being with your family showed Max what she was missing."

"Okay." Caroline seemed sincerely interested.

Spencer knew that Caroline would kill him if he hurt Max. And she'd probably have Zander's backing. And Zander would probably have Michael and Theo's help. They could dispose of his body easily. And they'd come up with a great story that even his own mom and dad would believe. So he had to convince Caroline that what he was feeling was real.

"I realized I can help us both."

Caroline studied him. "What do you mean?"

"Earlier today, Max and I talked about how she could be an amazing mom because of what she *didn't* have. She would work to give her kids the things she didn't have but missed. And I realized I could be an amazing boyfriend because of the things I don't have that I want. Instead of looking for someone to give me those things, I'll give them to Max. Making her happy makes me happy."

"What kind of things?" Caroline asked.

"I want a safe, happy, comfortable home, with people there who take care of each other. I want to come in at the end of the day, and find someone is there for me. I want there to be smiles and laughter, noise and dinner, and a relaxing routine where I can balance out the craziness and chaos of my work day."

Caroline didn't say anything. She just listened.

"Max never had any of that. Certainly not consistently where she could count on it, and it was a comforting, happy thing. She often came home to an empty apartment where she'd spend the evening alone. She had to cook for herself, entertain herself, put herself to bed."

Caroline's expression softened. "Yeah, I know," she said softly. "I didn't know for a long time when we were kids, but once I found out, it broke my heart."

His too. He almost couldn't think about little girl Max on her own, making her burger and beans, putting herself to bed to the sound of the neighbor's TV, so she didn't feel alone, being kind to *rats* because she wanted to nurture something.

"Max said something today that made me realize that instead of looking for someone else to be all that for me, I need to create it for myself. She did it as a little girl with no resources. She made her home as comfortable as she could. She found a way to make it hers. I'm a grown man and can imagine and create any home and routine I want," he said. *"But* I can make all that happen *for Max* too. Ever since the wedding, I've had this strange urge to be close to her and be *with* her, but I didn't understand it because we're so different. Now I've realized *this* is why. We need each other to make this home life we both want and need deep down."

"Are you drunk right now?" Caroline asked.

He laughed. "No. Not at all."

Caroline leaned in. "And you really will give her all of those things?"

"I can sure as hell try. We can give them to each other. I think Max deserves to have someone to come home to. And someone who wants to come home to her."

Caroline nodded. "I agree. She deserves to be appreciated, loved, and taken care of."

Spencer narrowed his eyes. "You don't think I can do that?"

"Of course I think you can if you want to. Though you have a crazy schedule and a job that can sometimes be a bit unusual."

At those words, a surge of confidence and pride went through him. He was proud of his job. He did think it was important, cerebrally, but he hadn't *felt* it in a while.

Again, it was because of what Max had said to him today that he could say out loud, "What I do is vital. And I'm damned good at it. I need to keep doing it, but I need to be with someone who feels that way about it too."

Caroline finally nodded. "Okay. This all sounds good. And interesting. And I can't wait to see what happens. And, of course, I'll not only kill you if you hurt her, but I'll do it slowly. Piece by piece."

He nodded. "Of course."

"Okay, then."

That was as much of a blessing as he was likely to get until he could prove to Caroline that he was crazy about Max.

Not just crazy.

"I'm here to pick up some food to take back to the cottage for lunch. And then I'm hoping you'll come over tonight and stay with her while I have a meeting with the guys."

Caroline sobered. "Yes, of course. I hate that she's here for protection, but I also love that she can come here for protection."

"I feel the same."

"What can I get you, Spencer?"

He turned to greet Ellie Landry. She had long gray hair that she typically wore woven into a braid that fell to her lower back. She needed a step stool behind the bar to wait on her patrons, but her personality, attitude, and heart were those of a giant.

"I put my order in with Cora," he told her with a grin. "How are you?"

"I'm fabulous knowing that I get to see Max again so soon. And you too, I guess." She gave him a wink. "Seems like you're gettin' smarter, so that'll make it easier to put up with ya."

"Smarter, huh? Why's that?"

"Makin' sure that feisty redhead didn't get away."

Ah. Well, Ellie had a point. "She made me work for it."

"If she's worth it, she won't ever stop. But it goes both ways." Ellie pointed a finger at him. "It's okay to need a hero once in a while, too, you know."

"What are you talkin' about?" He smiled at her, but he felt a tightness in his gut.

"You boys with the badges," she said, casting a glance at the table behind him. There was affection in her gaze and a touch of exasperation. "Always wanting to be the heroes and not realizing that bein' saved—havin' someone *see* you and decide you're worth it, and bein' willin' to jump in and pull you out of whatever it is that's threatening you—is maybe the best damned thing that can happen to a person. Everyone should know what that's like. Even those of you doin' the savin' most of the time."

Spencer had heard his cousins talk about how their grandmother's advice and wisdom sometimes just came out of the blue and smacked them upside the head. The way her hand would do at times when they were growing up, and she needed them to listen and learn. But he'd never experienced it himself.

He swallowed hard. "I will keep that in mind."

"Just take her hand, Spencer. Every time Max reaches out for you. Sometimes she might be reaching so you can pull her up. But sometimes, she'll be reaching to pull you up. Both times you want to take her hand."

He nodded. Yeah, he sure did.

"Now I gotta get back to work," Ellie said. "Quit distractin' me." She gave him a loving swat on the arm and headed for the other end of the bar and the new patrons who'd just taken seats.

Spencer looked at Caroline. "Wow."

She nodded. "That's how most people feel after they've been Ellie-ed. At least the first time. Though, for me, it never gets less 'wow'."

He laughed. "Ellie-ed?"

"We finally decided it needed to be a verb."

He couldn't disagree.

"You should go sit with the guys while you wait," Caroline said, gesturing toward the table where her fiancé sat.

The men sitting with baskets of fried catfish, boudin balls, and coleslaw looked far too serious.

"What's up?" he asked, kicking a chair out and dropping into it.

Zander jutted his chin toward the table near the windows. Leo was there talking with two guys Spencer didn't recognize. Not that he knew every citizen of Autre. But a lot of the regulars who frequented Ellie's were at least familiar to him.

Spencer regarded his cousin. "What's the deal there?"

It was hardly unusual to see Leo Landry talking and laughing. He did it with strangers every day. Patrons of Ellie's were strangers for only about five minutes. But Zander seemed unhappy about this interaction.

"You remember Lionel Sharpton?"

Spencer nodded. Sharp had partied with them a few times in high school.

"Sharp got mixed up with some guys who've taken over an old abandoned cabin down on the bayou."

"And it's a problem?" Spencer asked. Obviously, it was.

"Was more suspicious than problematic at first," Theo said.

The big man wasn't very chatty. He didn't need many words. His size alone was more than enough to get his job as a game warden done most of the time. People misbehaving straightened up pretty quickly when the 6'5", broad-shouldered, bearded, tattooed man approached. So when Theo shared information, it mattered.

"They're stockpiling guns. And have quite a tech set up out there. Satellites, high-tech cell phones. It's like they're preparing for the apocalypse or something."

That made Spencer sit up a little straighter. "Have they caused any trouble?"

"Only in as far as they are trying to recruit locals," Zander said. "They've offered jobs to some locals who are out of work."

"What kind of work?" Spencer asked.

"Very vague. They don't give out details until someone shows up at the 'job site'. But it's big money. 'On call' stuff. They want guys who have trucks and vans, especially."

Yeah, that sounded suspicious.

"We've made it very clear that they're not welcome here. And that recruiting local guys is not a good idea. So far, they've been turned down by everyone in Autre other than Sharp. Since he started working for them, he's been staying at the cabin more often."

"But no idea what they're up to?"

Zander shook his head. "Not specifically."

Spencer didn't like any of this. But unfortunately, it wasn't illegal to be sketchy and have a bunch of guns and a satellite dish.

Still, he was thankful Zander, Michael, JD, and Theo were keeping an eye on the guys.

"So, what's up with Leo being so friendly with them?"

"I don't know," Zander said, his scowl deepening. "This is the first time I've seen them in here. I intend to ask my grandfather about it as soon as I have a chance, though."

Spencer knew and trusted Leo Landry. The older man had lived in this area all his life. Spencer had to believe Leo had a good reason for being friendly with these men.

"Let me know if you need any help or backup," Spencer said unnecessarily. He knew the guys were aware that he would always have their backs.

"Yeah, we'll see what Leo tells me later." Finally, Zander met Spencer's eyes. "So we're meeting later?"

Spencer nodded. "Yeah, I'll fill you guys in on what's going on, but there's not much so it shouldn't take long."

Michael smirked. "In a hurry to get back home tonight, I suppose?"

"As a matter of fact..." Spencer said, leaning back and assuming a casual posture.

"Well, now that I've... met... Max up close, I see why," Michael said.

"The offer to beat your ass has not expired," Spencer said easily.

Caroline dropped into the seat next to Zander. "He's in love," she told her fiancé.

Zander's eyes lingered on the woman he was clearly head over heels for before returning to Spencer. "Is that right?"

"You don't seem as surprised as Caroline did."

"Can't say that I am. I saw the sparks between you from the very beginning."

Caroline nodded. "Me too. Sparks don't mean love. At least all the time."

"Yeah, well, these were this-girl's-gonna-turn-his-life-upside-down sparks," Zander said.

Caroline leaned in with a grin. "You know about those kinds of sparks?"

"I'm an expert," Zander told her.

The sparks between Zander and Caroline were obvious, even just sitting at a table in a bar with them.

Spencer looked over at Michael and JD and Theo. "Let me know if I get like that?"

Michael snorted. "You're just about there, buddy."

JD rolled his eyes. "You're going to be disgusting too?"

Zander chuckled. "He's just jealous. JD's a romantic."

Spencer laughed. "Are you?"

The firefighter lifted a shoulder. "You get drunk one night and tell the guys that there's a girl who got away, and suddenly you're 'romantic'," he said, lifting his fingers in air quotes.

"You mean a girl who got away who you came to Louisiana to win back?" Michael said.

"You followed the girl to Louisiana?" Spencer asked.

"It's complicated," JD said. His tone indicated he very much wanted that to be the end of the conversation.

"Sierra," Michael said. "Gorgeous, funny, sweet, kickass flight nurse. And a really nice—"

"*Okay*," JD said.

"You know her?" Spencer asked Michael.

"I do. She knows Lexi Moreau. I met her when we were all hanging out at Trahan's. But I do a lot of trainings up in New Orleans, and I've run into her several times," Michael said.

Lexi was an ER nurse in New Orleans and was married to Caleb Moreau, a firefighter who was a good friend of several of Spencer's cousins here in Autre.

Michael pinned JD with a look. "I am *not* the only one who's noticed her."

"Shut up, LeClaire," JD muttered.

"Here's your food," Ellie said, dropping a bag on the table in front of Spencer. "Tell your girl that while this will be the best burger she's ever had, I expect to see her in here eating gumbo before she leaves."

"I will tell her," Spencer said. "I'll let her sample mine."

He pushed back from the table as Zander whistled. "Man, it is love if Spencer is sharing his gumbo."

It was love. And Spencer wanted to share his gumbo, and a hell of a lot more, with Max. .

———

MAX HAD TRIED to work while Spencer was gone, but she didn't get very far. She did post her story, though, on her own social media page. It was clear it was not from the *News*. It was also clear that there were ties between Gordon Ridgewood, the men who had been arrested, and the types of chemicals confiscated. She hadn't *said* that Ridgewood had ordered the dumping, hired the men, or even that the chemicals belonged to his company. But she had pointed out that his company was the only one seeking to expand production, the only one that had been turned down for permits, and one of only three that produced that specific chemical by-product.

Fuck Gordon Ridgewood. If he was mad, he could call her. She'd love to talk to him in person.

Some of that confidence was definitely because of Spencer's encouragement. She always had so many people warning her and telling her to be careful. But Spencer understood that when dealing with criminals, sometimes you had to take risks. Criminals didn't play by the rules, so thinking outside the box was imperative when it came to keeping them in check.

Coming from the guy who seemed more protective of her than anyone in her life, ever, that was especially meaningful.

But of course, now she had to wait to see if there would be any reaction.

She might never know if Ridgewood had seen the article himself. Even if she got another threat, she couldn't prove it came directly from him. Unless he called her himself. Or showed up on the porch of the cottage.

He might have minions in place to monitor things like this and respond. Someone lower on the totem pole might take offense before it ever reached the upper levels of Ridgewood's world.

That drove her crazy. Did she want to take him down? Of course. Did she want to know that she was getting to him and making him miserable? Yes. If that was all she could have.

But she didn't even really know that she was doing that. She couldn't believe that in all of the years she'd been pursuing, publishing stories about, and helping bring down white-collar criminals, Gordon Ridgewood was unaware of her. And a man in his position, doing the things he was doing, had to worry and wonder what she knew about him.

But they'd never interacted directly.

Did she want to interact with him directly? Maybe.

She wanted him to know her name. She wanted him to know Phil's name. She wanted Ridgewood to know that she held him personally responsible for what had happened at that warehouse.

Whether or not she could ever do anything about it, she at least wanted him to know that there was one person walking the planet who blamed him directly and would never forgive him. Sure, that might not ruffle a single feather or prick his conscience for even a second, but that wasn't a reason to not let him know she was here and wasn't going anywhere.

She heard pots and pans clanging in the kitchen, and she couldn't help but smile.

Despite all her whirling thoughts about Gordon Ridgewood, the sounds of Spencer banging around in the kitchen could make her smile. That was something.

He'd come home from Ellie's with a bunch of bags, but he hadn't wanted her to look inside. He'd blocked them with his body, grinning and laughing and telling her it was a surprise. He'd been almost giddy.

It had been strange. But no stranger than how her heart had melted at the whole thing.

Who was this guy?

Who was *she*?

She didn't like surprises. At. All. She liked to be in control of what happened in her life. She was always in charge. No one told her where to go and what to do or when to do it. Hadn't since she'd been a very little girl.

Now Spencer was not only keeping a secret, but her stomach felt swoopy, and she was smiling about it?

Ugh. He was so annoying. And charming. And cute.

Spencer Landry being cute was going to be her downfall. Sexy she could handle. Charming, she could even steel herself against to an extent. But cute was something she was not prepared for.

As they'd eaten lunch—a burger that might have ruined Monte's for her—he'd told her that he'd run into Caroline and that she was very interested in the fact that the relationship had turned from pretend to real.

Max had groaned. Now she was going to get the third degree tonight. Caroline was going to make her try to explain her feelings for Spencer.

Then again, maybe it wasn't that hard to explain. Falling madly in love didn't take that long to say.

After lunch, he'd sat down with his computer, and they'd both worked quietly together at the table.

But when it was dinner time—even though she'd insisted she wasn't hungry again—he'd hustled her out onto the back porch and helped her get settled, with her leg propped on a chair and more ice. Then he'd returned to the kitchen to make dinner.

Spencer Landry was *making her dinner.*

The guy who had a woman-cooking-for-him fetish was making *her* dinner.

And she wanted to be in there watching.

Sure, guys who could, and would, cook were hot. But Spencer cooking? Especially hot because this was not in his wheelhouse. But he was doing it for her.

Damn, maybe this dating thing could work out after all.

"Okay, it's ready."

She looked up to see Spencer leaning out the back door. He could clearly hardly contain his excitement.

She laughed and set her computer to the side. He was beside her in a second, helping her up from the chair.

"Seriously, Spencer, my knee feels so much better. You don't have to do that."

"I want to be sure," he told her.

"I can walk on it normally. I got around the cottage the whole time you were down at Ellie's."

He frowned. She'd told him that earlier as well, and he hadn't been pleased that she'd been up and around without him.

"Would it kill you just to let someone take care of you?" he asked.

She stopped and looked up at him. "Maybe. I don't know. I've never really had anyone do that."

He only hesitated for a moment before he bent and tossed her over his shoulder.

"Spencer!"

His big hand settled on her butt as he strode into the cottage. "What?"

"So this is how it's going to be? You forcing me to be taken care of?"

He stopped by the kitchen table and let her slide down the front of his body. Slowly. When her feet touched the floor, he pinned her with her gaze. "Yes. If necessary. You deserve to be taken care of, Max. And I'm starting to understand that I'm the best one to do it."

She was a little breathless. Being pressed up against his body always did that to her. "And why is that? Seems like you spent an awful lot of time being the one taken care of."

He nodded. "Exactly. I know how it feels. I know how great it is. You deserve it. Can you just enjoy it?" He skimmed his hands down the sides of her body to her hips. "I know this is new for both of us, but that's what makes it great. We'll figure it out together. I'm definitely going to be annoying sometimes, but you're the perfect person for me to do this with. You'll tell me to back off. You'll call me on any bullshit. You'll know when I'm not sure I'm getting it right, and you'll reassure me."

She stared at him. That all made sense. Which was the crazy part. How could they know each other so well so soon? How could these feelings be so strong?

"You know it's possible once we aren't stuck together in this little cottage all the time that some of this will fade," she said, voicing one of her worries.

"Maybe. And that will simply mean that I'll be able to walk into a room where you are and take a deep breath. I'll be able to think about something other than you for five consecutive minutes. And I won't care about things like, what does golden brown mean when it comes to melted cheese?"

That was romantic and funny and sweet, and it did not make her feelings for him diminish in the least. She laughed and looked toward the table. "This includes golden brown melted cheese?"

"It does."

"I take back everything I said about you taking care of me. You should've led with the cheese."

He reached down and swatted her on the butt. "Don't try to convince me you don't like me carrying you around. I know your panties are a little wet right now."

And then, in the midst of being sweet and romantic, he could be just dirty enough to make that panty thing accurate. Okay, even more true. Because yeah, she liked the carrying thing. More than she *ever* would have expected. Or admitted.

She didn't answer. Instead, she turned her attention to the table.

She took a step forward. "Are these enchiladas?" she asked, focusing on something other than Spencer for the first time. "Oh my God. They smell amazing."

"I know, right?"

His tone had her looking back over at him. Again his expression reminded her of a little boy excited to show off a project he'd completed all by himself.

"Tell me that walking into a room and smelling a delicious home-cooked dinner isn't one of life's simplest and most incredible pleasures."

She took another deep breath. "You know, it really might be."

He focused on her. "You really *never* had this?"

"I mean, not enough that it imprinted on me."

Emotions flickered across his face before he ushered her into one of the chairs, then took the seat across from her. "We're fucking fixing that, Max. I'm serious. My list of girlfriend criteria has now changed. It's the perfect *boyfriend* criteria, and it's all yours."

She shook her head. "Spencer, I don't need that. There's more to—"

"But you don't even know," he cut her off. "I want to give you the simple pleasures. The home, the comfort, the feel of family. You didn't have that. And I don't think you know what you are missing."

She pressed her lips together. He was right, of course. She didn't know what she'd been missing. So she didn't miss it. And she thought she turned out pretty well anyway. He seemed to be pretty crazy about her.

But as she watched him dish enchiladas on her plate, she

couldn't help but wonder if maybe he had a point. How could she say she didn't want something she'd never tried? And this seemed important to him. At least he had adjusted his viewpoint from thinking he needed to find someone to provide all of this for him. Of course, she knew she wouldn't walk in the door at the end of every day and find him in an apron with a big smile. Their jobs wouldn't allow that. And that wasn't what she was looking for. But if he would do this every once in a while, she couldn't be upset. Hell, maybe she would even learn to do it too. And that was a hell of a change-up in a very short amount of time.

He passed her the plate, and she waited for him to dish up his own. Then she picked up her fork. She was excited about this.

They both cut into the cheesy tortillas and lifted their forks.

She took the bite and chewed.

Then frowned.

She looked across the table.

Spencer was scowling.

"Um. This doesn't seem quite right," she said around her bite.

He lifted his napkin and spit his food into it. Then he cut his enchiladas open. "Why isn't the meat cooked all the way?"

Yup. That's what it tasted like—raw chicken.

She followed suit with her napkin and took a big drink of iced tea. "I don't know. Did you cook it?"

"I put it all in the oven. Doesn't that cook chicken?"

Max shrugged. "I would think so. Why wouldn't it?"

He shoved his chair back from the table and crossed to the counter where his phone was lying. He jabbed at a few buttons, then lifted the phone to his ear. "Jordan, how do you cook enchiladas?" He listened for a moment, then said, "Yeah, but start at the very beginning. What is the first thing you do? How do you get it ready for the oven?" He paused again, then swore. "Why do you have to cook the chicken before putting it in the oven?"

He paused. "No, I didn't fucking know that. Cora didn't put that in her note."

Ah. He'd gotten the directions from Cora. The woman probably assumed people knew some of these basic things. Or she'd simply skipped a step that was so automatic she didn't think of it.

He looked over at Max. "Well, she eats medium-rare burgers."

Max looked at her plate and shook her head. Eating a medium rare hamburger and eating not fully cooked chicken were two entirely different things.

Spencer swore again and then said, "Thanks. Don't tell Fletcher or anyone about this, or I'll teach your baby words that make those swearing parrots blush." His tone softened a bit and he almost smiled. "Thanks."

Spencer jabbed a finger at the phone again, clearly disconnecting.

"Well, so… that's not how to make enchiladas exactly."

Max looked at him, knowing that she shouldn't laugh. He was obviously devastated. But honestly? This was still the sweetest thing anyone had done for her in a very long time.

"Spencer—"

"Don't say it. Don't try to make me feel better. Don't tell me that it's the thought that counts."

"I was actually going to offer to make *you* dinner."

He shoved a hand through his hair. "I'm asking this only because I don't want to go to Ellie's and get food because then I'll have to tell them why the enchiladas didn't turn out."

"You made a big deal of making the enchiladas for me tonight when you were up there?"

"Yeah."

God, yeah, he was cute. She was so screwed.

She grinned. "Okay. What's your question?" She already knew.

He looked at her with apprehension. "What would you make?"

"One of the things that I make at home a lot."

"Please say peanut butter and jelly. Please say peanut butter and jelly."

She laughed. "Macaroni and cheese and hot dogs."

He groaned. "Woman, I *really* need to take care of you."

Yeah, maybe he did. And maybe he was already doing a pretty damned good job of it.

"Let's go raid Heather's pantry," she said, pushing her chair back and reaching for his hand.

CHAPTER ELEVEN

Max let Caroline and Fiona in while Spencer was still getting ready in the bathroom.

"Hey, you two," Max greeted.

She was surprised to see Fiona but not disappointed. The wildlife rescuer was an interesting woman, and now that Max knew she had a royal bloodline, she couldn't wait to ask her more questions. She also knew that Fiona and Caroline had gotten closer since Caroline's move to Autre, and Max was looking forward to getting to know her friend's new friend better.

"I brought Fi along because I can't drink tonight," Caroline said.

Max frowned. "Why can't you drink tonight?"

"I'm on protect-Max duty while Spencer's gone. If I'm not one hundred percent, I have a feeling he'll kick my ass."

Max grimaced. "I wouldn't go that far. But yeah, he's a little..."

"Intense?" Caroline filled in.

That wasn't a terrible word. "Protective," Max said. "He's taking this threat very seriously. Which I appreciate. Of course."

"He's also madly in love with you. And from what Zander

has said, that is brand-new stuff. He's in new territory and seems to be overreacting a little."

Madly in love with you. Max felt that rock through her. Surely it wasn't true. They didn't know each other well enough to be madly in love. But things felt a little... mad. She definitely felt some nice, warm, swoony feelings for him.

Max cleared her throat. "Overreacting is kind of Spencer's M.O."

Caroline grinned. "Not according to Zander."

Fiona headed for the kitchen to set down the margarita supplies. "I can speak from experience when I tell you that it is all kinds of fun to have a big growly guy all worked up over you."

Well, no matter what she believed about the in-love stuff, he definitely seemed worked up. Max shook her head. "I don't know how to handle it. Seriously. No one has ever been this emotional about me."

"But they should have been."

Caroline's tone was serious, and when Max turned to face her, she found her friend looking almost sad.

Caroline grasped her upper arms and squeezed her. "You deserve to have someone worked up about you, Max. I'm thrilled that Spencer has seen that." She pulled Max in for a hug. "You have always been on my side for everything. You've always been there for me. And I don't think I was as good a friend in return. I am so glad you have Spencer on your side."

Max wasn't sure what to say. Caroline had always been a great friend. Even when her family had fallen into sudden riches and Caroline had moved to a new part of the city in a new school, she and Max stayed in touch. She knew that their friendship meant a lot to Caroline.

"Don't be ridiculous," Max told her, hugging her back. "You're an amazing friend. I love you, and I know you love me."

Caroline pulled back. "Of course I do. And I know that you

know that. But you deserve to have someone who is… intense about you."

"It's going to fade. This is all new. We're stuck here together in this cottage. Spencer's going through something emotional himself. It will all calm down."

Just then, Spencer strode into the room. He gave Fiona and Caroline a huge grin. "Evenin', ladies."

"Reporting for duty." Caroline saluted him.

"Yeah, I'm sorry I made you come over to see your best friend and drink margaritas." He gave Max, Fiona, and the blender a little frown.

"Relax. I'm not drinking. Fiona's in charge of that," Caroline said.

"Well, I *know* you can keep a secret," Spencer said to Fiona. "Did Caroline fill you in?"

Fiona and Caroline exchanged a look.

"Fiona," Spencer said, his voice low and full of warning.

Max felt a shiver go through her. She loved that growly, I'm-in-charge voice of his. Damn. She would never have guessed bossy would be a turn-on for her.

Fiona sighed. "Fine. Yes. She filled me in."

"She's good," Caroline rushed to assure him. "She deals with some real scumbags."

Spencer nodded. "Fine. But don't you be getting Knox all worked up about this."

Max didn't know Knox well, but she knew that the grumpy city manager was very protective of his town and its people. She hated the idea that her being here might piss him off.

Fiona seemed to see something on her face. "Hey," she said. "He's fine. Knox would want you safe. But you've got Spencer and the other badges, so there's nothing else he needs to know."

Max blew out a breath.

"Hey."

She looked at Spencer.

"Come here." He held out his hand, and she took it.

He tugged her to the door, then turned her and pressed her against it. He kept her face in his hands. "Do *not* feel bad about being here. This is where you need to be. With me. You're safe here. And I'm here for you. But so is everyone else. They don't need to know *why* you're here to care. Yes, we've got Zander, Michael, Theo, and Colin, and I'm going to fill them all in. But Knox, Leo, Ellie, Zeke, Sawyer… every single one of them will have your back and do *anything* for you, even without knowing the whole story."

She felt those words wash over her. They were so tempting. "I don't know how to have that many people caring."

He gave her a warm, affectionate smile. "You'll get used to it."

Her stomach flipped. She wanted to get used to that. She wanted to be a part of all of this. With him.

Minus the guy who might want her dead.

She wet her lips. "Okay."

Spencer lowered his mouth. He kissed her hot, deep, and for much longer than was probably appropriate with an audience.

When he lifted his head, he said roughly, "Be good tonight."

"I intend to be."

"I won't be gone long."

"Spencer, I'm fine. Have fun with your friends."

"I'd rather be here."

That warmed her. It shouldn't. She shouldn't keep falling for these things he kept saying. He was caught up in all of these new emotions and this fantasy-playing-house situation they had going on. But it still made her feel swoony. "I'll be here when you get back."

He bent his head and kissed her again. "Love that."

Then he turned her away from the door. "See you later," he called to the girls, then disappeared through the door, pulling it shut behind him.

Max turned the lock, slumped against the door facing the other two women, and blew out a breath.

They both burst out laughing.

"You're screwed," Fiona said.

"Oh, for sure," Caroline agreed.

"I have no idea what to do with him," Max said.

Fiona poured blended margarita into two glasses and then carried them toward Max. "Oh, I have a few ideas. Let's go out on the back patio, and we can talk about them."

Max laughed. "Well, in *those* cases, I'm covered. But he is just... so much. One minute we're fighting and annoying each other, and the next, we're screwing each other's brains out on my couch. Then we're fighting again, and then he's suddenly head over heels in love with me and wanting to take care of me and bend over backward to make me happy."

Caroline grabbed a bottle of water from the fridge. "That's how it should be, babe."

"I feel like my life has been turned upside down."

Fiona handed her a glass. "You know how we say that people come into your life?"

Max nodded. "Sure."

"Well, I've realized that *most* people come into your life. Some people just pass through your life. But there are a few who *arrive* in your life," Fiona said, making jazz fingers with one hand on the word "arrive." She went on, "It's like an event. Whatever things were like before are suddenly different and will never be the same after those people show up."

Max nodded. "That is exactly how this feels."

"Yeah, this is back-patio-cold-drink talk for sure," Caroline announced. "Let's go. This cottage is adorable, and I can't wait to see your view out back."

Max's phone dinged with a notification, and she pulled it from her pocket and checked it without thinking. It was a notification from the post she'd put up on Facebook earlier.

She opened it and scanned the comments as she followed the girls to the back patio.

She stopped just before she got to the doors.

Stephen White: Obviously, you think you're pretty smart. But let's see if you're smart enough to keep from getting stung now that you've stirred up a hornet's nest.

She read it three times. Yeah, every time that sounded like a threat. And the guy's name was familiar. It wasn't Gordon Ridgewood, of course. But this guy had definitely been involved in a couple of other situations—a money-laundering scheme and a million dollars that had gone missing from a political campaign last year—that circled back to Ridgewood.

But now, as she read this, she didn't think Ridgewood was behind this comment. Or the bomb threat. It hit her suddenly that this didn't *feel* like Ridgewood. It wasn't that he wasn't an evil bastard, but the truth was, he didn't need to issue threats. He'd just hurt her if he wanted to and thought he could away with it. And it wouldn't be physical harm. That was too messy for a guy like Gordon Ridgewood. No, he'd go after her reputation. Or her bank account. Or her job. Or her relationships. He'd stir up more lasting trouble. Trouble that would show her his power and connections.

Anyone could issue threats of physical violence. Hell, almost anyone could carry that out too.

Not just anyone could make a lie convincing enough to ruin someone's life. Not just anyone could get to someone's bank account and drain it. Not just anyone could spy on someone and mess with their personal and professional relationships. That took power and a network. And patience. And a huge grudge.

Max realized that's what Ridgewood would do if he wanted to go after her.

It was just like what she wanted to do to him. Except she was going to use the truth to go after him rather than making up lies to ruin him.

She wasn't sure he cared about her enough to do any of those things, but in case he did, she was going to ensure that he understood she had some power and connections as well. She hadn't been following and studying white-collar criminals all these years without learning a thing or two about how they operated. And about their egos.

Her conversation with Spencer from breakfast came back to her.

Could it be enough to just annoy the hell out of Gordon Ridgewood?

If that's all she could have, then yes.

"Hey, ladies, I'll be there in just a second," she called. "Bathroom break."

She turned for the bedroom and her laptop. But she came up short in the doorway. Her breath lodged in her lungs.

The room had been rearranged.

The bed had been turned, so the head of the bed was now against the wall where the TV was mounted in the living room.

Spencer had to have done this just before he left.

She felt tears stinging her eyes. He'd done it so she could better hear the television when she fell asleep at night. He'd not only remembered that story, but he understood the importance. He wanted her to feel safe and be able to sleep easily here.

Max pressed her hand against her chest, where her heart was suddenly pounding so hard she could feel it against her ribs.

Damn. Maybe the madly-in-love thing *could* happen this fast.

Wiping the tear that had escaped her bottom lashes, she grabbed her laptop and climbed onto the bed. She quickly pulled up her email, then searched for the email address listed on Gordon Ridgewood's business site.

She opened a new message and started attaching photos. Photo one was of a man named Reggie. Reggie had been arrested a couple of times for illegal gun sales.

Photo two was of Reggie and a guy named Anton.

Photo three was a picture of Anton and a woman named Jenna.

And photo four was of Gordon Ridgewood and Jenna at a party with Ridgewood's arm around Jenna and his lips pressed against her neck.

With those all attached, Max included a few simple words. *I'm not the only one that stirs up hornet's nests.* Then she hit send.

These photos were the kinds of things that her editor would never let her publish. She also would not post them on social media because they didn't prove anything.

But she didn't mind letting Gordon Ridgewood know that she had these photos and that she had noticed the connection between them.

Satisfied, she closed her laptop and headed for the back porch.

They'd only been talking about men and drinking margaritas for about ten minutes when she got another notification.

This was an email.

The sender was Gordon Ridgewood, and the message was *What do you want?*

She was tempted to write *For you to take a leap off the High Rise.*

Her reply was simply, *Just wanted you to know that I know.*

She sent that off and then shut down her email.

She didn't need to do anything more than that. She didn't need to talk with him any further. There might come a time when she could bring Gordon Ridgewood down. If that opportunity came, she would gladly take it.

But she could also keep digging up dirt, exposing it to the public when appropriate, and making sure Ridgewood knew that she had it when it wasn't appropriate for public consumption.

Being a constant negative presence in his life the way he was in hers could be enough.

She lifted her margarita to her lips and smiled at the two women on the patio with her. Then she thought about the big, hot man who had kissed her before he'd left and who was coming home to her tonight.

Yeah, she could put Gordon Ridgewood away in her pocket,

shut him off, and enjoy not constantly thinking about him and her work after all.

"Hey," she asked Fiona and Caroline. "Do you girls know how to make brownies by chance?"

"I'M NOT LETTING that Irishman anywhere near my sausages."

Theo strode onto Colin's back patio, a pair of metal tongs in one hand and a package of brats in the other.

Zander gave Spencer a wry grin. "Whenever we come to Colin's, he wants to barbecue. He's terrible at it."

They were at Colin's house tonight because it was the only place other than the bayou cabin where they could talk freely, and Spencer had asked if they could stay a little closer to the bed and breakfast.

He'd made it sound as if it was because he wanted to be closer in case anything happened, but all of the men were on to him. Clearly, he didn't want to be too far from Max for long. He didn't want a long boat ride out to the cabin and then back. He already wished that he hadn't had to leave her at all.

Not because he was afraid for her safety. He just wanted to be with her. He'd felt that way for a long time. Even after the wedding, and certainly, after the night he'd spent with her, he couldn't get enough of her. But now, after admitting how he felt, it was like a dam had broken. He was sure she was right that some of this would fade as it became a regular part of his life, and they spent more time together, but right now, he just wanted to wallow in it.

Still, he needed to fill these guys in so he had some back-up here in Autre, and Colin's house was the only one that wouldn't have other people showing up while they discussed sensitive matters.

Michael's son Andre was at his place with Michael's mom babysitting.

Zander and JD both lived at the end of Bayou Road, a dead-end road with five houses now occupied by JD, Zander, his brothers, Zeke and Fletcher, and their cousin Mitch. There was no way they could all gather at either of those houses without the other men noticing.

Theo was the only other one with a house in Autre, and his cabin was out on the bayou like their headquarter cabin. Spencer simply didn't want to spend the time on the travel.

So the guys had agreed to gather at Colin's. He did have roommates. Cian and his best friend Henry lived with Colin, but Cian was conducting one of the nighttime swamp boat tours, and no one was quite sure where Henry was.

Spencer wouldn't have minded having Henry around. He had served as Cian's bodyguard for several years. When Cian had been in line for the throne of the small island country of Cara, he'd been assigned protection. Now that his brother, Torin, was heir apparent, the security around Cian and their other siblings had been relaxed. But Henry and Cian were very close friends, and as long as Henry didn't have a better offer, he seemed content to hang out with the young prince.

Knox and Fiona lived behind Colin, and again, it would've been obvious to Knox that there was a large gathering of the men barbecuing on the back patio, and he had not been invited, but Knox had taken Fiona's daughter Saoirse to New Orleans to see her new best friend Stella Trahan and they weren't expected back for a couple of hours.

So these guys had a little time to cover the essential points that Spencer needed them to know.

"What Colin does to meat personally offends me," Theo said, arranging the brats on the grill.

Colin rolled his eyes and lifted his bottle of beer to his mouth. "Perhaps being so picky about how your meat is handled is why you're single and so hard to get along with."

Theo chuckled and shook his head. "Honey, you are wasting that charm on me."

Colin snorted. "If I turned it on, you wouldn't be able to resist. But you are not my type."

Spencer didn't know Colin well, but it looked like the man was fitting right in around here.

"So why *are* you single?" Theo asked.

"Because *I'm* picky about how *my* meat is handled," Colin said with a grin.

They all laughed.

Satisfied with how the brats looked on the grill, Theo lifted his beer. "Here's to finding women who can handle us."

"Amen," Colin said.

The other men all agreed—even Zander, who very much had a woman who could handle him—and lifted their beers.

"Okay, so, Spencer, fill us in while we're all here, sober, and no one's calling 9-1-1," Zander said.

Michael and JD were both on call tonight.

"Great." The sooner he ran down the situation, the sooner he could get back to Max. "I'm just looking for a little extra help keeping eyes and ears open for anyone new in town asking about Max, the *New Orleans News*, or anything related."

"Zander said it was a bomb threat?" Colin asked.

Spencer nodded. "Delivered by hand to the news. But no one saw the guy. Or at least they don't remember seeing him. No one stands out in anyone's memory. It was addressed to her and specifically threatened her. She did a story about chemical dumping in the bayou. Five guys were arrested in the raid on the dock where the dumping was supposed to happen. They're all still in jail, so it wasn't any of them. Now we're looking into known associates."

The men nodded.

"The names of the men arrested are public," Colin said. "Did Max name anyone else in her story?"

"No. But she did name some men who have worked with

those arrested and one company in particular in a social media post," Spencer said.

"And those are the ones you're looking at," Michael said, pointing out the obvious.

"Right. None of them have any connections to any past bombings or bomb threats in the databases."

"The men you picked up aren't talking?" Theo asked. His voice was deeper, and he looked pissed.

Spencer knew that the big man had become a game warden because he genuinely cared about the bayou and the environment and wanted to protect it. He loved camping, fishing, and hunting in this area and wanted others to be able to do all of those things as well. But he wanted it done safely—for the people, animals, and ecosystem. Spencer knew the idea of people dumping chemicals in these waters and threatening plants, animals, and people around here would enrage the man.

"They gave up one guy. He was the one who recruited them for the job. Told them how much they'd make, where they were supposed to meet, told them what they'd be doing," Spencer said. "But he wasn't there that night."

"And that guy?"

"Denies all of it, and we haven't found any proof of what the men are saying. Yet," Spencer added when Theo's jaw tightened.

"And there's no one else? No one tied to *him*?" Zander asked.

"Lots of known associates," Spencer said. "We're working on them."

Colin nodded. "Good. Let me know if you need any private help with… anything."

Spencer met the man's eyes. There were things that Spencer couldn't do as a law enforcement officer. Like, show up on Gordon Ridgewood's front steps to inform Ridgewood that Spencer would kill him if anything happened to Max.

Not that he'd have Colin do *that* specifically, but having a man trained as a special forces operative on his side was nice.

"Thanks."

Colin just gave him a single nod.

"So for now, we just need extra eyes and ears on Max," Zander inserted. "Actually the *places* Max will be. I'd think specifically the cottage, bed and breakfast's main house, and Spencer's truck. If the guy likes bombs, he'll have to plant one somewhere he knows she's going to be. I think the rest of the town is probably safe because there's no way he could predict where else she might be without watching her for a while and we'll notice him before he gets enough intel to work with." Zander glanced at Spencer. "And that's all assuming he ever finds out that she's here in the first place. I don't know how he'd track her. It was smart to bring her here."

"I'll be here with her for as long as I can," Spencer said. "Pretty much twenty-four-seven." But he didn't know how long this was going to take.

He would need to return to work in another few days. Leaving her in Autre was the only option when that happened if they didn't have someone behind bars. He would have to leave her here with the people he loved and trusted most.

"You know we've got your back. And Max's. We will make sure nothing happens to her." Michael's tone and expression were completely solemn.

The rest of the men looked just as serious.

Spencer knew that these men understood keeping people safe. He also believed they would protect Max even if she weren't important to him. They would do whatever they could. But her being connected to him made her even more important. Still, it didn't feel like enough.

"You guys," he started. "I just need you to know that this is the most important thing I've ever asked you. I need to know that she is safe every second while she's here. I don't know if you get it—"

Zander cut in. "We get it. Losing Caroline would be like

having my heart ripped out. The only people I would trust her with *implicitly* if her life was in danger are you guys."

The other men nodded.

"Saoirse is like a daughter to me," Colin said of Fiona's little girl, the girl he'd protected as a bodyguard for the past ten years. "I would die if something happened to her. And I would choose all of you if I needed someone to protect her with me."

"We're with you, Spencer," Michael said.

Spencer reached out and rested a hand on Michael's shoulder. "You're right. I'm sorry. You have a son. And I know you understand this."

Michael just nodded.

JD gave a soft little laugh. "He's not thinking about Andre right now."

Michael shot him a scowl. "I would give my life for my son's."

JD held up both hands. "Man, I know that. Everyone knows that. But when Spencer talks about Max, you're thinking about Ami. Admit it."

Michael didn't deny it. He didn't confirm it either, but that was enough. Spencer peered at Michael. "Ami Landry? Charlie's sister?"

Zander blew out a breath. "I knew you weren't okay that night."

"I was fine," Michael bit off.

"You were not fine," JD argued.

"You're new around here. You're the rookie. How about you mind your business?" Michael asked.

JD didn't look a bit intimidated. "And I work with you more closely than any of the other guys. Zander saw you that night, but I saw you that night and *after*. You were not okay. And I don't think you're okay now."

Spencer cut in. "What the fuck are you talking about? What night? What happened?"

"Ami was in a car accident the night of the wedding," Zander said.

"Charlie and Griffin's wedding?" Spencer asked.

"Yeah. It was late. After you left."

Spencer hadn't heard any of this. "Holy shit. I had no idea. Is she okay?"

Nobody answered immediately, and JD finally said, "She's alive. And she's improving now. But it was pretty serious. She was in the hospital for several days. Unconscious for a couple. I think she's home now, right?" he asked Michael.

"She's home." That was all Michael said.

Spencer had to agree that it was pretty obvious that Michael was not okay. "I didn't know you had feelings for Ami," he said.

"I didn't either," Michael said shortly. "And I don't want to talk about it."

Spencer didn't know Ami as well as he knew Charlie. Ami, Charlie, and their other sister, Abi, had come to Autre in the summers like Spencer and Wyatt had. They'd all run around and raised hell together. But Ami was a few years younger and had a different group of friends. Wyatt probably knew her better than Spencer did. But he was surprised his parents or grandparents hadn't said anything about a second cousin being in a bad car accident.

Spencer knew that the Landry and LeClaire families were very close. Michael's grandmother, Rosalie, was Ellie and Cora's childhood friend. The two families spent a lot of time together, and a couple forming from those two families would be like Autre royalty.

But it could also be complicated. Especially if something didn't work out.

"Sorry, man. I hope she's okay."

Michael just nodded.

"You should go see her. Or call her," JD said.

"No advice about women from you," Michael said crossly.

"You're the one who followed a girl to Louisiana because you're crazy about her but still haven't even told her you're here."

All the attention shifted to JD, just as Michael had expected.

"You haven't even told her you're here?" Zander asked.

"That sounds really stupid," Theo commented.

JD sighed. "Sierra and I have known each other a long time. It's complicated."

"Were you together?" Colin asked.

"Kind of. No. Not really. I don't know."

They all laughed. That was a hell of an answer.

"She works in New Orleans, but she's been on flights that have lifted patients out of here," Michael offered.

There was a beat of tense silence, and Spencer assumed that Sierra had been on duty the night of Ami's accident. Apparently, JD hadn't been on scene when she'd arrived. Or she hadn't recognized him if he had been.

"She came down to Louisiana from Omaha," Michael went on. "She worked with JD's sister on an ambulance crew there. She relocated down here when she got her nursing degree, JD followed her down here, but she has no idea he's here."

"What the hell, man?" Spencer finally asked. "I don't know you very well, but it seems to me that if you uprooted your whole life for this woman, you need to at least tell her."

"Yeah, well, the last time we were together, she told me to call her when I had my shit together."

"And?"

"I'm still working on it."

Again, they all laughed softly, but it wasn't quite as jovial. Spencer understood wanting to be the right man for the woman he was in love with.

"Yeah, well, you better get to work getting that shit together," Michael said. "I saw Sierra at a conference last week. She looked gorgeous, and I was not the only one who noticed."

JD groaned. "What are you trying to do to me?"

"Light a fire under your ass." Michael paused. "No pun intended," he added to the younger firefighter.

They all snorted, and some of the tension left the group.

Spencer checked the brats that Theo had just pulled off the grill. Then he tipped his beer back, wondering how much longer he needed to hang out.

He loved these guys. And he loved catching up with them. This was the first time they'd talked about relationships and not just hook-ups. It seemed that at least a few of them were thinking about getting more serious. This was interesting stuff.

Seeing Zander madly in love was something. Witnessing Michael torn up about a woman, especially one Spencer was related to, was interesting. As was getting to know JD and Colin better. But he had his own relationship to be thinking about now. He had a gorgeous redhead back at a cozy bed and breakfast cottage and could think of a lot better ways to spend his time right now.

"Colin!"

They all looked over to see a little girl running across the backyard toward them.

"Hope we're done," Colin said with a huge grin as he started across the grass to meet her.

Zander chuckled. "I think we're done with any intel anyway."

"Saoirse, right?" Spencer asked.

"Yep."

They watched Colin catch the girl in his arms and give her a huge hug.

Knox ambled across the grass behind her and met Colin in the middle of their shared backyard. The men shook hands, and Colin grinned as he listened to Saoirse tell him some story.

"That's got to be tough," Michael commented.

Spencer looked at him. "Why? They seem good."

"They are. Colin's really happy for them. Knox and Fiona are great. Knox is a fantastic stepdad to Saoirse. She loves him. But

Colin practically raised her. He went from essentially being her dad to seeing her only once in a while. I think he misses the hell out of her."

Spencer studied them. Saoirse was lucky to have all of these adults in her life loving her and supporting her, but he hadn't thought about Colin's side of it. The man had been Saoirse's bodyguard for ten years. He'd started when Fiona was pregnant. So yeah, he'd been around all of the little girl's life.

"I hadn't thought about it that way."

Michael nodded. "I can't imagine sharing custody of Andre even with his mom."

That wasn't an issue. Lauren, Andre's mom, had been killed in the same explosion that killed Spencer's grandmother. The same one that had killed Theo's brother, Wade. A lot of people had been touched by that tragedy.

"My long shifts are hard enough," Michael went on. "I miss seeing him off to school or to bed those nights. FaceTime saves us. And I'm sure that Colin and Saoirse stay in touch. But it's just so different. She now has a new father figure in her life and is living with Knox and Fiona. Colin is just kind of an extra now. He went from the center of her life to being more of a fun uncle."

Just then, Spencer's phone dinged with a text. He pulled it out and looked at the screen, hoping it was Max giving him a great excuse to go home.

It was Chris. *Have an update. Call me.*

This was what he'd been waiting for. "Need to make a call." These men all got calls like this regularly, so they all just nodded. He stepped away and lifted his phone to his ear.

"What's up?"

"A guy named Stephen White commented on Max's Facebook post today," Chris said.

"Who is Stephen White?"

"He's on the list of known associates with two of the guys arrested. But it wasn't just that. He threatened her in the comment."

Spencer's hand tightened around his phone, and he scowled. "What did he say?"

"That he wondered if she could keep from getting stung now that she'd stirred up a hornet's nest."

"Fuck," Spencer swore. It wasn't a *direct* threat, but the meaning was pretty fucking clear. "Okay, so what are we doing?"

Spencer wanted an address. He wanted to go straight to the guy's house and show him what *stinging* felt like. But his badge kept him from doing that. He glanced at Colin but shut that down quickly and focused on Chris.

"Well, before anyone could do anything, one of the guys who's been watching the *News* building reported a car circling the building three times before a man got out, walked up to the front door, checked the directory, then went back to sit in his car. He waited forty-five minutes without moving. They ran the plates, and it was—"

"Stephen White."

"Bingo."

"So, he saw her post, threatened her in a comment, and then showed up at the *News*."

"Yeah. But commenting on a Facebook post isn't illegal. Neither is going to a public building and sitting in the parking lot."

"Then he just left on his own?"

"Yeah."

"Is his association with the other guys enough to get a judge to let us surveille him or tap his phone or anything?" Spencer asked, already knowing the answer.

"I asked. No."

Spencer shoved a hand through his hair. "Okay. So what's the call?"

"Keep your eyes open. Keep her close. I'm sending you a photo of him and a description and plate for his car. Of course, let us know if he shows up there. They're going to keep an eye on the building. They've also got guys watching her townhouse. If he shows up there, that means he knows who she is and where she lives. That's a whole different thing. And it's possible that a judge would let them watch him more carefully then. They can make a case for stalking even if they can't tie him to the threat."

"Okay. Thanks for the update."

"You bet. How are things going?"

Spencer hesitated. Chris had been his partner for years. They'd shared a lot. Spencer knew Chris's wife and his daughter. "Things are good. Really good. Let's just say that keeping close to her isn't going to be a problem."

There was a pause on Chris's end and then a soft laugh. "So I wasn't imagining those sparks the other day."

"No. Those are very real."

"Well, good for you, man. Just don't let it make you less objective. Or less attentive."

"You got it. It's probably going to make me more attentive. I'm gonna make her crazy."

"Crazy is better than dead."

That comment sucked the air right out of Spencer's lungs. He coughed and made himself breathe. "Yeah. I would agree."

"We'll stay in touch," Chris said.

"You bet."

They disconnected.

Spencer needed a second before he could return to the group. He sucked in a few more breaths. Then he stepped in next to Zander. "I need to get back to the cottage. A guy made a veiled threat on Facebook toward Max and showed up at the building where she works. They can't do much more now, but I want to be close to her."

The guys all nodded.

He forwarded them the photo of Stephen White and his car and license info.

"I'll have Colin head out there later on and do a perimeter check," Zander said.

"I'll head down the bayou too," Theo promised.

"I'll have deputies drive by and just keep a general eye out," Zander said. "We're all just a phone call away."

"I appreciate it. You guys really do make me feel better." He shook all their hands, waved to Colin, and then headed out the door. He knew he had backup, but he needed to get his hands on Max right now.

CHAPTER TWELVE

SPENCER STRODE down the path toward the cottage. His heart rate picked up as he drew closer, and he realized it was because he was coming home to Max.

The cottage was lit up, and he felt the comforting warmth seeping through him. He started for the front door but then heard sounds of music and laughter that led him around the side of the cabin. The three women were up on the back patio talking and laughing. Caroline was seated in one of the chairs with her feet propped on another while Max and Fiona danced to music coming from one of their phones. They both also held margarita glasses.

Spencer paused in the shadows and just watched for a moment. His heart thumped hard, and he realized he didn't need to step inside and smell the aroma of a freshly made home-cooked meal. He didn't need enchiladas or lasagna or brownies. He needed to see this woman like she was now. He wanted to come home to this.

He stepped into the light spilling onto the rear path. "Sounds like you guys are having fun."

Max spun toward him, her eyes lighting up. "Spencer!" She started for the steps and met him at the top. She launched into his arms. He caught her, her arms and legs wrapping around him.

He laughed, balancing himself on the steps. "Hey, there."

Caroline rose from her chair. "She's had a few of those." She nodded toward the glass in Max's hand. The green liquid had sloshed over the side.

Spencer chuckled. "Is that right?"

He thought he might like to see a tipsy Max. Maybe it would help some of her walls come down. Though she had shared a lot with him in the past couple of days. He felt close to her. Protective, yes, but like she'd let him in. Told him things that most people didn't know.

She pulled back to look at him. "I'm glad you're here. But you're early."

"Am I? Sorry to disappoint."

She laughed. "No, not disappointed. But I was going to surprise you."

Fiona crossed to them and took the margarita glass from Max's fingers. "I think it's time for Caroline and me to go."

"Knox and Saoirse are home," Spencer told her as he stepped the rest of the way onto the porch.

The smile that lit her face was full of love. "Oh, good."

"Is Zander still at Colin's?" Caroline asked.

"They were just starting to eat," Spencer said, carrying a clingy Max into the cottage. He liked this. He enjoyed carrying her anyway, but he certainly liked that she was the one initiating the embrace.

"I might have to stop over there. Or maybe I'll go home and dirty text him the whole time and see how long it takes him to come home."

Spencer laughed. His hands were full of Max's ass, and she rested her head on his shoulder. He couldn't have been happier. If Zander stayed away from his opportunity for the same, he was crazy.

"I give it about two minutes," Spencer said.

"Oh, did you boys talk about girls when you were together?" Caroline asked with a grin.

"We did. I had no idea that Michael had feelings for Ami."

Caroline's smile faded a bit. "Yeah, he's taking her accident hard. He was very shaken up about it."

"Sounds like it was bad."

"I think she's past the worst of it. But it was touch and go there for a while."

"Damn," Spencer said softly. "I had no idea."

"That night was busy for a lot of people," Caroline said. Her gaze landed on Max, and her expression was full of affection. "Some of it was really good, though."

He hugged Max tighter. "It definitely was."

Fiona gathered up all of the margarita paraphernalia, and she and Caroline headed for the front door. "This was fun. We'll do it again soon, Max."

Max lifted her head and gave them a little wave. "Love you guys."

"Love you too," Caroline told her.

That warmed Spencer from his chest through his gut. He loved Max. But he really wanted her to be loved by everyone. He wanted her to know that she was surrounded by people who cared about her.

They pulled the door shut behind them, and he crossed the room and locked it. Then he looked down at Max. "So? Is it bedtime?"

His body always liked the idea of bedtime with Max. But especially with her wrapped around him like this and all of the new feelings swirling through him.

"Oh, not yet." She wiggled, and he let her slide down his body. "I was going to surprise you, but we didn't get around to it. We started talking about Caroline, the FBI, Fiona, her giraffes, and everything, and time just got away."

"It's okay. But what do you want to do?"

"I want to make brownies."

That wasn't even on the list of things he'd expected her to say. "You do?"

"I wanted to make them earlier, so the place smelled delicious when you walked in. Like you always wanted."

He reached up and cupped her face. "I don't need brownies. Not if you're on the other side of the door."

She pressed her cheek into his hand. "You are so cute."

He lifted an eyebrow. "Cute? I don't think anyone has called me cute since I was probably about three."

She lifted a shoulder. "Well, it's true. I still want to make brownies. Let's do it together. That would be cool. Then neither of us is making it for the other one or for ourselves. We're doing it together." She grabbed his hand and started for the door. "Yes, this is great. Let's make brownies together. They'll be so fun and so… symbolic." She threw one arm wide, enthusiastically, and almost whacked him in the face.

He caught her hand and pressed a kiss to the back.

He knew she was tipsy, but speaking of cute, Max Keller fit that description. Her hair was wild around her face from the breeze outdoors on the back porch. Her cheeks were flushed from the alcohol and she was talking fast and excitedly.

He let her pull him out the front door and down the path.

"We're going to raid Heather's pantry again?" he asked. "Do you know what ingredients we need?"

She waved her hand. "I looked it up before. She'll have every-thing. It's really basic."

They snuck into Heather's kitchen. At least Spencer was sneaking. Max was giggling, and she hit the leg of the chair with her foot with a loud *whump*.

"If you bang around and get Heather down here, she'll want to make the brownies for us."

That didn't seem like such a bad idea, actually.

But Max shook her head. "No, we have to make these together ourselves."

Spencer loved that she wanted to do this. "Okay, then you need to be quiet."

She giggled and put her finger to her lips. "I'm being quiet."

That was definitely not quiet. He pulled her up against him and covered her lips with his. He kissed her sweetly. It could've gotten heated, but he pulled back as she started to slide her fingers into his hair and arched closer. "Let's get the stuff and go back to the cottage. You don't have to be quiet there."

He had some ideas about activities he'd like to participate in where he wanted her to be very loud.

She pulled him into the pantry and started handing him items off the shelves. Then she crossed to the refrigerator and did the same with the eggs and butter. He took the opportunity to lean in and kiss her neck.

"Mmm," she responded.

She pressed her butt against him, and he was sure she could feel that he was already hard for her.

"You smell so good," he told her gruffly. "And your skin… fuck, I'm still addicted."

"I'm getting kind of addicted to a lot of things about you too."

Her head tipped to the side, and her hair swung away from that side of her neck, exposing more of the delicious skin he wanted. But it was her words that hit him in the gut and heated his body.

He dragged his mouth up and down the side of her neck. "Let's go back to the cottage."

She stepped back and closed the refrigerator door. "Definitely."

She turned in his arms. His were full of brownie ingredients, but she stretched up on her tiptoes and hooked her hand at the back of his neck. She pressed her lips to his. "I really more than like you, Spencer."

"I really more than like you too, Max."

He'd already told everyone else that he was in love with her.

He should probably inform her of the same. But he wanted her fully sober for that conversation.

They made their way back to the cottage, and she made a lot more noise getting bowls and spoons out of the cupboards and drawers. Soon the countertops were strewn with utensils, and she had flour down the front of her dress and all over the floor.

But she was laughing, her eyes sparkling, and he kept stealing kisses, and, quite honestly, this new version of Max was pulling him in and wrapping herself even more tightly around his heart.

As they poured and mixed, she insisted that she knew the right amount of everything. But Spencer gave her the side-eye when she dumped sugar into the bowl without measuring. For a woman who'd never cooked beyond the simplest of childhood favorites, he sincerely doubted she could accurately eyeball a cup of sugar.

She was stirring with a fork instead of a whisk or even a larger spoon. She'd had to fish eggshells out of the batter when she'd cracked the eggs. She had sugar dusting her arms and, somehow, on her cheek. She had cocoa powder on her bare shoulder and also on her cheek. She was making an absolute mess. Still, watching Max attempt to make brownies for him in her tipsy state was the sexiest thing he'd ever seen.

He crowded behind her, pressing his cock against her ass. He swept her hair away from her neck and leaned in to kiss the exposed skin. "Why do I want you so damned much?" he asked, repeating the question from the night at the wedding.

He was still a little baffled by the intensity of his desire for her, but her appeal was becoming clearer all the time.

Maxine Keller was something special. And she'd let him close. He knew she didn't let that happen very often. It made him feel like a fucking king.

She pressed her butt back against him. "Because I am clever, witty, bold, and beautiful?"

He loved that she could quote those words back to him as well.

He spun her, bracing his hands on the counter on either side of her hips. He pinned her with a serious stare. "Yes. That's exactly why. And so much more."

"And because I'm a goddamned marvel in the kitchen!"

She lifted the fork she'd been stirring with, and Spencer pulled back quickly to escape being stabbed in the eye.

He couldn't avoid the flying bits of brownie batter, though. He felt the drops hit his face, and he just grinned.

"Oops." She giggled. Then she tossed the fork over her shoulder, wrapped her arms around his neck, and stretched on tiptoe. The fork clanged against something on the counter, but he didn't care what. Max's tongue was licking off the chocolate that had splattered just to the side of his mouth. Then the bit on his chin. Then the drop on his cheek.

He took her chin between his thumb and finger to hold her still. He reached behind her and dipped a finger into the bowl of batter. Then he painted it over her lower lip. "My turn," he said gruffly.

She let out a shaky breath just before he licked his tongue over her lip.

The batter tasted great like this. But his senses only registered the flavor of *Max*. He took her mouth in a deep, hot kiss. He stroked his tongue inside, claiming hers immediately. She pressed her entire body against his, and his hands went from the counter to her hips, gripping her and pressing her into him. She made a delicious moaning sound, and her hands gripped his shoulders as she tried to climb up even closer.

He reached for the batter again and dragged it over her collarbone and down to the upper curve of her breast.

He pulled his mouth away, breathing a little faster. "Oops."

She was also trying to catch her breath, but she laughed. "Oh, no, whatever will we do about that?"

He lowered his head, running his tongue over the chocolate in long, slow strokes.

Her head fell back.

He slid the strap of her dress off her shoulder, then reached for the bowl again.

But her fingers were already there.

Spencer lifted his head and met her eyes. Their gazes locked as he drew the bodice of her dress down, and she painted brownie batter over her nipple.

He groaned. "Holy fuck, Max."

He lowered his head again, licking and sucking until there was nothing but creamy skin and a hard, wet, pink nipple.

"I suddenly *love* brownies," she told him, her voice soft and husky.

"Need you naked. Right now."

"We have to get the brownies in the oven."

He shook his head. "I don't need brownies, Max. I need you."

She kissed him again. "Why do I want you so much?"

He gave her a cocky half-grin. "Because you deserve to be adored, and no one will ever do it better than me."

He'd meant to give her a flippant response that had to do with his big cock and magic tongue, but instead, the truth came out.

She simply nodded. "I think that's part of it. I'm getting pretty used to that already."

He squeezed her hips. "Good."

"Come on, let me finish making your brownies."

"Fine. But we're making each other brownies." For some reason, he wanted that to be clear.

"Yes. Right." She gave him a bright smile that almost knocked him on his ass.

He dipped his head for another kiss, unable to resist. He took her mouth fully, backing her against the counter and pressing close. His hands stroked from her hips, up her back to the back of her neck. He held her head, drinking her in. She tasted fucking amazing. She sounded fucking amazing. She *felt* fucking amazing. He needed more. All of her.

"Spencer," she finally said, almost a gasp, as he let her up for air.

"Finish the brownies," he said, his voice roughened. "Quickly."

She nodded, her bottom lip between her teeth. He stepped back, and she pulled her dress up as she crouched in front of the cupboard where she'd pulled out the mixing bowls. She started pulling pots and pans out, the metal banging loudly against the wood floor. He grinned at her desperate moves.

"*Finally.*" She held up a glass baking dish.

He took it from her, dumped in the brownie batter, spread it out, and shoved it into the oven. He ignored that the batter didn't quite look right.

Spencer turned and reached for her.

Max dodged his hands. "Hang on." She slid around him and turned the oven on. "There." When she turned back to him, her smile was huge. Proud and mischievous at the same time. "Now we have about twenty-five minutes."

He reached and snagged her wrist. "I can make you come at least twice in that time."

Her breath caught. "Spencer."

He swept her up in his arms and started for the bedroom.

He dropped her onto the mattress and reached to pull off his t-shirt. He watched as she propped up on her elbows.

The sundress bunched high on her thighs, and her hair was tousled. She still had chocolate and sugar on her face and arms, and he couldn't wait to run his tongue over every inch of her.

"I love that fucking dress."

She reached for the hem and pulled it up, revealing the panties she wore.

He growled. "You changed."

She was now wearing the leopard print underwear he'd seen in her drawer in New Orleans.

"Thought you might enjoy these."

"I've decided I love all your panties. Especially when they're on the floor."

Her eyes widened. "I love when you're dirty."

He reached for the panties, hooking his thumbs in the sides, stripping them down her legs, and tossing them to the carpet.

"I love being dirty with you. When we first met, I knew there would be sparks, but darlin', you set me on fire."

He unbuttoned and unzipped to relieve some pressure on his cock but kept his jeans on as he leaned onto the mattress. He knelt between her knees, making her spread them, but braced himself with his hands, holding himself up as he caged her in, just staring at the sexy image beneath him.

"You moved the bed," her voice was soft. She lifted her hand to his cheek, rubbing her palm over his stubble.

"I moved the bed. I want you to be comfortable and happy all the time."

"You make me comfortable and happy, Spencer."

He lowered his head and kissed her again. He dragged his mouth over to her cheek where she had sugar and cocoa, licking, then dragging his mouth down her neck and over to her shoulder. He pulled the bodice of her dress down, tasting every inch of skin he exposed, kissing, sucking, and licking. He got to her nipples again and spent time making them hard, causing her to writhe against him, gasping his name. He loved the feel of her fingers in his hair, curling into his scalp as he wound her tighter and tighter.

He kissed his way over the bunched material at her waist until he got to the sweet spot between her legs. He settled between her thighs. He kissed up the inside of one, stroking his hand over the other.

"Spencer, God, you make me so hot."

"Ditto. As much as I love brownies, this is my favorite flavor." He leaned in and licked her with a long, firm stroke from opening to clit where he circled before repeating the pattern three times.

She arched hard against his mouth. "Oh my God, Spencer!"

"This is just the start. Come for me, Max." He looked up at her, then sucked hard on her clit when their eyes met. Her fingers gripped his hair, and she ground against his mouth. He slipped his hands under her ass, lifted her even closer, and feasted on her.

He felt her knees squeezing on either side of his head and knew she was close. He slipped two fingers inside her and felt the ripples of her orgasm start.

"Spencer!" she cried as she shot over the pinnacle.

At the exact moment he heard a piercing beeping from the other room.

What the hell?

He lifted his head and looked at her, then at the door.

Was that smoke?

Fuck. He pushed himself away from her.

She propped herself up, frowning. "What is that?"

"Stay here." He stomped into the living room and found that, sure enough, the smoke alarm was squealing.

And the stove was on fire.

"Son of a bitch!" He pivoted for the bedroom. "Max, get out here!"

She scrambled off the bed, her dress dropping to the floor. She met him in the doorway.

"Outside! Now!" He pointed at the door.

"Oh my God! What happened?"

She suddenly seemed completely sober.

"Just get outside. Grab your dress," he amended. "Then outside."

The fire seemed contained to the top of the stove, but there was smoke rolling into the rest of the room. Spencer looked around quickly for a fire extinguisher. He was sure that Heather had the place equipped, but he wasn't sure where the damned thing was.

He headed for the stove but felt a grip on his arm.

"Spencer, come on," Max insisted as she started tugging him toward the door. She was now wearing his shirt.

"I'm gonna put it out."

"What if it explodes or something?"

"The stove isn't going to explode,"

"Just come outside with me!"

"I'm going to find the fire extinguisher."

Max blew out a frustrated breath and stopped pulling on his arm. She pivoted and started toward the kitchen. "It's under the sink."

He caught her around the waist and lifted her. He turned, set her on the floor behind him, and shoved her toward the door. "Not you. Go outside."

"I'm not going outside without you."

"Max, don't be an idiot. We don't need to both be in here. It's a stove fire."

"I'm not—"

Then he heard the siren. The fire truck was here. Which meant Michael was here.

Spencer sighed. Well, great.

He walked to the sink, coughing as the smoke billowed around him. He leaned down and pulled the extinguisher out, pulled the pin, and pointed it at the stove.

The fire was out by the time Michael and JD came crashing through the door.

"Max! Spencer!" Michael shouted.

"Yeah, we're good," Spencer said, quickly coming forward.

"Holy shit!" JD swore as he looked around.

Just then Zander came through the back door. "Secure out back."

"Secure in here too," Michael said grimly, pulling his helmet off. "What the *fuck*, Spencer?" he demanded.

Spencer held up his hands, feeling like an ass. "We're okay. Set a dish towel on fire. No one's hurt. Nothing's wrong."

Zander did *not* look amused. "You set a *dish towel* on *fire*?"

"It was an accident, of course," Spencer said, trying to keep his voice steady as it was clear there was a lot of adrenaline pumping through the other three men in the room.

"How did you get here so fast?" Max asked.

"The whole bed and breakfast is set up on an alarm system that comes straight to us," JD explained. "With everything going on with you, we came straight over."

Max looked sheepish as she said, "Oh."

Of course they had.

"We're really sorry," Spencer said, still trying to calm the situation. "That was inexcusable. Thank you so much for getting right over here."

"Jesus, Spencer," Michael finally said, scrubbing a hand over his face and letting out a long breath.

"I know," Spencer assured him. An accidental alarm with everything going on with him and Max being here was a huge mess-up.

"What the fuck were you doing that you set a towel on fire and you didn't put it out before the alarms were set off?" Zander asked, looking around, still clearly very riled.

"We were in the bedroom, the alarm went off, we came out, and there was a fire on the stove," Max offered.

Spencer winced. He would have chosen to leave the bedroom out of the explanation.

Michael approached the stove. There was a scorched dishtowel on top covered in extinguisher foam.

"And?" he asked Spencer.

Spencer had also just turned off the stovetop burner.

"We were baking brownies. We obviously accidentally turned the stovetop on instead of the oven."

He glanced at Max. Her eyes widened, and then she pressed her lips together.

"And there was a towel lying on top of it that caught fire," Spencer finished.

"And you were in the other room?" Michael asked.

"Yes, I wasn't aware of the situation until the alarm went off," Spencer answered.

Now the men took in their state of undress. And clearly the full story clicked into place for them.

Zander sighed. "For fuck's sake, Spencer."

"I see," Michael said, rolling his eyes. But he looked less tense.

"Ah," JD added. He was fighting a smile.

Spencer sighed. Michael had seen Max's panties earlier. Now they would all see a hell of a lot more if she bent over or even lifted her arms.

Max propped a hand on her hip. "You can't be mad at us for getting distracted."

JD outright laughed. "Can't believe the whole place didn't burn down around you, honestly."

She looked sexy as fuck, of course.

"How's the goat bite, by the way?" Michael asked.

Spencer breathed out. His friend was obviously calming now that the threat of danger was over.

"I'm feeling great," Max said. "Not as great as I was about ten minutes ago in the bedroom. But great in general."

Spencer couldn't help his grin. He appreciated that. *Thank you very much, Max.*

"Maybe we should stick around and just make sure there are no more fire hazards. We wouldn't want you guys to be at risk." JD said with a smirk.

"I don't think there's any need for that," Max said. She put a hand on JD's arm and turned him toward the front door. "And I promise any screaming in the next hour or so is *nothing* to worry about."

JD gave a half choke-half laugh. "Damn, girl."

"I could stay and make sure your brownies turn out," Michael said, opening the oven. "These do *not* look right."

"Don't you worry," Max said. "The sweet stuff I'm going to be putting in Spencer's mouth all looks *just fine.*"

Her blatant innuendo caught all of the men in the room by surprise. And Spencer wanted to kiss her. She'd made Michael laugh and Zander was smiling even as he shook his head.

She pulled the door open and looked at the other men expectantly.

"We'll have to write up a report," Michael said, grinning broadly as he crossed the room. "All of the cabins have a fire and alarm system that alerts us and we have to report any findings."

Spencer nodded. "Be sure to mention how hot she looks in my shirt."

"Oh, that will absolutely be a part of the story," Michael said, giving Max a wink. "As will the fact that we were very rudely not invited to stay for the brownies."

Max gave JD another little shove toward the door. "Honestly, those brownies probably are going to suck. And as for the *other* sweet stuff… there's only enough for Spencer."

JD, Michael, and Zander laughed and finally stepped out the door. Spencer, on the other hand, was trying to keep from stomping across the room and throwing her over his shoulder.

Max Keller being that unabashed about their sex life and throwing Zander, Michael and JD out of the cottage was hot as fuck.

Max shut the door and locked it, then turned to face him. "Wow."

"Wow?"

"They just came charging in here to save us."

"Well… yeah." He studied her face. "What's wrong?"

She looked a little stunned. "Nothing. I just… They were really worried."

"Of course they were."

"But I mean, even after they realized it was not a real problem, it took them some time to let it go."

Spencer nodded.

"It felt like more than just a usual firefighter or cop thing."

He was starting to understand what she was working through. "It was," he said. "They were afraid their friends were in danger."

She chewed on her bottom lip for a moment. Then said, "I'm not used to having people break down my doors and charge in to save me. Or to even make me breakfast and leave it outside my door. I just… you all are… I feel…"

He crossed the floor, stopping directly in front of her. "Loved?" he asked.

She tipped her head back to look up at him and nodded.

He lifted his hand to brush her hair back. "You are, Max."

She gave him a wobbly smile. Then said, "Please tell me you didn't turn the oven on."

"No."

"Good."

"Why's that?"

"Because I want you back in my bed and I don't want you leaving for any reason for a very long time."

She stripped off his shirt, letting it drop. She stood there bare naked. Gorgeous. Feisty and bold. Sweet and vulnerable. And everything he'd never realized he wanted.

"There are really big windows and really bright lights on," he said gruffly, lifting a hand to her face. "I don't even know if the guys are all the way up the path."

"Then you better carry me into the bedroom where no one can see us."

———

SPENCER SCOOPED her up and ten seconds later, tossed her onto the mattress again.

Max's body was already hot and melty. She knew that she should be appalled at the fact that they had set a dish towel on fire when they were trying to make brownies, but she couldn't care. She needed to be naked with Spencer. And this felt totally different than the first time he'd showed up at her house. The first night had been amazing. But this time she knew she was crazy about him and that he felt the same way.

He shucked out of his jeans and boxers, kicking his shoes and clothes toward the foot of the bed.

She reached for him as he came down onto the mattress. He pressed her deeper into the comforter as he covered her body with his. He was all hot, hard muscle and rougher skin against hers as she wrapped herself around him.

His hand skimmed down to her ass, squeezing and lifting her against him. His cock was hard and throbbing between them. She reached for it. She wrapped her hand around his length, squeezing and stroking. She needed him stretching and filling her.

His hand slid around to the front, one long finger running over her clit and then dipping into her. "You're still hot and so wet."

"Of course I am," she arched closer to his touch. "I want you all the time, Spencer."

He growled softly and pumped another finger into her.

She squeezed and stroked him. "Need you."

"God, yes. You ready for me?"

"Always," she told him, honestly. She loved the foreplay. She loved his touch and his mouth. His damned tongue was amazing. But she didn't *need* it. His grins, his growls, his gruff words —all of it worked for her. The way he cupped her face, the way he carried her, hell, him turning the bed so that the headboard was against the TV wall, all made her hot and wet and ready for him.

He shifted and proved that he was even more amazing by producing a condom he'd clearly pulled out of his pocket before climbing onto the bed. He rolled it on and then moved between her thighs. She wrapped her legs around him, and he pressed forward, filling her slowly. The delicious stretch was torturous in the best way.

"Yes, Spencer," she practically panted.

"God, I love how you grasp me."

She wasn't sure if he meant the way she was digging her fingers into his back, the way her pussy clamped around him, or the way her heels were digging into his ass. Maybe all of it. She was wrapped around him and never wanted to let go.

He was braced on his elbows so he could look down at her as he flexed his hips, fully sliding home.

"You feel amazing, Max. This is the best it's ever been."

A few days ago, she would've thought this was simply pillow talk. That he was saying sweet things because they were having sex. But she believed him now. There was sincerity and a deeper emotion in his eyes. He was looking at her as if he *adored* her. As if he couldn't believe they were here and how amazing this all felt.

She flexed her muscles around him, and he groaned. "Same," she told him, honestly.

She'd had some good sex, but it was nothing like it was with Spencer.

He was easily the hottest man she'd ever slept with. Her attraction to him was a fourteen on a zero to ten scale. But she knew that this was more than that.

He pulled back and thrust again, slowly, almost gently.

"More," she urged.

"I'm taking my time with you." His voice was tight as if he was fighting for control, though.

He watched her face as he moved, and it felt incredibly intimate. Vulnerable too. But she met his eyes without blinking.

For the first few minutes, it didn't feel like they were chasing an orgasm or here for the pleasure. It was about being connected, about truly feeling one another, about being fully wrapped up in one another in a very literal and metaphorical sense.

But the heat and desire built, and soon the pace naturally started to quicken.

She arched against him, and he adjusted his angle so he could rub against her clit with each stroke.

"Yes, my God, Spencer."

"I have a confession," he told her gruffly, even as he thrust, hitting that spot that was making her toes curl.

"What?"

"In all of those sweet fantasies I had of coming home to dinner and a dog and cuddling on the couch, going to bed and fucking the hottest woman I've ever met to the point that she can barely remember her own name was never part of it."

Her muscles clamped around him, and she pulled in a quick breath.

"But now it is. Being like this with you every night? Kissing you until you're breathless, stripping you naked and licking you until you scream, and watching your eyes get that slightly dazed look when I thrust into you? Watching your mouth fall open and hearing you cry out my name? Feeling this gorgeous pussy clamp down around my cock, and knowing that I gave you the ultimate pleasure? That's all a new part of my fantasy."

"Oh God," she whimpered. "Yes. I want that. I want you to come home to me every night, and I don't care what's for dinner as long as you take me to bed, and I can feel you against me, around me, and in me."

Her words made another growl come from his throat, and his thrusts picked up both in speed and depth. He was thrusting hard and fast now, and she met him stroke for stroke.

She moved her hands to his ass, pressing him close and lifting her hips against him.

"Yes, Spencer, I'm so close."

He shifted and reached between them. His finger found her clit, circling and pressing as he continued to thrust.

It only took a few more seconds for him to wind her tight and then let her go.

She came hard, clamping around him and crying out his name.

Then he scooped his hands under her ass and pounded into her, following shortly with, "Max!" as he emptied everything he had into her.

IT WAS fifteen minutes before either of them lifted their heads from the pillows. Spencer was lying to her side, his arm and leg draped over her possessively. Max loved the heavy weight and heat of him, and she lay in spent bliss against the soft sheets, staring at the ceiling.

But finally, she stretched and scooted to the side of the bed. His hand clamped around her wrist. "Hey."

"Just going to the bathroom. "

"Well, all right." He let her go and stretched, the sheet he'd pulled over them slipping low.

Her eyes widened. He was getting hard again.

He caught her gaze. "You really have no idea what you do to me, do you?"

His voice was husky, and the look on his face was a mix of affection and lust that felt like it melted her bones.

"Maybe not. But I'm looking forward to you showing me."

"I'll go get us some water and straighten up the kitchen," he said, rolling to his side of the bed. "But get back here quick. Need you again."

Tingles tripped through her body, and she hurried to the bathroom.

She blew out a breath as she closed the door behind her.

Spencer Landry was a lot.

But she was getting used to the idea that all of it was hers.

CHAPTER THIRTEEN

SPENCER OPENED HIS EYES. Dammit. It was still dark. That meant that it was still the middle of the night. Or, if not the middle of the night, certainly not a time a normal person would be awake. Max's body was curled up next to his, her sweet ass pressed against his side. Her soft breathing helped calm his heart rate, but he was still awake.

He rolled his head to look at the clock next to the bed. Four fifteen. Fuck.

He'd awakened about one forty-five, which was typical. But he'd rolled over, kissed Max's neck, gotten a soft sigh and a wiggle against his hardening cock. He'd kissed her awake before teasing her nipples and clit to the point where she was begging him to do more. Then he'd eased into her from behind with her leg draped over his hip and made love to her before she drifted back to sleep. He'd fallen back to sleep too and had hoped it was for the rest of the night.

No such luck.

He eased out of the bed without disturbing her, pulled on his sweatpants, and headed out to the living room. At least if the television was on, it wouldn't wake her since she was used to sleeping with that noise. But as he pulled up his streaming accounts and started a random episode of *Schitt's Creek*, he shoved his hand through his hair.

He knew why he was awake. It was the same reason as every other night.

He'd hoped lying next to Max would come with better sleep. It'd been a romantic notion, he knew, but he'd hoped that she would be able to calm some of the turbulent thoughts that disturbed him at night.

But it was almost worse now. His thoughts wouldn't quit spinning and his gut was tight.

They'd been *baking brownies*. One of the nicest, most normal activities there was, and they'd nearly burned the cottage down.

Okay, that was dramatic, but they *had* started a fucking fire.

His stolen sweet, sexy, amazing moments with Max had caused three of his friends to be terrified that either the guy who was after Max had found them or they were trapped in a house fire. And if something *had* happened to him or Max, those men would have never fully recovered from it.

Of course that hadn't happened, but this was how his middle-of-the-night thoughts went.

Chris had told him to stay hypervigilant. And what had he done? Gotten so distracted that he hadn't noticed a *fire* in the next room.

Typically, his can't-sleep angst-ridden thoughts spiraled along the lines of: in the time he'd been laughing and badly baking and making love with Max, dozens of crimes had been committed, and lives had been turned upside down. There had been more than one assault, a few robberies, possibly a rape. And if nothing else, the man who had made a threat to harm Max was still walking around. But tonight, on top of those typical, more general fears, and worries, and guilty realizations, he had a very specific situation to feel bad about.

When the bedroom door swung open, Spencer realized he had missed nearly half the episode.

Max looked sleepy and sweet as she padded toward the

couch. She was wearing his shirt again. She sank down onto the couch next to him and he moved his arm from the back of the couch to loop around her shoulders and pull her up against him.

"Did I wake you?" he asked, kissing the top of her head.

"No. This is my usual time."

Oh yeah. *That* would take getting used to when they lived together.

"What are *you* doing up?" she asked.

"Couldn't sleep."

She looked up at him. "Is everything okay?"

"I don't sleep very deeply," Spencer told her. "I'm up in the night almost every night. I'm usually up more like one a.m., sometimes two. But then I'm up for an hour or two."

"Oh, I'm sorry. That's pretty tough." Her hand came to rest on his stomach. He was shirtless and her hand was warm. But it wasn't a sexual gesture. It felt as if she was trying to comfort him. He moved to put his other hand over it.

"Is that why you were awake a couple of hours ago?"

He gave her a half-grin. "Yeah. Though I did enjoy having something to do with my time rather than pace or watch TV."

She smiled but her fingers flexed against his stomach. "Well, I was very happy to help."

He chuckled softly. He lifted the hand from her shoulder to run it through her hair. God, he loved her hair. He rested his hand against her head.

They were quiet for a moment. Then she asked softly, "Why don't you sleep well, Spencer?"

He should have known she would sense there was a reason for it.

He knew he had to tell her about this. If they were going to be in each other's lives, they needed to know these things. He pulled in a deep breath and blew it out. "The job."

"You can't turn your brain off?"

She probably understood that. He could imagine there were

nights when she lay in bed, going over a story or facts that weren't fitting together quite right.

But that wasn't really it for him. "It's guilt," he said simply.

Max leaned back so she could look at him more fully. "Guilt? Why?"

"The idea of sleeping while bad things happen," he admitted.

Max frowned.

"My dad was a crappy sleeper too," Spencer went on. "One time when I went down to check on him, he told me one time that he had a very hard time with the concept of a peaceful night's sleep and knowing what was out in the world and what people were dealing with." Spencer looked down at her. "The old saying *I don't know how they sleep at night*? Some of us don't."

Her frown deepened. "But that saying refers to the people causing the trouble or doing the bad things. Not the guys investigating it and trying to make it right."

Spencer pulled his fingers through her hair again, feeling calmed by the way the silky strands moved over his skin. "His sleep problems were long-standing. Even when he was a practicing physician at the hospital, he would let cases get to him. But it got so much worse when he was elected coroner."

Max was quiet for several seconds. Spencer was sure she understood. Yes, she found crime and even murder fascinating but he knew she would understand how traumatic it could be for those working in investigations.

"Why did he stay with it if it bothered him so much?"

Spencer's hand stroked through her hair again. "That was also guilt, in a way."

"How so?"

"Did you know the Orleans parish coroner also examines any alleged victim of rape or sexual assault if the case is under criminal investigation?"

Max shook her head. "I didn't."

"They also have a mental health division that's available

twenty-four-seven. They respond to mental health crises and can issue involuntary commitments."

"I didn't know they did all that."

Spencer nodded. "So he's seen some stuff."

"I'll bet."

"I asked him that exact question about why he stayed and he said once he knew the things that happened, and things people were going through, and the way he could be a resource for questions and closure and help, he couldn't step away. He felt like he needed to be a part of it. He wanted to be a part of it." Spencer was quiet for a moment. He'd always been so proud of his dad. And yet so worried. His father had been amazing at his job, but when he'd decided not to run for re-election and to return to only part-time practice, it had been a huge relief for their whole family. Spencer worried less about his mom now too.

"He felt it was his responsibility to stay and do the hard work," Spencer said. "Not everyone can do it. And he was very good at it. He didn't feel like he could leave."

Max sat quietly for nearly a minute. Then she took a breath. "It's okay to take care of your own mental health though," she said softly.

Spencer didn't respond to that right away. He just kept stroking her hair. He knew she was right, of course. It was what he worried about most.

Finally, he said, "That's where my mom came in. The harder it got for him, the more she stepped up to make it better for him at home. She helped him balance it out. She was a full partner. She agreed with him that he had to stay and do the work. That all of the reasons he wanted to be the coroner were important. So she told him she would do whatever it took to help him do it well and to be as happy as he could be."

"Did he know about his clinical depression before that?" Max asked.

"Yes. But I don't think he realized how the job was going to affect him."

"And did he ever get any help dealing with it? Therapy, medications?"

Spencer shook his head. "Not therapy. I think there might've been medications. After the alcohol. But with my mom, he handled it."

They sat quietly again. Then she asked, "Do you want to be an FBI agent?"

His hand went still on her head. It was a fair question. He could already feel her tension. The things she was sorting through. The fact that his job got to him, he had depression in his family and his history, and he was seeking balance. And that he wanted *her*. She was smart. She was putting it together now and wondering how she was going to fit into all of this. The little girl who had only ever had herself to worry about. Who didn't even have a pet.

"More than anything," he answered.

"Really?"

"Absolutely. I believe in what I do. I'm good at it. And we have to have good guys. Sure, there are a lot of bad guys, but that's why the good guys can't give up."

She shifted back so she could look at him more fully. "You think you're letting down the rest of the good guys or letting the bad guys win if you step away?"

"Of course. But more than that I would be letting myself down. I want to be part of something important. I want to be one of the good guys. I just have to make sure that I take care of myself."

"Absolutely, you do. You *have* to take care of yourself. No matter what, but especially when you're aware that something is affecting you."

His hand started moving through her hair again. "And when I find something that works, I need to hang onto it."

Her breath hitched. But there was worry in her eyes. "What do you mean?"

He had to reassure her. "Just like you said—I need to make

my own brownies. Obviously, I need to work on that literally—" he said dryly. "But metaphorically I can take control of my happiness. I can go out and find what I need to be happy and balanced and make sure I have it. But, in addition to that, I like being a part of creating happiness for other people. I love making you happy, Max. I love that we're doing that together and for each other. It feels good."

She just studied him, clearly letting her thoughts spin.

Finally, she gave a little nod. "Okay, I have an idea. Maybe it would help if you know that I'm awake now, and I'm going to sit at my computer and do some work to take care of some bad guys. Maybe you can go back to bed and sleep knowing that someone is taking care of crime and corruption while you rest."

He thought about that. It was worth a shot. Then he nodded. "Okay."

She lifted and pressed her lips to his. "At least try it."

He kissed her again and then stretched up from the couch. But he paused in the bedroom doorway. "Hey, Max?"

"Yeah?"

"I think I should warn you about something."

"What's that?" She looked nervous.

"I'm falling in love with you."

She looked startled, but her face quickly softened into a smile. "Yeah, I'm falling in love with you too," she told him.

His heart kicked hard against his ribs. He took a step forward and she grinned, then pointed at the bedroom. "Go sleep. We can do that later."

He laughed "So you do realize I want to walk over there, throw you over my shoulder, and bring you back to bed."

"I do realize that," she told him, honestly. "But I also know that you need sleep and...." She wet her lips. "I'm worried about you. I want to know that I can help you feel some peace to sleep restfully."

That stopped him in his tracks. She wanted to take care of

him. She didn't really know how. She wasn't the nurturing, oh-baby-let-me-hold-you type maybe, but she wanted to help him.

He had to at least try to sleep. For her. "Okay. But prepare for me to tell you how I feel again later. And to spend a lot of time today naked."

She grinned at that. "Deal."

And five minutes later, he was dead asleep. And he stayed that way for nearly four hours.

———

SPENCER'S PHONE rang and Max looked up from her laptop. They were sitting at the kitchen table where they'd just finished the buttery croissants, homemade jam, and fruit and yogurt parfaits Heather had delivered. It was only morning two and Max knew she was going to think of these breakfast baskets every time she ate a protein bar or cereal in the morning after this.

Now she and Spencer were both working quietly on their computers.

He frowned at the display then lifted the phone. "Landry."

God, she loved that deep, commanding FBI agent voice of his.

She also really liked this homey domestic thing they had going. As long as she didn't think too hard about all of the expectations that Spencer was putting on all of this.

She blocked out what he was saying and tried to concentrate on her screen. But it didn't work well. It hadn't been working for the past hour. She couldn't stop thinking about their conversation before he'd gone back to bed.

It had shaken her a little. She'd used the word "intense" to describe Spencer, but it sounded like he came by it naturally from his father.

And now she couldn't ignore the niggle of trepidation at the back of her mind.

Spencer didn't sleep well because he felt guilty resting and relaxing when bad things were happening out in the world. How would that ever not eat at him? He thought being at home with *her* would help him block that out? Ignore it? She wasn't sure.

And she wasn't sure she was up to the task.

His mother had relied on casseroles and puppies. Okay, probably not really. But she'd obviously leaned hard on routine and keeping things balanced and even.

That wasn't Max's style. She never knew what her day was going to look like. She was not only used to some chaos in her life, but she liked it, and didn't expect that it was going to change as long as she was doing what she loved. She also still stood by the decision to not have a pet if she and Spencer both had crazy schedules.

But this man that she was falling in love with was looking to her to be his safe haven from all of the darkness that he found in his work. It was like he was already convinced that he was going to be depressed and traumatized from his career, and he was just resigned to it.

She knew he couldn't just *decide* not to deal with depression if he didn't want to, and she definitely wanted to support him through any dark times, but it couldn't be her responsibility to *fix* it either.

"I have to go into work." Spencer shoved his chair back as he disconnected the call and stood.

Her eyes flew to his. He looked upset. She frowned. "Oh. Is it about the bomb threat?"

"No." He looked grim. "I wasn't expecting this."

Her stomach tightened. "What's wrong? Is it something bad?"

That was a silly question. Spencer was an FBI agent. It wasn't like his job was painting beautiful works of art or helping a mother cat have kittens or teaching third grade. If he was called in, obviously something bad had happened.

She thought about that. Yeah, his job had a lot of pressure with it and he saw a lot of bad stuff. Every time his phone rang, it was potentially something awful.

Her stomach twisted. That had to be so hard. She was torn between wanting to go to him and just hug him. And get far, far away where she didn't have to feel responsible for making him feel better at all.

She would suck at that. He had to know that now that he knew her better. Why would he even want her to try?

"It's the cold case I told you about," Spencer said.

Max focused. "The teenager?"

He nodded. "We questioned his parents two days after you and I… talked."

She snorted. They had done so much more than talk. But she smiled, proud that she'd given him that idea.

"We also put the detective in charge of the case on leave for doing such a shitty investigation."

Her eyes widened. "No way."

"Yeah. It was a good lead. We went back and interviewed both of them." His scowl returned and he held up his phone. "Turns out his stepfather lied to us, though. They're bringing them in today and they want me there for the questioning."

"I assume you want to be there for the questioning."

"Yes. But I don't want to leave you here alone."

She took a deep breath. "I don't feel alone here." She was surprised to realize she meant that. "I know everyone here has my back."

His expression softened. "They definitely do. You'll be safe. I just…"

"You always want it to be you."

That piece of his personality was partly why his job was so much pressure for him. He was a natural hero. He wanted justice, to right all the wrongs, and he was willing to put himself out there to make sure that happened. When he took on the responsibility for something, he wanted to see it through. They shared a lot of those characteristics. But it was messing with his mental health, and she hated that.

"I don't want you here alone at the cottage though. Especially with Stephen White prowling around the *News*."

"He doesn't know who I am. How would he know I was here?"

Spencer shook his head. "I just don't want to take the risk. These guys have a large network and lots of resources."

Cold trickled through her as she acknowledged that point. "So what should I do?"

She could tell it mattered to him that she asked and that she was willing to follow his direction today. But she wasn't stupid. She needed to stay safe.

She also did not want Spencer worrying about her all day. If he had to go to work and deal with this other case, she wanted him to be able to focus on that. He didn't need the additional stress of what was going on down here. She would be fine.

"I'll drop you off at Ellie's. You can hang out there for a while. I'll find out what Zander, Theo, and Michael have going on today. I'm sure somebody will be able to stick with you."

"I don't need a babysitter."

"No, but I would like you with people. Maybe you can go on the swamp boat tour since we missed ours yesterday."

"That'd be fun. I'm happy to do that. Don't worry about me." She rose and stepped close, giving in to the urge to wrap her arms around him.

His arms came around her immediately. "I'll always worry about you, Max. Kind of part of the deal now."

Yeah, she didn't like that. He'd been looking for a sweet third-grade teacher he wouldn't have to worry about. Maybe that was best for him. Maybe she should try to get Liv's phone number for him.

Of course, that made her feel sick. The idea of Spencer with anyone else made jealousy churn through her, hot and acidic.

"I'm going to head in and shower," he said, kissing the top of her head. "I'll be back tonight, but I don't know what time."

"I'll be here. Just text me when you're on your way back."

She could tell going in for this case was bothering him beyond just leaving her. The case was horrible. A kid had been killed and it was possible that his parents had something to do with it. She hated that might be the truth and that Spencer was going to have to dig into it.

She definitely wanted to be home when he got here tonight.

She looked around the cottage. This wasn't home. They were staying here temporarily, playing house. This was not how things would be when they were back in New Orleans. This was a bubble. A fantasy.

THIRTY MINUTES LATER, Max had been escorted inside Ellie's, put on a stool at the end of the bar, kissed soundly, and given instructions to stay with Michael, JD, Colin, Sawyer, or Leo, then kissed one more time.

She watched Spencer leave and then met his great uncle's gaze.

Leo just lifted his coffee cup with a little smile.

"He's been a little worked up lately. I apologize for all of that," she said, sure that her cheeks were a little pink.

"Never apologize for someone caring about you, sweetheart," Leo said.

"Well, he's overreacting in his caring. We're just… new together, I guess. Figuring out this boyfriend-girlfriend thing." Wow, that sounded stupid.

Leo chuckled. "No offense, but Spencer's had girlfriends. You're a lot more than that."

Hearing Leo say that, made her heart give an extra hard thump. It wasn't like she didn't know Spencer had an extensive dating history. He could have his pick of a number of women who would be perfect for him. Women who would check off his whole list.

She leaned in. There was something about Leo Landry that made her think she could sit and listen to stories all day.

And more, tell him stories.

"Why haven't those relationships worked out?" she asked. "Why hasn't Spencer found his perfect girl yet?"

"Well, she didn't walk in until 'bout a year ago," Leo said, like it was the most obvious thing. "And then it took him a bit to figure out why she was drivin' him so nuts." Leo's eyes found his wife behind the bar where she was pouring beer and laughing at something a patron on the other end of the long expanse of wood had said. "Not all men are blessed with the ability to recognize true love when it's soaking wet with bayou water and yellin' words that would have made my granddaddy blush."

Max couldn't help her smile. "You knew right away?"

"Nah. Took me probably five minutes." He lifted his cup again.

She shook her head. "You really think Spencer's just been waiting for me, huh?"

"Of course."

"You know that I think *that's* over-the-top too, right?"

He nodded. "That's okay. A lot of people think a lot of things we take for granted down here are over-the-top. Don't bother me any. Just means they haven't been having as good a time or been bein' loved as hard as they should have."

Max felt her heart squeeze at that and she had to swallow hard. "Oh."

Leo studied her face. He didn't seem apologetic about clearly hurting her feelings. "Don't worry. You're here now. We'll make up for all of that now that we've got you."

Max felt her eyes stinging and she had to swallow again, not even able to manage an *oh* this time. *You're here now. Now that we've got you.* Those both sounded very… permanent.

And very nice.

Leo just lifted his cup again, seeming content to give her time to gather her thoughts and emotions.

She cleared her throat. "Do people come to you for advice a lot?" she asked. "You seem like the type people spill their guts to."

"Nah." He tipped his head toward Ellie. "They get most of their advice from her."

"Oh." She wondered if Ellie would have any words of wisdom for her.

"They get stories from me."

Max focused on him again. "Stories?"

"Yeah." He set his cup down and folded his arms on the top of the bar. "Advice is usually pretty short and sweet. Ellie gets to the point. Stories take time."

Max felt a smile teasing her lips. Ellie was hustling behind the bar, doing three things at once, talking and laughing while keeping things running. Max had the impression she knew exactly what was on every person's plate and how much was left, as well as their general mood.

Leo was clearly more laid back. He was simply sitting at the bar with a cup of coffee. He wasn't in a hurry. Didn't seem worried about anything. He had the air of a man with more time than anything else. Or maybe more stories than anything else.

It seemed Max had something in common with the older man. "I love stories," she told him.

There was no one else from the family around for the time being. They were all tied up with work and Leo was the only one able to just hang out with her. She still hated the idea that people had to go out of their way to spend time with her today, but she was starting to think that maybe Leo didn't mind a bit. Maybe he needed a new audience for stories the others had heard a few times.

"Okay, about Spencer, first," Leo said.

That got Max to lean in.

"His mother has been telling him that he needs someone to soothe him for years."

Max lifted a brow. "*Soothe* him?"

Leo nodded. "Someone to care for him. She worries. When he and Wyatt left for school, it nearly sent her over the edge, not being able to be there all the time and make sure they were alright."

"But they were? Weren't they?" she asked.

"Yes. Until their grandmother died." Leo's mouth pressed into a grim line. "That explosion rocked our community. And for those boys, it was the first time they had to face that bad, unfair, completely unexpected things could happen to people they loved. Spencer wasn't here when it happened, but Wyatt was in town. He hasn't been able to stay overnight in Autre since."

Max understood that. It had been traumatic, she was sure.

"So all of that really shook their mother too. She didn't know how to help the boys through all of that."

"I thought it was his dad who had some mental health issues."

"Oh him too," Leo agreed. "They found each other, I think, in part because he wanted someone to fuss over him and she wanted someone to fuss over. They're a great match."

Max felt her stomach drop. She was happy to know that perhaps Spencer's mother had been happier than Max had suspected in her marriage, caring for a man with so much pressure and so much angst around his job. But if Spencer was looking for someone like his mom, someone to "fuss over him", *she* was not the right woman.

"And she worries about Spencer even now?"

"All the time. I think some of the women Spencer has dated have been an attempt to make his mom feel better. If he could find a woman to settle down with, Mary Jo would feel better."

Max wrinkled her nose and Leo grinned. They were sitting perpendicular so Leo could watch her with his piercing blue eyes. The man was in his mid-70s, but he seemed at least ten years younger. His sense of humor was sharp like Ellie's, and Max could tell that not much in his family got past him.

She wondered if that extended to guests and the love interests of said family.

She'd been surprised many times by how insightful Spencer was. She wondered if Leo was going to be able to read her as easily. She'd always thought being such a loner made her less emotional, but maybe it just made her worse at hiding her true feelings because she'd never had anyone to hide them from.

And did she want to hide them? The way Leo was watching her right now, made her want to open her mouth and spill her guts.

"Well, Mary Jo is going to be very disappointed in me if she wants Spencer to be with someone like her," Max said.

"At the end of the day, she just wants Spencer to be happy," Leo said. "And you're the right one for that."

Max wanted that to be true. She really did. But what did she know about taking care of another human being's emotional needs?

"I don't know what he sees in me," she blurted.

Leo didn't even blink.

"I don't know how to be a caregiver," she said. "I grew up as an only child, on my own a lot. I take care of myself and I kind of expect other adults to do the same."

Leo simply listened.

"If something went wrong, or I needed something, I figured it out," she went on. "If I was hungry, I figured out how to make food. If I got a bruise, I figured out how to take the pain away. If I was scared, I found ways to comfort myself." She swallowed. "I don't know how to be nurturing."

Finally, Leo spoke. "Don't you?"

She frowned. "No. Obviously."

"You were nurturing for yourself."

She stared at him. "What?"

"You took care of yourself. You had a need, and you found a

way to take care of it. You nurtured yourself. All you have to do is apply that to someone else. Figure out what he needs, and help him get it."

"I can't even make him brownies."

Leo gave her a smile. "I said figure out what he needs. Not what he thinks he wants."

"You don't think he needs brownies?"

"What are the brownies really about?" Leo asked.

"Home. Fun. Comfort. Normalcy," she said easily. Even Spencer realized that.

"Exactly. Give him those things."

"But I'm not home until late at night sometimes. I don't have a normal job or schedule. He thinks my candelabra and my crows are weird. That doesn't comfort him. He wants a dog. We can't have a dog, Leo." She knew she was talking fast and probably not making sense.

Leo reached out and took her hand. "Give him what he needs. Not what he thinks he wants."

She took a deep breath. "Other things can be comforting besides enchiladas and dogs?"

Leo chuckled. "A million things."

"Will he believe that?"

"Show him."

Max shook her head. "I don't know how."

Leo squeezed her fingers and then reached to push her iced tea closer. "You will."

"But *how*?" She really wanted him to *tell her* how to do this.

"You see those three guys over at the table by the window?" Leo asked, picking his cup up again and keeping his eyes on her.

She glanced in that direction. Three men in their late thirties were sitting together eating an early lunch. They wore t-shirts, jeans, and work boots. One had a ball cap on. They looked like every other guy in the bar. She nodded. "Yes."

"They're mixed up in something. I don't know what. They spend time down deep on the bayou in an old cabin that's been fixed up. According to Zander and Theo, they've got a stockpile of weapons and computers."

Max's eyes widened. "Who are they?"

"Don't know. They're not from around here. And Zander made it very clear to them that they're not welcome if they're coming around Autre tryin' to recruit anyone for any shenanigans."

"But he's okay with them eating in here?"

"No, he is not," Leo told her. "But I reminded him it's not his bar."

"Why are *you* okay with them being in here?"

"Because it's harder to mess up a place where you feel you belong and harder to hurt people you know."

Max thought of the stories she'd written over the years and what Spencer was dealing with today. She shook her head. "I don't know about that."

"I'm not sayin' people never hurt people close to them. But it's harder."

"So you're getting to know them and making them feel welcome as a form of protection for Autre and your family?"

"Something like that," Leo agreed. "I know people often turn to groups like that when they feel unheard, desperate, or angry. They're human. And when we treat them that way and realize there are things they need, sometimes we can reach them. Not always. But it's worth a try."

"Do you think you're reaching them?" Max asked, fascinated.

"Well, it all started one day with me giving the guy in the ball cap a sandwich. Now he's sittin' in here with two of his friends. In about two months, I've tripled the number of people who feel comfortable walking in here. I figure that's triple the number of people who are going to think twice about doing something to this place or the people inside it."

"A couple of months? And you started with a sandwich? You are a far more patient person than I am," Max said. "I like to blow things open and burn things down."

Leo chuckled. "I understand the sentiment. I was like that when I was younger. And sometimes, that's the right approach. But the little bits matter, Max. Especially when it comes to people. And it can go both ways. You can slowly push people away, antagonize them, and build up walls brick by brick. Or you can slowly break down the walls, chip away at them, show them who you are a little at a time, and take those steps closer."

Max sat with that for a moment. Both applied. She could slowly and consistently annoy the ever-living shit out of Gordon Ridgewood, and maybe someday, it would mean that he would slip up and make a mistake that would allow her to take him down. Or maybe she would just torture him bit by bit for the rest of his life.

But it also applied to Spencer. Maybe she didn't know right now how to fix everything for him, how to be the perfect woman, how to make a home for him that would be absolutely everything he needed all the time, but she could do little things. She could try. And maybe, over time, they'd figure it out.

"For what it's worth, I really like your stories," she told Leo.

"Oh, darlin', that's one of the short ones. We're just gettin' started."

She chuckled.

Ellie appeared across the bar from them and slid a bowl in front of Max.

Max looked down. "Gumbo? Isn't it a little early?"

"It is never too early or too late for my gumbo."

The aroma hit her, and Max's eyes widened. It smelled amazing. "Well, I—"

Just then, a man moved up to the bar. "Any of you know a Maxine Clermont?"

Max sucked in a quick breath.

This man knew her pen name.

Leo gave her a look. It was quite clearly a *be cool and don't say anything* look.

He swiveled on his stool to face the man. "Why are you interested in her, Denny?" Leo asked.

So the man wasn't a stranger to Leo.

Ellie leaned in onto the bar. "Yeah, who's asking?"

"Just some guy. Gave me a hundred bucks to come in and find out. Anybody in here know her? Or seen her around?"

Max held her breath.

"Yeah, I know her," Leo said.

Maxine stiffened, then worked on breathing normally. She leaned over and took a bite of gumbo, trying to cover her sudden nerves. Obviously, the man didn't know she was Maxine Clermont. But who was asking about her? And why were they asking about her down here?

Out of the corner of her eye, she noticed the three men at the table by the window were paying attention to the conversation.

"The guy just wanted to know if anyone knew her. Specifically, if she's been around."

Leo shook his head and said, "I haven't seen her in a long time. But, I'd like to know who's asking the questions."

Denny shrugged. "Don't know his name."

Leo narrowed his eyes. "Is he from Autre?"

Denny shook his head. "Nope. New Orleans."

"So, you're just takin' money from total strangers and then poking around in our business? Come on, Denny. We should look out for our own, don't you think?" Leo asked.

"I didn't think this Maxine was one of ours. Are you saying that she is?"

"No, I'm not saying that," Leo said easily. He gave Denny a look that seemed to imply the other man was stupid. "What I'm saying is I don't like you coming in here and asking us a bunch of questions about who we know for some stranger from the city."

Denny scoffed. "It's just a question."

"Well, tell your new friend that none of us have seen her. And I'm not giving any information about my friend anyway."

"So she's a friend?" Denny asked.

Leo regarded him for a moment without speaking.

Come on, Leo. Say no. You don't want more trouble.

"Yeah, she is," Leo finally answered.

Worry slithered through Max. Denny had done his job. More or less. He'd found someone in Autre who knew Maxine Clermont.

Someone else might come to town to ask more questions, and they might not be "polite" about Leo's refusal to answer. Yes, he'd said he hadn't seen her in some time, but would this person believe that?

"Like I said, I'm just asking a question," Denny said. He pushed back from the bar and ambled toward the door. "See y'all later."

Leo watched him go, his eyes narrowing.

"I hate that guy," Ellie said.

A moment later, the three men by the window were on their feet and crossed to Leo's side.

"We're going to go talk to Denny," the one in the ball cap said.

"Oh yeah?" Leo asked. He didn't seem surprised.

"Yes, he's poking around about a friend of yours. We can find out who asked Denny to come."

"And we can tell them to knock that shit off," another of the men, this one wearing a gray t-shirt, said.

"You all know Denny?" Leo asked.

"We know him well enough," the third man said. "Well enough to make sure he listens."

Leo studied the other men. It took him a few seconds, but finally he said, "Thank you, boys. I'd appreciate that. I don't like having strangers looking for my friends without an explanation."

Max felt a little shiver trip down her spine. There was an ominous note in Leo's voice. As if he didn't care what these guys did to get the information from Denny or to warn him off. And maybe he didn't. Clearly Leo Landry had spent most, if not all, of his life down on this bayou. He fiercely loved a big, boisterous family and a group of friends who were like family. Max wouldn't be surprised if Leo was willing to do *anything* to keep them safe. And Leo wasn't the type to naively believe that *please* and *thank you* were always the way to get things done.

"No problem," Ball Cap said. "We feel the same way."

Leo gave him a nod.

The three men turned and headed after Denny.

There was a beat of silence, and then Max blew out a breath. "Holy shit."

Ellie reached over and grabbed her hand, squeezing. "You'll be okay. Obviously he doesn't know who you are."

"Yet," Max said.

Leo turned back toward the bar, looking unaffected.

Ellie narrowed her eyes. "You look pretty proud of yourself."

"My new friends are going to take care of the problem. Knew they would."

That was why he'd admitted Maxine Clermont was a friend. He'd known that would get those three guys on their feet and helping him.

Max was impressed.

"Your new friends," Ellie repeated. "You need to be a little more careful about who you trust, Mr. Landry."

"Didn't say I trust them. But I knew they'd return the favors I've extended. I've been kind to them and proved I'd get Zander to let off a little as long as they're not doing anything wrong. Now they're doing me a favor. And they're gonna be a lot more persuasive in telling Denny to back the fuck off than any of us would be."

"You still need to tell Zander," Ellie said, obviously agreeing with him.

Max also had to admit that Leo's friends did seem the types to be most convincing with Denny.

"I'll tell Zander. But I'm gonna wait and see if those guys get a name from Denny."

"The name of the man asking about me?" Max asked.

"Yeah. Denny knows who he is. Or has a photo or something. That man's entirely too paranoid to just be talking to some stranger without getting some information. Wouldn't surprise me if he has the guy's damned license plate."

Max suddenly felt a little better. Not that she trusted this Denny person either or the three men who had been eating sandwiches by the window. But one thing she had learned in her years of following criminals around was that no one knew criminals better than other criminals.

"Well, everybody, do *me* a favor and promise not to tell Spencer about this until he gets back to town tonight."

Leo gave her an interested look. "Why is that?"

"He has a lot going on today," she said. "He doesn't need anything more when things here are fine. He left me in your care, and you are absolutely taking care of me."

Leo grinned. "Always, darling. You're part of the family now."

Max was suddenly choked up, and Ellie obviously noticed. She nudged the bowl of gumbo closer and refilled Max's tea. Then she moved off without a word.

And as she took another bite of amazingly delicious gumbo that warmed her from the inside despite the hot, humid Louisiana summer day, she understood how comforting food could be.

CHAPTER FOURTEEN

"HEY," Spencer greeted Colin as he approached the cottage at the end of his day.

His very fucking long day.

Colin closed the book he'd been reading and stretched up from the Adirondack chair. "Hey."

The man was dressed in athletic shorts, a t-shirt with tennis shoes, and a ball cap. He looked like every other good ol' boy down here. But Spencer knew that he was not only a sharp-shooter but could probably kill a man six or seven different ways with his bare hands.

Spencer liked seeing him sitting on the front porch when he knew Max was inside.

He'd gotten a text from Colin that Max had finished lunch at Ellie's and had taken a swamp boat tour, and was now back at the cottage working. Colin had assured him that he could stay until Spencer got home.

But this cottage wasn't home.

That reality had crashed into him today as he'd returned to work.

The drive into work had been enough to make him realize that, but the reality had been hammered home all day long.

Wearing his suit and tie, questioning a suspect—who, as it turned out, had murdered his stepson—the paperwork, the sandwich from the deli, had all been so *real* he hadn't been able to ignore the fact that the cottage in Autre had felt like a fantasy.

Still, he'd found himself anticipating getting back to the cabin. And Max.

As he walked to his car in the parking lot, he'd been thinking about how much nicer it would be if he were only driving a few minutes to her townhouse or back to his apartment. He just needed to see her. It wasn't the cottage that mattered.

"How was your day?" Colin asked.

"Fucking sucked."

Colin gave a nod. "Figured."

"Thanks for your help."

"Of course. And anytime. Hope you know that."

Spencer dipped his head. "Ditto."

With that, Colin descended the steps and headed for his truck.

Spencer appreciated a man who didn't need a lot of conversation.

He let himself into the cottage and immediately homed in on Max.

She was sitting at the table with her laptop open exactly as he'd pictured on his drive. Her hair was pulled up into a messy bun, she had glasses perched on her nose as she peered at her screen, and she was in the same casual clothes he'd left her in at Ellie's.

She was just so fucking gorgeous.

And it had nothing to do with what she was wearing or how she wore her hair. It was just her.

He took a long deep breath but was frustrated to find that he still felt the tension through his shoulders and knew he had a sleepless night ahead.

She pivoted on her seat and pulled her glasses off her nose. "Hi."

"Hi."

She rose, and he met her halfway across the floor, folding her into a hug.

He loved how much more comfortable she was with the embraces. It had only been a couple of days ago that she'd thought him hugging her was strange.

She leaned back to look up at him. "How'd it go?"

"Long day."

Her brow furrowed. "Well, yeah, you expected that, right?"

"Yeah. I did. He's behind bars now. So I guess it turned out well."

That was true. A bad guy was off the streets. But he'd fucking killed his stepson. And there was a long history of abuse against his wife.

That made Spencer's gut turn. If they'd done a better job investigating before, the guy would've been imprisoned long before this. Hell, if they'd done a better job investigating, the local cops would have realized the stepfather was wanted for selling guns across state lines and the FBI could have gotten involved a lot sooner and maybe *they* would have put the other pieces together.

"So fill in the blanks," Max said. "What did he lie about? What happened?"

Spencer blew out a breath. "I don't want to talk about it. Let's talk about something else. And what do you want to do for dinner? I'm starving."

She frowned. "Ellie and Cora sent a care package. They figured you might be home late and didn't want to subject you to whatever I was going to come up with."

That tugged a small smile out of him. "Sounds good. I'm going to go change."

She let him go and stepped back. He left the room without another word, but he felt restless. He didn't know what else to say. He didn't want to talk about the case. He wanted to leave it at work. This was the first night he and Max would be together as a couple with him back at work, and he wanted to believe things could be normal. They could have dinner, sit on the back porch, watch the sunset, go to bed, and make love. He'd probably be awake around two a.m., but fuck, that *was* normal for him.

Still, their conversation from that morning had been nagging at him all day whenever he stopped long enough to let it in.

His dad had put a lot of pressure on his mom to help with his happiness. Or his mom had put a lot of pressure on herself. Or both. But no, his dad had never sought therapy. He'd never needed it because of his wife. He'd been able to leave the darkness at work and surround himself with happiness when he was at home.

Spencer changed into shorts and a t-shirt, and when he emerged, the scent of spices filled the room. He took a deep breath. That was more like it.

Max turned away from the stove. "Jambalaya. They told me I just had to heat it up."

"Awesome." He crossed to the cupboards and withdrew dishes. Within minutes, they were sitting down to eat. Along with the jambalaya and rice, there was a salad, bread, and more sweet tea.

It was practically perfect.

They ate in silence for a few minutes. Then he asked, "How was *your* day?"

"Good. The swamp boat tour was fun. Leo and I had a nice talk. A bunch of people came up for lunch. I think Leo called them in to make me feel at home."

Spencer smiled at that. Leo probably had, but Spencer had no doubt everyone was happy to meet and spend time with Max. "Did it work?"

She nodded. "I really like your family and friends. They're awesome. We laughed and talked for a couple of hours. The gumbo was amazing. When they all had to get back to work, I came down here. Colin came with me."

"Did you get work done?"

She broke off a piece of bread and chewed, watching him. "I've exchanged some emails with Gordon Ridgewood."

Spencer frowned and sat up. "What kind of emails?"

"Last night, I sent him some photos I have. Nothing I could have published but I wanted him to know I had them."

"What was his reaction?"

"He asked what I wanted. I told him I just wanted him to know that someone knew what he was up to. Then this afternoon I got another message saying that he could be a very good friend to have. But he could also be a very bad enemy."

Spencer's eyes narrowed, and he felt anger surge through him. "That son of a bitch."

Max shook her head. "No. It's good. He was thinking about me. He didn't just let it go."

She looked pleased.

"What did you say to that email?"

"Nothing. I'm going to let him stew. Or think he's intimidated me and shut me up. And I'll send him something else next week.".

Spencer studied her. "You don't think he's behind the bomb threat, do you?"

He didn't know how he could read her so easily, but sometimes he knew exactly what she was thinking.

Max leaned onto her forearms on the table. "I was considering what I know about him. When I could get past my emotions a little bit, I realized a bomb threat is too messy. Too broad. If he was angry with someone and wanted to get back at them for something, he would go directly at them. He would do what I just did and email me directly."

"He could find Maxine Clermont on the *News* website?"

She nodded. "Yes. And he wouldn't make a bomb threat. Not something that I could go to the police with. It would be something more subtle. Again, more like what I'm doing. Little bits. Picking and prodding and annoying me. Getting into my head."

Spencer knew she had a point. A bomb threat was aggressive. More an act of anger and the need to cause chaos. Gordon Ridgewood seemed more polished than that.

At least, until a certain tenacious, daring redhead had come after him for a few years. Max could wear him down. Make him a little paranoid. Maybe make him sloppy. At least make him look over his shoulder every few minutes.

"I also wrote a story about a man whose neighbor built a garage next door. The edge of the garage was *right* on the property line, and the garage blocked the man's view of the flower garden in the park across the street. So he worked his way through local politics from the school board to the elections board to the city council simply so he could propose and pass a bill that would make the garage illegal."

Spencer laughed. "Seriously?"

"Yep. I admire his persistence and audacity."

"Took him a long time to get to his goal."

"But he got there. A little bit at a time. Not everything can be big sweeping changes all at once."

Something in her eyes and tone made Spencer think that all meant something more.

"I guess that's true."

"Like the case that you wrapped up today," she said. "Just because it took a while doesn't mean that it doesn't matter that in the end, you put him away."

Spencer sighed and sat back. "I don't want to talk about it, Max."

"Come on, I told you about my day."

"But your day was good. Mine was full of murder and evil. A horrible person did a horrible thing."

"But you locked him up."

"Yes. Finally."

"So tell me about it."

"No." He frowned. "I just want to forget about it for a few

hours. I'm going to be thinking about it at two fucking a.m. Just give me a few hours of good stuff first, please."

Her eyes filled with concern. "Spencer—"

He shoved back from the table. "I know you love the murder and mayhem, Max, but I'm not going to rehash every case with you every day." He took the dishes and stomped to the sink.

He heard her sigh and then push her chair back. "I made you something."

He braced his hands on the edge of the sink and took a deep breath. Then he turned. "Yeah?"

"Don't get excited. I didn't bake anything or make lasagna. But I was thinking about you all day, and I do have this one thing I make when I want something sweet that does make me feel good and… I wanted to share it with you."

His chest felt tight, but her smile was bright, and he had to treat this with some levity. He peered into the bowl she carried over to him. "Why is everything you make brown?"

She swatted his arm and laughed. "Macaroni and cheese is not brown. "

"Fair enough. What is this?"

"Okay, here's the story. My mom never had time to bake, so I usually showed up empty-handed when I had to take treats to school. Once in a while, they would remember and leave me money so I could go to the store and get something there, but not very often."

He smiled at her even as, once again, his heart ached for the little girl who'd had to fend for herself. "Ho Hos and Oreos?"

"Yes. Except for this one time, somehow Steph, the woman next door, found out that I needed treats for school and showed up with a pan of homemade bars. Do you know what Scotcheroos are?"

He frowned. "Rice Krispies bars with chocolate on top, right?"

Her eyes widened. "Oh, they're so much more than that. Steph is from Nebraska, and they're a big thing in the Midwest.

The Rice Krispies bars have peanut butter in them and the chocolate layer has butterscotch."

Wow. That sounded amazing. Now Spencer wasn't sure he'd ever had a true Scotcheroo. "I'm with you so far," he said.

"So I took them to school, and not only was it the first time I showed up with homemade treats, but apparently these were the best things anyone had ever tasted," Max said, her smile so bright, his heart ached.

"That was the best school party I ever had," she said. "They became my favorite dessert just like that. But of course, I didn't know how to make them. So, I did this instead. And I still do it when I want something sweet or when I need comfort." She met his gaze. "I understand your brownie thing, Spencer. I really do."

He lifted a hand to her cheek but said, "These do *not* look like bars of any kind."

She laughed. "I know. These are deconstructed Scotcheroos. I just melt chocolate chips and peanut butter and butterscotch chips and then stir in Rice Krispies. You get all the tastes even if it's not the right form. And I can make them in small batches, and they're super quick."

"And you figured all this out all by yourself?"

She shrugged one shoulder. "I figured a lot of stuff out all by myself."

Yeah, he supposed this was minor compared to some of it. He dipped a spoon into the bowl and took a taste. She was right that all the flavors were there.

And more, she'd shared this with him knowing he'd had a hard day. His throat felt tight when he said, "Thank you, Max."

"Sure. I know they don't make the whole house smell good."

He shook his head. "I'm figuring out that's not what I really need."

Her expression softened. "Really?"

"Yeah."

"So, what *do* you think you need?"

"Just you. Just coming home and taking a deep breath and knowing there's a place where I can forget all the evil shit for a while."

Her gaze dropped back to the bowl, and she stirred the spoon through the chocolate-coated cereal.

He watched her, wondering what she was thinking and when she would speak. Because he knew she wasn't going to stay quiet.

"There's something you should know," she finally said, lifting her gaze to his.

Spencer felt his entire body stiffen. "Okay." This was not going to be good. He could sense it.

"A guy came into Ellie's looking for me today."

Spencer's eyebrows slammed together.

Surprise, anger, and fear ripped through him. "What do you mean?" He was already pulling his phone from his pocket.

She reached out and took it from him. "A guy came in looking for Maxine Clermont. He was someone everyone here knew. He said some guy offered him money to come in and ask around about me. Leo covered and some guys that he's been making friends with—"

"What guys?" Spencer was aware that his voice was low and ominous.

"I don't know. Some new guys that have been around lately. He's been letting them eat lunch at Ellie's. He said that he told Zander to back off."

"Son of a bitch." Spencer grabbed for his phone. But she held it away from him.

"I'm telling you because I want you to know about all the things in my life. Even the scary, bad things. At first, I was going to keep this from you. I knew you had a hard day and didn't want to add to it. But I'm not going to be that person, Spencer. I will not keep the bad stuff from you, even at home. I am sorry for what your dad went through, and I'm glad your mom was there for him. But I don't think that's healthy. I don't think one person should shoulder all of the burdens for the other person. And if that is what you're looking for, I'm not the right girl. Likewise, if you're looking for someone who will never have anything bad to tell you… that's not going to be me."

Spencer froze, staring at her. "What are you talking about?"

"You want our house to be a haven. And I want that, to an extent. Everyone needs home to be a comfortable and safe place where they feel loved and supported. But keeping the bad stuff away from you is not the way I'm going to do that. I am not going to keep the fender benders away from you. I am not going to *not* tell you when I've had a bad day. And I'm going to tell you when I'm scared or angry or hurt. Just like I want to tell you when I'm happy and excited and feeling great."

He focused on her face, trying to push away the rage and fear he was feeling. She was shaken up. A guy had come to Ellie's asking about her pen name. Someone had paid someone to ask about her.

All of that was sinking in.

Spencer reached out and grasped her upper arms. "I don't want you to keep this stuff from me."

"But you want to keep *your* stuff from *me*. I wanted to tell you about Ridgewood's emails. I'm not solving that problem any time soon. That's going to go on for years. I may *never* solve the problem of Gordon Ridgewood. I may rant about that man twice a week until I'm ninety. But I want to tell you about it when he emails and pisses me off. I want to tell you when he emails and freaks me out. And I wanted to tell you about today. I was going to protect you, and then I realized I can't be that happy-all-the-time person for you."

He stared at her, his thoughts and emotions churning. "I want you to tell me everything."

"And I want you to tell *me* everything. And if that means that we can only be friends, that maybe we get together once in a while and have a drink, and we spill about our work then—"

He crushed her to his chest. He could not just be her friend.

He didn't want to have drinks with her. He wanted her in every part of his life. He wanted to come home to her. He wanted to wake up next to her. He wanted to take care of her goat bites, and he wanted to have the TV running low while she fell asleep. He wanted her to get to know his friends and his family. He wanted to see her happy. But he also wanted to see her sad, angry, upset, scared, sleepy, and every other emotion possible.

"I want everything, Max."

She hugged him tightly but then pushed back. "Then you have to give me everything too, Spencer. You don't have to talk about things the second you walk through the door. You can have time and space. But you've been trying to get by without talking about it *at all*.

"Our home *will* be a safe, and comfortable, and supportive place for you. Full of love and…" She glanced toward the kitchen. "…mediocre food, but you can't come home and just shut it all off. You've been trying that. You've been seeking this place where you can just shut off your work, and you haven't been able to because it's a part of you. The brownies, puppies, and Schitt's Creek are just band-aids. Everything that's going on underneath is still there. And it bubbles up at night and won't let you sleep. Don't you see that's a problem?"

He saw all of that. And it scared the hell out of him. "I know. But I don't know what to do about it."

"These last couple of days, you realized that *you* could be in charge of finding that happiness," she said. "That you don't need someone else creating it for you."

He frowned. "I took you to see a goat, and you got bit. I wanted to cuddle on the couch, and you fell asleep. We tried to make brownies and almost burned the cottage down."

"You're being dramatic."

He felt the frustration knot tighter in his gut. "None of it's working, Max. Not when I go looking for it. Not when I try to make it happen myself."

She tucked his phone into her back pocket and put her hands

against his face. "It's *all* working. You're focusing on the fact that the outcome wasn't perfect, but you're not seeing the whole picture. We watched Sawyer and Cian argue before going to the petting zoo. When I fell asleep on the couch, it helped me tell you a story about my childhood that brought us closer. And the brownies… that was kind of funny. Not to mention the amazing orgasm I got while things were catching fire." She smiled at him. "You're focusing on the fact that things are not perfect. But things are *never* going to be perfect, Spencer. Again, if that is what you're looking for, I am not the right girl."

He stared at her. He didn't know what to do. He didn't know what to say. He wanted her, but all of this felt so fucking messy.

"I have to call Zander," he said, focusing on the only thing he could—his damn job.

"No, you don't," she said stubbornly, backing up, so her pocket and his phone were pressed against the counter. "The men Leo's befriending got a name from the guy asking about me. They told Zander who paid him, and Zander called up to New Orleans with the name, he and his deputies started patrolling to see if he was still in town, and Colin came straight over to be with me."

"Who was it?"

"Stephen White."

"Goddammit."

Her grip on his face tightened. "No. It's good. They found him and picked him up for questioning."

Spencer stared at her, processing that. "Why didn't they tell me?"

"You were busy today."

"Not too busy for this."

"This wasn't your job. You're here for personal reasons."

"I still want to know."

"Sucks to be left out, doesn't it?"

Frustration coursed through him again. "Max, I—"

There was a knock on the front door, and they both froze.

"Stay here," he told her firmly.

He started for the bedroom for his weapon, but Zander called through the door, "It's me! Zander. I have news."

Spencer pivoted and opened the door. "Why the fuck didn't you call me?"

Zander's gaze flickered to Max.

Spencer felt his spine stiffen, and he turned. "You told him not to call me?"

She crossed her arms. "Yes, I was trying to protect you."

"I want to know what's going on with you. Always."

"Ditto," she said, her gaze boring into his.

"I'll tell you both what's going on," Zander broke in. "Stephen White confessed to sending the bomb threat. He was tasked with heading up the chemical dumping. He managed to escape and hide the night the dock was raided, but when every-thing went to hell and the dump didn't happen, he got pulled off these 'special assignments' where he was making extra money. Then when you put his name in your social media post because of his known past connections with the other guys, the company fired him altogether, which pissed him off and made him come after you," Zander said to Max. "By the way, he also gave up the men who ordered him to set up the dumping."

Spencer glanced at Max and saw hope on her face.

"Who are they?"

"Gregory Axelrod and Anthony Shipper," Zander said. He looked between Spencer and Max. "Names sound familiar?"

Max sighed, and her arms dropped. "Yes. Known associates of…" She waved a hand. "All of the rest of them."

"Direct ties to Ridgewood?" Spencer asked.

She shook her head.

"Okay, well, we have him in custody. He's locked up. You don't need to worry about him anymore. Sounds like his beef with you was personal between just you and him, and no one gave him orders to do anything to you."

Max nodded. "Thanks, Zander."

"No problem. Turns out I should probably thank my grandfather's new friends."

Spencer scowled at him. "Seriously?"

Zander huffed out a breath. "Man, I don't know. It's not like I trust them. But Leo says that they may be worth having on our side. Or at least not having firmly on 'the other side'. But no, I'm not gonna talk to them. They want nothing to do with me."

Zander said good night, and to call him if they needed anything, and left.

Spencer turned the lock and then took a deep breath. "So—"

"So we can go back to New Orleans now," she said.

It felt like an icy bucket of water had just been dumped over his head. She was right. The reason they were here was no longer a reason.

"Yeah. We can."

And that was for the best. The longer they stayed here in this sweet little cabin with the back porch that had a sunset view, and the deconstructed Scotcheroos, and the bed where he'd made love to someone for the first time in his life, the longer he'd keep believing that all of this could be real and that this was all it would take to be truly happy.

They stood just staring at one another for several ticks of the clock.

Then, at the same time, they stepped forward.

His hands went under her ass as her arms looped around his neck. Their mouths crashed together. His tongue stroked into her mouth as she moaned, and he started walking her toward the bedroom.

If he was going to lose her after they left this cabin, he had to have her one more time. She clearly felt the same way.

He dumped her onto the mattress and immediately stripped off his clothes. She had everything off but her panties by the time he was done, and he slid them down her legs in one swipe. She reached for him, but he knelt at the side of the bed, pulling her ass to the edge. With no warm-up or warning other than a low growl and a gravelly, "Need you," his tongue found her clit. Her hand grabbed onto his hair, gripping tightly.

He thrust two fingers into her slick heat and licked and sucked until she was crying his name and coming hard. Then, he flipped her onto her stomach.

"Oh my God, Spencer."

He stroked his hand over her ass. "You good?" he asked with absolutely no finesse.

"Yes, so good."

He moved one hand to fist his cock. He was aching for her. "Condom or no?"

"No," she moaned as he stroked her butt again.

He wasn't going to ask twice. He grasped her hips and pulled her up on hands and knees, then climbed onto the mattress behind her nudging her forward until he was fully supported. With a hand between her shoulder blades, he pressed her upper body down, keeping her hips in the air.

He lined his cock up with her opening and thrust forward.

She was hot and ready for him, and he sank deep immediately. Again she cried out his name, and the sound, the feel of her around him, and the knowledge this might be the last time made his strokes hard and fast.

He reached around and found her clit, circling and pressing, taking her to the summit again.

She cried out and clamped down around him within minutes, and he pounded into her, somehow needing this frenzied release.

He felt his orgasm bearing down, and he stroked three more times before pulling out, grasping his cock, and coming over her ass and the back of her thighs.

It was hot as fuck, and he was unapologetic that this was the way they'd done this the last time. Anything sweeter or softer would have been far too difficult.

She slumped forward onto the mattress, resting her cheek on

her hands, her eyes closed, breathing hard. He flipped the sheet over her to cover her and then bent to retrieve his clothes.

"I'm going to shower, and then I'll pack." He quickly shut himself in the bathroom.

When he finished, he left the room so she could also clean up and pack.

They walked out the cottage's front door less than an hour later.

Max had written a letter to Heather thanking her for everything she'd done for them and telling her they needed to return to New Orleans unexpectedly, but they couldn't wait to come back.

There was no reason for anyone else to know their relationship was precarious.

Precarious. It was a pretty word for the dark, swirling emotions that were churning through Spencer.

He couldn't imagine a future without Max. The same woman who had seemed completely wrong for him only a week ago.

They didn't talk all the way back to New Orleans.

He pulled up in front of her apartment and shifted into park. He couldn't leave it like this, though he had no idea what to say. He turned to face her. "Max."

She shifted in her seat. "Spencer, I'm in love with you."

He opened his mouth, but nothing came out.

"That hasn't changed." Her voice was soft, and her eyes full of affection. "It's stronger than ever. I hope you can believe that's why I'm saying this."

"Saying what?"

"I can't be responsible for all of your happiness. And I can't be expected to ignore what you do for a living and how it affects you. I want you to be happy. But I don't want you to think brownies and puppies are the keys to happiness. You need to work on figuring your stuff out for real."

He ran a hand through his hair. "I wish I knew how. I need you, Max."

She nodded. "Maybe. In some ways. But you can't need just me. You need professional help. You need a therapist."

He straightened. He shouldn't have been shocked. She'd mentioned therapy in connection with his father's issues before. "You think it's that bad?"

"Nothing has to be 'that bad' to seek out help." She shook her head. "But I want you to take control. Like when I said that you need to learn to make your own brownies, and you realized in the last couple of days that you can be in charge of the happiness rather than waiting for someone else to do it for you? *This* is a way to take control of how all of this impacts you. A therapist can help you delve into why you feel this way and help you with coping strategies."

He blew out a breath. Could he talk to someone about his issues? The things that kept him up at night? His fear of sinking into the darkness? He studied the face of the woman beside him. To make her happy? Of course he could. "I don't know how long this will take. It might be a while till I'm fixed. If I ever really am."

She leaned over the console and grabbed his hand. "It's not about you getting *fixed*. You don't have to be 'fixed' for me, Spencer. You just need to take control of your happiness, so you're not looking to me to do it for you."

"I really wish you could believe that you can take care of people and understand how to love them," he said, lifting a hand to her face. God, he loved her. He wanted to heal the little girl inside her and show her that she not only could be loved but that she could love as fiercely as she fought for justice.

She nodded. "During this time with you I've realized that I've also spent a lot of years thinking I'm fine and just throwing myself into work to distract myself. I want to figure out how I can love you and everyone around me the best I can. I'm going to start talking to someone too. And I know figuring this out isn't going to happen in one fell swoop. It's like everything else we've been talking about. None of this can happen in one session. Or one month of sessions. Or probably even a year."

Right. Steps. Little pieces. Persistence over time.

Maybe he couldn't just say *I love you, Max,* and give them both everything they needed. But even if taking her to the petting zoo and making brownies and the couch-cuddling and back-porch-sitting hadn't turned out exactly as he'd planned, they'd managed to fall in love anyway.

He cupped the back of her head and brought her in for a kiss, but it was soft and sweet, and when she pulled back, she simply said, "Goodnight, Spencer."

"'Night, Max."

He watched her walk into her townhouse and somehow made himself point his truck for home.

But he was calling a therapist first thing in the morning because the idea of Max falling asleep alone in the dark was almost too much.

———

TWO WEEKS LATER, Max was in the kitchen at the stove when an arm suddenly snaked around her, and a hand covered her mouth. She gasped and stiffened.

The man's voice was gruff against her ear. "You broke into my apartment?"

She grinned. Spencer was still wet from the shower, his big body hot against hers.

Max pressed her ass into him and realized he was only wearing a towel.

"I'm making you dinner." Of course, it came out muffled because he was covering her mouth.

He dropped his hand and turned her, bracing his hands on either side of her, crowding her into the counter at her back. "You know I thought you were an intruder?"

"Kind of like the first morning when you broke down my door?"

"I would've let you in."

"I wanted to surprise you."

God, he looked good. She was glad she was leaning against the counter because her knees were actually weak.

It'd been fifteen days since she'd seen him. They'd stayed apart because they'd wanted to start therapy and get into that routine and work on a few things on their own without the new relationship pressure on top of it all. They texted a few times, and talked twice on the phone, but they'd wanted to figure out if the crazy-in-love surrounding them at the cottage would work in reality.

She lifted her hand to his cheek. He'd been in the shower, but he hadn't shaved. She ran her hand over his stubble. "Very real."

His eyes were hot as he looked down at her. "What?"

"Everything I felt at the cottage is very real."

His voice dropped to a husky growl. "God, yes."

He was hard behind the terrycloth pressing into her belly. She rose on tiptoe, and his mouth came down on hers hungrily.

They kissed for a long moment. One of his hands tangled in her hair, and his fingers stroked through the long strands. He wrapped her hair around his hand and tipped her head back, pulling his mouth from hers.

"I'm so fucking glad you're here."

"Me too."

Today after therapy, Max had felt like it was time.

She'd been talking with her therapist about how she felt like she wasn't supposed to depend on other people, and how she also didn't feel that people should depend on *her* for nurturing that she couldn't give, among other things. Spencer had shared with her that he was talking with his about how he took on the responsibility for all the bad things that happened during his downtime and that he needed to take more control of the things that gave him joy. It had only been two weeks, but they both felt good about talking through their issues.

And now, she was ready to see Spencer and start their relationship in the real world—their New Orleans apartments, their jobs, their routines, and lifestyles as a part of that.

He'd agreed two seconds after she'd texted and said he'd be on her doorstep at eight p.m.

It was seven-thirty now.

"I can believe you know how to pick locks, but how'd you get past my security system?" Spencer asked.

"Chris let me in."

"Did he?" His hand was still holding her hair.

"I wanted to make you dinner."

He pulled in a long breath, pulling in the scent of what was in the oven. "Enchiladas?"

She smiled. "Take out. I'm just warming them up."

"I don't care. They smell amazing, and you're here."

"But," she added. "I also thought we could make Scotcheroos together. I brought all the ingredients." She ran her hand over his chest. "I thought it would be symbolic. Instead of them being deconstructed, we take all the pieces, and we make them whole."

The look he gave her was full of heat and love. "I already have all the ingredients."

Her eyes widened. "You do?"

"Been eating them a lot. And it turns out, I like them deconstructed. I don't mind all the little pieces. Turns out that the flavor can be there even when things aren't put together perfectly."

She gasped and gave him a big grin. "That's beautiful, Spencer."

He laughed. "I'm an excellent therapy client. Or so I've been told."

Finally, she couldn't resist anymore. She slid her arms up around his neck and pressed close. "I've missed you so much."

"Ditto. And I *need* you so much."

Her hands were already at the front of his towel and she had it unwound and on the floor before he even finished the sentence.

Max wrapped her hands around his already hard cock. He lifted her onto the counter and bunched her skirt at her waist. "Thank you so much for wearing this dress.

She raised it higher and spread her knees.

He groaned. "And thank you very much for not wearing any panties."

She laughed. "My pleasure."

"Oh, it's gonna be."

She guided him into her. He sank deep, and they both moaned. They moved together like that for a few minutes but soon, he scooped her up, keeping them joined, and walked to the couch.

"I do love it when you carry me," she said against his neck.

"Where do you want to go?"

"Couch. It's closer."

He lowered her onto the cushions and immediately started thrusting. Soon they were climbing to the peak together, gasping, her fingers digging into his shoulders. He reached for the bottom of her dress, stripping it over her head. He lowered his mouth to her nipples, taking one in his mouth and sucking hard. That made her pussy clench around him, and they both groaned.

"Love you," he said against her breast. "So much."

She came apart. "I love you too, Spencer."

He followed her with a deep groan.

They came back down, holding each other tightly.

Until Max noticed the smell of smoke. She groaned. "You've got to be kidding."

He lifted his head from the curve of her neck. "What?" The next moment he realized what she was talking about. "*Fuck.*"

He pushed up off the couch just as the smoke alarm started squealing.

He rushed toward the smoke detector, fanning it with his

towel, and Max headed for the oven. She pulled the reheating enchiladas from the oven and dumped them into the sink, running water over them. Then she opened the window over the sink, hoping to air out the smoke and quiet the alarm.

Finally, the squealing stopped.

They looked at one another.

And burst out laughing.

"There's a fabulous Mexican place just up the street," Spencer said. "Amazing enchiladas."

She laughed. "Do they deliver? Because I don't have any panties."

He laughed even harder. "This might be the best problem I've ever had."

She crossed to where he was standing, naked under the smoke detector. She wrapped her arms around him. "Ditto. Very much. Ditto."

He bent and kissed her. When he lifted his head, he said. "And we're definitely not telling Michael about this, right?"

She shook her head. "Absolutely not. Ever."

EPILOGUE

Six months later

IT TURNED out that he hadn't been right about *everything*.

Spencer had always believed that nothing could be better than walking into his house at the end of the day to the smell of dinner in the oven, a beautiful woman, and a dog with a wagging tail by the door.

That was all pretty damned great.

But it turned out that already being home to watch Max walk through the door of the townhouse they'd bought, pause, and take a deep breath of the dinner-scented air, smile the soft, sweet, happy smile she didn't realize he saw, just before being nearly knocked over by their three dogs was the *epitome* of happiness for him.

"Hi, everybody!" she greeted, dropping her bag and dropping to her knees to embrace Joey, the mutt they'd gone to the shelter to rescue, Harry, the Pitbull they'd fallen for as well, and Sally, the twelve-year-old German Shepherd who'd been there for almost ten months without being adopted. The dogs adored her almost as much as Spencer did.

He had three dogs.

And a woman who loved the dogs. *Loved* them. Spoiled them. Had photos of them on her desk at work. Sent him photos of them on her days off.

Yes, she now took days off. So she could hang out with the dogs. Well, more accurately, she worked from home more often so she could hang out with the dogs. Still, Spencer fell further in love with her every time he got a "puppy text" from her. And none of these dogs were actually puppies. He didn't even mind the fact that they all loved her more than they loved him.

She hugged and kissed and talked to the dogs for a few minutes, then climbed to her feet and caught Spencer's eye. She gave him a smile that made his heart squeeze hard, but he knew it would still be a few minutes until he got *his* hug and kiss. There was still more to their usual evening routine to complete before that.

He'd just come in from the balcony where he'd fed the crows. Yep, it was a new balcony, but there were crows here too. Or the same crows. He wasn't sure, but he wouldn't be surprised if the birds had followed her. He could certainly understand following her no matter where she went.

He opened his hand, showing her the two shiny gold paper-clips the crows had left for her. She grinned and he crossed to the glass jar they kept on top of her roll-top desk, especially for the collection of baubles from the crows.

Except for the ruby. They'd had that appraised and sure enough, it was real. It was now set in a gold heart that hung on a chain around her neck to remind her that she was loved by a great number of people and creatures and was never alone. Which was exactly what Spencer had told her when he'd given it to her.

"Hi, honey," Phil greeted Max, rolling his wheelchair across the foyer from where he'd been giving her space with the dog.

He was the dog sitter while Steph prepped dinner. The couple came over from the assisted living facility that was only a block from the townhouse to help out on the nights Spencer and Max worked late. Which was most nights.

They'd come up with a harness and had worked on training the dogs so Phil could take them for a walk in his motorized wheelchair. Not only was the walk good for the dogs, but the dogs were fantastic for Phil's mood and the activity gave him an important sense of independence.

The arrangement was a win-win for everyone. It gave Phil and Steph a chance to participate in activities they enjoyed, gave them some extra money, and absolutely helped Spencer, Max, and the dogs.

Joey, Harry, and Sally loved Phil and Steph. Phil and Steph loved seeing Max and being able to help her out this way. And having the dogs cared for and dinner ready when they got home helped Max and Spencer with their unpredictable schedules.

It had turned out beautifully and Spencer was grateful to Max's therapist for the suggestion that Max have a deeper conversation with Phil and Steph about how they could be a more meaningful part of each other's lives. She'd had some important conversations with her parents as well. Max was learning that she could be nurturing and that others could depend on her and that leaning on others sometimes was not only wonderful, but encouraged. Just like he was learning that he could take control of his own joy and could be a nurturer himself.

He was nurturing the hell out of that woman, and watching her bloom from it had shown him that he was making the world a better place every damned day. He was forever grateful for that chance.

"Hey." Max crossed to Phil and leaned in to kiss his cheek. "I got that prescription picked up and the new pillows will be delivered on Wednesday."

"Thanks, kiddo."

"Of course."

"Hi, Max." Steph came out of the kitchen. "Everything's

ready to go. Just took the casserole out of the oven. Just let it cool for a few minutes."

"Thank you." Max hugged Steph too. "And Caroline, Charlie, and Naomi will be here around eleven on Saturday. I thought we'd take them to Blue's for lunch before we shop. What do you think?"

Steph nodded. "That sounds wonderful."

"Great, I'll pick you up."

"Bye, Spencer!" Phil called as he and Steph headed out the door and down the ramp Spencer and Wyatt had installed off the side of the front steps.

"See you guys," Spencer said.

Sally went up on her hind legs to watch them leave through the front door while Joey and Harry ran to the window in the living room to do the same.

Spencer knew Phil would pause and wave at the dogs from the sidewalk, but the dogs wouldn't leave the windows until Phil and Steph were out of sight.

Max kicked her shoes off by the door and padded toward him.

Spencer opened his arms and she stepped into his hug.

They both gave a sigh as they wrapped themselves around one another.

He just held her for a long moment, absorbing the fact that this was his life. He actually had it all.

She pulled back and looked up at him after a minute. "Hi," she said with a smile.

"Hi."

"I love you."

"Love you too."

"What's for dinner?"

"Chicken and broccoli casserole."

"Oh, yum."

He grinned. She meant that. It had only taken one try and she'd fallen for broccoli and chicken. But her favorite was lasagna.

They headed into the kitchen to set the table, moving around the room in a wordless, synchronized routine that was now a near-daily habit.

Once they were seated, the food dished up, and they'd taken the first few bites, Spencer said, "I have some news."

Max paused with her fork halfway to her mouth. "What kind of news?"

"Work news."

She took the bite, then nodded as if the chicken and broccoli was going to help her brace for whatever it was.

They talked about work a lot. He shared what he was working on—as much as he could without sharing confidential information—and she told him about her stories.

He also slept through the night about five nights a week. He still woke up around two a.m. some nights, but he could often roll over, gather Max close, and lay with her on one side and a dog at his feet and two more snoring on the floor and at least drowsily drift rather than get up and pace the house.

He'd even talked to his dad about dealing with some of those work demons.

Sam had admitted that he'd never found a great way to quiet those voices and he still had sleepless nights. He hadn't said he would seek counseling himself, but he'd been glad to hear that Spencer had found therapy helpful. Spencer figured that was something.

His mom, on the other hand, had been thrilled to know that Spencer was getting help and she, of course, loved Max.

Mary Jo had flat-out sobbed the first night they'd had her and Sam over for dinner with Spencer, Max, Wyatt, Phil, and Steph. She'd sat on the couch with two dogs' heads in her lap, had eaten Scotcheroos, and had absolutely blubbered about how all she wanted was for Spencer to have people around him who loved him and could they please find a girlfriend for Wyatt.

"I have someone willing to testify that Gordon Ridgewood's accountant has been fucking around with his taxes."

Her eyes widened. "Really?"

He nodded. "It's going to take time to piece it all together and it's nothing flashy, but we could start to put some pressure on the accountant to give up bigger fish or more information. Of course, Ridgewood *could* say he didn't know what his accountant was doing, blah, blah, but it's something."

She nodded. "Is it an FBI matter?"

"He's got business dealings in multiple states," Spencer confirmed.

She tipped her head, studying him. "Is it a Spencer Landry matter?"

"It is."

"You don't have to," she said quietly. "I'm *very* happy, Spencer. The things you've given me… the *life* you've given me… is so much. You don't have to give me Gordon Ridgewood too. You know that, right?"

Spencer reached out and took her hand. "I will give you everything and anything I can. Always." He squeezed her. "But I'd be interested in Gordon Ridgewood's business practices anyway. And, honestly, if I could pick a way to take him down for you, it'd be way bigger and louder than tax evasion."

She laughed and squeezed his hand back. "I know. And I'll keep working on it too. If there's more, I'll find it. Eventually."

He lifted her hand and kissed it. "I know you will."

"Hey, Spencer?"

"Yeah?"

"Will you marry me?"

He froze, his lips against the back of her hand.

She went on quickly. "I know it's incredibly selfish. You've always had family and friends and dinners and dogs, but dammit, Spencer, I haven't and now you've given me a taste and I just want *all* of this all the time now and I don't want it with anyone else. So I figured I should just lock it all down right now before I buy any more creepy candelabras or you get sick and realize that I *suck* at taking care of people when they don't feel good or you find out that I've been feeding a cat at work and I'm probably going to bring it home as soon as it lets me close enough to touch it."

Spencer just stared at her. This woman was… everything.

"Um… yes," he finally said. "Fuck, yes."

"I mean, eventually. It's not even been a year. We still need to take this slow. We still have pieces to work on and—"

He was out of his chair and had her swooped up, her chair toppling over, and her gasping, "Spencer!" before she finished her thought.

The dogs were on their feet, barking, not sure if this was good or bad. They were used to him carrying her around, but not necessarily chairs falling over, and dinner being left on the table.

"Quiet, guys," he commanded reassuringly, striding down the hall to the bedroom.

Max was laughing. "Hey, I was eating."

"It's broccoli. It can wait."

"I *like* broccoli."

He shook his head with a grin as he tossed her on the bed. The dogs scrambled up, clearly having realized this was fun and nothing to be concerned with.

"You forgot to shut the door," Max pointed out. When they came into the bedroom for sexy times, they had to be sure to shut the door or they would have company.

"Nope, they should be here."

Her brows rose.

He crossed to the dresser and retrieved the package he'd purchased and wrapped nearly two months ago.

He returned to the bed and held it out. Surrounded by dogs, Max propped herself up on the pillows, one of his favorite positions for her in this bed. She tore open the paper and then stared at the gift.

It was a package of tan panties.

She started laughing. "Thanks."

"Keep going."

She unrolled the panties and inside found the little black velvet box. "Oh."

Spencer reached out and took the box. He popped it open, showing off a beautiful diamond engagement ring. It was simple, but stunning.

It was a very Spencer ring.

He knelt on the mattress next to her as she covered her mouth with one hand.

"I could have picked an elaborate jewel with an exotic history or a funny story behind it, or an unusual stone in a one-of-a-kind setting. But just like I love every one of your eccentricities, I want you to wear this classic ring, and every time you look at your hand, I want you to think of this by-the-book, traditional guy who loves you with everything he is and somehow, inexplicably but amazingly, fits with you anyway."

Her eyes were wide but she nodded and he knew she understood what he was trying to say. Just like they'd blended everything else in their lives, he wanted that simple symbol on the hand of the most extraordinary woman he'd ever met.

"Max, since the day you marched into Ellie's bar the first time, you've been making me look at everything I thought I believed differently. Some of it I was wrong about. Like panties. I *love* tan panties. More than anything."

She giggled behind her hand and his heart thunked against his ribs.

"Some of it I was right about—like dogs and dinner."

Her hand seemed to instinctively go to Joey's head where he lay beside her.

"But you managed to make those things even better than I could have ever imagined."

Her hand fell away from her mouth and he could see that she was pressing her lips together.

"You've made *me* better in every way and I know I have a long way to go, but I can't imagine eating a cookie or an enchilada, or petting a dog or a goat, or waking up in the middle of the night or in the morning, for that matter, without wanting you there. So, will you do all of this with me forever and eventually, sometime, will you also marry me?"

She started nodding her head rapidly. "Yes. Yes, yes. Forever. Eventually. Sometime."

He leaned in and took her mouth in a hot, deep kiss. She cupped his face in her hands as he pulled her down against the pillows and pressed into her.

Suddenly there were three dogs on top of them too.

He lifted his head as they both laughed.

"I have one more question," he said.

"Okay. Anything." The love shining in her eyes was the most beautiful thing he'd ever seen.

"Do you think you can bring the cat home this weekend?"

Tears welled up in her eyes. "I think so."

"Good." He kissed her again.

Then her stomach growled, and he laughed, rolling off of her and pulling her up. "Now let's go finish dinner."

They walked back to the kitchen holding hands, her left hand now with a pretty, sparkly diamond ring on it.

Spencer wasn't sure he'd ever been happier. He took a deep, satisfied breath.

Just as the timer on the oven went off.

They looked at one another, puzzled.

"Is that..." He started as he pulled the oven door open.

"No way," Max said with a laugh. "That's perfect."

Inside was a not-even-slightly-overdone, delicious-looking pan of brownies.

And Spencer had to agree...

It was *all* perfect.

Thank you so much for reading Max and Spencer's story! I hope you loved Gotta Be Bayou!

Michael and Ami are up next in **Bayou With Benefits!**

Michael LeClaire is small-town Louisiana. A firefighter. A single dad.

And Amelia Landry is New York City. A social media influencer. A *model.*

Of course they're friends too. But there can't be any extra "benefits" in this relationship. Even if she is sleeping just down the hall…

ജ
Find all of my books at
ErinNicholas.com
including a printable book list!

And join in on all the FAN FUN!

Join my **email list!**
bit.ly/Keep-In-Touch-Erin
(be sure you get those dashes and capital letters in there!)

And be the first to hear about my news, sales, freebies, behind-the-scenes, and more!

Or for even more fun, join my **Super Fan page** on Facebook and chat with me and other super fans every day! Just search Facebook for Erin Nicholas Super Fans!

MORE FROM ERIN'S BAYOU WORLD!

Want more from my bayou world? I've got so much more sexy fun for you!

Boys of the Bayou
My Best Friend's Mardi Gras Wedding (Josh & Tori)
Sweet Home Louisiana (Owen & Maddie)
Beauty and the Bayou (Sawyer & Juliet)
Crazy Rich Cajuns (Bennett & Kennedy)
Must Love Alligators (Chase & Bailey)
Four Weddings and a Swamp Boat Tour (Mitch & Paige)

*

Boys of the Bayou Gone Wild
Otterly Irresistible (Charlie& Griffin)
Heavy Petting (Fletcher & Jordan)
Flipping Love You (Zeke & Jill)
Sealed With a Kiss (Donovan & Naomi)
Say It Like You Mane It (Zander & Caroline)
Head Over Hooves (Drew & Rory)
Kiss My Giraffe (Knox & Fiona)
Better Safe Than Safari (Colin & Hayden)

SPENCER'S FAVORITE FUDGE BROWNIES

BROWNIES:

- 1 cup butter
- 2 cups granulated sugar
- 2 eggs
- 1 tsp vanilla extract
- 2 cups all-purpose flour
- ½ cup baking cocoa
- 1 cup chopped walnuts (opt)

FUDGIE FROSTING:

- ½ cup butter, softened
- 3 ½ cups powdered sugar
- 1/3 cup baking cocoa
- ¼ cup milk
- 1 tsp vanilla extract

DIRECTIONS:

1. In a mixing bowl, cream butter and sugar. Add eggs, one at a time, beating well after each addition. Beat in vanilla.

2. Combine flour and cocoa; add to creamed mixture just until combined. Don't over mix. It's a very thick batter!

3. Stir in walnuts if using.

4. Spread into an ungreased 13 x 9 in baking pan. Bake at 350 degrees for 23-28 minutes or until a toothpick inserted near the center comes out clean. Don't over bake. You want them fudgie in the middle. Cool on a wire rack.

5. For frosting, in a mixing bowl, beat butter until fluffy. Beat in the powdered sugar, cocoa, milk, and vanilla until smooth. Spread over brownies.

Yield 2 dozen.

ABOUT ERIN NICHOLAS

Lover of coffee, cats, cookies, and other c-words (also tacos) **Erin
Nicholas is the NYT and USA
Today bestselling author** of over sixty romances.

If you want to have a latte, and chat about all things
New Orleans, anything Schitt's Creek, or socializing stray cats,
she's your girl. And, of course, if you
love rom coms with swoony heroes who fall hard, amazing
found families, and quirky small towns.
She lives in the middle of the US with her husband and too
many cats (his opinion, not hers).

Find her and all her books at
www.ErinNicholas.com

**And find her on Facebook, BookBub, Goodreads, and
Instagram!**

Editor: Lindsey Faber

Cover design: Beck and Dot Book Cover Design

Paperback ISBN: 978-1-952280-52-8

Digital ISBN: 978-1-952280-31-3